# THE OTHER ALEXANDER

## BOOK I OF

## THE BOW OF HEAVEN

A NOVEL OF ANCIENT ROME

BY

ANDREW LEVKOFF

cover illustration / design by Lynnette Shelley
www.lynnetteshelley.com

ISBN: 0983910138
ISBN-13: 978-0-9839101-3-8

In the greatest, foulest city in the world, love, mayhem and betrayal are waiting for the slave, Alexandros. Given as a gift to the richest man in Rome, he soon discovers that intrigue and murder stalk the house of his master. Alexandros can solve the crime, but if he does, the worst punishment may prove to be his own.

---

**2011 Gold Award, Historical Fiction - eLit Book Awards**

**2012 Silver Award, Global Ebook Award, Historical Fiction**

**Editor's Choice – Historical Novel Society, Spring, 2012**

---

**Praise for *The Other Alexander***

Thoroughly researched, beautifully written, and cleverly staged. Superb. - *Foreword Clarion Reviews*

The world of Republican Rome is brought entirely alive in these pages. - *Historical Novels Review Online*

*The Other Alexander* is superb: a beautifully-crafted, electrifying example of just how good historical fiction can be. Don't miss it. - *Open Letters Monthly*

Beautifully written and thrillingly good Roman historical novel ... crisp plotting and absolutely infectious narrative drive. Enthusiastically recommended. - *Historical Novel Society*

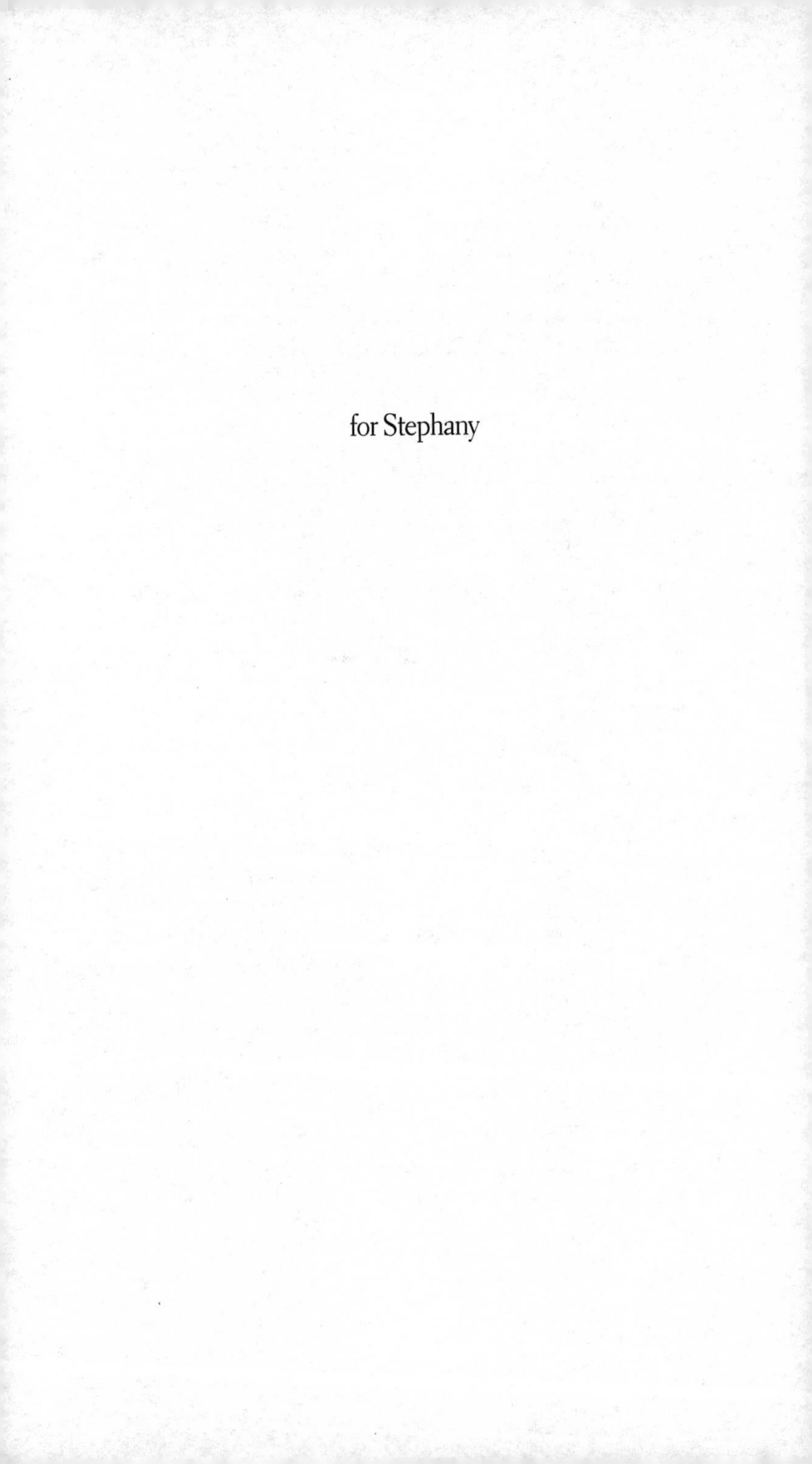

for Stephany

•••

*In 2010, archaeological students from the University of Athens, working with Dr. Kostas Vranas at the Artemonas dig site on the Greek isle of Sifnos, were contacted by workers of the nearby stone quarry. They had made a remarkable discovery: buried in the soft clay just west of the excavation were three chests lined with layers of tin and beeswax, containing over two hundred scrolls of parchment in almost perfect condition. An additional chest of writing tablets was for the most part ruined, the wood frames rotten, the inscribed wax melted or eaten away.*

*The translation by the author is an unprecedented account of events preceding the demise of Republican Rome, authored by Alexandros of Elateia, a slave in one of Rome's mightiest houses. As was the custom, Alexandros identified the passage of time not by the number of the year but by the names of the consuls elected to lead the senate for their annual term. To give the reader a more useful frame of reference, we have divided the narrative into both parts and chapters, added the BCE convention to denote the year, and provided the season and place. A glossary is included at the end of the text.*

•••

# PROLOG

## 20 BCE - SUMMER, SIPHNOS, GREECE

Year of the consulship of
Marcus Appuleius and Publius Silius Nerva

The boy comes bearing honeyed tea onto the blue tiled terrace with its too-white stuccoed walls. I shan't call him 'boy' to his face, though, or risk forfeiting my foot massage. Say what he will, his scars are almost thirty years younger than mine. Though his were earned in battle and mine are of a different nature entirely, to me Melyaket will always be "boy." Now he waits patiently for me to set down the stilus. I have long stopped trying to convince him that it is I who should serve him, for I know he will but smile thinly and ignore me as always. So be it. I am ancient and frail and the tea is hot and aromatic. Of course there is also the matter of my feet.

Enough of the Parthian bowman; how he and I came to this island sanctuary is a tale for another telling. This recounting does not belong to Melyaket, nor would I presume to lay claim to it for myself. This is my lord's story, and I pray the gods grant me strength and time to tell it. My master is long dead; few mourned his passing; fewer still recall his name with kindness. More than thirty years have passed since his ignoble death in the dirt at the feet of his enemies. The memory of that heat-drenched day, encrusted with grime and blood and clouded by the dusty haze of battle yet returns to me with glittering clarity. His mocking Parthian captors, their barbarism and bloodlust palpable as they towered over him, pricked him with their taunts and jeers, swords poised to pierce his unarmored heart. Yet when the moment came, they were robbed of the release the mortal blow would have granted both murderers and murdered. For it was Melyaket who slew my lord.

•••

There is much to tell. Nicias has sent men to scour the town for ink, reeds and parchment. I am anxious for their return, for these tablets are all but useless for my intention. It would take a forest of their frames to fill my need. I shall use them for my notes and musings. Now they sit before me, prepared with freshly melted wax, piled so high on my writing table that unless I rise from this cushioned chair, a feat for which I find I lack both the strength and the inclination, the splendor of the sea below, bronzed and burnished by the setting sun, can only wink at me between the cracks. I pull a simple string necklace from around my throat and find the single scallop shell that adorns it. With my thumb I absentmindedly rub its inside surface, grown glossy with age and use, admitting a rising tide of memory.

News has reached us from Rome: the standards of my master's legions, pried from the twisted fingers of their fallen bearers and flaunted under the shamed chin of

Rome for each day of their captivity have finally been ransomed, by no less a negotiator than Caesar Augustus himself. For thirty-five years they were held hostage behind the throne at Ctesiphon, the Parthian capital, a mockery of the invincibility of Rome. Though my body wrinkles and shrivels like a Persian peach forgotten in the desert sun, the memory of the day they were lost remains as ripe and raw as a newly drawn knife cut.

To the cruel and superstitious Roman, whether soldier or senator, these are more than poles covered in hide and metal, wood and bone. They are the very essence of Rome, imbued by the gods themselves with the divine mystery of its dominance and superiority. But to me they have always been absent and ironic reminders both of liberty and of loss. I care not, after all these years, that these eagle-festooned sticks have been returned to the bosom of Rome, a poisonous breast where I shall be pleased never to rest my head again.

Tulio writes that the return of the standards has caused such riotous celebration in the streets it is as though Parthia itself had been vanquished. The rabble's ignorance is as supple and resilient as its memory is arthritic. And what of the nobles who cling with a slippery and tenuous grasp to the tether that holds the mob in check? They must remain blameless, their pristine togas unblemished by any crimson reminders of our misadventure.

# PART I - SLAVE TO MASTER

# CHAPTER I

## 86 BCE - SUMMER, ROME

Year of the consulship of
Gaius Marius the Elder and Lucius Cornelius Cinna

If you are a citizen of Rome, you will not know the count of the year, because history, being a thing of the past, is of little interest to you. Rome concerns itself with today and tomorrow, but cares little for yesterday. So while we Greeks (the learned ones, that is) know that 690 years had passed since the first Olympiad, you Romans know only that which concerns you most: who is in power now. Which I suppose is a very modern, forward-looking attitude, for who can remember who was in charge seventy or eighty years ago? Should a Roman astound you with the ability to recall such a year, you may assume with some assuredness that some costly and bloody war was fought, a renegade noble took political matters into his own hands, or a rebellion of one sort or another was put down. Or perhaps a bit of each.

When I was little more than a boy, time had stopped altogether: the count of the year reset itself to 1, and would remain there the following year and the one after that, for so many turns of the calendar I cannot recall the count. Ah, invincible, immortal youth. You see, free men may make use of the passage of time as if each golden coin may forever be newly minted: lay plans, set goals, chart achievements. But never mind. However you set your clock, what I speak of now transpired sixty-six years ago. I was 19, about to be imprisoned for the next thirty-three years of my life, not in a cell, but to the will of a single man.

My, Alexandros, you whine like a stuck boar. Reader, pay no attention to the sniveling of a melodramatic ancient who has outstayed his welcome above ground. I have had more than my fair portion of satisfaction and accomplishment. I have even known love. And as you see, I am quite accomplished in the art of digression. Move along, Alexandros, move along.

•••

Who am I, you may protest, and with what credentials do I claim the right to chronicle the life of one of Rome's once venerable patriarchs? I am no one. I am less than no one. But I was there through it all, and now I shall bear witness. You of breeding and substance, you senators and aristocrats may dismiss with a wave of your soft hands the thread of my narrative should it not unravel to your liking. Nonetheless, I shall tell what I know for truth's sake and my master's honor, and the glory of Rome be damned!

My name is Alexandros, son of Theodotos of Elateia. I may be bald, half-blind and more than a little wobbly on these eighty-five year-old willow branches that serve for legs, but my mind has yet to fail me; it is as keen today as the day I was made the property of my captors.

There is another word for what I became. It is dull, commonplace and prosaic, like the chalky base coat of a mural, necessary to fortify the coming of the artist's colorful strokes but ultimately invisible, its worth unseen. It is a word without bias or weight, like 'water,' or 'tree.' Unless you happen to be one. Then, the world becomes a simple but lopsided place. There are owners and there are the owned. And the latter, those afflicted with fits of common sense and introspection, must soon come to ask themselves in the black, sleepless hours, why? Why would the gods, in their unfathomable wisdom, give us life only to watch us fall to a state as low as this? What good could ever come of such a fate? There were those of us, I among them, who once blithely sought answers to the essence of being, who contemplated the meaning of existence with a pomposity only the truly ignorant may display. Without warning, the focus of our contemplation was wrenched from such esoteric heights and narrowed most effectively to the chafing sores of our ankle chains. The pursuit of knowledge is an inaudible whisper lost in the stentorian debate of an empty stomach, drowned out even by the quiet discourse of muffled sobs in the night.

What folly to once believe we were the masters of our fate, when at the point of a sword we may so swiftly and permanently become the mastered. In this world, philosophy must go begging. No, not so, for even a beggar may choose his street corner. To be a man, once, and then to be magicked so effortlessly to be transformed into a clay pot, a footstool, a nothing. I was not brave. I was not a soldier. I tried neither to escape, nor to end my servitude by my own hand. This is my shame, and I carry it upon my back like the sacks of rock my stooped and broken brothers and sisters bear in the quarry. Why do I speak of such things? Because if you are reading this you must surely be among the owners, not the owned, so of what possible interest could anything I have to say be to you? Do you wish to learn of greatness? Then abide, for one need not possess greatness to stand close by it.

•••

How my bondage came about was a study in cause and effect. My parents raised horses on our small country estate; I was riding before I could hurl an insult. (My mother claimed the first word out of my mouth was "stupid.") I was also quite bright: I was reading Aesop by the time I was five, bored with him at six, and laughing with Aristophanes a year later. Beyond anything to do with hippology or reading, I had no use for the continual stream of young, hapless playmates with which my mother was continually pestering me. As a result, any friends I might have made quickly became discouraged, if not by my disdain then by my stable-infused bouquet. In truth, I was an alarmingly disagreeable child.

My mother and father, being quite patient and forbearing parents, did their best, but even their gentle tenacity finally frayed and their restraint turned to resignation. By then, unfortunately, my acrimonious and antisocial behavior had all but calcified. And so, when I turned seventeen, they threw their hands toward

Olympus and packed me off to the urbane, marbled wonder that was Athens. Perhaps my compassion would expand with my mind, they prayed. I do miss them, and shall forever wonder what fate they suffered.

In the city I found a new love, but became just as single-minded as I had been with my previous equine obsession. Its name, or rather his name, was Aristotle. I ate his words as if no other food could sustain me. Obsession being my only way of shutting out all that I saw that was wrong with the world, I soon had no interest in anything other than the continuation of my studies at the Lyceum. In my arrogance, I presumed to think that some day I might even teach there. Finding spare but adequate lodgings near the school, for two years my eyes would not be torn from the parchment of my texts, my ears would heed only the words of my teachers.

Oh, how the fierce devotions of youth are easily diverted!

When not in class, it was my occasional habit to go for long walks, not for exercise or with any destination in mind, but to digest what I had learned that week in school. On one of these peripatetic strolls, I found I had taken myself to the very steps of the library at Plato's Academy. I ventured within and before my eyes had adjusted to the indoor light, I beheld a raven haired, blue-eyed girl pushing a trolley of unfiled scrolls. She turned and spoke to me, asking if I required assistance, and I was immediately undone. From that moment on, my walks became neither random nor infrequent.

But the Academy was Plato's school. No matter. It became clear to me in a heartbeat that the focus of my studies was far too narrow. After all, to become a truly enlightened philosopher, one must have a generous and open mind, mustn't one? Without so much as a letter home I rushed to matriculate where I might be nearest to her, trading philosophical heroes faster than the time it would take to barter for a handful of figs in the market. In the end, it made no difference – the same fate awaited both schools.

Like the Academy, my infatuation was doomed. Phaedra had no interest in anyone with a pedigree as poor as mine. Never spurning me outright, she gently yet firmly directed me to an outer orbit of her admirers. In retrospect, a little more overt derision on her part might have dampened my obdurate campaign to humiliate myself. I could not comprehend a universe which could allow a love as pure as mine to languish unanswered. How could I feel this deeply unless her heart stirred as well? I was achingly naïve. Phaedra was my first encounter with the brittle, wintry truth that alas, love is often a skewed affair. I returned to my studies, vowing never to love again, unaware that I hadn't yet loved at all. Eventually even I tired of my pitiful pining and determined to redirect that wasted energy back toward my studies. I was at the center of the philosophical universe, and there was much to learn and little time to waste. But by then it was too late.

Plato's school lay northwest of the city walls in a park along the southern bank of the Kephisos. The Academy was an idyllic spot close by the gymnasium and formal gardens, and we students debated and discussed as much and as often wandering through leafy glades as we did in the halls of learning. But it had not always been so.

Centuries before, to celebrate Cimon's victory over the Persians, the vast spoils of that war were used to both fortify and beautify the city. Had not my forebears chosen to turn the dusty, neglected hills north of the city into a verdant paradise, Plato might have founded his school elsewhere. But no, to honor Athena, Cimon had planted there a grove of sacred olive trees, irrigated them with care and transformed the forlorn northern suburb into a bucolic haven. The goddess of wisdom blessed the grove and the trees grew thick and tall. A hundred years later, Plato arrived to find the place a perfect setting for contemplation and learning.

Alas, my thirst for knowledge withered when it came near the heat of the aspirations of a Roman by the name of Lucius Cornelius Sulla who, in ruthless and systematic fashion, laid siege to fair Athens. His engineers chanced upon the Academy's ancient grove north of the city walls. What was once a sacrament to a goddess now became timber for machines of war intent on the destruction of the city that bore her name. If not for Sulla, I might even now be strolling, perhaps with the aid of a walking stick, or better still with a young, attentive maiden supporting each arm, through the gardens of the Lyceum, my students crowding behind, hanging on every word of my discourse. Afterwards, they would bring me honey, bread and wine, and we would devote each day to the simple yet sublime pleasure of seeking knowledge in all its forms. A pretty picture, that.

But this was a life imagined, never lived. For like one of our sacred trees usurped to make their siege engines, I was harvested and swept up to feed Rome's insatiable appetite for the tens upon tens of thousands of men, women and children upon which that lumbering beast's survival depended.

In those first days, I was bitter, despondent, terrified. I never knew what became of Phaedra. Did I hate Rome? Most certainly. Why had she come pounding at Greece's door? What had we done to deserve invasion and annexation? It was only later that I discovered why it was that Sulla had crossed our borders, a tragic example of cause and effect. Was it not to avenge the death of tens of thousands of his own countrymen at the hands of the King of Pontus, with whom Athens was allied? Shall I then lay the blame for my bondage at the feet of Asia Minor's treachery? Or were they, in turn, simply trying to expel an invader? If you ask Melyaket, he will tell you it was my own foolish lust for a library girl that put chains around my ankles. But he is a lover of pain, and likes the rap of my knuckles upon his Parthian pate as payment for his insolence. In the end, what does it matter? The gods set me down in the right place at the wrong time. Now, time has brought me here to this moment where right and wrong have become little more than words, drained of meaning. Over the years I have grown ... philosophical.

•••

Not long after I was captured I was given by Sulla as a gift of thanks to one of his generals, and it was he I served first in fear, then faithfully for thirty years. It was not the life I would have chosen, but who among us is fortunate enough to choose his own destiny and see it fulfilled as planned? Who, indeed, is fool enough to make such a plan?

Lest you think I skipped merrily from student of philosophy to master of one the great houses of Rome, let me assure you, the road was long and bitter. Those first days of my shame and humiliation still prickle with crisp memory; I yearn for a cup of forgetfulness from the river Lethe, but it is yet beyond my reach. I cannot forget, but neither can I bear the thought that you will condemn me or call me coward for allowing myself to become the man you shall discover. I shall tell you of those early days, with the hope that in the end understanding may be accompanied by forgiveness and forbearance. As for you Romans who have not already tossed this narrative aside, I hope for and ask for nothing.

From my hiding place in the library I was discovered and at first praised Athena I had not been skewered then and there. I lived to regret that answered prayer. I was thrown shackled into a cart identical to those used to transport wild beasts to the arena. Our oxcart joined a dismal procession of countless others, the yellow dust cloud of our passing clogging our lungs and eyes and turning day to dusk. As we passed the Lyceum I beheld a sight that caused me to shove my way to the wooden bars and groan aloud. I was purple with rage, yet reluctantly grateful as well. Dozens of Roman soldiers were systematically emptying the library of its contents, packing thousands of scrolls carefully into a line of waiting covered wagons. Much of the rest of the city was aflame, yet Sulla was saving the works of Aristotle. This Roman was a strange and perplexing man.

Although my traveling companions and I were total strangers, we soon became intimate. For days, then weeks we rode at the back of Sulla's army as it cut a swath first through Greece, then into Italy. The rough roads and bare wooden wheels conspired to make close acquaintances of us all. We stumbled and tripped into each other, there not being enough room for all of us to sit on the hay-strewn floor. There were countless carts like ours, and we passed many more thousands chained and on foot. We were the pretty ones, I suppose, destined for labor outside the quarries. Most of my cart-mates were women, plus a few children and six other young men. It took three, maybe four days before we no longer bothered to turn away at the sight of one of us squatting to piss or shit. The bronze butt of a *gladius* in the gut quickly taught the men not to aim their arcs outside the cage. Soon we no longer tried to avoid our own reeking waste. The soldiers laughed, raised up by the depth of our abasement. The few days it rained, in spite of the chill we pressed close to the bars, washing ourselves as best we could. To our captors I am sure we resembled nothing so much as a troupe of ardent beggars, arms outstretched, hands cupped to catch the drops, a paltry blessing from the gods who had otherwise abandoned us.

Our return to Rome was hastened by consul Lucius Cornelius Cinna. Fearing that Sulla's victories in the East would obstruct his own ambition, Cinna raised an army and drove them hard to meet his enemy before Sulla could once again set foot on Italian soil. But the Italians thus conscripted had no stomach for the hardships of a forced march across the mountains of Illyria. Facing Sulla's seasoned legions with no prospect of booty held less allure than the thought of returning to their farms. Which they did, but not before stoning the despotic Cinna to death. When news of the consul's fate reached Sulla, it inflamed that which Cinna had feared the most:  Sulla's lust to don the mantle of dictatorship. He took five of his seven legions, marched through fallen Athens, past Corinth and northwest to Patrae, dragging his spoils behind him.

In those three weeks, except for the occasional snarl over a maggoty hunk of bread, or an ineffectual attempt at comforting a terrified child, none of us ever spoke a word to each other. Ever. We could barely look each other in the eye. From Patrae, we sailed to Brundisium, and as I stepped blinking from the dark hold, I set foot for the first time in Roman Italy. It looked liked any other country on the Adriatic.

But it was not.

•••

The moment Rome learned that Sulla had landed in Italy without disbanding his troops was the signal for civil war. There were many battles waged on our march toward the center of the Western world, and Sulla's senatorial antagonists, especially Marius the younger and consul Gnaeus Papirius Carbo knew that after what they had done to any friend of Sulla they could catch, they were fighting for their lives. There would be no quarter. And there was not. Carbo was eventually cornered, but managed to escape to Africa. Then, three day's march southeast of the city, Sulla gave Marius a furious thrashing and sent him and what was left of his army running back to Praeneste.

Sulla pursued him and laid siege to the town. Since we were to rest there for some weeks, we were brought to the baths and given fresh tunics. A medic came and applied some greasy salve to the sores on my ankles, but my chains were left in place. I was given the first piece of goat's cheese I had had in a month. Then, as a special gift to the company of legionaries behind whom we were dragged, my cart-mates and I were each assigned to an eight-man *contubernium*, or squad, one of us per tent.

I don't know what happened to the others, but my new life depended upon a single and all-consuming duty: to service the needs and whims of these sweaty, filthy and exhausted men. When stripped to their tunics, you could hardly tell us apart. Yet if I was not quick enough with water, if I did not scrape the mud from the soles of their *caligae* to their liking, if I was not pliant or willing enough in the dark, I was beaten senseless. It was then I wished that death would come, but I had neither the will nor the courage to take my own life. On those few nights when my rest was brief but uninterrupted, I dreamed of Athens and the Academy. Each dawn I returned to Hades. The days passed like this, one after another, for over a year.

My life was taken from me, and often were the times when I pondered the irony of taking it back by ending it. Suicides among new captives could reach as high as twenty of every hundred. Were these men and women the brave ones, and we the cowards? I would not presume to judge them, but I chose a different path. To live - not to thrive or protect family or leave something of value for the next generation - but simply to take the next breath and the one after that, I submitted to abuse of any kind, allowed my spirit to crumble to dust, knowing all the while I was crippling my soul for eternity. Yet I was unable to bring an end to it. I clung to a life which was no life. I rose each morning in a stupor, with barely the strength to wish that this day would be my last. Is it cowardice to choose life? Any life at all?

I slept outside my legionaries' tent, a thin, tattered blanket my only shield against the chill. One morning, well before the *cornicines* had sounded the call to awaken the camp, I was disturbed by a noise and rose shivering to one elbow, hoary rime clinging to my hair and blanket. Two soldiers were dragging a body by its heels. It was just light enough for me to see the slashed wrists from the man's upturned hands, his arms trailing above his head in a jostled pose of surrender. Blood still leaked from the wounds, leaving slug-like trails, black in the pre-dawn light. As they passed close by, I recognized the suicide: he was one of the six other men in the first cart that had taken us from Greece. The two Romans, whispering happily about the end of their watch, would take him outside the gate and dump him into one of the defensive ditches surrounding the camp. I strained to see the dead man's expression, hoping foolishly to find the trace of a smile, or at least the hint of a look of peace. There was nothing. There was no expression at all. It was just a corpse.

It was in that moment that I decided to choose life. I set my heart and mind on living with an act of determined will. And to justify that choice, to suffer all the degradations that lay ahead and the sorrow of remembering the life left behind, I chose to believe that those of us who survived did so not out of cowardice, but for the slimmest and most fragile of unuttered hopes that one day our lot would improve.

I was to discover that even when such miracles are granted, and life's burdens lighten, hope comes not as a solitary friend, but is joined by confederates of guilt and shame that sit like harpies in judgment over every goodness that fortune bestows. I survived, and some would say I flourished. But never think for an instant as this tale unfolds that mine has been an easy life. Even in the best of times in the house of Crassus, even after I had opened the smallest of places in my heart where I secretly, silently call him 'friend,' he was still and forever my master.

# CHAPTER II

## 82 BCE - FALL, ROME

Year of the consulship of
Gaius Marius the Younger and Gnaeus Papirius Carbo

Sulla's enemies fell one by one. He commanded the bulk of his legions to abandon the siege of Praeneste in a final push to win his civil war at the very gates of Rome. But the general's dream of dictatorship was almost crushed at the base of the city walls. All would have been lost if not for Marcus Licinius Crassus, only thirty-three years old, who with 2,500 Spaniards fighting on Sulla's right broke the flank of the defenders at the Colline Gate. The city was now Sulla's. He had paid for it with the lives of fifty thousand Romans. The peaceful life of study and contemplation I had hoped to live was buried beneath an avalanche of carnage. I watched the ashes rise from the pyres that burned for weeks about the city and mourned not only for the Athens I would never see again, but also for the lives of these strangers who choked the air with their ascent into a foreign sky.

I quickly learned that in this place, treasure had no value unless it was accompanied by victorious war, political gain or domination over multitudes. Learning, education, philosophy - these things, pursued for their own sake were worthless. Strength, influence, power - this was the currency of Rome.

Which left me utterly destitute. Yet it was my education that saved me. Although the fighting was over, the slaughter continued. Before Sulla's armies had breached the city's gates, Marius the younger had sought to create a majority of senators and supporters by eliminating any voice that might be raised against him. Politicians and patricians known to be partial to Sulla were murdered in their homes and in the streets. Whole families were destroyed. The Forum ran with blood, festooned with the heads of those loyal to Sulla. In this Marius was much like his father, the elder Marius, who five years earlier sought to destroy the irrepressible Sulla when his duties as a Roman general called upon him to abandon the city to put down the rebellious king of Pontus. Two victims of that earlier purge had been Crassus' father and his only remaining older brother.

•••

The officer of the century in which I served was gifted the captives from the ten *contuberniums* under his command. With the money he got for us at auction, he might buy drink and whores to last a week, and perhaps have a bit left over to replace his fraying belt. That is, if he could find a shop or a tavern that was open for business. The city was in chaos. Gone were the days when no armed soldier was allowed within the *pomerium*, the city's ancient boundary, unless it was for the brief span required to celebrate a *triumph.* To my bleary eyes this was a celebration of slaughter, and those who did not take part stood vigil over a once great city devouring itself whole. Rome was ruled by gangs of vicious and undisciplined children playing at king-of-the-hill. It was a terrifying time, for these "children" had devoted, armored men at their backs, their swords bright and bloody.

The gates which Sulla's army had fought so hard to breach were now barred shut. No one could leave, and the screams of those who had sided with the vanquished echoed all around us. We marched south, single file through narrow, stinking streets, our passage often made unbearable by the bodies through which we were forced to tread. In spite of my own chattering teeth, I thanked Athena that the fetid smell was blunted somewhat by November's chill. Even so, all too often the ropes that bound us to each other would pull us off balance causing one or more of us to fall, wrestling for a horrid and frantic moment with the stiffening corpses. We struggled to our feet, Roman blood staining our faces and hands. As we trudged on, our ankles became spattered with a fruitage of butchery so copious at times it flowed in rivulets down the street's central gutter. In the worst passages we gave up trying to avoid it; our toes were stained and slippery, our sandals sticky with clotting blood.

The centurion led us into a wider street, the Vicus Patricius, where we turned southwest and walked until we came into a crowded neighborhood - a valley called the Subura. That is to say it felt as if it *ought* to be bursting with people and activity, yet the street and alleyways were empty, save for the occasional squad of Sulla's soldiers going about their grisly business, their captains gripping scrolls of the damned. It was oddly quiet here. Like birds calling to each other, the silence was pierced now and then by the cries of the dying. The merchant shops were shuttered; the apartments above full of fearful eyes. We could feel their stares upon us but could not see them, did not wish to see them. In our state, there was no gaze we were eager to meet.

I never made it to the auction block.

Soon we heard many voices raised, not in agony but in commerce. We turned into a wide courtyard where it was evident that the business of selling an endless, hapless multitude fallen to the lowest strata of human suffering was not only open, but brisk. Soldiers anxious to cash in on their human booty milled among the braver citizens hoping for a bargain. Other than legionaries, these were the first living Romans I had seen since entering the city. The wooden holding pens on either side of the single raised platform were full. The auctioneer and two assistants were quite well organized, moving people up one side of the auction block and down the other into their new owners' care at a steady and rapid pace. Being the newest arrivals, before we were crammed into one of the cages we were greeted by a mercenary with a rusty, bent gladius and an armload of blank wooden boards. He began at the end of our line, questioning each captive, writing down the replies on the board, then hanging the identification plaques around each neck. Afterwards, he copied the information into a ledger and moved to the next man.

This efficient process was interrupted by the appearance of a lone mounted officer who rode into our midst with the casual confidence of the victor. The man was frighteningly magnificent in his gleaming armor, his red horsehair-plumed helmet blindingly bright when the sun momentarily sliced through the clouds and smoke hanging over the city. He sat with ease upon the largest steed I had ever seen, but was not dwarfed by it. I was toward the front of our miserable parade and heard him tell our centurion that he was looking for talent. Our officer, whose name escapes me, was still caked with the grime, sweat and dried blood of battle. I was struck by the difference in appearance between these two officers - it was as great as that between owner and owned.

Our centurion snorted a short laugh and wiped his arm across his nose with no noticeable improvement. "Talent?" he said. "Take a look. There's no fucking talent in this lot. What's he want with 'em, anyway?" he asked with more impertinence than sense. For answer, the military tribune reined his mount and walked the huge horse down the line.

"Any of you Greeks speak Latin?" he asked in the language of Rome.

I barely hesitated. Before me stood the auction block with what horrid assortment of futures I could only guess. Finding a place where my education might be put to use had to be better than any other fate. To be given this choice, well, it was as close to freedom as I had had since my capture. I opened my mouth to speak, but before I could utter a word the captive next in line elbowed me aside and rasped his assent. If the last four years had reduced me to a reed, this one was a blade of grass. And just as sturdy, for in his haste to edge past me his leg irons tripped him up. Breeding outraced the instinct to survive and I placed my hand on his elbow to steady him. He jerked his head toward me, ready to wrench free of my grip and strike me. Stunned, I let go of him. It had probably been the only non-hostile touch he'd felt in years; at first he could not recognize it. Understanding dawned. He gave me a quick bow of his neck, down and up, and as one we lifted our eyes to the glamorous and impatient officer.

"You, too?" the tribune asked.

In as loud a voice as I could muster, I recited in perfect Latin, "'Education is an ornament in prosperity and a refuge in adversity.' My lord," I finished, "I am seeking refuge."

The fat auctioneer interrupted his harangue when he heard me quoting Aristotle. The merchant had been selling a thin, dark Numidian, the plaque around his neck stating the man's name and confirmation that he was free of epilepsy and had not tried to run away or commit suicide. He pointed a grubby finger at me and addressed the centurion. "I'll give you 150 *sesterces* for this one. 200 for both." Before our weary soldier could get the word "Sold!" out of his mouth, the tribune held up his hand, gave the auctioneer a fiery glance and commanded our centurion to cut the two of us loose. Our officer stood very still for a moment, as if weighing the odds of success in further argument. He fooled no one. Finally accepting his delay in obeying as his sole victory, he begrudgingly untied the lengths of rope around our waists. These had kept us bound in line, and we marveled at this tiny freedom. The centurion secured his slightly poorer inventory, grumbling not quite under his breath all the while.

"Where did you serve?" the tribune asked him as he bent to unlock our chains.

"With the third on the left flank. What's it to you? Sir."

"We were hard pressed on the left. How did you fare?"

"Three Samnites right up against the wall," he said, patting his sword as he stood. "Then it got a bit hectic and I lost count." The tribune motioned to our officer to toss him the lengths of rope that had held us in line. Pommels rose from both the left and right side of his saddle. To these he looped our ropes and let them drop on either side of his mount. Without being asked, I grabbed the nearest one and my new companion trotted around the horse to take the other.

"Do you understand what will happen if you let go?" he asked. We assured him we did.

"Good. I've seen men trampled by horses. Makes quite a mess. Many animals shy away from it. But Lightning here quite enjoys it. You there!" he said, turning to the auctioneer. "Pay this Roman officer the 200 *sesterces* you promised him."

The auctioneer was dumbfounded. "But I ... you ..."

"General Sulla has asked me to repeat how much he deeply and personally appreciates your offering of thanks to his legions for your liberation and our victory over the illegitimate Marius, the traitorous Carbo and the vicious, godless Samnites." The tribune turned back to our centurion who was now beaming and said, "Carry on, soldier."

As we reversed direction heading back down the narrow side street that had brought us to the courtyard the tribune said, "One more thing: read and write, yes, in both tongues?" His right hand rested gently on the butt of his sword. I said of course, and assumed that on the other side of the tribune's horse the other man nodded, for I heard nothing and the Roman continued on.

•••

The tribune marched us through the Subura. Ahead, in the "v" of our restricted vision formed by the four and six story apartment buildings that looked as if they could topple down upon us in an instant, we caught glimpses of white marbled temples and basilicas of brick and stone. From a pack slung across his saddle, the tribune pulled a fair-sized hunk of bread, tore it in two and held his hands down at his sides. Miracle of miracles, it wasn't even stale! I tried to consume it with dignity, but after one small bite manners were overwhelmed by hunger, even gratitude. The best I could manage was to be discrete while wiping away a tear that formed as I chewed.

"If Rome is the heart of the empire," the tribune lectured unnecessarily, "then the Comitium is the heart of Rome. There lies the Forum and the Curia Hostilia where the senate deliberates, and you should thank the gods you lived to get a glimpse of it." Before getting any nearer, the Roman turned his horse sharply to the left. "Don't expect to ever lay eyes upon it again."

We had come onto a wide, flagstone paved street that sloped gradually uphill. "I would not stain the Sacra Via with your unworthy and pestiferous feet, but this is the shortest route." I could not help but look back the way we had come to stare at the seat of Rome's power, but my head was jerked around abruptly by the tribune's pull on my rope. Clearly, my unworthy and pestiferous eyes had lingered long enough.

This new street was also lined with merchants' stores, now deserted, but these were finer and no doubt traded in goods beyond the reach of any but the richest citizens. Well behind these single and two-story shops we could see the roofs of the homes where those wealthy patrons must live. To my right, a roughly rectangular hill rose a few hundred feet, its base graced by a grove of trees surrounding a columned, circular temple. The top of this hill was studded with many ornate villas, but several of these were now burning. Our route took us to the top of the Sacra Via on the hill opposite. The homes of the wealthy graced both sides of the broad street, but our view was blocked by high walls, broken now and then by the doors and displays of a *tabernae* catering to the richest Romans. As we approached a pair of tall, iron gates, two guards threw the bolt and gave us access.

It was as if we had passed beyond the veil of the living and entered a miniature Olympus, a place inhabited by immortals. I was at once dumbstruck, and almost immediately thereafter afraid. I did not belong here. The sight of such wonders could only bring misfortune, like Actaeon stumbling upon Artemis as she bathed. The Huntress turned him into a stag, then caused his own hounds to tear him apart. Our tribune broke this dreadful reverie by yanking on my rope to pull me forward into the grounds of the estate. Startling a lethargic peacock draped across the white gravel path, we passed a spouting fountain, marble statuary and flower gardens, the sight of which would calm the most agitated eye. Though I remained uneasy, I was compelled to look. It was not long before another sense conquered my fears and completed the seduction. I found myself stealing great breaths of fragrant air, saturated with a harmony of herbs and flowers that made my knees weak. Suddenly overcome, I fought to keep my eyes from welling.

The tribune led us down and around to the back of the home where we and the soldier's horse were tied haphazardly to the same column supporting a semicircular balcony above our heads. He took our fragile hands, the ones that held the free ends of the rope, and with his own calloused, giant fingers squeezed with such force that my knuckles cracked. We were admonished in a low whisper that to move or speak was death. The fullness of my belly made me giddy; as the officer strode briskly into the house, I almost called out after him that we would do our best to keep his horse quiet. Sanity prevailed, but was soon to be abandoned.

# CHAPTER III

## 82 BCE - FALL, ROME

Year of the consulship of
Gaius Marius the Younger and Gnaeus Papirius Carbo

Several men and women were busy pruning and trimming the flowered garden that sloped gently down the hill that overlooked the way we had come. I almost smiled when I realized the view to the northwest looked directly down upon the Comitium. The tribune would have insisted that I avert my gaze. I took great pleasure in allowing my eyes to linger over every building and temple.

Men were talking on the balcony above us.

"... the one at the very top of the Palatine?" a deep voice, well-pleased with itself was saying.

"The one on fire?" asked another. This one sounded much younger than the first speaker, his voice constricted by nerves. I did not know it as I eavesdropped, but I was soon to become a poorly wrapped gift, and Marcus Licinius Crassus, the man who had just spoken, the arrogant recipient.

"The very same. That is the ruins of the house of old Marius. I shall build my estate upon its ashes."

"Sir, may I ask why you have called me to the Carinae? As lovely as the view is from this hill, I must see to my Spaniards."

"Good men all. My best medics are already on their way to your camp to tend to the wounded. Relax, Marcus. I've a special surprise for you which should be here any minute. Take a cup of wine. It's from your vineyards after all."

"Sir?"

"This home has been abandoned by the previous owner, along with all his property and wealth. Not coincidentally, he abandoned the field of battle as well, his tail well-tucked. A coward such as Carbo deserves no finery such as this. I doubt he'll be making any claims from Africa. Today, I give all his possessions to the hero of the Colline Gate."

"Words cannot express my gratitude, general. But my father, may he rest peacefully in Juno's arms, would never approve of such a display of immoderate wealth. Our family home was a third as large." The man's barely contained joy was proof that he was not his father.

"And your father," the first man countered, "could have afforded an estate ten times as grand, so let us consider this a fair compromise. Come Marcus, we must begin to rebuild the wealth Marius stole. We take back only that which rightfully belongs to you. My mind is set on this - though of plebian ancestry, the Licinii Crassi have sacrificed more for the sake of Rome than most nobles: a father and the two eldest of three sons? It is enough. You must make your mark for their sake."

"My lord ..."

"No. You have your own family to consider. How fare your wife and son?" Evidently there would be no further argument.

"My wife and *sons*, if my offerings are accepted. When I left Tertulla in Lavinium last year to join your campaign, she was with child. Her letters have yet to find me; I pray Mercury lends mine swifter wings. Girl or boy, the next Crassus should be a year old by now. Young Marcus will turn three next month." Even from my lowly vantage point I could hear the pride in his voice.

"This is magnificent news. You honored the memory of your brother when you took Tertulla in."

"She was just a child. Only thirteen and married to Lucius less than a year the day he was cut down. I do honor his memory, but I would have seen it served in any other way than this. Thanks to the gods that Tertulla was visiting her parents, or her name would have lengthened the list of the dead. It is a marvel, but these past five years I have come to cherish her as if I had been the first to woo her. Yet that is of no account. What I did is unremarkable; any decent Roman would have done the same."

"Decent Romans," the older man mused. "Roman decency is a rare commodity nowadays. For proof, one need but take a stroll through almost any neighborhood of the city." I grimaced with disgust; the man was oblivious to the fact that at least half the carnage in the streets could be laid upon the edge of Roman swords. The senior officer continued. "Wait a few weeks before summoning Tertulla back to the city. A woman's eyes ought not to lose their sparkle from the sight of what men must do to keep them safe. Although it's never too early for the son of a Roman to begin his education." I prayed to Reason that no son of Rome would ever call me father. As it turned out, Reason would attend. The boy I grew to think of as a true son would hail from quite another quarter, a fugitive who would find his home with me.

There was a short silence after which Marcus Crassus appeared to acquiesce tacitly to his benefactor's generosity by changing the subject. "So, Carbo escaped, then?" he said.

"Don't trouble yourself. I've sent young Gnaeus Pompeius after him with his three legions. Do you know him?"

"We've never met. I hear his ability to command far outstrips his years. Wasn't it he and Metellus who engaged Carbo in the north? It makes me feel unworthy being the recipient of such bounty." My ears strained to catch each word of this lofty conversation.

"Look there. That villa will be his upon his return. You'll be neighbors! Be at ease, Marcus, it has at least one peristyle more than yours. Will that give Pompeius his due? Fine. It is settled then. Let's eat something while we wait. I'm famished." In a different tone, one I had heard often from countless men since my abduction, he barked, "Bring it outside."

Several more people approached, there was the scraping of furniture and the gentle clank and clatter of trays being carefully laid down. The man next to me took no notice; he sat cross-legged, his head tilted back against the column. Jaw slack. Eyes closed. My foot was at the ready should he start to snore.

After a few moments of quiet, the man who I assumed was older than Crassus laughed out loud. "You should have seen their faces," he said. "As white as their togas, I swear by Jupiter." He was talking with his mouth full. The implication made me salivate. "The Curia was no fit place to address what was left of the senate. I would not speak to them standing on the still fresh blood of my friends. So this morning we shepherded them all up the Capitoline to the Temple of Bellona. An unhappy coincidence, since close by my legates had assembled the remaining, captured Samnites on the Campus Martius. There they would pay in full for their insurrection." The man bit into some kind of fruit. I could hear the juice fly. "Only open field with enough room to herd 'em all," he said, his mouth once again overfull. I swallowed back unbidden saliva, almost losing track of the conversation.

"How many were taken prisoner?"

"Oh, maybe five, six thousand." Crassus made a sound of acknowledgment. "The cries of the ones in the rear who could see their fate approaching worked our venerable legislators into a frenzy. And my intention had been to calm the senators and reassure them. It really was quite funny. They thought they themselves would be next to fall under the sword. I had to leave the rostrum to compose myself while my men shepherded the terrified conscript fathers back to their places. When I stopped laughing and regained my dignity I returned and told them I had come to save them, not slay them. I could see it in their eyes: everything I said fell on ears plugged with wax manufactured from the screams of the dying Samnites.

"Marius and his gang were their true enemies. If he had had his way the assemblies and the plebs would have stripped the senate of all real power. Jupiter! His thugs killed off more than half the original three hundred. We need to do something about that, Marcus." He paused a moment. "We need to protect the old ways. I shall tear down the Curia and build a new, larger one, this time with enough room to hold twice as many togas."

"But the law only allows three hundred senators."

The older man's tone grew dark. "The law shall be rewritten." Then he brightened. "And we must see that the seats are filled with our friends, with men who are loyal to Rome, eh, and to me? You shall have a seat," he said, suddenly inspired.

"General, I am honored, but I have yet to embark upon the *cursus honorum*."

I could envision the wave of a dismissive hand. "It is a done thing. What a pity it would have been had my dreams died at the very gates of the city. Your role was not insignificant, Marcus. We will speak no more of it."

I smiled outright. The tribune who had marched us here had been so proud of his Curia; now it would be razed. But a breath later my smile fled, my lips pressed to flatness by widened eyes. I tried to rationalize my stupidity: I was exhausted, starving, a blood-spattered wreck. Still, logic should have prevailed and shaken me before now. Above my head stood Lucius Cornelia Sulla, conqueror of Asia Minor, plunderer of Athens and thief of the life of Alexandros, son of Theodotos. My heart used my stomach for a drum and I gripped the column for support. Here was the man at whose feet could be laid every injury, insult and degradation I had endured these past four years. In that time, all that I once might have been had been ground away until what was left was more stone than man: cold, weathered, inert. Knowledge wrenched me back to myself; I was suddenly, sharply awake.

Much more was said, and of that heartbreaking tale I shall speak again. But the nearness of General Sulla was causing me to become increasingly agitated, like a fly unable to reach a pile of offal. There was nothing holding me save my word, my own voluntary grip on the centurion's rope and the promise of a summary and certain demise. Even so, I imagined myself stepping out into the light, armed with arrow and bow to wreak glorious justice upon Sulla, claiming as my prize a death that would make an end of my travails.

My impotent and weaponless daydreaming was cut short by the sound of a prisoner being brought before Crassus and Sulla as they waited on the balcony. To tell it briefly, the man was executed and beheaded on the spot. The head escaped its executioners, rolled out off the veranda and onto the gravel path below. I followed the sound of a moist thud and there, almost at my feet I met the open and discomfiting gaze of the victim. His facial muscles still twitched in a parody of communication, either from the fluid still draining from his neck or from the jarring effect of his flight and abrupt landing. I leapt back, stumbling over my sleeping companion who, having been trampled awake began a diatribe of reproach interrupted by the sight of the severed head. The gardeners froze, their hoes and rakes motionless, but then like the well-trained servants they were, they continued as if this barbarity were an everyday occurrence.

The chains of fear that had kept me from myself suddenly fell away. I could act, not at the whim of my captors but of my own volition. Sulla had emancipated me, for who among the hundreds of thousands shackled by this brutish man's armies had ever stood so close to the taproot of all that misery? I was free! Free, but with only one act to choose, only one decision that was mine alone to make. I would die, and deprive these Romans of any further use of me. I laughed to think that I had once believed my lot could ever improve; to wish for a return to a life of dignity was a vain and empty hope. I would deceive myself no longer and take back my life, if only for a moment. A meaningless gesture was my only weapon, but I intended to wield it with skill and accuracy. I have heard that the moments before death can bring unrivaled clarity and lightheartedness. It is true.

Running out into the sunlight, I grabbed a hank of black, oily hair and hoisted the staring head high: Alexandros, son of Theodotos, a demented Perseus. "General, I see you've lost your head!" I shouted in Latin. "Shall I toss it up to you? Catch it, then, and bloody your hands. May the stain never fade."

The conqueror of Rome leaned over the marble railing and glared at me. He turned away and said something I could not catch. Any moment now. The rumble of many feet came rushing down the stairwell.

Soldiers poured out the doorway but Sulla shouted for them to hold. The military tribune's horse shied and was led away, almost trampling my bilingual friend. He scrambled to his feet only to be pressed against the column by the points of several threatening *gladii.* Seeing me bloodstained and wild-eyed, holding aloft the severed head, despite the ring of soldiers hemming him in my fellow Greek began mumbling incoherently and making signs against evil.

"It feels good, you know," I said, breaking the moment of silence when the world grew still and even the breeze held its breath.

"Please," Sulla mocked, "Do describe this brief elation before I end it."

"Why, having the great General Sulla do my bidding."

"Ordering me about, are you?" He laughed along with his subordinates. "And what is it you expect me to do?"

"You have already done it." I would say no more, for fear he would rescind the order for spite and spoil my plan. A moment later the audience for this little entertainment parted and an archer appeared, swinging his bow up and over the balustrade.

"Don't bother throwing it up. My men will fetch it once you're dead." He nodded to the archer. I dropped the corpse's head and spread my arms, chest out, face turned to the infinite sky.

"General! A moment." It was the voice of the tribune who had led us to this place. "Forgive me," he said, "but that is one of the two translators you had me fetch for ..."

"Damn! Marcus, this was to be another gift. Carbo's slaves are mostly Greek, they speak no Latin. When we took the house my men met with some resistance and we were forced to thin them out – the house translators were among the dead. I'll shoot this one and get you another. There has to be a more compliant candidate left alive in the city."

"A shame," Crassus said. "His Latin is perfect."

"Archer!" I called. "Do you love your vocation?" And in Greek, "I hope so, for 'pleasure in the job puts perfection in the work.'"

"Aristotle!" cried Crassus. Then, almost apologetically to Sulla, "I am an admirer." I got the first look of my master as he appeared at the railing. A soldier in his prime: hair close-cropped, brows knit over a slightly bent nose; thin lips, strong chin and eyes care-worn yet masterful. Like most of the men peering down at me, he looked worn out, yet comforted by the mantle of victory. He leaned over the railing and called to me in Greek, "Apologize, and you yet may live."

"If you are a true student of philosophy, good sir, you will not interfere," I said. "You will know that 'the very best thing is not to have been born, to be nothing. The second best thing is to die soon.'"

"As much as I admire the Greek thinkers," Crassus said, "Aristotle missed the mark this time. Live awhile and prove me wrong."

"Sulla!" I implored desperately. "Will you let all these witnesses make you a laughingstock?"

"You have spirit," Sulla called. "But there's no meat on your bones. What good is a weakling, insolent slave? I can't let this go, Marcus. Archer ...." I closed my eyes. The bow overhead voiced a single, creaking complaint as the string was pulled back.

"I like his impertinence," Crassus pressed. "And with all humility, may I remind the general why it was you had him found? If you still intend him as a gift, perhaps the *lorum* will tame his arrogance. Will this suffice?"

Sulla considered. "See how he perplexes me? I had quite forgotten. Well ... he is yours now; the decision belongs to you as well. But damn it, Marcus, I cannot allow *any* man to speak to me thusly with impunity. And this ... I mean look at him. Archer, shoot him in the leg. And somebody bring me my head!"

# CHAPTER IV

## 82 BCE - FALL, ROME

Year of the consulship of
Gaius Marius the Younger and Gnaeus Papirius Carbo

A word of advice: if you can possibly avoid it, do not get shot. The arrow pierced my right thigh and exited out the back of my leg with force enough to spin me off-balance. My wounded leg flew backward, tripping up my other leg as I twisted from the impact. I was screaming *before* my fall broke the feathered shaft as I hit the ground face down. Unable to stop my momentum, I rolled over until the protruding iron arrowhead stabbed the back of my other thigh. I'm told the complaints streaming from my mouth were insufferable; Sulla ordered a legionary to rush up and knock me on the head with the butt of his sword.

•••

Now that I have told you how my new master ruined my first and only attempt at escape from bondage, I return to the events that happened only moments before. They concern the condemned man whose blood Crassus refused to allow to be washed from the balcony's stones for as long as he lived in that place. So let us go back to the moment he was dragged before Sulla and Crassus.

•••

There was a commotion at the front of the house: the slap and murmur of leather armor, the clamor of studded *caligae,* the stumble of an out-of-step gait shoved from behind. "Your next gift approaches," Sulla said to Crassus. As this procession marched out onto the balcony, the sound of a sword being drawn was accompanied by these words from the general: "Lucius Junius Brutus Damasippus, I accuse you of the murder of Quintus Mucius Scaevola, *pontifex maximus.* In the blinking brightness of day. In front of scores of witnesses. In of all places the most sacred Temple of the Vestals. A crime so bold and heinous it is a reeling affront to everything for which Rome stands. Do you deny it?"

There came a coarse cough of laughter, then a new voice spoke with venom made potent by the hopelessness of his plight. "I deny nothing. I cut the priest's throat with my own *pugio* and watched his blood run down the steps of the temple."

"And do you deny that Gaius Marius Minor, the last holdout of those who have raised arms against me, he who is now held under siege at Praeneste, holds your leash?"

"This is too pretty a place for an execution, Lucius Cornelius, and far too private for your purpose. What are you playing at? I appreciate the view, but if you expect repentance, I shit on your ignorance. Do what you brought me here to do."

"The dead make no demands: I give no credence to the words of a ghost. For history's sake, I *will* make an accurate accounting. Marius gave you a list."

"We have it here my lord," a soldier said. There was quiet as Sulla scanned it.

"And did you ...?"

"To the last senator," spoke Damasippus. "You'll find them at the bottom of the Tiber. Togas make excellent shrouds. By the way, you'll find the high priest Scaevola down there as well. You see, we did try to clean up after ourselves," the villain added.

"You were loyal, Brutus; you served faithfully, first the father, then the son. This I do not hold against you, for it is this quality I seek above all others in my own allies. You may have truly believed, as did Marius, that the people require more representation than what they already have from the senators whom *they* have elected. Or maybe you simply gambled that your sword would be wielded on the side of the victor. Either way, you have chosen unwisely. Yet even this I might be inclined to overlook, but for the cruel and vicious streak in you. I take no pleasure in restoring sanity to Rome. I do what must be done. But you, you are ... overzealous. I cannot abide intemperance in any form."

"Then chide your tongue," Damasippus snapped. "This endless prattle offends my person more than any blade." There was a blunt *whump* and the prisoner became silent. My neck ached. I rolled my head to relieve the strain of looking up, as if that would improve my hearing.

Sulla spoke again. "Marcus, come close. Do you know this man?"

"There is something familiar about his face." A pause. "YOU!"

"Hold, Marcus." A short scuffle. "He will be yours in good time. Before I could breach the walls of the city, this traitor had already discharged his bloody commission from Marius the son, but five years earlier, the faithful cur performed the same bloody tricks for Marius the father. I wish these good souls assembled here to know the full measure of his perfidy. Remember, Marcus Licinius; purge yourself of the memory."

There was silence for a long while, then Crassus spoke hoarsely, but I could not make out the words. Sulla's stentorian growl, though, fell hard on my ears. "This is the man, Marcus! More than this house, more than any treasure I have yet to bestow upon you, I warrant you will value him as my greatest gift to you. Most of him, that is. I shall retain his head for another purpose."

Crassus found his voice, each word of the retelling slowly stoking his anger as the memory took shape and form till it was once again a live and twisting thing in his gut. "You were bearded then." The sound of measured steps fading then returning: Crassus circling Damasippus. "Bless the gods for their kindness – they took my mother the day I was born; she would be neither witness nor victim of that day's work. My eldest brother, Publius - he too was fortunate. He died honorably, killed in the last war against our rebellious Italian allies.

"But on the day of which you would have me speak, general, the day my family's honor and life was gutted like a gasping trout, I was the *lucky* one." The word came miserable and shriveled from Crassus' throat. "My brother

Lucius had just returned ... ." A breeze blew through the needles of the stone pines lining the garden border and carried his next words away on the chill wind. I pleaded with their great, rounded crowns, swaying like giant mushrooms on spindly stalks, begging them to be still. To my amazement, they heard my prayer and ceased their lofty chatter.

"They never found me," Crassus was saying. "But through the cracks of the garden shed I saw what happened. Pallus, the gardener and two of his Egyptians had gone there with me to fetch fertilizer and tools. If not for them ....

"How ironic that my father once supported Marius. He was always a man of the people. But his taste for politics soured once the killing began. He became devoutly apolitical and withdrew from public life altogether. Which is why he looked mildly surprised when a squad of soldiers marched up to his home, led by *this* man. I never learned his name, but his deeds made the memory of his face indelible. Damasippus, you say. I have it now. You never gave it when my father demanded it of you. Why should it matter to me now? But it does, you see, because there is a perverse balance in the knowing. In my heart, the names of my kin are forever linked to their kind and gentle ways. Until now I had no name to connect the profane acts of that day. Marius may have given the order. But never has such a heinous command ever been executed with such joyous devotion. By you. Damasippus.

"You gave my father a choice. You must have known of him: consul, censor, governor of Hispania Ulterior, a patrician proclaimed *imperatore* by his troops and granted a triumph for his victory over the Lusitani, yet *you* gave *him* a choice. Fall on your sword, you said, and spare the life of your son. My father was no fool. He knew the sun above his head would be the last to shine upon him. He did not beg or ask why or hesitate for one second. He said, 'Spare the lives of the rest of my household, my children and their children.' Lucius cried out and struggled against the two that held him. 'Be brave, my son,' my father said as the rest of the soldiers pushed roughly past him to search the house. 'Take anything you like ....'" Crassus' breath caught, it became clear he was crying. 'Take it all,' Father said, 'but spare all who live under my roof. Swear this. Swear on the honed tips of Diana's unerring arrows and upon the blessed curls that grace your mother's head.' And you swore. You swore.

"My father called for Plocamus, our steward, to assist him, and he shuffled bravely out from amongst the servants. But he was old and frail. You pushed him aside and ...." Crassus faltered. "You told him he could not lift a sword, let alone brace it."

"I know damn well what I ..."

"SILENCE!" Sulla bellowed. "Go on, Marcus."

"I cannot. Rage and sorrow both have stopped my mouth. Oh gods! Will you not let me avenge them now?!"

"Draw your sword," said Sulla, "for its thirst shall be slaked. I have heard the tale, my friend, and would be your voice, for the story eats at me and must out. This traitorous whoreson took his own sword and knelt before your father, bracing the butt against his boot. Publius Licinius addressed the house, but his gaze was fixed on Lucius, his eldest remaining son. 'Mourn not,' he said, 'for

I happily sell all my remaining days to make this purchase. When Marcus returns, express my sorrow at not being able to say goodbye.' He looked down at his murderer and added, 'Be not forsworn,' and then he fell upon the blade."

"I could not go to him!" Crassus cried with a voice aged with five years of guilt and anger. "Three men held me fast, their strength doubled to save their own lives as well as mine. Pallus whispered 'forgive me' in my ear as he clasped a hand over my mouth."

"A foul business," Sulla said. "And here is the worst of it. Before the sword could inflict a lethal blow, Damasippus thrust a hand up to your father's shoulder, arresting his descent. He nodded to the men holding your brother and smiled as they slit his throat. Seeking your father's eyes once more, he grinned as he said, 'Marius bids me say thusly: you and your family shall become as dust, your coins melted, your works dismantled, and your household utterly destroyed.' He cast his stiffened arm aside, your father fell, and Damasippus laughed as the light went from his eyes. You and your three brave servants were the only ones to escape."

The sound of weeping came from above, and more cries than the sobs of Crassus swept down to me on the wind. There soon followed silence. I strained to listen, my breath a caged captive in my chest.

Sulla said, "Marcus will kill you now, Lucius Junius. You will receive no rights of burial. Your body will be cast into the Tiber. Your possessions and property will be proscribed and your family and all that called you friend will be hunted down and put to the sword. When you are slain, I will take your severed head and send a message with it, more convincing than any inked on parchment. I shall catapult it over the walls of Praeneste so that the son of Marius will know his battle for Rome is over. For him, like you, all is lost."

There came a thud as the condemned must have been forced to his knees. Sulla said in a solemn voice, "He is yours, Marcus."

I had seen these executions before and cringed at the thought of what was going on above me. Crassus must have stood behind his victim, placed his sword point at the base of the neck and with both hands thrust straight down. I heard nothing, but the deed must have been done.

Because then they took the head.

# CHAPTER V

## 82 - 81 BCE - WINTER, ROME

Year of the consulship of
Gaius Marius the Younger and Gnaeus Papirius Carbo

There was a girl, maybe ten or eleven. Perhaps twelve; I've never been good with children. They puzzle me. She stood by wherever it was I lay and stared at me with an intensity that, had I the strength, would have made me look away. Green eyes the color of a hummingbird's back. I tried to smile at her, but I don't think my face cooperated. She began to whistle, backing away into the middle of the room and dancing to the rhythm she set. Her long hair, as red and gold as a Piraeus sunset, spun about her face as she twirled. It made me dizzy to watch her, but I was transfixed. The back of my head throbbed like a second heart. Before I lost consciousness again, a thought lurched past, irrelevant and nonsensical: her tresses are silken and she has no freckles. Unusual for a redhead.

•••

My legs were brittle fire. If I moved, they would crack and break apart like charred paper. Someone replaced the cloth on my forehead with one dampened by cool water and aromatic oils. Ecstasy. The blanket soaked with my sweat was pulled away and someone gasped. "Livia, get out," a woman commanded. Footsteps retreated and next I felt the pressure of gently probing fingers. I groaned. My heart had abandoned my chest altogether. Now it fell to my thigh, thumping against its swollen tightness. If I moved, it would burst free from the inside.

A man's voice: "Will he live?"

The woman answered, "If the fever breaks. I must drain the wounds." She began her work in earnest. There came a most disagreeable scream, after which I spun out of consciousness.

•••

Two weeks later, I was summoned. Sabina, the Greek healer responsible for my recovery, guided me from the servants' wing through the house. But for her, I would have perished in the delirium of infection that spread from my thigh until it ran up against the unyielding ministrations of my savior. As clarity returned, I found myself in the middle of a perplexing dilemma. A captive quickly learns that the odds of survival are greatly improved by *not* drawing attention to oneself. Yet here I was, propped up on pillows (rough-woven homespun stuffed with seed hulls, but pillows nonetheless), spoon-fed hot broth by either the healer or her daughter, and given a gift withheld for so long I could scarcely count the days since I had last received it: comfort. Never in all my life had I craved someone's attention as much as I did this spare, hard woman. Her face, once beautiful, had been weathered down to handsome. She was tall but never seemed to stand to her full height, as if her trials were a constant weight against which she strove. She was not quite old enough to be my mother, but each moment spent in her company brought painfully sweet reminders of family, and home.

A non-ambulatory servant will test the patience of the most understanding Roman, so I drank Sabina's potions, hobbled about as long and as often as I could endure it, and did everything I could to assist in my own convalescence. On these brief walks down dark hallways, my arm gripping her narrow shoulder, her strength supplying most of what kept us vertical, my best conversational skills were not enough to draw Sabina out. In two weeks I learned little more than that she was from Attica and had been married. Her husband had been killed almost a year ago, I know not how. Like me she had only recently come into the service of Crassus. She evaded all my queries; I did not even know if she was bought or free. Yet there was some part of her story she could not conceal. An unknown hardship lived just beneath the surface of her smile, etching lines of care about her eyes. Sometimes I would catch her standing silently, staring off in some sad reverie from which I was loath to startle her. It saddened me to see this, and to know there was no way I could help.

But oh how she brightened when Livia alighted in the room, which the child did whenever her own chores were done. Then, the gremlins that tormented Sabina dropped their detestable tools and fled the moment she set eyes on her daughter. Livia was ready with a quick and fervent hug, but flitted off again, questioning this, examining that.

The girl could not keep still; when she wasn't talking she was whistling, and the whistling inevitably led to dancing.

Her mother tried to channel some of that energy by handing her a dust cloth, then a broom, then a mop. Sabina claimed the servants assigned to housekeeping were sufficient for cleaning barns and sties, but little else. Sabina was neat the way a Roman pine was coniferous. I have found her on her hands and knees scrubbing the grout between the flagstones with an old tooth rag and a bucket of diluted vinegar. And then again three days later.

Livia did not grumble when asked to help; her vitality needed an outlet and almost any activity would do. She sang and scrubbed, creating dance steps that used the mop as a partner. More than once Sabina had to remind her they were no longer in Salamis. Romans, she admonished, find dancing vulgar. So Sabina, too, had learned the benefits of remaining invisible. A lesson yet to be absorbed by the dazzling and willful Livia.

"Then Romans," she replied, fixing me with an impish leer, "are the thing you see when you lift a horse's tail."

I stifled a guffaw as Sabina exclaimed, "Livia! You must never speak like that." She glanced toward the hallway, a reflexive movement common in non-Roman conversations: were we being overheard, there would be consequences. Roman consequences. "Where ever did you learn such a thing?"

"At home, of course." And she was gone, twirling off at speed. Sabina called her back unsuccessfully. The sadness came rushing back into her expression, a thief of joy intent on stealing a mother's smile. "Home?" I tried. "But this is her home." Sabina ignored me as she refilled my water cup from a terra cotta pitcher. "Keep drinking," she said, her healer's demeanor restored. She ruffled my hair with genuine affection. I ached to know more, but dared not pick further at a scab that was not my own.

•••

By the time we reached the entrance to the *tablinum,* sweat dotted my forehead; Sabina steadied me, her arm an oak branch under my own. The study was small, crowded with the work assigned to one of Sulla's new favorites. The day was surprisingly warm; curtains had been pulled so that the room was open to the adjacent peristyle. Iron rings discouraged a spray of scrolls from going outside to play with the occasional breeze. There was room for but one chair, and its occupant was unlikely to give it up to the bandaged young heron wobbling before him. Sunlight fell from the columned garden onto Crassus' outstretched, sandaled foot, the leather lacings only a few shades darker than his tanned calf. His bare arms draped languidly over cedar armrests, hands hanging down in repose. The man I must now call lord wore a tunic hemmed with silver thread; the only other adornment was a band of iron on his left ring finger. His form begged to be sculpted; his face belonged on coins. Marcus Licinius Crassus, one of Rome's new masters, had just turned thirty-four. As my eyes rose to meet his, I saw that he was studying me as intently as I had been taking account of him.

"You live," he said.

"Apparently."

"I am pleased."

I did not respond.

"I've decided I am not going to have you whipped."

"I am pleased," I said with emphasis.

There followed a second of silence in which I tried to hold his gaze, but faltered. "Take him back, Sabina," Crassus said with a flick of his wrist. "Give him another day's rest, then have him report to Pío." We turned to go, but he stopped us. "You studied philosophy, did you not?" I nodded. "Next week," he said, returning to his work, "you'll spend an hour each day tutoring my son. Why should we hire out when we have our very own expert on the Greek thinkers."

"But how did ...."

Crassus did not look up. He took another scroll from the pile, but his lips curled into an involuntary smile. "We keep excellent records on captives' backgrounds. Unlike some, I read them."

"Isn't Marcus a little young?" Sabina asked.

"When the other boys start at seven, he'll be that much further ahead. Just an hour a day; enough to whet his appetite."

"Yes, *dominus,*" Sabina said. She elbowed me.

"Yes, *dominus,*" I repeated dully, marveling at his knowledge of me, and that he had bothered to discover it.

Crassus spoke again. "Now we shall ascertain if your educational gifts equal your prowess as an archery butt."

My face reddened. Was that a dismissal? Crassus read his parchment while we stood there, stuck in a hot, uncomfortable limbo. I shifted painfully on my leg. Finally, he said, "Oh, one more thing." He looked up, his expression impenetrable. "Pío is a Laletani - Hispanic. His Latin is passable but rudimentary. He does not understand sarcasm. He boasts twice my weight and half my sense of humor. Need I say more?" he asked with eyebrow raised. I stared at him in mild surprise. Was he trying to look out for me, or was he merely protecting his investment? Dare I ask? Too late. The interview was over. Crassus had returned to his work and the moment to wave the banner of my own ironical sense of humor had passed. Timing is all.

In any case, my stamina was flagging.

That was the extent of my first conversation with Marcus Crassus. I would not have another for three months.

# CHAPTER VI

## 82 - 81 BCE - WINTER, ROME

Year of the consulship of
Gaius Marius the Younger and Gnaeus Papirius Carbo

Two days later, the morning rose surly and bitter, wrapping itself in a thick cloud blanket against the cold. Crassus had left early for the senate. From there he would ride to surprise his wife on the Via Laurentina as she returned to Rome from Lavinium with her two children, one of which Crassus had never set eyes upon. As the morning progressed, I quickly discovered that when the cat is off in search of other game, the mice in this house had better keep their mouths shut and their whiskers well hidden if they didn't want them plucked out one by one.

I was owned by Crassus, but my quotidian fate rested with the Spaniard, Pío. He was the kind of man whose features are difficult to describe: the moment you set eyes on any one of them you are struck with the need to look quickly away. I do not make a practice of such thoughtless prejudice: just because he looked like an unwashed, overfed barbarian did not necessarily mean he wasn't the sweetest of men. So to be clear as an Alpine lake, let me set your mind at rest: Pío was *not* the sweetest of men. Crassus had found him during the months he had been forced to flee the city. Publius, Crassus' father, had been governor of Hispania Ulterior, and his fair and prosperous rule had gained him many friends. Vibius Piciacus was among them. When the disheveled son of his murdered comrade sought refuge, Piciacus did what he could to keep young Marcus safe from the spies of Cinna and Marius. There was a large cave by the sea on Piciacus' estate, and there Crassus and his few retainers hid for the better part of a year. Piciacus, fearing reprisals should his generosity be discovered, would not visit his guest himself, but sent his manservant Pío there each day with food and anything else Crassus might require, including the company of two young women paid well for their silence and their service. When news of Cinna's death reached Hispania, Crassus came out of hiding. As a reward for his constant and discrete care of his charges, Pío was given his freedom. He chose to return with Crassus to Rome; Piciacus must have been glad to see the last of him.

My first encounter with Pío occurred in the dining room. Appropriate, considering his capacity for consumption. He had stripped the meat off a roast leg of goat and was absentmindedly gnawing the bone to splinters. With his free hand he held a serviette beneath the machinery of his mouth to catch the falling detritus. From this visage of dainty gluttony my eyes fled to his feet, but the sight of those broad, hirsute plains sloping to the grimy boulders of his toes gave them no shelter. I know he wore a belt; I could see the leather escaping his sides to find sanctuary across the broad expanse of his back, but head-on there was no sign of it: the sagging lozenge of flesh had overwhelmed and smothered the sweat-stained band. Crassus had not employed the man as his *atriensis* - an archaic term for the manager of his household which Crassus still favored - for his good looks. Was it the Spaniard's talent or my owner's sense of obligation that had moved him? If talent, it was well-hidden.

The house was preparing a feast for the masters' return that would double as the start of the seven days commemorating the Saturnalia, the most raucous of Roman holidays. I limped into the room on my own with Sabina by my side, who watched my progress closely. She had furnished me with a staff, but warned that I should use it as little as possible if I wanted to strengthen my wounded leg. I did indeed want that, but more immediately wanted not to lose my balance and fall crashing to the ground. I clasped the crutch like a lover.

Livia came in, carrying a small tripod table which she carefully set down near one of the couches. She waved at us, then ran back to the kitchen, skidding to avoid a servant heading the other way. A little bird chittered after Pío picking up verbal crumbs. Pío spit directions that were barely Latin at the bustling servants who were mostly Greek, and this little man translated. I didn't recognize him at first for he was washed, shaved and healed of all his sores and bruises. But then another serving girl got in his way and he elbowed her aside to regain his position near his master. The familiar rudeness also jostled free a memory: a bedraggled chain whose links could barely be called men, trudging without will toward whatever unplanned future the auction block held in store. Here was my bilingual companion-in-misery, saved from a choiceless fate (almost at my expense) and thrust into one of his own making a lifetime ago. I hobbled to him with one arm outstretched, but to my surprise he backed away and Pío's giant hand came down between us.

"This is Alexandros," Sabina said. "He is the second translator for the house. You know Nestor?"

"So that is your name," I said, peering over Pío's flattened palm. Nestor gave me a look that would freeze the Kephisos in summer.

"Keep him away from me," Nestor said with a mixture of pleading and revulsion. "He's insane, Pío."

I started to protest, but upon reflection could not argue; with what Little Nestor knew of me, even I was forced to credit his opinion. He was, after all, witness to my botched attempt at suicide before the great Sulla. Pío's voice matched his countenance: its assault on the ears made one want to retreat a step; two would be better. Stalwart, I held my ground as he said, "You love your father?"

Now that was unexpected. "I beg your pardon?"

"You love your father," Pío insisted. "I love *my* father. When he with my mother fifteen years, master Piciacus allow him bring carpenter to build fine cabinet to hold my mother's clothes which he bought. Twelve years I had. Every day this man come to work on cabinet. My father work in fields. My mother spread her legs for this man. My father killed him. Slow. Then they killed my father.

More quick. The carpenter's name was Andros. I do not like this name. I do not like your name. Here you will be ... Alexander. Like the famous one. I think maybe you will not be so famous? This name I like - Alexander. Sabina, show him to kitchen and let him see that cook's meanings are pure. No mistakes like last week. You, Nestor, you will speak for everything but kitchen? Good."

With a word from that Hispanic grotesquerie another chip from my old life fell to the tiled floor. I am certain he had no idea how cruelly this arrow had hit the mark. At home in Greece, no human property was allowed to keep his or her own name - new ones were always assigned by their owner. It was purposefully dehumanizing, and completely sustainable, in my opinion. I never dreamed it would be happening to me, and not for any practical reason, but on a whim, because Pío didn't like the sound of it! How absolutely rich! The sting of it burned as deeply as the wound in my leg. Well, that is an exaggeration, to be honest. But it did hurt; you need only imagine it happening to you. Sabina barely took notice, accepting the tyrant's ruling without comment. "He is well enough to take quarters," she said. "Where do you want him?"

"Who has empty bed? You, Nestor," he said, pointing a fat finger, "you have empty bed. Translators share room."

"No!" Nestor protested.

"I've an empty bed," offered a servant wearing the tunic of the wine steward.

"No," said Pío. I sensed he was the kind of man who believed thoughtful reconsideration to be a sign of weakness. "Translators together."

Fuming impotently over the theft of my name, I wanted to lunge at Pío. I, however, am the kind of man who believes thoughtful reconsideration to be a sign of manliness and strength. In any case, before Sabina could lead me out of the *triclinium,* others had performed what pride and fear were about to suppress. Oh, I was scathingly articulate and brutally eloquent when complaining about someone to someone else, even if that meant talking to myself. Given the opportunity to actually vent directly to the object of my anger, I was as ferocious as a puppy, as outraged as an oyster.

A young, be-freckled woman with honey hair, tied in fraying braids intertwined with daisies marched into the dining room, her bare and muddied feet marking her determined passage. No one had dared remind her to don a pair of indoor sandals, six of which, in varying sizes, lined every entrance to the house. Her face, as flushed from the sun as her tunic and knees were begrimed by yard work, was set and grim. She walked straight up to Pío and knocked the napkin out of his hand, bits of goat and bone, so fastidiously gathered, now littering the floor. With her other hand she slapped him as hard as she could, and before he could make a grab for her was out the way she had come.

Medusa would have applauded the frozen and stony silence caused by this performance, and a second was just beginning. Keening rose from the direction of the baths, a flooding river of sound that crested with the arrival of another woman, her face streaked with tears. Pío spun to face her, comical with rage and discomfiture. She was upon him, spearing his eyes with a look that needed no translation. Looking up at him, she paused for the barest of moments, then spoke her terse jeremiad with hoarse and indignant fury: "How *could* you?"

Rhetoric at its finest, for it demands, nor permits reply. Pío, of course, did not know the rules.

She turned to leave, but he caught her by the wrist. "I owe you nothing," he said, spoiling the purity of her lament. She yanked free of him. "Not even the explanation," he called after her. The woman's sobs grew, then receded till they became not-so-faint reverberations echoing from the chamber of the baths.

"Pío controls the slave larder," Sabina said in response to my raised eyebrows. We spoke Greek as we walked to the kitchen through the atrium. The chill air swirling down from the open *compluvium* made us quicken our pace. "There's enough for everyone, unless he wants something from you. Then you find less on your plate."

"You must go to the master," I cried. Take note how quick I was to say 'you' and not 'we.' Sabina cocked her head, taking her own turn to raise an eyebrow. "Oh," I said, chastised. "A foolish question. Pío is favored for an old debt. He cannot be touched. And even if the paterfamilias should have him punished, he would find ample opportunity to take his vengeance." Sabina nodded. "But how then," I asked, "could that first woman slap him with impunity?"

"Tessa? Oh, it's just part of her little act. She likes to be the center of attention, and she's a little carefree with her charms, if you take my meaning." She paused. "And, besides, I think he likes it."

We entered the crowded kitchen filled with the pungent smell of *garum* and baking acorn bread. Sabina introduced me to the Roman cook and his three Greek assistants. She turned to go but I stopped her in the doorway. "What about you? Are you safe?"

"Pío is a bully," she said, dismissively. As if that answered the question.

# CHAPTER VII

## 82 - 81 BCE - WINTER, ROME

Year of the consulship of
Gaius Marius the Younger and Gnaeus Papirius Carbo

Later that day, the fourteenth before the *Kalends* of January, we were to stand outside the villa's entrance, eleven of us plus two house guards, Betto and Malchus, shivering in the cold to greet the paterfamilias and his wife. Everyone who was not free wore the *pileus,* a brimless, conical felt cap traditionally presented to newly manumitted freedmen in a ceremony that included, for some nonsensical reason, head shaving. This was supposed to represent the freedom dangled before us during the Saturnalia season. A cruel joke. The little cap was optional for freedmen only; servants owned by Crassus were forced to wear it. Pío chose to wear his proudly, unaware how ridiculous it looked atop his rockpile of a head. The pate of Ludovicus the handyman was bare. We Greeks celebrated the autumn planting as well, but at least in my family's house we had never made such fools of ourselves or such a mockery of those who served us. The hat was yet further proof that cultural distinction was sadly deficient in Romans; they stole everything from everyone: culture, gods, clothing. The *pilos* had been worn by Greek sailors for centuries. It is a marvel to me that a people so successful in subjugating all they encountered could at the same time be so vacant of any original idea that did not in some way assist in those conquests. Roads, bridges, engines of war, I grant them those.

But I digress. In any event, Sabina had told me that later in the week there would be gifts, games, a suspension of work, and general revelry. The household would even sit at a banquet served by our masters; the meal, however, would be prepared by us, the table cleared by us and the dishes cleaned by us.

As usual in those first days after my injury, I was late getting to where I was supposed to be. I limped through the vestibule, trying to get my *pileus* placed securely while struggling with the staff. It had been a bad day for my leg: I had already been on my feet too long. Pío was not about to let me shirk my duties, and I was not about to ask for any favor that might put me in his debt. I leaned up against the wall to catch my breath and peered out at the group huddled outside. My glance fell on Sabina standing behind the soldier Malchus, her hands lightly resting on Livia's shoulders.

They were both wearing the *pileus*.

•••

Somehow, three-year old Marcus escaped the far side of the carriage even before it had stopped. With delighted screams he came racing around the back and right into the young senator's entourage of six armed horsemen. Pío stepped forward with surprising speed. He placed his left hand on the snowy chest of our owner's horse (the beast came to an immediate halt) and with his right arm whisked the kicking bundle of male energy into the air. Only when Crassus had leapt from his white stallion did the chief of staff put Marcus down. The little treasure turned and kicked his savior in the ankle as hard as he could before rushing past his father to get back to the carriage.

Children.

Crassus was even more intent on reaching Tertulla than his son. As the door opened, he scooped the boy up, hung him upside down by his own ankles (an apt punishment until I saw how hard it made little Marcus laugh) and dropped him, gently, back into Pío's arms. Marcus began to struggle; Pío whispered something to him and the boy lay still. The senator grasped the big man's shoulder in gratitude, then with a whoop, turned and leaned inside the open door. There sat Tertulla, young and elegant, a wide-eyed baby boy in her lap. Crassus reached underneath his wife with both hands, and accompanied by her shouts of delighted protestations, gathered both mother and son up in his arms. He spun twice round in the gravel, the two parents laughing so hard we who watched could not help but smile.

"Welcome Tertulla," Crassus cried, "queen of this house, of our assembled *familia,* and most assuredly of me!" He set his wife down as we cheered, then reached for the baby. She whirled away from him, her ice blue eyes on fire. Realization dawned on the master and he apologized deeply, with only his enthusiasm to blame. She turned once again to face him, standing an arms-length apart, formally erect. All became terribly still as Tertulla bent and placed the baby at his feet. It squirmed uncomfortably, its swaddling picking up bits of gravel, but did not cry out.

If the paterfamilias walked away, the child would be taken to the outskirts of the city and abandoned. A father could legally do this if the babe were female, deformed, or if the idea of another screaming mouth in his house were just too tiresome to bear. The practice was the same in Athens.

No such thing would happen to this child. Crassus swept him up in his arms, lifting him high over his head. "I give you Publius Licinius Crassus!" he cried. "Io Saturnalia!"

"Io Saturnalia!" we all shouted in response, I less enthusiastically than most of the others. I mean, honestly, it was freezing. Truth to tell, Pío returned little Marcus to his mother's arms with remarkable tenderness. I would be moved, if I cared a whit for these strangers. What were they to me?

I looked over at Sabina. She had removed her cap. We began to follow the family back into the house. I waited for Sabina to pass but when I tried to speak to her, with eyes averted she mumbled that she was needed by the master and hurried past.

•••

One son of Marcus Crassus would marry and grow old with little to remark his passing. There was, however, one disturbing exception: he became, for a time, quaestor to Julius Caesar. It was one of life's small, ironic blessings that Crassus did not live to see his progeny in the service of his enemy.

The other child was doomed to die a hero's pointless death.

•••

Before I could reenter the *domus*, I was waylaid by Ludovicus. He was five years younger than Sabina, a hard man with a soft center. I always liked him. Except on that day, when he threw an extra cloak over my shoulders and led me into town. Somehow he had come by the knowledge that when it came to women, I had none. He had taken it upon himself, in a festive, holiday mood, to rectify what was, in his opinion, a dreadful oversight. I don't care how smart you are, he told me cryptically, you'll never understand how little you really know till you've had a woman.

I do not wish to speak of the incident, only to tell you that it was a failure of less than spectacular proportions. By which I do not mean to employ a double negative, nor to imply that it was in any way a success. We arrived at a house with which Ludovicus was well-acquainted and his custom well-received and appreciated. My guide through these dark waters even supplied the coin to tip the ferryman. Which only made matters worse: is a man who does not pay for his whore less of a man? If he is twenty-three, terrified, and the cerebral sort who cannot help but take this simple, single string of reasoning and obsess about it till he has built a smoking Vesuvius, then yes, he is less of a man. And being thus diminished, by definition, therefore, he is less capable of performing this manliest of acts. Why couldn't we just go home? I looked in vain for Ludovicus, but he had already paired and departed for the bounteous paradise of his favorite Ligurian, leaving me to my personal Hades.

The longer you keep your virginity, the harder it is to get rid of it. If you are male and past a certain age, the more concerned you become that nobody wants to relieve you of it. Which makes it more difficult to perform when given the opportunity. Which confirms your original supposition. Which makes you still more afraid that nobody wants it. And so on.

For a young boy who has not spilled his first seed, sex is a frightful and abhorrent thing to contemplate. As a young teen, it is the *only* thing worthy of prolonged consideration. A visit to the brothel or an early marriage quickly dissolves both tension and ignorance. But what if chance, lack of opportunity or becoming a spoil of war interrupt the natural progression into adulthood? Then, the difficulty of the mathematics of prolonged virginity rises exponentially with age. Until you solve this equation, it will remain a barrier between you and the rest of mankind.

The girl was sweet enough, the room relatively clean and quiet. She took my hands, guided me to her pallet and bade me sit. Standing before me, she slipped from her tunic, her oiled breasts and thighs bronzed by the lamplight. She began touching herself, hardening her nipples between thumb and forefinger and making little animal sounds, either of pain or appreciation. Her facial expressions indicated the former, but I could not be certain. Her hips moved in ways that no man could mimic. Was it arduous practice or some differential physiognomy that enabled such gyrations? Her movements and her hands began to converge about the darkness between her legs. What did she expect of me? Was I supposed to sit and watch or wait for an invitation to become an active participant? And what was I to do exactly? I had no idea and was too embarrassed to ask. I did not know where to look; my eyes darted about, dragonflies flitting over an exotic pond where no resting place promised a safe landing free of humiliation. My confusion was compounded when of a sudden her ankle bracelet began to jingle; she pivoted, dancing in a slow semi-circle till her glistening buttocks gyrated just inches from my face. The oiled dimples of her taut lower back were shining eyes, pleading with me to do I knew not what. Finally, since it was easier to find courage when direct eye contact was not a further dissuasion, I gathered what little I could salvage from my trembling core and in a small voice spoke to her undulating backside, admitting my lack of experience and need for guidance.

For answer, she turned round and smiled with a knowing coyness that gave me credit in an account that was pitifully empty. I was less than bankrupt, for bankruptcy connotes there is something of value to lose. Lying down on her back, she raised her arms behind her neck and interlaced her fingers amongst the tousled thickness of her hair. She raised her knees, planted her feet flat on the orange bedsheet and let her legs fall open. Her hips began a slow rise and return to the bed, over and over, requiring quite a good deal of abdominal strength. Now what? There was no doubt as to my objective: there it beckoned, a miniature cavern whose secret entrance the girl was even now unveiling with painted fingernails. What is it with these women? Do they think that such a log jam of disuse such as I, presented with a scented, lithe and willing female is enough to unleash a lusty and adept Priapus. Was I to touch it, massage it like a sore muscle, plumb its depths with the pitiful limp thing between my quaking legs? Gods awaken! Was I supposed to kiss that moistened, bearded mouth?!

She did not love me. Most likely she did not even like me. Why should she when we had met only moments before? This was all an act; there was no genuine feeling here. Even when she took me in her oiled hands to bring life to the dead, I could not stop thinking that the only reason my prick was in her hands was the coin Ludovicus had placed in it earlier. Then I began thinking about Ludovicus touching her hand, and her hand touching me, and the oaky lengths she was beginning to coax from my staff quickly began to shrivel. Yes, I understand there was far too much thinking going on in that tiny room, but that is my curse. I thanked her with another small coin and retreated to the lobby. There I sat waiting for the lusty Ludovicus to reappear, as comfortable as a failing student sent before his favorite teacher. I supposed I would just have to wait until I came across some understanding woman who found my obsessions a blessing. And that is all I wish to say about the matter.

•••

It was late by the time we returned, Ludovicus conciliatory, myself dejected and consigned to a still deeper pit of virginity out of which it seemed I would never climb. The feast was over and the last guest had departed, content and full by the look of the domestic disarray. Crassus and his wife had long ago retired. My wouldbe benefactor and I pitched in to help clean the house and restore its pristine opulence. An hour later we were about to retire to our respective quarters when there came a knock at the front entrance. The soldier Betto admitted a dark, bearded man wearing one gold earring and long robes striped blue and purple. He was followed by two of his own protectors. Rome was not a safe place to be out and about at night.

Livia, a small bag slung over her shoulder, came running up to her mother. Sabina hugged her daughter fiercely and would have remained till dawn in that embrace had not Livia gently broken free. "Good night, mother. Will I see you soon?"

Sabina's chin trembled and her eyes widened in that trick we use to keep the tears from falling. "Soon," she managed. Livia turned toward the strangers, but Sabina reached to trace her hand down the full length of her daughter's outstretched arm. As Livia moved away Sabina let the fabric of her daughter's tunic pass through her hand, then the softness of her child's arm till at last only their hands touched, fingers intertwining. Finally, fingertips shared the last brief spark of connection. Livia giggled at this little game, then ran to the stranger.

"Can we not keep her," Sabina asked, "at least till the end of the Saturnalia?"

"She is promised elsewhere," the dark man said with a compassionate tilt of his head. His accent was strange. He smiled down at the girl and held out his hand. She took it. They stepped back out into the night. As the front door was being barred shut Livia began to whistle. In a few moments the sound receded into silence.

Dumbstruck, I stood staring at the closed door. "What just happened?" I turned toward Sabina, but she had fled. Betto, the young door guard was standing at his post, fussing with a strap on his leather breastplate. "Who was that?" I asked.

"Boaz. A Jew," he said, his head bent in concentration over the lacings. As if that explained anything.

"And?"

Betto looked up at me, irritated. "He has a contract with the house." I had no idea what he was talking about. "Boaz is our slave merchant," he said as if talking to one of those pitiful god-touched souls wandering aimlessly through the stalls of the Subura market. He spoke in sharp-edged barbs of rising inflection. "He owns the girl. She was only here on a rental."

•••

Earlier in the day Sabina had shown me where I would be sleeping from now on. It was near the end of the servants' hallway; a small room right next to Pío's much larger quarters. I limped there now, stung, numb and so very tired. It was very dark and I had to feel my way. Pulling the curtain aside I saw absolutely nothing. I had to stand there for a few moments until my eyes regained some of their sight. There was a shape on one of the two sleeping couches. Nestor faced the wall; I could not tell if he was asleep or feigning; either way I doubt he wanted to engage in conversation. Fine by me. A narrow table stood between the beds; trunks sat at the foot of each. That was all. There was barely a foot between the two couches. No window. No ornamentation. Home.

I undressed and slipped beneath the heavy blanket. Sleep would not come. I tossed like a beached fish, stared at the ceiling and replayed all that had transpired that day. Finally, I decided my foul mood needed company. "Nestor," I whispered. No response. I tried again, louder this time. And a third, louder still.

He whipped around to face me. "What do you want?" he hissed. "Are you crazy? Do you know the time?"

"To talk. No. Yes."

"Leave me alone." His tone sounded more frantic than was called for by the occasion.

"Yes. No."

"You *are* insane. The master should lock you away and make you eat hellebore leaves till you come to your senses."

"Why did you not acknowledge me earlier today? I thought you would be happy to see me."

"This is *my* home. *My* position. I asked for it first. I don't need you."

"Well, we won't go into the manner of your 'asking,' beyond acknowledging that shoving me out of the way was a rude and inelegant gesture from one Greek compatriot to another. Be resigned, Nestor, I am here. I am not your enemy. We can help each other."

"Really?"

"Yes! We are fellow countrymen. Does that not count for something?"

"Did it count for anything when we were in chains? Did we ever pass so much as a word between us in all those many months? No, it doesn't count for anything, not then, not now."

I was not expecting such chastisement. All the more scathing for its accuracy. "Forgive me, Nestor. You are right. Those were difficult times."

"The only difference now is a bit more food and a bit less mud. Now let me be."

I awoke some time later lying on my side facing Nestor's bed. It was empty. From the room next door came again the sound that had roused me - a couch scraping on the floor. There it was again, then two men talking. No, not talking. I rolled over and tried to wrap the long, narrow sleeping pillow over both my ears.

# CHAPTER VIII

## 82 - 81 BCE - WINTER, ROME

Year of the consulship of
Gaius Marius the Younger and Gnaeus Papirius Carbo

It was late the next morning. None of the family had come out yet; the house was oddly quiet. No one was wearing their *pileus* except Betto, the guard, but he was doing it as a joke. I had just finished translating cook's instructions for the evening's meal when Sabina came into the *culina*. She beckoned me to follow her outside into the garden. Cook flapped his permission with the cloth he used to battle the permanent film of perspiration on his forehead. Limping to my room as fast as I could, I grabbed my only cloak and met her outside. A bright sun was burning the dew away.

Swiping a hand across the marble bench where she stood waiting, I sent a small wave of condensation onto the dead grass. I laid the cloak across the veined stone and we sat watching the steam rise off the artificial pond. "I'm sorry," Sabina said after a short while.

"This is a terrible place." I kept still, letting her take her time.

She was not quite ready, but skirted close. "Livia is quite fond of you, you know. She told me she likes embarrassing you."

"An unremarkable feat, easily accomplished. Only yesterday we were practicing the finer points of how to butcher a boar. Cook was demonstrating, I was translating. The staff laughed at every word I spoke; puzzling, since I could not imagine a subject less humorous. The more they laughed, the angrier I became. How dare they humiliate an invalid with a cane? I chastised them sternly, wagging a finger at their disrespect; the laughter became uproarious. A noise from behind caught my attention; I turned to discover your daughter standing there barefoot, wearing an old brown wig, holding two long sticks with stuffed, white gloves attached to each end. She had snuck up behind me to pantomime everything I did."

"I heard all about it."

"I glared at her, but my heart wasn't in it. She grinned sheepishly and waved at me with one of her 'hands.' It really was quite funny. Even cook laughed."

"For one so young, you are very good with children. Marcus, too. I know you've been teaching Livia Latin."

"She's a fast learner. If only we had more time."

Damn myself for a fool. I had inadvertently broken the spell. For a moment, we might have been mistaken for two companions enjoying the morning air. "I have not been honest with you," she said.

"You owe me no explanations."

"I feel that I do." She bent to pick up a pebble, then tossed it underhand into the pond. "We seem to have become friends, haven't we? Not an easy accomplishment." She sighed. "I was ashamed, Alexandros. To confess to you that my station was no better than yours. I thought I would be free, and Livia with me; that I would be gone from this place. Such an insult to you!" She turned to face me. "Can you forgive me?"

"There is nothing to forgive. You have only shown me kindness. You and Livia have been the only brightness to shine upon me in years. The real tragedy is to learn that you and your daughter are not free."

"They will be looking for us soon. I must tell you quickly."

"You don't have to say a thing. Come, let us go in." I started to rise but she caught my arm.

"No. I must do this." She steeled herself. "I was pregnant when we married. He was Roman, a soldier for Marius. It wasn't a formal ceremony, we weren't citizens, but we were free and it was legal - he walked me to our apartment with a few of his legionary friends to bear witness. I wore the flame-colored veil and the amaracus wreath. I was such a romantic. My parents were dead, and he was estranged from his. A clue which I completely ignored."

"What was his name?"

"I won't speak it. Soon after we were married, it became clear his love for me paled beside his passion for gambling. He was obsessed by the chariot races; whenever the cheers from the Circus Maximus echoed through the city, he would disappear, probably with those same men who had followed us to our threshold. I didn't notice the losses at first; he didn't confide in me. And honestly, I was so wrapped up in my daughter, I wasn't paying attention. I had never been so happy." I nodded. "I suppose that's why two years ago when I came back from the market and he gave me the news, I fainted. See this scar?" She leaned toward me; I saw a thin white ripple just below the hairline near her left temple. "I fell and cracked my head. When I got up a few moments later, blood was seeping between my fingers; he steadied me and put me in a chair. I brushed him away and made him speak again so I would know I had not misheard him. He spoke slowly, defeat and regret coating every word. To pay his debts, he said, he had been forced to sell our daughter. I looked around frantically, realizing we were alone. I screamed at him, 'Where is she?!' but she was already gone."

"I cannot bear this," I said.

"I would have killed him then, had I been able. His gladius was in the corner and I ran for it, but blood was getting in my eye and I tripped."

"Please, Sabina, let's go inside."

"Some head wounds look far worse than they are," she continued. Her eyes were focused on a sight I could not behold, on the memory being reborn as she spoke it. "If only I could have killed him," she said wistfully, "none of this would have happened."

"I don't understand."

"That man tried to bandage me, but I preferred to bleed rather than have him touch me. He boasted he had gone to the forum to find the most reputable of merchants. It was Boaz. By the darkest sorcery, Livia, my flesh and my heart, had been transformed into a lifeless pile of cold, worthless coins. He tried to explain how well off we were; showed me the money that would be left after he paid off his creditors. Even tried to put the coins in my hand – the equivalent of 4,000 *sesterces* in forty small gold *aureii*. 12,000 *sesterces* for my daughter to pay 8,000 in debts. He gambled away almost nine years' wages. The sorry bastard I married had only served for ten."

"How could he get so much money on a soldier's wage?"

"Where do you think? Over half of it was mine; money I'd saved working as a healer. Foolishly I thought my girlish love would pave the road to infinite trust. I gave him the money to manage. The rest he must have borrowed. A clever snail, he was, I'll give him that. He put a false bottom in the small money chest that held our savings. When he needed to take out more than the 925 *sesterces* he was putting in each month, he'd raise the floor to make the level of coins look unchanged. That's how he stole from us.

"He actually thought he was being noble, giving me charge of all that gold. But he left me with but a third of what I would need to buy Livia back, and that was only if Boaz would make the exchange profitless. I took the coins, cupped them in my hands and spit on them. Then I flung them in his face as hard as I could. I cut him, and hit him in one eye, but it wasn't enough. Nothing will ever be enough. Within the hour he had left to rejoin his legion. I never saw him again.

"That night I awoke with a start and lit a candle. I crawled on the floor till I had collected every *aureus*. I put them in our water bucket and the next day bought another one slightly smaller. I broke the staves and set them aside, muffled the coins with a rag, pressed them into the false bottom and calked it."

"Your husband's trick in reverse. Ingenious."

"Then I put it under the basin stand and prayed to our house god to keep it safe. I kneeled by our hearthside *lararium* till the flames became embers. My prayers twisted into thoughts of how I might undo my husband's betrayal and reclaim my daughter. I awoke on the floor, cold and alone.

"My biggest regret is that the man did not die that day, for while he lived, my fate worsened. I was taking work anywhere I could find it: baking pies to sell to the troops, sewing, anything. I starved myself trying to save every *as*. But it was taking too long. It would take forever. Then Sulla marched on Rome. My husband was among those defending the gates.

"Four months ago, two men came to my door. They weren't his friends, and they weren't soldiers. They showed me the leather bag from his kit. It bore the mark he had carved on the flap. There was a large tear on the front that went through to the other side. Dark stains made their meaning clear."

"Shall I offer condolences?"

"I wouldn't accept them. Anyway, he was killed, but not before he had gone into debt again. I was so stupid; legionaries, whoring, gambling - just different names for the same word. Those men had come to collect. They showed me the contract; his mark was on it, there was no denying it. And they knew about the forty *aureii*. I tried to stop them, but they came in and found the hiding place within minutes. I thought I had been clever, but they had experience. We save anything that might be reused - I never discarded the broken staves; they found them in my trunk.

"But how had they found you?"

"Before the battle my husband must have told them he had given me the money. I hope they tortured him."

"Why do you insist on calling him 'husband?' It borders on profanity."

"I do it with purpose. He *was* my husband. Our marriage was not arranged. I chose him, Minerva help me. Livia is gone because I could not govern her father. I call him 'husband' to remind me."

"If you hadn't chosen him," I said quietly, "she would not have been born."

"She would have been better off." Her tears came now.

"You cannot think so."

"I can. And do. Look at the world I have given her."

"It was never yours to give."

"I am her mother. I am responsible."

"You are not a goddess, Sabina. If every bride stopped to think upon the odds of their family's future, there would soon be none left to risk the vows. You can only do so much."

"Say what you will. I have not done enough."

I wanted to find more words of comfort but did not know where to look. They were not within me, of that I was certain. Her story had made me feel like a scoured gourd.

"You do not yet know the worst of it," she said wiping her eyes and composing herself. "The forty in gold was not enough to settle this new debt - he owed four thousand *sesterces* beyond what those men stole from me. My loving husband's estate, his gift to me upon his death," she said bitterly.

It took me a moment to digest this new information. Suddenly, it dawned on me. "Tell me you did not do this thing."

She glanced at me, then away. "I did. I went to the slave merchants' quarter. I found three, but none would give me more than two thousand *sesterces*. Pretty young girls fetch so much more than mothers in their thirties. Finally, I found Boaz. He was not hard to locate; he supplies the finest houses in the city. I was wrong about him. He tried to talk me out of it; getting in, he said, is so much easier than getting out. For me, the choice was simple. In the end, he gave me twice what I was worth - four thousand *sesterces*. I was his for less than a week, then he resold me to the house of Crassus."

Sabina, indentured by her own hand. Such love and sacrifice; how I envied her steel-edged purpose. And how I despised this life! "But your healing skills, surely they were worth a premium?"

"I may not be voluptuous and my hair may be cropped close, but I should like to think I have not fallen so far that a buyer would mistake me for a man. Most Romans insist that included among their doctors' salves and instruments one may also find a pair of balls."

I laughed, or tried to. "Then why did Crassus take you on, if not to use your skills?"

"As a wet nurse for the baby."

"Then your debt to your husband's creditors is paid."

"In full."

"Which leaves you?"

"A little more than half of what I sold myself to Boaz for: twenty-three hundred *sesterces*. It's not as bad as it seems. He has taken pity on me, Hera knows why. If I can but raise a total of eight thousand *sesterces*, he will sell her back to me when he can and take the loss."

"Why would he do such a thing?"

"Who knows? I never stopped to question him, only to fall to my knees to kiss the hem of his robe. Are not all men sons?"

"I hated him when I saw him take her away."

"There are many things to hate in this city. This man should not be counted among them."

I found that hard to believe; how could you not despise such a person? Every new admission of Sabina's gave me more to ponder. "Perhaps he is fond of you."

"I have no interest in men."

"But if he were, might he not free your daughter himself?"

"Do you think I have not begged him? There are contracts; leases with clients for ... for Livia ... which he must honor. She must be available a certain number of days each month."

"When do they expire?"

"I could not bring myself to ask."

I shook my head. "Tell me, is it permissible for a ... for you to buy Livia's freedom before your own?"

"No. But what good is flour, water and salt to a baker without an oven? First things first: the money.

"5,700 *sesterces,* Sabina. How can we raise such a fortune?"

"I don't know. I'll find a way."

"I'll try to help if I can." Empty, hollow words. I thought of the girl, and of the future she faced.

Sabina sat uneasily with that barely restrained tension of hers, her hands palm down on her thighs. I took one of them in both of mine and held it. I had no idea how to comfort her. It was such a clumsy act it forced a smile from her. Encouraged, I said the only thing I could think of to turn both our thoughts away. "When did you learn the healing arts?"

Sabina gently reclaimed her hand and patted my own. "My husband's father was a doctor."

"Truly? Surely he would help if he knew your plight." Words came racing ahead of thought. She would not have left any option untried.

"You are right. They would have done anything for their granddaughter. But they sided with Marius."

"Ah."

"Otho was an unusual man, nothing like his son. He believed aptitude deserved nurturing wherever it settled because to him, it was a gift from the gods. If they saw fit to bestow it upon a woman, who was he to argue? When his son was off with his legion for months on end, I learned from him. Sometimes my father-in-law was called away to an accident or to perform a complex surgery. He would grab me and yank me out the door, all excited about the chance to show me something new, or to try something new himself. Livia would hold up my kit for me to take, tears streaking her little face. She broke my heart, she was so sweet, so brave. My mother-in-law would shoo us on our way, promising she'd look after her. I was torn; now I wish I'd stayed with her those few extra hours, just to have had them."

"Sabina," I said, a thought suddenly furrowing my brow, "how is it that Livia spends as much time with us as she does? Wouldn't Pío have to approve, and make the arrangements?"

She didn't answer, but pointed with her chin to the other side of the peristyle. The man himself was heading this way. That was twice I had asked her about him without getting an answer. An awful light revealed something I desperately did not want to see.

"Leave it," she whispered urgently, then stood and walked briskly away from both of us. I tried not to look where my imagination tugged, but sometimes our minds are our worst enemies. Pío beckoned to me impatiently and I rose to do his bidding.

# CHAPTER IX

## 81 BCE - SPRING, ROME

Year of the consulship of
Marcus Tulius Decula and Gnaeus Cornelius Dolabella

Over the next several months a change came over the house. Many profited by it, others suffered. I refer, you understand, to everyone excluding my master's family. Crassus, his wife and children never faced anything more troublesome than a boring houseguest or a hangnail. Both the start and the culmination of this transformation were each marked by an absence. The first was cause for celebration; the second spurred me to an unthinkable confrontation. It all began with Nestor's bed.

Some days life was easier to bear than others. This had been one of the difficult ones. It was near the end of Martius and Livia had been reclaimed by Boaz that morning. After a week's stay helping to prepare for and then cleaning up after the festivities surrounding little Marcus's fourth birthday, we were just getting used to having her around. I'm not much of a drinker, but that night I had four cups of *lora*. I might have shown more restraint had not the mistress herself set two pots of honey out for us, surplus from the party. With this nectar, the wine was made less bitter, but not I. Euripides said "wine is the happy antidote for sorrow," yet I retired both foul of mood and stomach. I doubt a libation as insipid or as astringent as *lora* had ever passed the playwright's lips.

So it was that late that night I rose to relieve myself and perhaps find a scrap of bread to sop up the choppy seas of my gut. Nestor was snoring lightly. Down the hall in the opposite direction from Pío's room lay the female servant's wing. Midway between, running at right angles was the short hallway leading to the men's latrine on the right, women's on the left. A trench four inches wide and almost as deep ran down the middle of that floor; you could hear the gurgle of fresh water from the aqueduct running through it as you approached. Crassus' Palatine villa was richly appointed: normally such luxury was reserved for the master suites.

Sleeping in a sitting position on his small cushioned bench at the intersection of the two hallways was our young guard. An oil lamp stanchioned in the wall flickered above his head. Malchus had a room to himself, but when he wasn't patrolling he preferred to rest here. The hallway was so narrow no one could get past without stepping over him. He woke at my approach.

"*Salve,* Malchus," I said quietly so as not to wake the rest of the house.

The lanky soldier wiped his mouth and looked up at me appraisingly. "Too much *lora,*" he said. It wasn't a question. I nodded. "I'll join you if you promise you won't puke." I told him life held few guarantees. He shrugged, stood up and took the lamp out of its holder. Stretching and yawning, he left his short sword by the bench and followed me to the toilets. The small room was divided by the fresh water channel and fed from a spout extending a foot off the floor of the far wall. On either side of the trench were two benches with hinged lids; each had two holes on top for sitting and two smaller openings on the front for cleaning. On the floor were two large covered buckets and two taller, narrower ones with long handles protruding from their open tops. Malchus lifted each covered bucket by its handle to test its weight.

"This one's full," he said, tapping it with his foot. He opened the other one and we urinated into it together. I finished first; when Malchus was done I closed and latched the lid. Malchus reached up under his tunic, pulled down his *subligatum* and took a seat on the bench nearest him. "So what's troubling you, translator?"

I sat down across from him, letting my bad leg stretch out before me. The limp was barely noticeable now. "Why should anything be troubling me? Troubles are for adults; children need only obey. I am a carefree child."

"You know, my friend, your face won't shatter if you manage a smile once in awhile. I see you, don't think I don't, moping around the house all day. That's not going to make things any better."

"Why didn't I think of that?" I said, smacking my forehead. "I simply have to look happy to be happy. Genius."

"Think about it - your lot could be a lot worse."

"Really?" I felt myself beginning to mope, but didn't want to give him the satisfaction of seeing it. The best I could manage was a crooked, tepid smile.

Malchus, however, was the type who would grasp at any sign of encouragement, even a false one. "That's better," he said. "Don't worry, you'll get used to the place in time. Crassus is a good man. I've been with him since he came back from Hispania, going on three years now. Betto and I joined up when he passed through Perusia, our village."

"He's never around. Do you think he even knows what goes on in his name?"

"Oh, so that's it. Can't you just stay out of Prick Pío's way?"

"As easily as I can avoid the air. It's not just for me, you know ..."

"*Dominus* owes Pío a debt of honor. Hang on." Malchus' face glazed with concentration, then relaxed. There was a soft, wet thud beneath him. "Ahhh ... a thing of beauty. Where was I. Pío. Yes. Unless he murders someone, my friend, Crassus will never give him up. Pass me the *spongia,* will you?" I pulled the dripping sponge stick out of the cask of fresh water and gave it to Malchus, handle first. He turned it around, inserted it through the small hole between his legs and cleaned himself.

"You could help us, if you'd a mind to."

"No chance. Pío's shit, my friend, if you've ever had the luck to be in here when he's about the business of making one, smells like mountain laurel and columbine. And he knows it. I'm not saying I'd do the same as him in his place, but you know the old saying: swing a big cock and somebody's gonna get fucked. That's just how it is."

"So you do see how he treats us, then?"

"I see it. And do you see it's got nothing to do with me?" Malchus stood, dropped the *spongia* back in its receptacle and rearranged his clothes. He saw the look on my face and said, "Look, it's rotten luck, but let me tell you something my father taught me. The world is always changing, right under our noses, even if you think it's not. Most of the time it happens so slow you'll miss it if you're not paying attention. That's the trick, see. You've got to pay attention so you know when something's changing."

"An interesting theory, but what use is it to me?"

"I wish I could help you, translator, but I'm just a sword for hire. I've got a skill and I get paid to use it. You're smart, you'll think of something. Hey, it's the ones who can think that come up with most of the change, right? Just make sure when you go mixing things up you leave me out of it. I like my job; things are fine just the way they are."

•••

In the servants' kitchen, I found half a loaf of something under the breadbox. It was fresh enough for me to tear off two chunks, one of which I chewed upon thoughtfully as I padded barefoot back to our sleeping quarters. I turned into our wing, passed Pío's and my room and found Malchus back at his post on the bench in the hall. He had covered himself with his cloak; his head was tilted back against the wall and his mouth hung open. I dropped the other hunk of bread into his lap. He opened one eye, grinned and said, "You're a good man, translator. From now on, I'll ignore what everyone says."

"It heartens me," I replied, "to know we are so well protected by the alert and ever-vigilant Malchus. Brigands, blackguards and thieves beware!"

"Don't let this come as a shock," Malchus said, his mouth well-stuffed, "I'm not guarding you, I'm guarding you, if you follow."

"You're doing a superlative job either way," I said, heading back to my room. When I turned aside the curtain and slipped into bed I realized that I was alone. Nestor was gone.

•••

Indeed, over the coming weeks it seemed as if I had the room to myself at night. Nestor continued to behave as if our recent paths were not literally chained together, as if his claim to this place was somehow greater than mine. If it were mine to give, he'd be welcome to it. I would have welcomed his friendship, but that tree was obviously not going to bear fruit.

There was, however, a direct correlation between Nestor's absence and Pío's demeanor. Dare I say it? The man's disposition was becoming almost sunny! The more time they spent together, the less the Spaniard preyed upon the rest of us. Food rations were no longer withheld, sexual blackmail vanished and the household in general brightened several shades. It was spring, and Pío and Nestor were in love.

But no good thing comes without a price, and it was Sabina and her daughter who paid it. With the house settled back into a normal routine, there was no need for extra help; Pío refused the "coin" with which Sabina had paid him so that she and Livia could be together as much as possible. True, happiness had tamed his more repulsive habits, but it had also made him faithful. And as bad luck would have it, Crassus took Pío to task over the house accounts. Not that there was any lack of funds, but to the master, "more" was always better than "enough." Livia came to us no more.

I could not bear the sight of frustration and heartbreak in Sabina's eyes. While I lacked the courage to stand up for myself, it welled up of its own accord on behalf of my friend. Malchus had said something about being a sword for hire; that gave me the kernel of an idea. And so it was I found myself standing alone before the *dominus* in his *tablinum*.

"You wished to see me?" Crassus chose an apple from a bowl and offered it up to me. I declined gracelessly, only able to manage a grunt and a head shake. He shrugged and bit into it himself. What was I doing here? Was I mad? Before I could get my vocal chords to function he saved me by asking, "How are you settling in?"

"Well," I managed.

"And how goes it with Marcus? Give us a progress report."

"Well ..." I repeated. Do I tell him the truth? I don't see what choice I have. "He's keen on mathematics. At least, that is, he understands that when I take two blocks away from three he is left with only one. It, uh, is easier for him to grasp the ... conceptual aspects once he stops crying."

"I see."

I had no choice but to forge ahead. "He's quite entertained by some sections of The Iliad. I'm afraid his favorite part - I've had to repeat it to him almost every day this month – is the death of Hector." Crassus smiled at that. "He's learning his Latin letters, but truth to tell, *dominus,* Greek is as yet beyond him." I waited, but Crassus was silent. "We've started with a little history, the Punic wars, but forgive me, lord, I cannot hold his attention for more than a few minutes."

Crassus stroked his chin. He let out a long breath and I could have sworn he was about to send me to the mines. Instead, he said, "I suppose, then, we'll have to leave oratory and the Epicureans till he's four."

"That might be, I mean to say, four is perhaps ..."

"I am in jest, Alexander. Let him play."

"*Dominus*?"

"I was wrong to start him so young. Does he like you?"

"I think he tolerates me. He loves his mother, and Sabina. And you, of course."

"Alexander!" he snapped. My sandals almost left the floor. "You are not a client. And I am not your patron. Patronize me again at your peril."

"Yes, *dominus.*"

"You're a good man, Alexander," he said with softer tone. "I know, because my son knows. You cannot fool a child. I note you have omitted Marcus' progress with his riding lessons."

"*Dominus*?"

"Your hands and knees must be raw, from what he tells me."

"Oh."

"Oh indeed. Continue as you see fit. He'd miss his time with you were I to postpone his "lessons" for another year. Now what's this you say about Sabina?"

"My experience with children is quite limited, *dominus*. Limited, indeed, to myself. An only child. No playmates to speak of. Sabina has been a great help with Marcus. Which, if I may ...."

"What is it?"

Now we'd come to it. I felt as if the past few minutes had helped my cause, but I was too nervous to see anything objectively. By the Dog, curse my trembling, perspiring body. I did my best to ignore my uncooperative physical self and concentrate on my ideal, non-corporeal self. "I have a proposition, *dominus*."

Crassus hoisted the semaphore of a raised eyebrow. Was this permission to proceed, or a manifestation of 'how dare you?' His next utterance would tell. Remember, don't patronize. Like a barrel rolling downhill, I plunged on, waiting for the moment when my staves would explode. "It is an idea that will unite a family, bring good to many in your name and procure another able body for your house at no cost to you. I would humbly beg that you allow Sabina a *peculium*."

I paused for a response. "If you are finished," Crassus said, "then my answer is 'no.'"

"Finished? No! Out of politeness, I merely wanted to give you the chance to voice your initial thoughts."

"You just heard them. Never let manners stand in the way of making your case. The great orators barely take a breath between sentences to frustrate any chance of interruption. Plow on, Alexander. I don't have all morning."

"Here it is, then." I took a breath and expectorated my argument as quickly as my pasty tongue would allow. "Livia, Sabina's daughter, was sold by her father to pay his gambling debts. She is owned by Boaz who on occasion leases her to this house. Sabina is a trained healer whose talents go tragically unused. Purchase Livia for the sum of 8,000 *sesterces;* Sabina will contribute 2,300 of the cost. The balance she will repay from the profits from her *peculium* - as a healer. Livia will be reunited with her mother, both will become your property and your reputation as a sage and canny patrician will increase."

"Qualities by which I am already known. I thought you said it would cost me nothing."

"Eventually."

"How did she come by such a sum?"

"She sold herself to Boaz."

Crassus nodded. "Would that all Roman mothers acted as nobly, when Roman men succumb to their failings."

I could not help myself. "Sabina is Greek."

Crassus eyed me. "And no less noble for it. Why does Boaz sell the girl so cheaply - she could fetch twice his asking price."

"This I cannot explain. I think he likes the mother."

"I will not have strangers with gods-know-what sores and ailments tromping through the house. I will not allow any such unfortunates near my children or my wife. She may not ply her trade here."

"The empty apartment that faces the street could be used as a *taberna*. It has its own entrance and is used only for storage. It's completely separate from the main building by at least two hundred feet of garden."

"I know where it is; it's my damn house!"

"You could charge her rent," I said in as small and unobtrusive voice as possible.

"I *would* charge her rent. But tell me, Alexander, has your convoluted scheme considered this? What citizen would make the trek up the Palatine when there are plenty of doctors, *male* doctors, throughout the city?"

"A well-placed word or two from Crassus would push the stone from the hilltop. Word of mouth would soon cause an avalanche. In reverse, so to speak."

"I see. More work for me. Next I suppose you will tell me that you yourself are living proof of her skills. You needn't bother. I began looking for your replacement the moment the fever came upon you. Few survive its grip. She has a gift, without doubt."

I held my breath. At last Crassus spoke again. "The plan has merit. Get the money from Pío and see that the girl is here by nightfall."

"*Dominus*!"

"So help me, Alexander, if you fall to your knees or begin to blubber, I shall strike you. Get some backbone in you. I have no use for cowards. You belong to a noble house; best you act the part."

There is a nasty miniature of me that lives inside, a small but persistent voice that would spoil any triumph, sour any accomplishment. How it came to reside in my head is a mystery. I would excise it if I could; and yet I do enjoy arguing with it. Since coming to the house of Crassus I have given it a name. I call it Little Nestor. Well, here was a perfect opportunity for the daemon to be heard, and he did not disappoint. In that instant of my master's acquiescence, I experienced real joy, a feeling that had eluded me since my abduction. Little Nestor could not let that go, and I heard him whisper: *his words are free, but you are not. Act the part, he says. As long as you remain here, like an actor never allowed to leave the stage, you will never be yourself. So act the part. Slave.*

That day, I managed to ignore him, enough to say, "*Dominus,* I am very pleased. And on Sabina's behalf, I offer gratitude. There is but one thing more; actually two. Please do not tell her this was my idea. Take credit yourself, or perhaps give it to *domina,* whatever you think best."

"Why would we do that? Your suggestion is an act of kindness she will not soon forget."

"First, the act is yours, not mine. Second, she is my friend; I want no debts between us. Lastly, Sabina is proud almost beyond measure. This would sit better coming from the master of the house."

Crassus rose from his seat. "Stay here. I must fetch my wife." He walked back toward the atrium and I heard him call for Tertulla. In a moment, the two returned, followed by Sabina, who led a wobbly, grinning Publius by the hand.

"*Columba,* a word. Sabina, if you wouldn't mind, take Publius for some air."

"Yes, *dominus.*" Sabina left, looking back over her shoulder to fling a nervous 'what's-going-on?' face at me. I replied with a look of feigned innocence and hoped that it appeared genuine. I was never much good at dissembling.

"Alexander! What have you gone and done now?" Tertulla took both my hands in hers and held them while she spoke. Her smile was so broad and genuine I felt my face redden. "He's so good with Marcus, husband. How's the leg, Alexander?"

"It heals," Crassus answered for me, sounding slightly irritated. He bade Tertulla sit in his chair and began to recount the details of my proposal. He stood next to me, so close I could smell his perfume. I hoped that my own scent did not offend. If only I could step further away unnoticed. I am most comfortable on the outskirts; being at the center of anything unnerves me, the center of attention in particular. To endure, I composed my features into one I hoped gave the impression of self-abasing, modestly proud interest. No mirror presented itself, so I attempted to breathe normally and instead let the vision of my mistress consume me.

Tertulla's hair was long in those days, and as black as any Nubian's. She wore it piled at the back of her head, held with gold butterfly pins. Two long tresses escaped this binding and fell down either side of her neck. It was a style that made her look regal, yet utterly feminine. Her sleeveless *peplos*, pinned at the shoulders with more gold butterflies, was pale blue, a foil to the darker seas of her eyes. She left one shoulder bare by draping her *palla* as a long, diagonal sash. Her toenails were painted to match her *peplos* and her long-laced sandals were gold. She was nineteen, five years younger than I; precisely the sort of girl who wouldn't give me a second look or a first chance back in Athens. She was as beautiful as Phaedra, my youthful infatuation at the Academy, but where Phaedra was a siren, Tertulla was Venus.

# CHAPTER X

## 81 BCE - SPRING, ROME

Year of the consulship of
Marcus Tulius Decula and Gnaeus Cornelius Dolabella

"Why didn't Sabina come to me?" Tertulla asked when Crassus had finished. "That child is a delight. I would have purchased Livia in a hummingbird's heartbeat had I known."

"Of course you would, *columba,* because little doves don't know the value of money."

"Don't patronize me!" she said with playful indignation. The irony, however, was lost neither on me nor on Crassus, who glanced sideways at me with a weak smile.

"Never again," he proclaimed dramatically, dropping to one knee. Tertulla laughed and slapped his hand away. "But Alexander's plan," he said conspiratorially, "has more financial merit. With your permission, of course." Their playfulness with each other was embarrassing, yet wondrous to witness. Irony was everywhere this day.

"I have only one suggestion," Tertulla said, standing and pulling her husband up with her. None present, especially the lady herself, believed that she would ever limit her opinions to just one. "Pay Boaz Livia's full worth, love. I know that Jew; he's as soft-hearted as a lamb. How he ever chose that trade is a wonder. How he survives in it is a miracle."

"You needn't worry about him," Crassus said. "His family's been in the business for generations. He may choose to keep a modest house in the Subura, but his accounts are overflowing. He has an eye for talent, and a keener lookout for profit. I suppose that gives him the latitude to make exceptions when he chooses."

"So you will pay him the 16,000 *sesterces*? Sabina is sure to be a success and your purse will yet be made whole. When you think of it, a little more time, not money, is all that will be required."

"And we forbid women the practice of law! If I refuse her," Crassus said to the air above, "though the cost could not be counted in gold, its sum would be far greater."

"Isn't it wonderful to have a husband who comes complete with both ears and heart?" she asked, also to no one in particular. I felt completely useless.

Crassus answered her nonetheless. "Much depends on where you find them. They're not much use in the senate."

"Oh, one more thing. Let Sabina keep her coins. It is a trifle to us, but a treasure to her."

"Let us wait a moment, Alexander," he said, finally addressing me directly. "There may yet be more."

"No, I assure you I am quite finished." Crassus nodded and turned back to his scrolls. "Oh."

"Yes, dove?"

"Of course, Sabina should only be required to repay 2,300 of the total. If we choose to offer more to Boaz, that is not to be counted against her."

"Agreed." Now Crassus waited.

"No, no, I am quite finished. The good commander knows when to leave the field. I retreat and leave you to carry on." She whispered, "I shan't say a thing. Let's tell her when we put the children to bed, shall we?" Without waiting for an answer she kissed her husband lightly on the cheek and turned toward the peristyle. "Sabina! To me, please."

Tertulla had not gone ten steps when she stopped and called back, "Husband - interest free!" Crassus waved her off.

"I wasn't going to charge the woman interest," he muttered.

"Um," I ventured after making sure that Tertulla was completely out of sight, "I have something more, if I may. It concerns my tutoring duties?"

"Why, are you tiring of them?"

"On the contrary, I think I may have found my calling. Teaching suits me. Which is what gave me this thought: Running about the house translating Pío's instructions seems inefficient for both myself and the staff. I am constantly repeating myself and being interrupted by someone looking for a word here or a phrase there. I should like, with permission, to make the process more formal."

"How?"

"A school. Imagine an entire bilingual staff - their value would increase two-fold at least, if I understand the market. Communication and work would flow smoother throughout the *domus*. And we needn't limit instruction to language: any skill required by the *familia* could be taught. Gardeners could teach gardening, cook could teach, well, cooking, so that more than one of us would have the same skill. Should one become sick, others could fill in. And if *dominus* feels the need to sell one of us, we are bound to fetch a higher price."

"And where would you organize this school?"

"The apartment has two large rooms. Plus two smaller closets."

"You've been headed here all along, haven't you?"

"When I thought of Sabina's plight, I went to look at the apartment - the idea dawned on me then."

"Why so timid, *grammaticus*? As you learn to know me, you will find that I am quick to appreciate logic, especially when logic leads to profit. Now I must find my wife and contradict her, gods protect me. News of this importance cannot wait for nightfall. Sabina should not have to wait an extra minute to be reunited with her daughter. Go straight to Pío and have him see to the girl's return personally."

"*Dominus,* what if Livia has been sent to work at another house?"

"Tell Pío to find her and remove her. He can take Betto and Malchus with him. The three of them should be persuasion enough. And if Boaz requires more convincing, remind him his asking price was two; we are paying four. If that should still prove insufficient, I will buy out any open contracts. But I shall want to *see* them first. Send Pío to me if any of this is unclear to him."

•••

The next morning I had been released to prepare the schoolroom. Secured in my tunic was a purse containing two hundred fifty *denarii*! I went to the forum shops and purchased supplies, including writing tablets, paraffin, *stili*, paint and brushes. My plan was to whitewash one entire wall then use it to write my lessons so all could see them. The student would practice with his wax tablet and stilus, then I would paint the wall and start again. Letters, syllables and some phrases would remain constant at the top of the wall; more ephemeral lessons would be painted over.

When I returned I went right to work. Since the outside door to our new *taberna* (I had a key!) was on the far side from the main house, at first I saw no one upon my return. I was pouring white paint from the heavy pigskin into more manageable bowls when I heard a noise from the inside entrance. Expecting Sabina or Livia, I was surprised to see Boaz smiling broadly in the doorway.

"*Salve, paedagogus*," he said. "May I be among the first to wish you *mazal tov*. Congratulations!"

"Boaz. It may be a little premature to call me teacher. When I have students in this classroom and when they have actually learned something, then I may be worthy of the title. But thank you, and *salve*, just the same. What brings you up the Palatine?"

"You."

"Me?" I said, replacing the stopper in the pigskin. "We have no business together." If he was here, he knew.

"That is true." He reached inside his robes and pulled out a lambskin cloth. "For you," he said, holding it out in his open palm. "*Todah rabah.* Many thanks, my friend, many thanks."

I stayed where I was. An irrational fear gripped me: if I got too close, he would snatch me up and carry me off; another addition for his collection of human souls. I did not want to like this man. Yet the things I had heard about him, and witnessed, belied his occupation. No compunction marred his laughing eyes; his warmth and good cheer were not only genuine but infectious. How could such a man do what he did and live without shame? Instead of asking him, I said, "If you are here because of Livia, it is the lady of the house you should attend."

"No, it is you."

"It was she who doubled your asking price."

"It was you who braved the lash by going before your master."

"There was nothing brave about it," I lied.

"I suppose, to be fair, we must admit that it was only a matter of time before Sabina herself begged for Livia. If she had not done so I would have proposed an accommodation myself."

"You?"

"Why not? We Jews know all there is to know about slavery. From both sides of that coin. Half the people in this city are owned by the other half. If looking down upon us helps a Roman get a good night's sleep, eh. But I ask you, who better than a Jew to see that these unfortunates are treated as humanely as possible? As long as they are in my care, that is what I do."

"Will you not be judged by your god?"

"Hah! My God loves owners and slaves alike. As long as there is balance, there is no problem. Everything works unless someone puts an entire people under the lash; then comes the fire and flood, retribution and death. Remember Egypt? Anyway, why worry about such things? I don't hear anybody complaining. And business has never been better.

"But you, teacher of language; you, a new slave with no standing and nothing to gain - of all of us, you were the first to act. You know, in the East, there are people who believe that everything we do in life, both good and bad, return to us three-fold in like kind. Perhaps that paint you are stirring is an emblem of your act of kindness. I have another. Please, take it."

He stepped closer, his arm again outstretched. Curiosity got the better of me and I reached for the small bundle. When I did, he grasped my hand and pulled me close. My irrational terror flashed again. He put his other hand on my shoulder and squeezed. "Take heart, teacher. You are a good man, in a place where goodness is rarely rewarded. But sometimes, with luck, good men rise."

He released me and I unfolded the lambskin to discover a signet ring. It's metal glowed dully in the room's soft light. "I still don't know how it was you knew to come to me."

"Do not blame Malchus. He, too, has a good heart, but sometimes it beats so loudly he doesn't notice that his mouth is moving."

"This ring is gold," I said. I had never held anything of such value, even when I was free.

"The inset is carnelian, but the ring is unfinished. The stone is blank, its surface smooth. A patrician would have his seal engraved there. Perhaps someday, you will carve your own mark."

"You are generous, and I bid you gracious thanks. But you must know that gold, gemstone or iron, it is all the same. I have no right to property. This cannot be mine."

"And *you* must know that Boaz is nothing if not a negotiator for the ages." He laughed. "I have already spoken to your master. The ring is yours. Keep it, sell it, do with it what you wish. Think of it as your own first *peculium*."

The ring was large, but it slid perfectly onto the middle finger of my right hand. It made me feel uncomfortably important.

"Still the troubled look! Be at peace, friend. I am not here to take thanks but to give it."

"It's not that. It is only ... I am thinking of the girl."

"Livia? A delight, no?"

"I must ask, is she pure?"

Boaz's smile shrunk. "This is her master's business now."

"I see." I removed the ring and held it out to him.

"Attend me," he said. "I have the luxury of choosing my clients, and I sent her only to those I trust. All I can tell you is each time she returned to my house, she was almost always whistling. The child is happy. If for nothing else, keep the ring to remind you of the part you played to reunite mother and child."

Years later, any time the subject arose, Livia has always been quick to tell me I would have been a fool to give it back.

# CHAPTER XI

## 81 BCE - SPRING, ROME

Year of the consulship of
Marcus Tulius Decula and Gnaeus Cornelius Dolabella

I was lending a hand in the kitchen, dredging chickens with flour. Everyone was busy except Pío and Nestor who were playing a game of dice on a corner table, their backs to the activity and bustle behind them. Cook had asked twice for another pair of hands but Pío waved him away. A moment later, Crassus came wandering in, still wearing his purple-striped toga from the senate; he was looking for a snack. Cook had just handed one of his Greek assistants a last-minute shopping list. The young woman looked at it, made a face and brought it straight to me. I started to translate but she protested, "Too much, too much! Write it down, for pity's sake." I held up my flour-coated hands and called to Nestor to please, if he wouldn't mind, jot it down in Greek for Eirene.

"I'm busy," Nestor snapped. "Wipe your damn hands and do your job."

There came the sound of a patrician 'ahem;' both Nestor and Pío leapt to their feet to find Crassus standing behind them. "*Dominus*," said Pío, "forgive me."

"Why? Have you done something that needs forgiving? Nestor, lend a hand, or lose it."

"Yes, *dominus*!" Nestor took the list and Pío shoved a *calamus* and a pot of ink toward him, looking as nervous as if he himself had spoken harshly to me. Nestor took the pen in hand and studied the list intently. Crassus chewed on a date and asked cook to review the evening's menu. As they talked, Eirene waited patiently at Nestor's side, but as yet he had done nothing but look at the list, turn it over and stare at it. He was becoming increasingly agitated.

Pío and I came to the same conclusion simultaneously. He moved to distract Crassus and I went to Nestor, wiping my hands on my tunic as best I could. I took the list and the pen from his shaking hands and translated it into Greek as fast as I could. Pío used his bulk to block us from view.

When I handed the list to Eirene, the poor, polite thing said, "Thank you, Alexander," and our impromptu scheme was undone. Crassus turned round, gently pushed the big Spaniard to the side and saw Eirene holding a list dusted with flour.

"Who wrote that?" he demanded.

"Nestor's writing is next to illegible," I began. I was about to say more, but Crassus stopped me.

"Remember that lashing I spoke of when you first arrived?" I assumed correctly this was a rhetorical question. "Please do not lie to me. Nestor, bring me the list."

Nestor obeyed. Crassus looked it over and handed it back to him. "Read it." Nestor began reading the list, but Crassus interrupted him. "Wonderful. Now try the side written in Latin."

Nestor turned the scrap to the side written in Latin and pretended to read, stopping when his memory failed him. "I cannot," he said, looking down at the floor.

"Look at me," Crassus said. The moment Nestor raised his head Crassus slapped him hard. The surprise and force of the blow almost knocked Nestor off his feet. "Unlike you, I have an excellent memory. When general Sulla asked how he might be of assistance, I asked for slaves who could both read and write in Greek and Latin. Did you tell the general's man that you could do this?" Nestor nodded. The left side of his face was turning pink.

"Disappointing," Crassus said. "Very disappointing. You are to be congratulated for deceiving this house as long as you have." He adjusted his toga on his shoulder and turned to go. "Pío," he said as he walked away, "there are limits to my good nature. Were it not for you, Nestor's deception would not be tolerated."

•••

Livia had been spirited into the house while Sabina was in the garden helping Tessa cut bouquets. Publius was at their feet, chortling with delight at every worm he could wrest from the dirt. Crassus and Tertulla summoned Sabina to their private quarters; the shriek of joy could be heard throughout the house. At supper that evening, an unusual night in that Crassus and his wife were neither entertaining nor being entertained, they called the entire staff into the atrium to make the announcement. This was superfluous, of course, as every ear had the gist of the tale poured into it practically before mother and daughter had left the masters' bedroom. *Dominus,* however, thought it important to make a formal declaration. As he spoke, cook passed around a tray of spiced wine; not the cheap *lora,* mind you, but one of the sweet vintages served to company. I emptied a cup and reached for another. "Your *domina* and I have decided ...," he said, making eye contact with everyone in his or her turn, "... well, is there anyone present who does *not* know what it is we have decided?" Everyone laughed, although it looked as if Nestor would speak up till Pío put a hand on his shoulder. "Let us say only that our family has been most joyfully increased by one."

On cue, Sabina and Livia came into the atrium, hand in hand.

"Welcome home, sweet Livia!" Tertulla cried.

Crassus waited for the applause to subside, then described the healer's new clinic, which he encouraged everyone to visit. He spoke fleetingly of the school, but this was Sabina's moment. She stood next to Tertulla, dabbing her eyes with the white linen *orarium* given her by *domina.* The square of cloth was wet from one end to the other by the time her happy ordeal was over. Livia clung to her mother but reached across to take Tertulla's hand when Crassus announced that the girl would be taken into *domina's* personal service to be taught spinning and weaving.

I felt a foolish tear play about my eyelid and quickly banished it. Watching Sabina's own eyes water as she fussed with Livia's hair, a spark of clarity illuminated the parody before me. Why should I allow this pretty scene to make me cry? Twigs of frustration fueled an anger I could not vent. Here was one poor child being sold from one place to another, nothing more. A business transaction, profit for the master. Had the comfort of this new life clouded my vision so quickly and thoroughly that I could no longer recognize the chains that bound us to this place or feel the invisible walls that confined us here? What cause was there for celebration? Could there ever be justification for separating a loving mother from her daughter? Instead of applauding her return, we should be outraged that they had ever been parted. But no, we must show gratitude to our masters for their generosity. The *taberna*, Sabina's *peculium*, all of it - we were no more than pigeons, scrambling to peck at the crumbs flung into our midst. The wine in my belly soured and I turned to flee.

"Alexander," Ludovicus called, "where are you going?"

Was I the only one to lament that the price of this reunion was the freedom of both Sabina and her child? "I am no witless, feathered scavenger!" I said, knocking over an incense burner in my haste to depart.

"He's overcome with emotion," I heard someone say.

"He's drunk!" said Tessa, the gardener, with surprise.

They were correct, the both of them.

•••

Crassus and Tertulla kept their promise, taking credit for making Livia a permanent member of the household, but the girl had come back into our lives so quickly after my conversation with Sabina that she was naturally suspicious. Suspicious enough so that every week until her departure a fresh bunch of flowers appeared on my schoolroom table. She spoke to me about it but once. It was the day of my first class, a week after Livia's return. The benches and tables had not yet arrived, but no matter. We sat in a circle on the floor: three students from our house and three staff members from the homes of some of Tertulla's friends. Each of those placed coins in my hand when they left. I looked at them and thought to myself with pride, now you are a professional. Little Nestor tapped me on the shoulder and snickered, *yesterday you were a slave; today you are a slave with a few coins.*

Livia and I were playing a game of *tali* after everyone else had left. Sabina came through the door adjoining our two rooms. She watched us quietly for several moments. I glanced up from the floor where we sat cross-legged and bid her join us.

"I cannot say what part you have played in this," she said, gesturing to her daughter, "or why you would choose to hide it." Livia was about to roll but held the knucklebones to listen. "I have decided that I do not need to know. However, *you* need to know this: you will always be in our hearts; no matter where the fates may take us, you will always be remembered." She left without further comment.

Livia asked, "What's she talking about?"

"You heard her. I'm in your heart."

"Well I might not remember you."

"Just roll."

"All right, be like that." She gave the bones a good shake and threw a Venus. "Hah!" she cried. "Victory! Just for that, I'm not giving you a rematch."

It was hard to be a curmudgeon, hard as I tried. One day I came upon Pío teaching Livia and Nestor a melody from the Laletani village of his childhood. Astounding to both eyes and ears. The sound of laughter and children playing seeded every hour: contentment took hold, grew and flourished. Even the food improved: Tertulla gave cook stacks of recipes from her mother's kitchen. He grumbled, behind her back of course, having no choice but to try them. When the quality of mealtime rose by several degrees, all he would say was that execution was everything. The weight he himself was gaining, however, was a belt-loosening contradiction.

From the first day Sabina opened her practice, her waiting area was never empty. Crassus was as good as his word. As that word spread, she became so busy Tertulla was forced to relinquish her as a wet nurse and hire another. By the end of the first month, even after she had paid the master for furnishings and rent, Sabina had put aside three hundred *sesterces* in the family books. In two years, maybe less, her debt would be paid and she could begin to apply her fees toward the purchase of their freedom.

At last the carpenters brought long tables and benches to my schoolroom, plus one for me as the master, and a most comfortable chair. With a cushion! The schedule was set: two hours, three times a week the house came under my tutelage, even Livia. Tertulla soon saw that my hours were doubled, easily convincing her friends to send their own servants. Crassus began dropping by late in the day; he found in me his own apt pupil; discussing an invigorating regimen of politics, philosophy and oratory. He never spoke down to me and always gave ear to my remarks with interest and thoughtfulness. He asked questions and invited debate when he could have commanded unilateral acceptance. The omnipresent imbalance of our status never left my consciousness, but it faded to a background noise, like the sound of distant surf. He made me feel valued, and by doing so, let me rediscover my manhood, which had been stripped away like bark from a tree.

Atop Rome's richest hill, we lived at the cold heart of the world, where distance made everything sparkle, and close inspection was almost never required. Our masters were kind and our bellies full; who among all the bustling, struggling throng below could say as much? We could forget who we were and how we had gotten there. Yes, we were actors playing a part, but every day was dress rehearsal, and with enough practice, we could become the characters we played. The days passed and without even realizing it, the small estate on the Palatine began to feel like a place where I belonged.

All might be well again.

Except that it could never be. Boaz's Eastern philosophers must have been mistaken. Perhaps there, at the edge of the world, life was more just, but here in Rome, one could never be certain that goodness would be rewarded in kind.

# CHAPTER XII

## 80 BCE - SUMMER, ROME

Year of the consulship of
Marcus Tulius Decula and Gnaeus Cornelius Dolabella

Sulla had given up his dictatorship after only a year, having needed only those few months to turn centuries of Roman law inside out. His enemies, allies of Cinna and Marius, were either dead or exiled. He had had himself elected consul along with his friend Metellus, but even that was a sham: Sulla had been dictator in all but name. No one dared dispute his "reforms," most of which shored up the aristocracy and eviscerated the plebian council, whose power to thwart the senate was neatly castrated. Ironically, it would be under the consulship of Crassus and Pompeius ten years hence that most of Sulla's legislative upheavals would be overturned.

Eventually, Sulla must have tired of staring at his bloodstained hands, for there was one nineteen year-old member of the *populares* who none could believe the new master of Rome would ever let slip through his sticky fingers. Recently married to Cornelia, the daughter of

Cinna himself, he was near the top of the proscription lists. This friend of Marius fled to the countryside while his supporters and family petitioned clemency. Sulla was somehow swayed and lifted the sentence of death, but only upon condition that the lad divorce the daughter of his hated enemy. In an act some would call reckless, others insane, the insolent, headstrong rebel refused. The gods clearly had grand plans for this impudent Julius Caesar, for only they could have stayed Sulla's outstretched hand of clemency from returning to its more accustomed role as wielder of the executioner's blade. He relented, but warned those that had lobbied for clemency: "in this one Caesar, you will find many a Marius." History would prove that it was Sulla, not Marius, that Caesar would eventually emulate, and unlike Sulla, Caesar would not tire of the role of dictator.

Rome, then, had settled into an uneasy peace. Not so the house of Crassus. Up from its chthonic bonds beneath the Palatine, Hades was about to break, and it was a damned soul once named Alexandros who had already unlocked the Gates.

•••

If Nestor had had any faith at all in his master, it never would have happened. Crassus would not dream of willingly causing harm to the man who had sustained him those many months in hiding while Marius and Cinna hunted for him. But Nestor left our *dominus* no choice. It was hot on the Kalends of Quintilis. All the doors had been opened, the curtains pulled back and a dozen fan-bearers rented from Boaz. Sabina had taken Livia to town to restock her rapidly dwindling supply of herbs and ointments. I had just finished the afternoon's last class in Latin grammar. The inside door to the front garden was open; so too the door to the street which I normally left bolted to discourage prying eyes and dampen street noise. Today the need for cross-ventilation bested privacy.

I looked up at the lesson wall, sweating like a Thracian wrestler. The layers of whitewash cried out for a good scraping and a fresh coat of paint, but it was hotter than Hephaestus' forge in summer. Happy with my procrastination, I had grabbed my bag of scrolls from the teaching table and taken two steps toward the street-side door in order to shut it when two men stepped through the opening into the schoolroom.

"Salve," I said. "If you're looking for the front entrance, it's the gate just after the next door down the street." I am pitifully unworldly, for one look at these two and anyone else would have known they would never come a-calling on any establishment other than a brothel, a tavern or a barn.

"Tall and skinny," one said to the other.

"Must be the one," said the other. "What's your name, then?" They stepped closer and I took a step back. It is laughable how good manners so often interfere with my survival. My sluggish instincts had finally flashed a warning, but rather than run from the room screaming for help, I hesitated. What if my apprehension was unfounded? How rude it would be for me to flee. Decorum demanded that I give them the benefit of the doubt.

"Alexandros," I said, swallowing. "Whom do you seek?"

"What, not Alexander?" The two looked puzzled and stopped their slow advance.

"You a teacher?" asked the second ruffian in a veritable lightening bolt of inspiration. My parents taught me never to lie. I nodded, my knuckles white on the edge of the table.

They looked at each other and said simultaneously, "Close enough." Each drew an iron dagger from his belt, and my wits finally connected with my mouth and I cried out for help. I couldn't take my eyes off the knives, so rather than turning to run I backed up, immediately tripping over one of the low benches. I landed up against the wall right next to the inside doorway, the air knocked out of my lungs, the overturned bench up against my feet. As I gasped for breath they advanced, the taller one tossing the knife between his left hand and his right, back and forth. The two men stepped over the bench at the same time.

I kicked out with both feet. The shorter one, the one on my left, tripped and slammed head first into the wall. He cursed and rolled away out of my line of sight, but the other one was lighter on his feet. He hopped neatly over the skidding bench and crouched by my side. The few teeth in his smile were not many shades lighter than his knife blade.

He gave me no time to plead for my life or even cry out. He was smiling, but he knew what he was about; do the job and leave. The other man called out, quite unnecessarily, "Do him, Quintus, and let's fly."

The knife was in Quintus's right hand; he must have been left-handed for he flipped it across his chest one last time to wield the blade where it was most comfortable. While it was still in mid-air, a half-eaten apple sailed threw the open doorway and hit him hard in the face. Close behind it came a blur of Betto and obscenities. The dagger clattered to the floor as our legionary flew at the bigger man. They crashed to the ground then scrambled away from each other, but the assassin had somehow come up wielding his knife. Circling round the room till they were side by side again came his partner, his own weapon drawn.

The two intruders had lost all interest in me and were focused on the one man in the room who might foil their escape. Their mission had failed; the door to the street held their only salvation. Everyone in the room knew it. The two men faced off against Betto.

"You're a young wisp of a soldier, ain't you," the taller one asked. "But we're a generous pair, we are, and not too proud to admit we've come to the wrong house. Stand aside, let us pass and you'll be bothered no more by us."

"Wrong house, came to the wrong house," Flavius Betto mumbled. "YOU'RE DAMN RIGHT YOU CAME TO THE WRONG HOUSE!" he screamed. Everyone jumped. The intruders took a step back. Then, as if to himself, in little more than a whisper, Betto said, "I knew I should have taken the roast squash. I took the apple, and now Ceres spites me for my choice. Typical."

"What are you on about?" the man called Quintus asked cautiously. The two assassins took a step away from each other. Betto answered by sidestepping to his right, moving between the killers and their only means of escape.

"My lunch, you thick-skulled clodpate. You interrupted my lunch."

"Now, now. No need for insults."

"Yes. Yes, there is need for that and more. But enough talk." Betto drew his *pugio*. His eyes were wild and bulging. "Put your knives on the ground, and follow them with your asses. Alexander, get to the house. Raise the alarm."

I couldn't do it. It was the right thing to do: what use was I in a fight? But I couldn't leave him. Two against one; what if I returned to find Betto dead on my schoolroom floor, murdered because I had abandoned him even as he fought to save me? I scrambled on all fours, not to freedom but to the teaching wall behind my table. The pigskin of white paint lay where I had left it, full and unused. Bless my laziness, I thought as I grabbed the neck and tried its weight. Gods, it was heavy.

The tall one, the one with a bit of apple still clinging to his cheek said, "Very brave, ain't he, Lucas? Doesn't even draw his sword. Now why do you suppose he ain't even drawing his sword?" They were moving further apart, flanking Betto left and right.

"Because my aim is much better with this." I heard a grunt, but by the time I looked toward the sound, the one called Quintus was down, Betto's knife sunk hilt-deep in his chest. While my protector was throwing his weapon, I saw the remaining assassin toss his own dagger in the air to grab it by the blade; he was bending his arm back to throw. I rose as the knife was released, knocking the legionary aside, holding my shield of pigskin before me. The knife sliced into the heavy sack right where Betto's neck had been half an instant before.

•••

"You should have seen him," Betto said. "He was a man possessed." Crassus was home from the senate and had assembled the stunned household outside the front of the house. Tertulla had insisted, not wanting to get any paint on the mosaic floor of the atrium. The surviving assassin was trussed and harmless, most of his face and chest splattered white. Malchus had drawn his *gladius;* the blade against the assassin's spine impressed upon him the need for stillness. "After the sack stopped this villain's blade," Betto continued like a proud father, "the teacher bellowed like a bull and came right at that poor bugger, swinging his pigskin like he was at the Olympics. The bag must've weighed sixty pounds! He spun round on one foot and that sack whistled through the air. It clopped the bastard right in the head, as anyone can plainly see."

I remembered none of this: the assassins came into the schoolroom, Betto's apple hit one of them, and the next thing I recalled was Crassus asking if I was all right, here outside the house. I do not know how I came to be standing here, though Betto and Malchus assured me they were with me, their new hero, every step of the way.

Crassus stilled any further chatter with a raised hand. He addressed the captive. "I do not know what chain of events has brought you into my home," he said in a calm voice, a disinterested voice. "You may have been a good man cursed by ill luck or lived your entire life outside the law. I do not know and I cannot care. Whatever choices pushed your life along its unfortunate path, they are of no consequence now, for your actions have reduced *my* choice to one. There are many ways a man may die - look at me - and here I have some leeway. Answer truthfully and I will give you a death you do not deserve, one reserved for men of honor. Lie to me and before we speak of death again we will speak of pain. And so I ask you, who hired you?"

"I never saw him," Lucas said, working to control his fear. His eyes scanned the people encircling him. "He's not in this lot, I can tell you."

Suddenly, Tessa turned sharply in her chair, causing one of the daisies she always wore in her pinned up braids to fall to the table. "Where's Nestor?" she asked.

A second later, his stern voice a thin skin unable to hide the stab of betrayal, Crassus asked, "And where is Pío?"

Cook, still flushed and breathing heavily from his run through the house from the kitchen, raised his hand. "He left early this morning, *dominus*. Didn't say why. Said he'd be home before dark."

Before Crassus dismissed us, he instructed Malchus to execute the assassin and arrange to have his body and that of his partner thrown in the Tiber. There was neither ice nor heat in his voice, no hint that these sounds strung together in a certain order meant a man would die. It was the first time I saw the unbending steel at my master's core.

"*Dominus*, Malchus said, "shall we keep this one alive till Pío returns? Just in case?"

"No. Give him a quick death. I was foolish to think this poisonous cake would only have one layer. Whoever hired these men put more than one face between the coin and the knife. Send word to Boaz. I want Nestor found."

True to his word, shortly before supper the Spaniard passed through the gates. He appeared genuinely stunned to be met by drawn swords and a quick escorted march to Crassus. Pío earnestly claimed he'd been to the temple of the Vestals to pray for his family as he had every month since he'd arrived in Rome. Crassus accepted the alibi, but without joy.

Nestor was gone, yet remained: in the sullen bark of our master's sharpened tongue, in the despair and sorrow that hung like weights from poor Pío's eyes, in the shame bore by the rest of us, knowing we served in the house of an apostate. The big Spaniard became lethargic, despondent, and the house sank into dark waters; we moved sluggishly, unable to talk to one another, afraid to meet the eye of either Pío or our master. Everyone knew that Crassus would not let the matter rest; his reputation had been sullied. Nestor, property of M. Licinius Crassus, by running away had in effect, stolen himself from his master. Boaz's men were searching throughout the city, and they knew where and how to look: each carried an image of the fugitive and a purse heavy enough to animate the most reluctant tongue. The law of *furtum* hastened the inevitable: to conceal a runaway was the same as theft, and theft could result in flogging or worse: consignment to the aggrieved with freedom forfeit.

Three days after Nestor's disappearance, young Marcus and I were sitting on the rim of the peristyle's fountain, building papyrus boats to see whose design would stay afloat the longest. A shadow came across the sun and I looked up, shading my eyes to see Pío looming over me. His huge hands cradled a bunch of flowers, which I assumed he was going to arrange at the shrine of the house gods in the atrium. Yet his demeanor struck me more like a mourner making a gravesite offering. He stood there, immobile yet tense, a bear sniffing out prey. His eyes rested on me like dead coals, staring down at me; no, not at me, through me. Spray from the fountain blew our way and Marcus laughed. I almost hushed him, as if to warn him of imminent danger. Pío glanced his way, then turned and walked away, allowing me to exhale.

Marcus tugged at my tunic; my eyes were drawn back to the boy, but not my attention. Why would Nestor want me dead? I could understand why Pío might help him flee, but was that where his involvement ended? Nestor did not seem the type to cultivate connections of such a base nature. The house was in a state of dreadful disruption, and at its vortex the fact that I was still alive. I did not understand, nor could I connect the logical points. Unhappily, I was about to be tutored, for it was only a moment or two before the sun was eclipsed a second time. Pío was still holding the flowers, but their stems looked crushed in his unwitting stranglehold. His stare was now direct and purposeful.

"Why you make change? You hate us? You make jealous?" I started to protest, but there was no room here for dialog. "You are like carpenter ..." Pío dropped to a knee-cracking squat and I flinched, but his attention was on the boy, not me. "Marcus, you be good boy and find mother."

I had a wild impulse to beg the five year-old to stay, and was absurdly relieved when Marcus protested. "Go now," Pío insisted. He smiled and handed the boy several flowers. The trade was struck and off Marcus ran, leaving a trail of pulled petals.

Pío remained squatting. He turned to me, the look of affection for Crassus' son transformed. "I see you, I think of carpenter who fuck my mother," he said. "You not fuck, but you come to my house. You do not belong here. Like him. After he come to my house, all bad." The animation left his face as he rose; he lumbered off toward the *lararium* to make his offering. Those flowers would be dead come morning.

It suddenly occurred to me that my consternation, which was palpable, was not rooted in fear, though by any standard it should have been. What struck me like a blow from a fist as I sat swirling my fingers in the fountain's waters, the sun polishing cabochons from each drop of spray, what pierced me like one of Sulla's arrows was the realization of the extent to which I had become accustomed to living in the house of Marcus Crassus. Though I would not have thought it possible, there were good people here. The days were not onerous and the nights, though lonely, were at least peaceful. I was finding my place, and the last thing I wanted was change. To what god could I pray to stop the sun and send it spinning backwards? Let Nestor be surly and Pío romantic, let knives not fly and halcyon days return. Had I faith, I would bend my knee to Kronos, god of time, a barbarous

Titan who had devoured his own children. I would do this, and fervently, too, for more miraculous than any myth of creation, I had begun to feel at home.

# CHAPTER XIII

## 80 BCE - SUMMER, ROME

Year of the consulship of
Lucius Cornelius Sulla Felix and Quintus Caecilius Metellus Pius

It was never proven whether or not Pío had helped his friend escape, but the look on his face when Boaz's men dragged Nestor back in chains six days later condemned him as surely as any confession. Even so, Crassus was loath to punish his *atriensis*, though as paterfamilias he could do so on a whim, with or without proof. Crassus was not a capricious man; his steps were thoughtful and measured. Still, he must have been asking himself how long could a man's past loyalty balance the scales against his present transgressions?

Malchus and Betto told me what had transpired when they met in the small guardhouse at the front of the estate on the far side of the gates, opposite the schoolroom and clinic. The men who found Nestor had not been kind. The lumps on the runaway's face ranged in hue from eggplant to urine. He floated between our world and a better one, in and out of consciousness. Crassus allowed Pío to revive him with sips of watered wine laced with *sambucus* and cinnamon, but would not permit his bonds to be undone so that he could hold the cup himself.

Present were *dominus,* Pío and Nestor, with Betto and Malchus close by, hands on pommels. Betto confessed he had fretted through the entire meeting, afraid that should Pío become enraged, he and Malchus would prove to be a man or two short in the effort to subdue him.

When Nestor was more or less himself, Crassus began the interview with a single word. "Why?"

Nestor sat straighter and winced with the effort. "We were doing fine without him," he said, jerking his chin toward the house. "We didn't need him mucking everything up." Pío held the cup to his lips, but Nestor turned his head away. "We had a system; it was working. *Dominus,* if you'd been here, if you'd spent more time at home, I mean I know you are an important man, but still, you would have seen it."

"You have shamed this house. Your crime is a capital offense. By all rights I should plant a cross in the front yard and nail you to it." No one doubted the senator's resolve; words now needed to be chosen very carefully.

"Mercy, *dominus.*" This was not Nestor, but Pío, who actually had tears in his eyes.

Nestor continued to speak as the aggrieved party. "This school," he continued, the pitch of his voice rising, "he devised it to be rid of me. I could see it, I could see what was happening. He knew you wouldn't need me, that you'd send me away. I'd be off to the mines." He looked up at his companion, his face suddenly soft and sad. "And Pío. Pío would be alone again."

Crassus stood considering, twice about to speak and once holding his tongue. "This interview is over. I shall ask no more questions regarding the attempt on Alexander's life, for I fear to hear the answers and what they will demand of me.

"Pío, you have served me well, but what would you have of me? There must be payment, and it must be public. This is my will: nine days hence you and this entire household will escort Nestor to the forum. There his crimes will be announced and *you* will mete out his sentence. You will bind him with a collar like the dog he is; upon its iron face you will have inscribed the words, 'PROPERTY OF M. LICINIUS CRASSUS. RETURN AND BE REWARDED.'

"After the collar is affixed, across his forehead you will brand him *fugitivus* with the letters FVG so that all may know his shame."

"No, *dominus*, no!" Pío cried. Crassus was unmoved.

"I know your part in this, Pío. Let your punishment be the administration of his. And consider yourselves fortunate that when that day is past you will both yet draw breath."

•••

Pío never had to carry out Nestor's awful sentence. I don't think he could have done it in any case, such was his feeling for the little Greek. It was the day before punishment was to be exacted. We were taking the midday meal at our place in the kitchen. Everyone was present except Sabina, whose patients were especially numerous that morning; Nestor, confined to our room with the aid of a leather collar bolted to the wall by a sturdy chain; and Betto, on guard duty.

Two days earlier Crassus had escorted Tertulla and the children to Lavinium. Sabina had been released from Tertulla's service to allow her to tend to her practice. Ostensibly, the purpose of the trip was a visit to her parents, whom Tertulla had not seen for almost a year. A fortuitous lapse; the bolt that came closer to the mark was that the family was not immune from the pall shrouding the household. They were due back tonight, in time for the spectacle the following day.

Livia was last to table, the exuberant frenzy of her thirteen years oblivious to our sour mood and thankfully ignorant of its cause. I put my hand on hers as she sat next to me to quell her delightfully irritating whistling. When she asked why everyone was so grumpy I answered by grabbing a few figs and passing her the bowl. She wrinkled her nose at them, shoved them to Ludovicus the handyman, and instead reached for the hard boiled eggs with one hand and the grapes with the other. Today her red hair was piled high and tied with multi-color ribbons. The back of her neck, long and pale, revealed a fine down of softest incarnadine gold. I realized I was staring and hastily reached for the bowl of figs, perhaps taking one or two more than was decorous. I do so love their gritty texture, their subtle, complex flavor.

Pío moved a few grapes around his plate with his finger. His expression was unnerving: grim, determined, his lips pressed together, holding back whatever was bottled up inside. The only one who spoke was Livia, and we answered her with as few syllables as possible.

Everyone ate hastily, happy to return to their chores. Malchus and I were the last to rise. As I stood, I became aware of a rushing in my ears. My heart knocked against my chest like a deranged woodpecker. Suddenly I felt as if I could drink the Middle Sea. I grabbed the pitcher of *lora*, sloshing it into my cup and consuming it with graceless haste. I went to pour another, but my fingers had gone numb. Malchus stared at me open-mouthed and said I'd better have a lie-down. I told him that was an excellent suggestion and stumbled off to my room, wondering how my voice had managed to emanate from some distant place outside my body, tinny and remote.

Nestor lay on his back, his arms folded behind his head. "What are you doing here? You'll get the lash," he said hopefully. "I'll tell, see if I won't." I ignored him and collapsed onto my own bed. Breathing was no longer an activity my body did without my participation: if I didn't consciously inhale and exhale, I felt as if I'd stop altogether. The paralysis was moving up my arm. Nestor kept up a steady, nattering invective. I ignored him until it dawned on me that his babbling brook of complaints sounded like no language I had ever heard. I turned my head to look at him: he stared back at me with unmoving lips. Be afraid, I told myself, but I did not have the energy. Call for help, I chided, but weariness lay on my chest like a stone. It was so much easier to simply lie still and look at the ceiling. The ceiling. It had come alive: fawns and nymphs cavorted and contorted in a slippery, slithering dance of copulation that was repulsively riveting. I supposed I'd been poisoned, but unless someone found me, there was no way I could summon help on my own.

Someone did find me. Pío was in the room, which was irritatingly vexing because, I am ashamed to admit, his bulk was blocking my view of the ceiling. He sat on my pallet, making room for himself by shoving me against the wall with a swing of his hips. I moved my head one way, then the other, seeking a better view of what lay beyond the mass of him. I beg not to be faulted, for my faculties were functioning well short of normal. That mortal danger had just made itself comfortable on my bed did not occur to me. Nestor, it became obvious, was also ignorant of Pío's intent.

"What are you doing?" he asked in a language I understood. I think it was Greek.

"Hush, sweet man. We go soon. I make justice first."

Now here is where the tale becomes a trifle cloudy. I remember the feel of Pío's calloused hands, one pressing down on my chest, the other covering my nose and mouth. Struggling against him was useless, quite literally, because I could not feel my appendages, much less use them. I realized now, and not without a little sadness that I was about to die. Twenty-five, and still a virgin. The imminent end of one's brief stay on this earth will bring clarity to the mind even while poison still works on the body. What a miserable thread the Fates had sewn for me; was I so undeserving of a full and productive life? Or was I just a random accident of happenstance from beginning to end. One thing was certain: if these were indeed my last moments, Pío's misshapen, straining countenance was the last image I wanted to take with me to Elysium. I closed my eyes, sending two tears down either cheek.

I felt a slight release of pressure against my face. Nestor was cursing and straining against his fetters. Here I need to rely on Sabina's recounting of what transpired next, together with my own feathery impressions. As had been her wont ever since Livia had been returned to her, she had arrived with a fresh bouquet for my room, hardly expecting to encounter this murderous spectacle. The fresh flowers fell from her hands; screaming Pío's name she demanded to know what he was doing. Frankly, I should have thought that was obvious. Pío returned to his work, ignoring her next assault: pounding on his back and head with her fists. This he found as annoying as a gentle Aprilis mist, so she leapt upon his back, pulling at the arm attached to the hand affixed to my face.

My mind stretched thin, a taut, plucked string whose vibrations created a tone both pure and celestial. I was beginning to lose consciousness.

Pío's right arm swung backward, knocking Sabina onto the floor against Nestor's pallet. He strained to reach for her hair, grabbed a handful and pulled with all his might, and thus awoke an infuriated, incandescent healer. The tigress now reached behind her and clawed at Nestor's arm till it bled. He cried out, released his grip and before he could scramble backwards found her straddling his chest, a scalpel pressing against his throat.

"Release him, Pío," she screamed, "or I swear by the Seven Sisters I will cut so deep the arc of his blood will reach your thigh."

Pío laughed, but he also took his hand away. The string snapped; the music fled; and rather curiously I found myself longing for the sound. I gasped, my lungs pumping like bellows, and without any conscious effort on my part. The effect of the drug was already fading.

"You not kill Nestor," Pío said. He was right - Sabina would not kill an innocent man. I wanted to remind her that Nestor was not innocent. Perhaps another time.

A look of terrible realization came over her: Pío was going to kill her if he could. Something inside him had been squeezed until it had ruptured like a burst appendix; the only antidote for this poison was for the *atriensis* to free Nestor or die in the attempt. She dug into the bag slung over her shoulder and withdrew a second scalpel, moved a safe distance from Nestor and prepared to grapple with her own dubious fate. His plan might have hatched successfully, she knew, but its one fatal flaw, discovery, had just smashed its fragile shell, thanks to her. Now there was only one hope for Pío and Nestor - leave no witnesses.

Pío had come to same conclusion and went for the most immediate threat. Sabina screamed for help, expecting none, for this time of day none but the four of us would be found in the servants' wing. There was little room to maneuver. She could not wait for him to strike first; if he caught her she was doomed. She leapt across the short space between them - desperation, fear and finally, a vision of Livia flooding her muscles with godlike strength. It burst from her body in a warrior's cry and continued even when she realized she was going to survive. Pío caught her shoulder in his left hand and inched his thumb toward her throat. Before he could crush her windpipe, she struck with both scalpels. With the right, she stabbed up into the tendons of the wrist that held her, sawing till she felt something give. At the same time her left hand swept across his neck, severing the vein that bulged just beneath the surface. There was irony in the choice of her attack, but there was much more blood.

Pío stood up straight, as if listening to the sound of a more urgent call. Inside him, a clock began its inexorable count backward to zero, every diminishing moment marked by a surge of escaping of blood. Suddenly it was as if Sabina and I were no longer in the room. He shoved her aside; with his good hand, he ripped the chain from the wall. He picked Nestor up in his arms and said, "Push hand here. Hard." Not waiting for Nestor's horrified muscles to awake from their paralysis, he took his lover's hand and pressed it to his wound. Blood bubbled between the little Greek's fingers and poured down Pío's side. Nestor was crying.

Sabina followed them, but it was impossible for me to rise. Pío carried Nestor through the house, out into the front gardens, gathering the rest of the astonished household as if he had walked through a spider web and everyone else was a captured fly attached by sticky ropes, unable to do ought but be dragged along. Betto and Malchus raced to him with swords drawn, but as they neared it became obvious their skills would not be needed. With each step down the gentle slope between house and gate, Pío's pace faltered. Blood trailed from his neck and wrist, painting erratic crimson lines on the white gravel. Nestor used both hands to staunch the flow but Pío's neck was slippery and his jolting steps made the task impossible. Nestor begged for Pío to set him down, but the man from Hispania had his heart set on the iron gates. In the end that heart would betray him; with each ragged beat it pumped more of his life out onto the perfect landscape.

At last Pío stepped onto the Sacra Via. Below him, the greatest city in the world sprawled like the octopus he used to spear as a child. Freedom, he had learned, could not be priceless, for its value was less than freedom and home combined. In this hard, unforgiving place, the salt spray tang never filled his nostrils, the smell of grilled mackerel and onions never made his mouth water, and the sight of fishing boats anchored in waters so clear that the red and yellow hulls seemed to float in mid-air, this was only a vivid but distant memory. The village of his youth had receded to a few faded images. He looked up and smiled; at least the same blue vault arced here and in his mind's eye. It was enough. Gently, he set Nestor on the paving stones and sank slowly to his knees. He was very tired.

"Pío!" Nestor keened, "don't leave me here!" He reached up with bloodied fingers. "Don't let them do this to me! Take me with you, I beg you!"

Pío looked down and said, "Yes, *amor*, you come with me." He lay down beside Nestor and put his once powerful hands about Nestor's throat. "*Momento*," he said. Their foreheads touched. "Can you see them?" Instead of tightening, Pío's grip relaxed.

In a little while, Malchus and Betto eased Nestor up off the stones and brought him back into the house. They came back with a cart for Pío and left him in the guardhouse; Boaz's men were there within an hour to dispose of the body.

•••

Of the nine of us present for that midday meal, four had not eaten figs: Pío, Livia and two of cook's helpers, Mercurius and that woman who cried "how could you" on the day I first met Pío. Her name, I regret, escapes me.

"I'm certain," Sabina told Crassus that night. "It was tincture of henbane." Tertulla stood uncomfortably by her husband, but was determined to participate in the running of their home. She had even insisted on helping with the cleanup, discarding her palla for an old tunic and scrubbing the tiles of the atrium on her hands and knees with the others.

"Diluted, henbane opens and calms the breathing passages," Sabina said. "The bottle I keep in my stores is gone. My records show that it was three-eighths full, so unless someone ate every fig in the bowl, the dose would not be fatal."

"And a non-fatal dose?" asked Crassus.

"Depending on how much was ingested, delirium, paralysis. Brief unconsciousness."

"You must put a lock on the cabinet," Tertulla commanded.

"There was, *domina*. It was broken."

"Find a stronger one."

"Yes, *domina*. As soon as the shops open tomorrow."

Crassus asked about the staff that had been poisoned.

"All are resting comfortably, *dominus*. I sacrificed a goat, roasted its bones and gave everyone a dose of bone black. Because Alexander ate half the bowl all by himself, I forced him to drink the bone black, plus a reduction of mulberry leaves boiled in vinegar. Everyone should be fine by morning."

"This makes no sense," he said. "Why sicken, but not kill? Why hurt others, if it was Alexander Pío was after?"

"I think," Sabina answered, "he thought he could get away with the murder. Alexander's love of figs is no secret. Pío wanted to make it appear like bad fruit had killed him. That's why he couldn't break his neck or stab him. He could leave no mark. If others ate the figs and became ill, so much the better: it would help mask the truth. Except that I chanced upon him in the act."

"And for that we thank you," Crassus said without emotion. "Do you always carry your scalpels with you?"

"Always. I never know where I'll be when I ..."

"Have to slit someone's throat?"

"*Dominus*, it was a miracle you did not return to find two corpses instead of one."

"A miracle, yes. How do you come by such fighting skills?"

"No skill, only luck." Crassus looked skeptical. "Why did you not flee?"

"I could not leave knowing Pío would finish what he had set out to do. I would never have been able to get help in time."

"So you killed him."

"I am deeply sorry, *dominus*. I meant to cripple, to incapacitate, not kill. I know how much Pío ..."

"And why," Crassus said, squeezing his eyes shut and pinching the bridge of his nose, "why have you been bringing flowers to Alexander's room? Do you wish a *contubernium* with him?"

"What? No! It was ... for Livia."

"Ah. I see." Crassus did not press her. "It is late, and we all need rest. Go to your beds."

•••

Crassus looked in on me before he retired. I was groggy and my limbs still tingled, but the ceiling had lost its animation. He rested his lamp on the nightstand and sat on my pallet just where Pío had of late been visiting. Putting his hand on my shoulder he asked if I recognized him.

"Of course, *dominus*. I am sorry."

"For what? It is I who must apologize to you. I am glad you are still with us."

"I am tougher than I look."

"I doubt that. Until I think of a more permanent solution, I want you to become my new *atriensis*. I'll go over what is required, but I need to know if you think you can handle the responsibility."

I was struck, not dumb, but witless. In times of stress and shock, when mouth outpaced mind and completely overran good manners, I fell back on my old standby, pedagogery. "Is not the original meaning of *atriensis*," I stammered, "one responsible for the care of the atrium? Later, as well-to-do Latin homes grew, it came to mean chief steward, but the modern meaning is hardly more significant than hall monitor?"

"Calm yourself, Alexander. We are not in your classroom. If you must know, and I see that you must, I prefer the role as defined by my father and his father before him: as my *atriensis* you shall be master of my household, responsible for everything and everyone that in any way touches my home or my family. Or would you prefer being elevated to hall monitor?"

If only he were serious. "What of the school?" I asked.

"You will hire a new *grammaticus.*"

"I am certain I would make a better teacher."

"As I say, it is a temporary post."

I expelled a deep breath. "Then I am honored to accept."

"Of course, there is the matter of Nestor's chastisement. Nothing today has changed my will on that score." He saw the appalled look on my face. "You're right. Not a fit assignment for your first day on the job. Never mind. I'll do it myself."

And he did.

# CHAPTER XIV

## 80 - 76 BCE - ROME

Year of the consulship of
Gnaeus Octavius and Gaius Scribonius Curio

I was very quick to make myself indispensable. My accounts balanced to the *as*, the larders were always full and my promotion was begrudged little, mostly because there was none but myself remotely suited to the post. Like the mark upon Nestor's brow, the shock of our tragedy receded to a dull throbbing, but never healed: it felt as if his collar were worn by each of us, and the sight of him skulking about his chores was a constant reminder of the shame brought down upon our house. Nestor was reduced to performing the lowest of household tasks, not by me but by Crassus himself: cleaning the toilets and collecting urine for the fullers. I could not bear the sight of him. True, I was the intended victim of his crime, but to see his sentence carried out firsthand, every day, grated against my nature, a pumice stone applied too long to the same callus.

In the early days, I was so fearful of criticism I worked into the black of night poring over every detail of every task. If the post was temporary, there was no long-term need to replace myself as teacher, nor any desire, so that was one task I let slip. The result was a workload that more than doubled. I managed, though I admit my success was insured in part by Crassus himself. Friction from almost any problem was easily greased with his ever-expanding coffers and willingness to enlarge my budget whenever the need arose. It arose almost daily.

Mind you, there was nothing in his manner that made my promotion seem anything but temporary. He would pass me on his way out the door and waggle a finger at me. "I'm on my way to another interview," he'd say. Or, "Still looking." Or, "You're just too young." I swear on one occasion I heard him chuckling as I raced off to do better, be faster, panic more deeply. I was eating little and sleeping less. I believe it was five or six months after I began this purgatory that Crassus finally took pity on me, or more likely that Tertulla convinced him to decide one way or the other and stop torturing me.

I remember it was a fine summer's day. A cardinal as red as a yew berry was singing his redundant yet not unpleasant song in one of the peristyle's fig trees. I was hurrying to the kitchen to confer with cook. Crassus came out from his study. I tried to nod a quick greeting but my body interpreted the signals from my brain as an order to cringe. As we passed each other, he reached out and grabbed the sleeve of my tunic. A poked frog could not have performed better. When I had settled back to earth he leaned in and spoke softly to me. "The post is yours." He smiled and continued on his way. Later that evening he announced his decision to the entire *familia;* I found the voice to thank him then, but at the time my pounding heart had stuffed itself in my mouth, choking all communication.

Now that Sulla was gone and the *populares* were trying their damnedest to pry back the cold fingers of the dictator's legislative legacy, Crassus' true genius had time and opportunity to flourish. His influence in the senate grew with every oration. He would hear almost any grievance, especially from plebian businessmen shunned by elitist *optimates.* These were granted a voice and advocacy by Crassus. He would argue on their behalf, breaking the legal barricades to their success with no other weapon than the ballista of his gifted tongue. The more he spoke, the more senators crowded to his side of the *curia,* for it was no small trick for a patrician to earn the trust of the equestrian class and the popular support of the people. Less persuasive legislators began to "cling to his toga," as the saying goes. While publically he performed these acts for the good of the people of Rome, privately he was gracious in his acceptance of both fees and percentages of future profits.

In his march on Rome, Sulla had been generous to the one legate of whom it could be said: without him the city would not have fallen. And so our master was given the house in which we lived, but also many others of lesser value taken from proscribed supporters of Marius and Cinna. These Crassus repaired, embellished and sold at multiples of their original worth. The cash was never idle, for Crassus used it either to buy more property or loan without interest to those senators who might some day need prodding to reassess their positions and vote with him. When I first became *atriensis,* my master's worth totaled three hundred talents, a vast sum about which the average citizen could only dream. By the time we left for Parthia, his wealth had grown twenty-five times as large.

We had been settled for less than a year in the house given to Crassus by general Sulla when he began building an estate to match his aspirations. It sprawled over a tenth of the entire Palatine, dwarfing our existing home. Some senators, led by Sulla himself, accused my master of displaying five million *sesterces* worth of ostentation, but Crassus had a simple theory: people respect wealth. Make your home a hovel and be treated like a pauper. Live in a palace and be treated like a king. I had a theory, too: an estate such as this would be all the revenge left to a man who had lost his family, his possessions and been forced to live as an outlaw. For Crassus, this meal of aggrandizement could never be anything but unsatisfying, but the building and sustaining of it would feed many mouths.

The site was to the northeast of the old *domus,* gathered from the razed homes of three proscribed senators, now dead, whose property Crassus had purchased from the state for a pittance. The new home took two years to build and was the marvel of the city. Its forest of columns, fields of terra cotta roofs and moons of not one but three domed baths looked directly down upon the forum. And every time the populace looked up at the top of Rome's first hill, the man they thought of was Crassus. He was only thirty-nine years old.

Within this opulent warren of fountains, formal gardens, heroic statues, tranquil pools and entertainment rooms that grew from intimate alcoves to the grand atrium, sequestered in the middle of it all Crassus had given to me a *tablinum* worthy of an elder patrician. There were two tables, several cushioned chairs, a *lectus* should I feel the need for a snack or a nap, and storage along two walls for hundreds of scrolls. A rolling cart contained writing utensils, cups, goblets and a small amphora of wine tucked neatly in the middle. At my disposal were rivers of parchment, forests of stili and fountains of ink. On overcast days, I need only look up at the groined vault of the ceiling to admire a painted blue sky cradling clouds of yellow and rose, lit from beneath by a rising sun. Double sconces on all four wall corners dispersed any gloom. The eastern exit led out into a peristyle so monumental that on a hazy day I could barely see the columns at the far end. Beyond the opposite curtains lay a small, verdant atrium open to the sky which I learned was my private refuge for contemplation and study. My office, I discovered with abashed pride, was adjacent to the one belonging to Crassus.

This bounty of space and privacy was more than matched by my private quarters. Though I would spend far too little time here, the miracle of this room was not its wall paintings or its size or the exceptional feature of a small window that opened onto my study's atrium. It was the location of my *cubiculum* that set my mind spinning between joy and bitterness, elation and shame. The room where I was to take my rest was not in the servants' wing. Just down the hall lay the family's quarters; no relay of runners need answer the call of the *dominus* to fetch me. The master himself could summon me by barely raising his voice.

When Crassus, giddy as a child with a new toy, first led me to my room, I was beset by a confusion of guilt and hubris. I thought of the cart full of captives that had carried me to this place. What had become of those innocents? How did they fare? Were they even alive? Even as my heart reached out to them, I confess a part of me did not care. I had survived the ordeal, and this was my reward. I deserved it, I thought, then reviled myself for even thinking such a thing for even an instant. What was so special about me, after all? I had suffered no more than they.

Crassus saw my consternation and said, "Come now, Alexander. Do not spoil this moment. Wait until tomorrow to do what you do best: think too much. For now, just accept your good fortune."

"I am grateful, *dominus,* yet I cannot help but think of those less fortunate than I."

"You are in Rome, man. You had better start thinking of yourself."

"But why," I asked him, "am I worthy of such magnificent lodging when in the old house even Pío slept under guard with the rest of the servants."

Crassus replied, "By Jupiter, I swear Daedalus himself could have engineered the labyrinth that is your mind. Satisfy yourself with this: *Servi aut nascuntur, aut fiunt.* Slaves are either born or made. Pío slid from between his mother's legs a newborn slave. His entire life could be distilled down to a single choice: obey or disobey. For almost all his years, till love found him, he was a good man – he obeyed. But you, you question, you argue, you think. In the end, of course, you too, must obey. But you make *me* think, a feat none such as Pío could perform. Study Alexander, learn all you can; teach me, challenge me, and do not cower like the rest. The more you know, the more valuable you will be to me. You are not like Pío; you have been made a slave, but damn it, man, it is just a word. Serve me, and I will fulfill every dream that that young Athenian philosopher ever had. This life is a greater life than any you could have imagined. Learn to trust me if you can, and I shall do likewise. Can you do this?"

"Until you decide otherwise, *dominus*, I am your servant."

Crassus laughed. "Yes, Alexander, you are. I hear the undercurrent of insolence in your tone and I relish it. You will not disappoint me." He walked to the doorway and turned. "Enjoy your quarters. You'll earn them."

•••

This was the humble start of many cerebral wrestling matches between us. I did not intend to lose. Of course, it fell to me to populate this self-contained village on the Palatine with furniture, landscaping, and ... people. So many people, in fact, that a separate, two-story barracks would be built near the main house. The irony was not lost on Crassus; he may have thought me capable, but there must have been an element of mirth in watching me squirm from on high. How would I handle conducting the purchase of my fellow man to serve this house? Would I bridle? Balk? Refuse? Any of these would have given him great pleasure and opportunity for discourse, let alone chastisement.

I decided that Crassus would be disappointed.

•••

In the first days of my promotion, I would find little time for rest, but when I could, I took it in a small copse toward the western edge of the estate, unique for its wild woods and lack of landscaping. As the new estate grew up around us, its crushed marble walkways and formal gardens, as breathtaking as they were, began to weigh heavily upon me. There was something claustrophobic in perfection.

Several foot trails tunneled through this forgotten forest's leafy shade, and while the place wasn't the hilly farmland of home, it did spark memories which I was not quite ready to surrender. At first Crassus wanted the architects to raze the site to make way for a shrine to Bellona, the war goddess whose hand had helped Sulla to victory and Crassus to staggering wealth. I talked him out of it with the truth: it was the only place I had seen in Rome that reminded me of Aristotle's Lyceum, and perhaps each of us might stroll there, separately or together, to collect ourselves and contemplate whatever inspiration the woods lent us.

It was after I realized I would soon be hiring servants of my own that I withdrew to this sanctuary to reflect upon the man I had become. I walked the dirt paths, listened to birdsong, inhaled the scents of spring and marveled at nature's unsculpted bounty.

I know I am cursed with a mind that will not remain quiet; it will ruminate and fret till rough rocks of ideas have been tumbled into smooth stones of logic, either that or into dust. As I walked, I considered my condition. Was it better to be born into bondage rather than as a free man reduced to such a dismal state? Better to exist in a perpetual fog of blessed ignorance, or to have tasted sweet self-determination, even for a little while? I say the latter, even though it is the way of pain. But why talk of choice when that commodity, once foolishly taken for granted, had become precious by its absence? The way of pain was my way. And since I have just stated that as my preference, I should have been content.

Even Aristotle believed in the natural condition where one man could be owned by another. "For he is a slave by nature who is capable of belonging to another - which is also *why* he belongs to another." If you *are* one, you deserve to *be* one. However, if you have the ability to reason, he argued, as someone might if he were, say, a student captured in the destruction of Athens, then the victorious society should hold out freedom as a reward. I wonder how Aristotle might have revised his philosophy had he himself been taken as a trophy of war. You see, I did not question the system so much as rail that I had fallen victim to it.

You, reader, live in a world where power and wealth are controlled by a tiny, fractional elite, men who claim to use their wealth and armies to serve and protect you. Your government is controlled by these same men who allow your senators to live unfettered by the rules they themselves legislate. You receive only so much grain for your bread and oil for your lamps. Your sweat and toil builds great homes and palaces; those who live within tell you how proud you should be of your glorious, gleaming accomplishment. But you are barred from setting foot inside. You may rise only so high as your rulers allow, for there is only so much wealth, and it has long ago been claimed by others. These few men let slip a coin here, an entertainment there, and this they know will feed the inertia that keeps you from making the effort to claim a larger share. This is what you call freedom, but are you certain of your claim upon it?

Crassus knew what I had at first failed to recognize; his error lay in not understanding that after four years in his service, I could at last see it as clearly as he. I was a slave. Yes, I could say the word at last. Do not tax your eyesight scanning back through these scrolls, I promise you it isn't worth the effort - nowhere in this manuscript until this very moment have I myself used it.

My owner was right: whatever place I had hoped to earn in the world, this is where fate had delivered me. I was a slave, but even slaves are given a single, awful choice: rebel, or rise as high as nature may permit within this unnatural state. My frail nature, even in my prime, was hardly rebellious. I was no Spartacus.

And so, the further freedom slipped from my grasp, the stronger my determination to become a paragon of slaves, a slave with money and power, as fine as any Rome had ever seen.

It was of significant help, I admit, that I belonged to the richest man in the city.

# CHAPTER XV

## 76 BCE - SPRING, ROME

Year of the consulship of
Gnaeus Octavius and Gaius Scribonius Curio

I should mention that in the spring of this very year, Melyaket, my brave-hearted companion and steadfast friend (I shall claim senility should he ever lay eyes upon these words), was born in a ravine at the base of the Sinjar mountains, a lonely range at the northwestern border of the Parthian Empire. To hear him tell it, on that day nothing less than the intervention of the gods saved him from a very short life span, not to mention a grisly and horrific death. Well, if the immortals did truly take such singular interest in him, then let them tell his tale. I do not have the time.

•••

In matters of the heart, I have observed that it is difficult to learn from our mistakes. On the contrary, we seem quite adept in making the same blunders over and over again. So when Sabina told me soon after we became friends, that she had had her fill of men and wanted nothing more to do with them, I had my doubts. Seeing my eyebrows elevate, she attempted to convince me by claiming the fault lay not with men, but in her own character. It was flawed, cracked, she said. How could she make such a monumental blunder in her choice of husband and trust herself to choose wisely ever again? Her logic made me falter in my skepticism, till I realized logic had very little to do with the mystical chemistry of the heart.

When it comes to love, we are the great architects of artifice. We construct elaborate stages, festooned with intricate sets, costumed brightly, aglow with candles incapable of illuminating any flaw, upon which we play our most convincing acts of self-deception. What convoluted excuses we spin to justify behavior we would find ludicrous in others. What pretty lies we tell ourselves.

You would think that Sabina was not the kind of woman to make the same mistake twice. That is unkind, for indeed, while the cause was redundant, the man was new. In three of the four years I had known her, she swore she would have nothing more to do with men. Her work, she claimed, captivated and satisfied her as no man's attention ever could. The gods know I am no expert, but surely there are certain thirsts which no occupation can slake. Sure enough, the siren call of these more physical requisites grew louder this past year, but unlike Odysseus, Sabina was not securely bound to any mast. The man waiting for her upon that dangerous shore? Steadfast, sturdy Ludovicus.

Who could blame her, honestly? Allow me to illustrate. I trust that by now you have a clear idea of my own physical shortcomings: too tall, too clumsy, too thin, too evocative of the aloof professor. Now imagine the opposite and there stands Ludovicus. Brawn to his fingertips, shaven pate, prominent brow over pale eyes, large, tan hands made for strangling, thrusting a sword or other such manly pursuits. Mind you, he was not unkind or malicious or indecent. In the end, however, he was just a man.

Maybe she only thought of him as a dalliance. I blush to say it, but once the needs of the body have been sated, does not the heart often command a strategic withdrawal. Not so with Sabina: she was an emotional lover; her attraction to any man needed to be more than physical right from the start. Otherwise her Lysistratan resolve would have prevailed and she would have had nothing to do with Ludovicus. She had had her eye on him for some time, but had been content to let the pressure build without action. Which is to say the moment he entered her clinic with a wrenched back she allowed her temple of abstinence to be ransacked.

Being in the room next door with nothing to do but work on lesson preparation or eavesdrop, I chose the latter. Sabina asked Ludovicus to lie on the examination table on his stomach, sounding completely professional and curt, her voice devoid of any of her usual compassion; by which I mean to say, she was a little flustered. He said he'd have to strip down to his *subligaculum*. She told him to get on with it; I could almost hear the rolling of her eyes. There was a pause without sound, but the smell of pungent Egyptian eucalyptus informed me that liniment was being applied.

Ludovicus made some insouciant remark about how good her hands felt on his back, then added, "What would you say if I told you there was nothing wrong with me."

"I'd say you are quite mistaken."

"What do you mean?"

"You're arrogant, presumptive and like the rest of your sex only look at yourself when you can get your hands on a glass that magnifies. You're also wasting my time. Get out."

"Perhaps you are the one who presumes. I never said there wasn't anything wrong with my back. I said 'what if.'"

"Either way, get out."

"Sabina, don't think I haven't felt your eyes boring through my back these past few weeks."

"That must be what caused the damage. Here's a 'what if' for you. 'What if' I call for Betto who's just outside at the front gates?"

"Be my guest. But I think we'd both like it better if you didn't."

"For the last time ..."

Now there was silence, then a loud slap. Then silence again. Then rustling and the table scraping on the floor.

All of a sudden, Sabina called out breathlessly, "Alexander, are you in there?"

"No," I replied. I collected my things and headed up to the house as quickly as possible.

# CHAPTER XVI

## 76 BCE - SPRING, ROME

Year of the consulship of
Gnaeus Octavius and Gaius Scribonius Curio

I had just spent a long day with Boaz negotiating over the purchase of dozens upon dozens of new slaves required for a senator of Marcus Licinius Crassus' growing stature. Reputation, not necessity, propelled the calculus of their number. The size of one's household was the most important badge a senator with my master's burgeoning eminence could and must display. Tertulla, being the mistress of the house, was the first to receive her new staff. She had a slave to help her dress, plus one to organize her jewelry; one to prepare her various ointments and another to apply them, one to put her makeup on, another to take it off; one to adorn her hair and one to curl it; one to organize her wardrobe, another to fold her clothes and yet another to inspect them for wear. One would accompany her to parties to change her footwear from outdoor shoes to indoor slippers, another to whisper in her ear the names of guests she might have forgotten. She had three bath attendants, including one whose sole purpose was to pluck away unwanted body hair. A bedchamber slave would keep her private quarters tidy, another would remain awake throughout the night should she or her husband wake and require a snack or a cup of water.

In the kitchen, beside the head cook and two subordinates, the staff would eventually include specialists for soup, pickling, meat pastries, desserts, dairy, fruits, and baking. Assisted, of course, by servers, fire boys, stewards for the pantry, wine and stores, a procurer, a menu preparer, an overseer of the dining room, a couch spreader, a table wiper, an ornament arranger, an announcer, a taster, a carver, and a cup-bearer.

As for Livia, she was apprenticed to the head seamstress; I heard she was as nimble and adroit with a needle and thread as she was with her tongue.

I myself required a personal secretary, two scribes, two purchasing agents, and three men to supervise the various subgroups of household workers: the baths, the kitchen, the gardens, the stables and all the rest of it. Over the coming months, by the time Boaz fulfilled all the positions required by the *domus*, our *familia* would swell past 100. It was a good beginning.

•••

I was hot, tired and needed a bath. On my way to my quarters I passed through the northern gardens. Near the center, encircled by the graceful, tapered columns of six cypress trees was a magnificent marble statue of Apollo holding his lyre. His wise and gentle gaze was fixed on the horizon, proof that no god inhabited that cold stone. If the Olympian had lived within, he would surely have bowed his head to behold Beauty lying asleep at his feet. Livia was curled up against the granite plinth, a damp sponge drying in her outstretched hand, her unpinned hair, the color of Armenian apricots, lay fine and abundant across her face, guarding the pale cream of her complexion against the intrusion of the fascinated sun.

Next month we would celebrate her seventeenth birthday.

The god gleamed from head but not quite to toe, for kneeling to complete her task, she must have succumbed to the persistent invitation of the warming day. Drowsy and safe within the alcove of trees, she slept peacefully at the foot of the god.

Apollo was naked, save for sandals and a cloak circling his neck and draped from behind over his left forearm. His hair curled in tight ringlets about his comely face, his body was smooth, muscled, proportioned, perfect. I pictured marble come to life and knew that here would be a human worthy of Livia's attention, of her devotion, of her affection. *They* would have made a beautiful couple, this flawless immortal and impertinent slave girl. For one arrogant instant, I tried to envision myself in the god's stead and was so repelled by the absurd image that I turned to flee. Something caught my eye, the glass-smooth inside of a scallop glinting in sunlight. Livia's shell bracelet lay untied beneath her outstretched wrist. It must have come undone as she fell asleep; the single shell lay in the grass just beyond the string's end.

Beyond her sat a bucket of water and a small stepstool. I pulled the latter close and sat so that no part of my shadow fell on her. I moved quietly, but knew I could not succeed without disturbing her. I know as do you, part of me wanted her to wake, wanted her to speak to me, to see me. All the while I could hear the churlish voice of Little Nestor inside my head: *you're too old, you're too skinny, you're unworthy; she'll want a warrior, not an accountant, she'll crush you with a glance, she'll scoff at your clumsy fumbling and the sound of her laughter will shatter your heart.* And I knew he was right. But the humiliation of her rejection would be much easier to bear than remaining silent forever. I had watched our friendship grow for years; the closer she matured into womanhood, the more dissatisfied I had become. Did she too yearn for more? How would I know if I did not ask? Every chance meeting with her left me feeling like a stone struck by flint. What better place and time than here and now to discover if heat would ever produce flame?

I had the shell on the string and the string almost tied above her wrist before she woke. "Alexander," she said, stretching luxuriantly. "I fell asleep." The movement of her arm caused the uncompleted knot to come apart. The single scallop escaped again and lay separate from its brethren. I reached for the bracelet but found myself holding Livia's wrist instead. I would have pulled away but she held me and said, "I dreamt of you."

"Truly?" The softness of her skin made the hairs on my arms prickle as if a thunderstorm were nigh; her resolute grip was hardly necessary. "The best dreams are gifts," I said. "In sleep we give ourselves the things we want but cannot have in our waking hours. Was yours one of these?"

Livia laughed, a light but ruffled sound. "It was."

"Well?"

"I cannot tell you."

"I see. Then you must ask your mother for a salve. You look as if you have tarried too long in the sun. Or perhaps those rosy blooms grow from a different stem?"

"You are impertinent." She pulled her hand away; was there reluctance, or was I merely dreaming for something I could not have? "What were you doing watching me sleep anyway? Oh ho! What's this? A garden growing in Alexander's cheeks?"

"Not at all," I said, lying poorly. "The day warms. I was passing and noticed your bracelet had come undone." I felt Apollo's eyes on me and resisted the urge to look up.

"Oh, this thing. It's always coming apart. Were you trying to fix it?" I nodded. "So now you are become both jeweler *and atriensis* to the house of Crassus. Congratulations."

"Merely an apprentice. Perhaps for both positions. Fixing your bracelet was not the hard part. Repairing it without waking you was the test I could not pass."

"I am glad of it."

She sat up, flicked a leaf from her tousled hair, and straightened her tunic. The many greens of her eyes, a sunlit forest suddenly thrown into shade, transported me for a moment to the woods of Elateia and home.

"Here," she said, holding out her arm once more. "Please?" I bent to add the last shell to the string but Livia said, "No, not that one. Keep it, you know, to think of me when you hold it."

There it was, the miracle that would silence Little Nestor forever. I worked to conceal my elation. "It's a good start," I said, putting the shell in my belt bag.

"Good start? You assume much, Alexander of Elateia."

"Do I?"

"What would you have of me then? Would my lord command me to forfeit even more shells? Oh, but we're not talking about shells now, are we?"

"I am not your lord." I retied the bracelet. When it was done, I bent and kissed the top of her hand. "And no, we're not. The truth is, Livia, though I shall treasure your gift for all my days, I need no token to keep you in my thoughts. You are rarely out of them."

"Alexander ..."

"No. Please do not speak if I have misjudged this moment. I could not bear to hear the sound of it."

"I cannot speak," she said, rising to her feet. I stood with her, but left my heart upon the ground. "I cannot speak," she repeated, taking both my hands in hers, "and kiss at same time. Can you?"

Our eyes locked to speak of an ardor I had thought one-sided. To learn otherwise fueled a strength I did not know I possessed. I wrapped Livia in my arms, pressing her own behind her back. Her yielding body sent suns bursting in my head; my ancient timidity shattered. She arched as our lips met, tender at first, then insistent. She pulled against my grip to free her hands, but I held her fast. She moaned, part complaint, part animal need. I released her. The moment her hands were free she threw them about my neck. Our kiss continued, interrupted only by the need for breath. My hands drifted through the unending seas of her hair, my closed eyes saw every curve and line of the face that had beguiled countless sleepless hours. Our mouths tasted and explored, giving and taking in equal measure. But my mind had no part in any of this. That Alexander, the analyst, the worrier, he was nowhere to be found. For the first time in my life, I felt without thinking, became utterly and completely present yet without any sense of myself. In my life, it was a moment without equal.

"I have been waiting for you," she said after we had paused to compose ourselves. We sat beneath Apollo, gently touching, kissing lightly, lost in this infinite instant.

"Why did you not make your feelings known to me?" A finger tracing an ear.

"I thought you would think me a child." A palm caressing a cheek.

"You *are* a child." A kiss more fervent than the last.

"And you are an old man. An old man who, with each passing day, grew in favor with our lord, and further away from the rest of us. I feared you would spurn me."

"A fear I mirrored. After today, I may never fear again." An embrace, an inhalation of intimately scented air.

"It was you, wasn't it?" she whispered. "You had me bought from Boaz."

We separated enough to see our flushed faces. "A mother reclaimed her daughter, a wrong was partially righted. What more matters?"

"And a certain tall, fair-haired servant saw a bit more of a young girl he fancied?"

"He is a great admirer of talented whistling."

"And now you have become great, second only to our masters."

"I am still Alexander. I would be your Alexander."

"I have already claimed you."

"Someday," I said thoughtfully, "you will buy your freedom."

"And yours!"

I laughed, and deep inside resisted the old Alexander who wondered just how that would happen. "Speaking of freedom, how is it you do not attend your lady? Why are you not at your loom?"

"*Domina* threw me out!"

"What on earth did you do?" The intertwining of fingers.

"Nothing more than my duty. It's your fault, in any case. You have 'saddled her' with too many slaves. She said she feels like a bee in a hive. And she thought I needed air."

"You are a little pale."

"You love my complexion; confess it!"

"You fish when your basket is already full."

"Of fish? There's a fine compliment!"

"Indeed. Your skin is as white as a flounder's underbelly, as soft as cheese, as smooth as cowhide." Livia punched my shoulder. "Rubbed with the grain, naturally."

"Hah! What of the day they carried you in like the prize in a boar hunt? Your face was as waxy as the masters' death masks."

"You remember? That was the first time I saw you," I said, watching as she pinned her hair. "You were twelve."

"You were a fool. Ruining one of general Sulla's fine arrows."

"Not as expertly honed as your sharp tongue." She pursed her lips and let the object in question dart out and in. How she aroused me! "Had I known this day would come, I would have been much less carefree with my life. Do you know you were the vision my eyes beheld when I first regained my senses? You came to my sick bed, dancing and whistling, your red hair unclasped and swirling like Charybdis aflame."

"I love the way you speak."

"Then let me speak true now. Shall I tell you of your complexion? It is fresh cream from the pitcher, soft as moonlight on a rose. You made me dizzy that first day, and the sight of you has kept me reaching for support ever since. I'm afraid, Livia, I've been in love with you for rather a long time."

"I am yours," she said with her usual determination. "Forever." She leaned into me and pressed her head against my chest. Then, almost to herself, "I wonder what mother will say?"

# CHAPTER XVII

## 76 BCE - SUMMER, ROME

Year of the consulship of
Gnaeus Octavius and Gaius Scribonius Curio

"Ah, Alexander. Good, good. Ludovicus found you. Come in."

It was the night of Livia's birthday celebration. Long after the party had ended, she and I had been walking in the smallest of our gardens, lit by a three-quarter moon, holding hands, saying little, pretending the distant rumble of Rome's commercial traffic was the sound of the sea at Cumae. A dozen runners had been sent to fetch me when I could not be found in my quarters but, Fortuna's backside, it was the newly appointed (by me) battalion commander who stumbled upon us. Even had Ludovicus not seen our hands quickly separate, what else could an assignation at such a late hour signify? Sabina would know by dawn. In our *familia*, if she did not know already, then she would be the last.

I was twenty-nine, over six years in the service of Crassus; once I dreamed only of freedom, now my sleep had room enough for visions of Livia, no more. Gone were the sweat-stained hours of darkest night when I would lie awake and berate myself, mocking my decision to make the best of it as just another way of calling myself a coward. I was no coward. I was in love. And lovers are nothing if not brave.

I took a tentative step through the doorway as Tertulla complained, "Marcus, not again! It's the *middle* of the night!"

"Forgive me, *domina*," I said. Taking my mistress too literally, with eyes downcast I added, "I am afraid it is well past the sixth hour; it approaches the eighth." It was the second time this month I had come to my masters' bedroom at an hour when even the gods lay curled in sleep. Tertulla glared at me as I stepped gingerly into the room. After Ludovicus found us, we each dashed off in separate directions: he to the stables, I to set the house in motion, and Livia to the room she shared with her mother. Would she slip unnoticed to bed, or disturb her roommate's slumber and face stern maternal interrogation? I could not help her now - momentous doings were afoot.

Glancing behind me, I jerked my head at the two men standing like statues in the hallway, motioning impatiently for them to enter. They hurried through the parted curtains holding two lamps aloft. Three more sleepy-looking attendants waited outside, each with two large leather bags slung over their shoulders. Every bag weighed almost twenty-five pounds.

Tertulla growled in exasperation. "Marcus?!" The blue ice chips of her eyes flashed, and in the warm light of the lamps her black curls glowed like spun obsidian.

"*Columba,* it's an adventure!" Crassus tried to kiss his wife, but she petulantly pushed his face away with a manicured hand. He grabbed it, found her forefinger and bit it. She replied by batting him over the head with a fringed cushion. This provoked a suppressed giggle from two of Tertulla's attendants. I glared at them and their vapid silliness was replaced by a genuine and more appropriate alarm.

"Oh come now, Alexander," said Crassus, "don't let the night rob you of your sense of humor. What little there remains of it."

"The night, or my sense of humor?"

"I want Livia," Tertulla said. "I'm outnumbered, and I'll wager her wit against the lot of you."

I made eye contact with one of my men and off he went to fetch the owner of my heart. Crassus said, "Take your rest, dove, I promise I'll be warming myself by your side in no more than an hour. Perhaps two."

"Hah! You'll be lucky to find me in the house. I think I'll wake the boys and take them to visit their grandparents."

"They won't enjoy either one."

A moment later Livia rushed in, barefoot in her dressing gown. "*Domina,*" she said. We made eye contact; Livia rolled hers to the ceiling. That was it, then. Sabina knew.

Crassus jumped off the bed, clad only in his *subligaculum.* Livia's eyes sought the floor as he put a hand under her bowed chin. Tertulla's favorite may have been a firebrand with anyone else in the house, but when it came to the master, she was well and truly cowed. "What's this then? The birthday girl. Did you enjoy your party?"

"Yes, *dominus*. Very much, *dominus*. Thank you."

"You are welcome," he said, scrutinizing the top of her head, his own far too close for comfort.

"Livia, come to me," Tertulla said. "These brutes want to take my husband from my bed."

"My lady," Livia said, her enunciation constrained by Crassus' gentle grip on her jaw, "it would seem they have been successful. *Dominus*, my lady calls."

Crassus raised Livia's head to meet his gaze. Her eyes widened like a doe's. "Does she indeed?" he said softly. "Then you must answer." Abruptly, Crassus' tone changed and in his deep, authoritative voice he said, "But first, answer me. Quickly now, whose side are you on?"

Livia's eyes grew wider still, her face still held captive. "Surely, I am on the side where my master commands me to stand." Crassus narrowed his eyes. "I don't know, *dominus*. Yours?" she tried.

Crassus shook his head sadly and released her chin. Livia tossed her red hair from her eyes without moving her hands from her sides. The gesture had an air of defiance.

Crassus sat back down on the bed. "Well then, child, let me assist you. Attend me, and learn. When you are with your mistress, you are on her side. When you are with both of us together, you are also on her side. And when you are alone with me, whose side ...?"

*"Domina's, dominus?"*

"That's right, Livia, you always take the side of your *domina.*"

"See how well I have him trained?" said Tertulla.

"Like a Phrygian bear," I said. "*Dominus*, must we not make haste?"

"*Columba*, see? My master calls. I must depart."

"Go then!" Tertulla said melodramatically, a forum actress, "go, and do not return!" She threw her arm across her forehead. She was only twenty-four; young enough to be excused, perhaps.

"Alexander," Crassus said, serious for a moment, "are you prepared? How much did you lay out?"

"The usual. Seventy-five thousand."

"Too much. It's always too much." Crassus eyed Tertulla's favorite. "Well, Livia, since Mercurius is obviously sleeping in a corner somewhere, would you mind doing the honors?" He opened his arms, palms outward to illustrate the state of his undress. Livia ran out of the room smiling. "Happy girl, that," he said. "Why do you suppose that girl is so happy? Anyone? Alexander?" he asked pointedly.

My eyes took a turn at inspecting the floor. Crassus winked, and I exhaled. Then, with resignation he said, "Bring it all."

Tertulla sat up and reached for the *peplos* thrown haphazardly over the edge of the *lectus*. As she drew it over her head, her pale nipples disappeared behind falling fabric. Her husband said, "Reminds me of lids closing over tired eyes. An apt analogy, considering the hour."

She caught his look and said impishly, "You can have them *now*, and everything that goes with them, but *not later*."

"Alas, business before pleasure."

"Your business *is* your pleasure," Tertulla said, pouting as she dropped back down on the bed.

Livia returned balancing a huge pile of clothing in her arms, using her chin to keep it all from falling. I said, "*Dominus* will suffocate if he wears all of that."

"I'm only following your example."

"I beg your pardon," I said.

"Did you not just bring to *dominus* more money than he will need, as a precaution?"

Crassus laughed as Tertulla clapped, "That's my girl."

"He's not going to wear the money," I muttered.

"Thank you, Livia," Crassus said. "I prefer a large selection when I dress. You may go." Livia raised her chin at me as she passed, a look of superiority more triumphant than the one she usually wore. As she reached the doorway Crassus added, "And try not to smile so much, dear. It is unbecoming of a slave." A year or two earlier, my gut would have clenched to hear Crassus speak thusly, even in jest. Now, I felt only a pinch of sadness that even his words had lost their sting. We were what we were.

*Dominus* threw on two tunics, one over the other to protect against the chill. Mercurius, his *ornator*, came rushing in holding a heavy but short riding cloak which he proceeded to fasten about his master's neck.

"Apologies, *dominus*."

"You are ill-named, Mercurius. From now on, I shall call you Somnus."

"Yes, *dominus*. Thank you, *dominus*." Crassus dismissed him, then turned back to the bed. "Not one kiss then?"

"You had your chance." Tertulla said, ducking back under the covers.

"Hmm. I think I deserve two." Crassus crossed from the doorway back to their bed, gauged where Tertulla's bottom was hidden and gave it a not-too-hard whack. She screamed, then laughed and finally cursed him, but I knew he must ignore her muffled baiting. If he delayed, who knew what damage would be done, what opportunities lost. Men and women were now running all over the villa, lighting oil lamps and sconces, preparing baskets of food, making almost as much noise as the rhythmic pounding at the front entrance.

"Would someone *please* open that door!" Crassus yelled. I snapped a finger and one of the lamp bearers ran off. "Damnation!" Crassus shouted, tripping over one of the only pieces of furniture in the bedroom, the small step stool used to climb up onto the *lectus*. Although the room was mostly bare, its walls were exquisitely painted with scenes from my own mythology; the floor, for example, had the light been better, would have revealed a mosaic of Xanthus and Balius, the immortal horses that bore Achilles in his chariot at Troy. The chariot was empty. Achilles kneeled in the dust before it, grieving over the news of the death of his friend Patroclus. The horses wept. An odd choice of inspiration for the bedroom. Or any room.

Crassus shouted, "Epimachus! Boots!"

"Can't you please send someone else?" Tertulla said in a muffled voice, letting a slender leg and way too much thigh slip out from beneath the coverlet. "Must you always insist on playing the hero?" She wiggled her painted toes. The gold ankle bracelet with the zodiac charms he had just given her for her birthday beckoned. For a moment, it looked as if the siren song of their tinkling would be enough to lure him back to bed.

"You're making this very difficult," he sighed. "But I must see to this."

Tertulla sat up. "Come here," she said. He obeyed. "I want to give you a reminder of why you should hurry back to me." She slid her arms around his neck and pulled him forward till his mouth met hers. Their kiss was long and languid. I looked away.

When at last they separated, he sighed and replied, "I'll be back as soon as I can." Stepping through the doorway, he glanced at the three waiting men. "That is all of it?"

"Six bags, three thousand, one hundred twenty-five coins in each. A total of eighteen thousand, seven hundred fifty *denarii*: seventy-five thousand *sesterces*. Precisely," I added, my tone daring contradiction.

"Precisely? Surely the count might be plus or minus a denarius or two?" I looked at him and smiled thinly. Crassus met my gaze and said, "How foolish of me to suggest it."

We headed for the front entrance.

# CHAPTER XVIII

## 76 BCE - SUMMER, ROME

Year of the consulship of
Gnaeus Octavius and Gaius Scribonius Curio

What drove Crassus from the arms of his willing wife was the memory of the eight months he had spent hiding in a cave near the town of Tarraco on the Hispania Citerior coast. He swore he would never, ever let himself be forced to live that way again. Cinna and Marius the elder had killed his father and brother along with many others, slaughtering them for no greater crime than their having been born into noble families. Crassus could not help the accident of his birth, but he could gird himself with what, in Rome, was inviolable armor. Money provided far more than just a roof over your head. It would buy influence, friends, arms and men-at-arms, power and protection, and he meant never to be without it. A great deal of it. At thirty-nine, he was making excellent progress toward that illusive, mythical amount: more. Since the day I was made his *atriensis,* it had been my task to help him achieve his goal.

Outside the vestibule to his villa, his horse was waiting, held by one of six torch bearers. There were also six armed bodyguards who looked like they could handle two or three times their number. Among them was Drusus Malchus, but not Betto, who was more energetic than stalwart. When Malchus caught my eye, he nodded and winked. The young legionary guard from the old slave quarters had grown in girth and strength over the past several years. He was no longer the skinny lad from the latrine, but one of the most massive of Crassus' fighting men. I was thankful he had taken a shine to me.

Crassus called good morning to the men, each by name. He mounted the black Hispanic stallion by stepping on the prostrate back of one of his stable boys. It was still several hours before dawn, and the streets were empty. Only the foolhardy or those in dire need ever ventured out after dark into the unnamed, unnumbered and unlit streets of the city.

"I can smell smoke, but see nothing," Crassus said squinting into the gloom. The Urbs spread out beneath us in unnerving silence.

Ludovicus said, "Just across the Forum to the Quirinal. Take the Alta Semita. You'll see the apartment house as soon as you start up the hill, two alleys north of the temple. Don't worry, when you get close, you can follow the sound of Septimus Corvinus' wailing."

"Corvinus, eh? I'm surprised he has any *insulae* left. He will insist on making them out of rotten timber and mud bricks."

"And four and five stories high," said Ludovicus.

"Hopefully everyone is getting out safely."

"The first brigade is on their way with two pump carts," the commander said. "We can use the Petronia Amnis. Plenty of water in it this time of year."

"Good work. What about the second?" Crassus asked.

"We'll be right behind you, just in case."

Crassus turned the reins and patted his mount. "Let's go, Ajax." With a kick to the horse's flanks, he wheeled and took off down the hill at speed.

I climbed up onto one of the two carts and my men handed me the six bags. Lifting the seat of the storage bench, I secured the money in their hiding place and nodded to Ludovicus to proceed.

Crassus had little difficulty finding the location of the fire. By the time the rest of us got there, the top two floors of the apartment were glowing like paper lanterns and smoke was billowing above the flat roof. It was indeed a mud brick and timber building, four stories tall. At any moment the flames would erupt. The first brigade was standing a safe distance away having already prepared the hoses from the nearby stream and primed the pumps. Crassus nodded to the lead slaves of the two pike crews who rushed not to the burning *insula* itself, but the two adjacent buildings. With their ladders and long, hooked poles they began dismantling the now-vacant buildings.

The narrow streets were full of hundreds of spectators who acted as if they were privileged guests at a *ludi* put on just for them. Yet closest to the pumps was a large knot of anxious onlookers in anything but a festive mood. These were the people who actually lived on this street. They were being held in check by a semi-circle of armed men belonging to Crassus. With one exception, no one in the growing crowd had much hope anything would be left come morning: they all knew that poorly constructed buildings like these were almost impossible to save, either from the flames or the intentional demolition. The exception was an obese man stomping up and down amongst them, gesticulating wildly. His toga was unraveling and his hair stood out at odd angles. His face was made more florid by the glow from above. He was followed, back and forth, by several bodyguards who looked menacing but helpless.

"Is everyone safely away?" Crassus asked, riding up to the pumps. He remained mounted to be sure that the crowd could see him.

"Crassus! What are your men doing? They're destroying my buildings!"

"Compose yourself, Septimus Florius. They're following my orders."

"Your orders?! Are you crazy, man?! My apartment house is burning!"

"We can't have the adjacent buildings ignite, now can we? No, of course we can't. Now tell me, Corvinus, does the whole complex belong to you?" The fat landlord nodded frantically, wiping sweat from his forehead with a perfumed kerchief. "The whole block? Oh dear," Crassus said, shaking his head. "I don't know how we're going to be able to save them all."

"If you'd stop talking and start doing something ..."

"You're quite right, of course. Men, man the pumps!" With well-rehearsed choreography, Ludovicus and his team flew into action, adjusting regulators, shouting at each other, tightening connections, checking hoses, readying the buckets and doing … nothing.

"Septimus Florius," Crassus said thoughtfully, "it occurs to me that no matter how successful we are, at least two of these *insulae,* possibly three will be forfeit. I am devastated that I could not get here quickly enough. I will make it a point to address this neglect of civil responsibility in the Curia. I feel personally responsible. Awful, just awful. Perhaps the best thing now is for you to cut your losses. It's not really my area of expertise, but I would be willing to take this block off your hands for ... say ... eighty thousand *sesterces*?"

"Pumps two, three and four primed and ready, sir!" shouted Ludovicus. The first hose team approached the smoking apartment house while the pikemen continued to destroy the buildings on either side, pulling debris away from their incandescent neighbor. Two other groups of Crassus' slaves hauled the rubble away to a safe distance almost as fast as the pikemen could create it.

"What? What?!" squealed Corvinus. "I don't want to sell my buildings. I want you to save them!"

"Wait a minute!" Ludovicus shouted. "We've lost pressure!" As he spoke, there was a dull thump from the top floor. Wooden blinds blew out of two corner windows in a shower of sparks, and flames exploded out the smoking holes. There was a sharp intake in hundreds of lungs as the crowd quickly pressed back against the storefronts opposite the fire. Corvinus slapped pudgy hands to his face, pushing his fleshy lips out like a corpulent fish.

"Goodness!" Crassus exclaimed. "I was afraid that would happen. I don't think it's possible now for me to offer full price. The best I could do ...," he sighed laboriously, "would be sixty thousand."

"I think we've got it now," Ludovicus called.

"Sixty thousand?! They cost me over a hundred."

"And I have no doubt you squeezed the most from every *sestercius*. Although, I hear they're doing marvelous things with concrete and fired bricks these days. A little more up front cost, but well worth it, I should imagine."

At that moment, one of the firefighters closest to the building called out. "I heard something! I think someone may be inside!"

Immediately, Crassus dropped his play-acting, leapt off his horse and grabbed a torch from an onlooker. "Stay back!" he yelled to Ludovicus. He dashed across the unpaved street into the building. His men stared at each other in disbelief. Ludovicus didn't know what to do. If he turned the pumps on the burning floors, the weight of the water might cause the already weakened structure to collapse on our master. If he ran in after Crassus, he'd be disobeying a direct order, and his back would bear witness to his insubordination. He settled on selecting several men with full buckets to wait with him a little closer to the doorway.

Crassus had given me no such order. I gave Ludovicus a look that said 'watch the money.' He nodded and I jumped off the cart and raced to follow my master into the building. I bypassed the *tabernae* on the ground floor, knowing we had only moments to search the upper floors. Crassus was already at the top of the stairs. Smoke hung in the deserted hallway, and the air was thick with the smell of burning wood as I joined him.

"Vulcan's prick, man ...!"

"I'll take the left," I shouted above the roaring and ran down the narrow hall. I might get a beating for it later, but at least now I could honestly say I never heard my master give me an order to leave. I was relieved to hear the thump of Crassus' boots heading in the other direction.

I ran into each apartment, calling out as loud as I could. With little furniture and only one or two rooms, they were easy to search. The second floor was empty. Crassus met me at the central stairway; as we bounded up to the next floor he threw me a glance but said nothing.

The heat grew alarmingly with each step. By the top of the landing, we could no longer stand. Fire flowed in waves across the ceiling of this hallway like an upside-down river. Crassus threw his cloak over his head and motioned for me to do the same. We called out again but it was almost impossible to hear anything above the noise of the fire and our own racked coughing. It was like inhaling the smoke at the top of a clay oven. There was a constant, deep rumbling over our heads. I remember thinking how ironic that it should remind me of pounding surf. If there had been anyone on the fourth floor, they were gone now.

These thoughts took but a second. We inhaled a lungful of air through the fabric of our cloaks and scrambled down opposite ends of the hallway, crouching low. The *cenacula* on this floor were empty as well. The heat from above pressed down on us like the hand of Hephaestus, forcing us to crawl. It was too hard to hold onto our torches, so we abandoned them. Looking for survivors was no longer our mission. Now our task was simply to make certain we would be counted among them.

We were scrambling toward each other on our bellies through thick, slowly curling smoke. Like me, Crassus held his cloak over his head with one hand and dragged himself forward with the other. His clothes were ruined, his face soot-stained, his eyes tearing. Another strange thought struck me: at this moment it would be hard to tell us apart.

My lord reached the stairwell just ahead of me. It couldn't have been more than a second that he hesitated, waiting for me to join him so we could descend together. That's when a section of the floor above came crashing down. A smoking plank hit Crassus in the back. It knocked him down the stairs to the lower landing. The hole in the floor above exposed an inferno. It wasn't bravery that made me leap from where I stood to the landing below. I was moved urgently and instantaneously by the overwhelming instinct to get away from that searing heat. Crassus was dazed and struggling to his feet as I landed hard, tripping and falling onto him. We tumbled down to the ground floor, rolling over burning wreckage.

Miraculously, neither of us was badly hurt. My arm had smacked into a piece of burning wood and my sandaled feet would take some time to heal, but nothing seemed broken. Crassus' cloak was smoldering. I unhooked the jewel-studded *fibula* that held it around his neck and tore it off him. The second it landed on the ground in a smoking heap, I dove for it again, ripped the clasp from the smoldering fabric, rose and handed the golden disk to Crassus. He looked at me in amazement and laughed out loud.

"Did you hear that?" I shouted.

The sound came from our right. "Anyone there?!" we called.

A thin voice answered, "In here." It came from a barbershop whose entrance opened on the lobby where we stood. We moved quickly into the shop and I saw that Crassus was limping. The store was empty. The voice called again and we could tell that it came from above us. A wooden ladder led to the loft found in almost all these small shops.

Crassus grabbed a rung but I said, "*Dominus*, allow me." I indicated his injured leg. He stepped aside and I climbed up through the trap door in the ceiling. In the smoky dark I could barely make out the narrow, cramped sleeping quarters of the old man who lay shaking on a pallet in the corner.

"You're safe now," I said. With Crassus helping from below, we managed to get him down the ladder. He was barely conscious. Once back on the shop floor, Crassus steadied the frail barber while I bent to pick him up and heave him over my shoulder. I staggered only a little.

We left the store, crossed the lobby and headed back down the vestibule. Smoke clinging to the ceiling was being sucked out into the cool night air. Ten paces before we reached the exit and safety, Crassus tapped me on the shoulder and held out his arms. I realized what he had in mind and carefully helped resettle the wisp of a barber over Crassus' own shoulder.

I followed Crassus out of the building, noting that the limp in Crassus' left leg seemed markedly more pronounced than it had only a moment before. Of course, it could have been the extra weight.

A huge shout went up from the crowd as we crossed to the other side of the street. The loudest cheers came from Crassus' own household. He gently set the old man down, who instantly reanimated and threw his arms around his savior, sobbing his thanks. Another huzzah. Crassus extricated himself, wished the barber well and left him to the care of the happy and grateful onlookers.

Ludovicus barged through the crowd and pulled up short in front of us. He looked at Crassus with shining eyes and trembling chin. He could hardly show his relief by throwing his arms around his master, but had no such compunctions with me. The massive, muscular battalion commander gripped me in a bear hug and told me I stank. I swear he wiped a tear away on my sooty shoulder before releasing me.

Crassus put his hand on that same spot. He looked me in the eyes, nodded ever so slightly and gave my shoulder a brisk squeeze and shake. That was all. That was enough.

Then he returned to business.

"Fortuna has smiled upon us this time," Crassus said to an even more disassembled Corvinus. If possible, he looked worse even than we. Crassus continued, "I shall make an offering to Pluto for sparing these good citizens. I suggest you do the same."

"Yes, certainly," agreed Corvinus. "Uh ... but ... what about my building?"

"Well, it's a corner building, that's something anyway. Ludovicus, what are you waiting for?!" Crassus shouted in false anger. At last, Ludovicus gave the signal to swing both streams of water directly onto the burning building. As we knew it would, after only a moment, the top two floors caved in and a fireball veined with debris, steam and dust rose into the night sky. Another collective gasp came from the crowd.

Corvinus sagged. "Sixty-five thousand?" he begged.

Crassus shook his head. "Fifty."

Corvinus whimpered like a struck puppy. "Done," he said, defeated. I clambered up onto the pump cart, retrieved one of the three heavy bags and handed the twenty-five thousand *sesterces* to Crassus who passed it to Corvinus.

"Here is half. Come by my house tomorrow, after your sacrifice, and I'll have the balance and the documents ready." It was sometimes necessary to offer all the cash on the spot to convince the landlord to sell, but Corvinus was completely deflated. He turned and slumped away with his guards.

From out of the darkness came a troop of twenty torch-bearing scribes. As they moved into the street, Crassus allowed himself to be hoisted back up onto his horse, favoring his leg, then turned to address the crowd. As he spoke, those of his men who were not busy with the actual firefighting switched roles and spread down both sides of the block, each bearing a lit torch. With the help of the still burning building, the street was now illuminated to festival brightness.

"Good people of the Quirinal. My name is Marcus Licinius Crassus. I am deeply sorry for this tragedy and the loss of your homes. As I am sure you are aware, the flats built and leased to you by Septimus Florius Corvinus were of an older, less safe construction." At the sound of the landlord's name, a chorus of boos and hisses rose to mingle with the smoke. "Now, now, each according to his ability and means. Corvinus did the best he could."

"To rob us blind!" someone shouted. The crowd cheered.

"Citizens and plebeians, this is what I propose. You see my assistants passing amongst you now. Please let them record your names, sign if you can or make your mark. Everyone present tonight, regardless of where they live, will receive my gift of two sacks of wheat flour." The crowd applauded, surprised and pleased. "Come to the granary tomorrow before midday. Countersign the list and you'll be eating bread and honey by sunset!" That will bake him a few votes, I thought, when he stands for *praetor*.

"For the people whose homes were destroyed tonight: when we depart shortly, please follow us back to my villa. A barracks in my compound is being prepared to receive you even as we speak." This earned sincere applause and nods of approval. "Now, it would make no sense to ask you to return to these same homes, those left standing, when we all know it will only be a matter of time before they look like that." Crassus pointed to the glowing rubble. The crowd murmured agreement. "Tomorrow, a team of my engineers will arrive at first light and begin the demolition of the remaining *insulae*." A cry of dismay rang out. Crassus raised his arms above his head to quiet them. "Do not be alarmed. Everything will be provided. My scribes will go to the Temple of Ceres and request the occupant records from the *quaestors*. At my own personal expense, you will be temporarily relocated while we begin construction on a new complex, built entirely of safe, sturdy and heat-resistant concrete and fired bricks!" The people were happy about the new buildings, but not so enthusiastic about the disruption of their lives. The cheering was less than tumultuous. But Crassus was ready for them.

"To compensate you for this inconvenience, each tenant will receive an additional two sacks of flour, two *amphorae* of oil, plus a cash allowance of one thousand *sesterces* to spend as you wish during reconstruction." This time, the crowd roared with unbridled enthusiasm. While they were cheering, Crassus added under his breath, "And of course new leases will be executed with nominal increases in rent."

As we rode home, the sky was lightening in the east. It looked like it was going to be another gorgeous morning. Crassus looked exhausted yet elated. He would have little rest before the days' *clientes* started arriving. He reined in Ajax and pulled alongside the cart in which I rode. "See the doctor before you retire," he said. He began humming a tune from the pantomime. After awhile, as we climbed the Palatine, he said, "Another solid night's work, Alexander. Another acquisition, another rung."

# CHAPTER XIX

## 76 BCE - SUMMER, ROME

Year of the consulship of
Gnaeus Octavius and Gaius Scribonius Curio

We were welcomed by a crowd from the household, mostly those who knew members of the brigade and were happy to see them return home safely. Among them were Sabina and Livia, stiffly holding hands. Well then, even without the direct order from Crassus, there'd be no putting this off. Tertulla was at the head of the little cheering throng and the moment Crassus was off his horse she was in his arms. Suddenly, she tilted her head back, having got a good whiff of him, pushed him to arms' length and saw the state of him in the growing light: charred, blackened and bruised. To our horror but his delight she thumped his chest with her fist, raising a small cloud of dust and ash. Sabina made to accompany him but he put up his hand.

"There are others," he said, nodding at me, "that are more in need of your skills. When you are finished with

Alexander, you may attend me in my quarters." They began walking to the house, at which point Tertulla immediately noticed his limp. She punched him again. "Enough," he cried, raising his index finger like a beaten gladiator. "Mercy!"

•••

Ludovicus leapt from his mount and raced to meet his lover and also mine, throwing his arm around the healer and smiling broadly at her daughter. Livia would have run to me, but her mother's grip was firm. It would be up to me, then, to go to them.

"Salve Sabina, Salve Livia."

"I have been waiting for you ..." Sabina said coolly.

"As have I," Livia said, her voice one part anticipation, two parts defiance. Ah, the politics of love: when affection is wielded like a club to gain independence from a disapproving parent.

"...for almost three months," Sabina finished.

Ludovicus, never one to fret over subtext, barreled along excitedly. "You should have seen our lad here!" he said, clapping me on the back. "He was Mercury himself. Sped into that flaming apartment house as if it was two-for-one day at the brothel. Your pardon, of course. I didn't mean ..."

"Thank you, Ludovicus. You neglect to mention that I was *following dominus*."

"Well, yes of course, a stunning bit of work by the master as well. You'll both owe Vulcan a couple of goats for letting you out of that one!"

"Why didn't anyone else try to help?" Livia asked hotly.

"Orders, miss, orders."

Livia turned to me. "You disobeyed a direct order from *dominus*?" she asked as if running into a burning building held the lesser risk.

"Not so much disobeyed as ducked under."

"You might have been killed. He might kill you yet!"

"Save me the trouble," Sabina said, not quite under her breath.

"Mother!"

"Did you hear they pulled an old man from the insula?" Ludovicus asked. "By Vesta's flaming toenails, he'd've burned to a cinder for sure, if not for those two."

"Sweetheart," Sabina said gently. "You're not helping. Why not see to the horses and I'll find you later?"

Before he could either answer or leave, Tessa ran up to us. "I just heard," she said breathlessly. "Gratitude to you both for rescuing *dominus*!" First, she threw her arms about me, then Ludovicus. Jealousy can be measured in fractions smaller than a thousandth of an hour, and Tessa's hug of the battalion commander lasted just one of those slivers too long. It went unnoticed by everyone, except Sabina.

Ludovicus replied, "'Fraid you've got it turned around, Tess. I didn't save anyone."

"Don't you need to freshen your daisies, *Tess*?" Sabina asked. Ludovicus colored, looking like a man with something to hide trying to look like a man with nothing to hide. "We're trying to have a conversation here."

"Well. No need to get snippy, I'm sure. I'll be off then. The flower beds need watering anyway, don't they?"

As soon as Tessa was out of earshot, Sabina said, "Look, daughter, let's just have out with it, right now. Are you still a virgin?"

"Of course I am!" Livia exclaimed.

"I think I'm done standing up for awhile," I said, suddenly gone all atotter. Ludovicus thrust an arm out to steady me.

"Fine. Livia, attend to your chores. We'll speak more on this later." The moment she was released, Livia ran to me and kissed my cheek. "Don't worry. You will always be my foolish, brave centurion," she whispered in my ear, then ran off before her mother could fling any more verbal darts at her. Sabina called for a litter and very soon I was being carried off to her office.

"These should heal fairly quickly," Sabina said tonelessly, spreading boar grease over both my feet, including the sandals. Then she went to her collection of knives and began sharpening one that looked to me to be already honed to deadly perfection. An image of how she had dealt with Pío flashed before me. I lay on her examination table, feeling not a little vulnerable.

"You should have come to me," she said flatly, cutting the laces that ran up the top of each sandal.

"I did not know how to express my feelings to you."

"Of course you didn't."

"And I was afraid."

"Of course you were." She began pulling the leather tongues away from my feet, applying a colloidal solution of honey, crushed lavender and silver as she went. I winced as she passed over one of the worst burns on the outside of my left heel. She did not apologize.

"I'll tell you why you were afraid. You knew if you came to me that no matter how much I cared for you, no matter how grateful I am to you, I would never condone such a match. You would never receive my blessing."

"Why not, Sabina? I would never harm her. I would care and provide for her, I would ..."

At that moment, little Marcus and Publius came stumbling in, tripping over each other in their haste. Nine year-old Marcus said, "We've come to thank Alexander ..."

"For saving Father," his six-year old brother blurted.

"I was telling it!" Marcus said, infuriated.

"Ooh, that's discussing," Publius said, wrinkling his eyes and nose at the sight of my feet.

"Disgusting, you dolt," Marcus said. "But he's right, you know. Will you have to cut off his feet?"

"Boys, go ask cook for some honey cakes and leave me to my work. Or I might slip and accidentally cut a toe or two right off, right before your eyes. Can you imagine the blood?" Two little jaws dropped in unison. They moved in, hoping for a display of carnage.

"Sorry, boys, no fountains of gore here today," I said, trying to sound confident. "Go, my little warriors. Let the healer concentrate." Pleading, followed by reluctance and resignation.

"Mother said she hopes you know what you're about," Publius declared as Marcus led him out by the hand.

"You've got a mouth as big as Polyphemus," Marcus said.

"Oh yeah? Well, you've got a pimple as big as his horn! Ow! Well, you do. Right there! Ow! Can I pop it? Hit me again and Father shall hear of the missing honey. So can I pop it? Please?"

When the sounds of their discourse finally faded, Sabina said, "It's obvious how you feel about each other. And it grieves me to deny you, but I must."

"I could go to *dominus*. Crassus could give his blessing to a *contubernium* between us."

"But you would never do that."

"No, I suppose I wouldn't." *Wouldn't I?* "I'll just have to find another way for you to find favor in the match."

"I won't. By Vesta's eternal flame, Alexander, if things were different, no one would be happier than I to tie the knot of Hercules about her waist on the day of your joining. But even if *dominus* gave his blessing, it cannot and must not be. Soon I will have enough to buy my freedom. I have already negotiated a price with the master. He will allow me to continue to work on the estate, free of rent. Then, in two years, maybe three, I will have earned enough to release Livia."

"And Ludovicus has already bought his freedom. Do you love him?"

Sabina hesitated. "I am doing the best I can."

"You will leave us?" I could barely get the words out.

Sabina had been wrapping my feet in washed linen. She stopped to look at me. "That has not yet been decided."

How could this be happening? This woman, my oldest friend in this place, was building a wall between my love and me, a wall neither logic nor force could breach. "I have a ring," I blurted. "And a *fibula*. They are very valuable."

"Oh, Alexander, you are wise in so many ways, but in this you are a babe on the altar. Don't you see, Crassus will never let you go; you are too valuable to him. My daughter must marry soon. By the time I have bought her freedom, she will already be past the prime age for union. She and I may never be anything more than freedwomen, but her children will be *born* free citizens of Rome. You want that for her, don't you?"

I exhaled the long breath that heralds tears. "Of course I do. I just ...." Sorrow choked off words and dammed my eyes, raising pools that blurred my vision. How could I argue with a plan for freedom? Especially for Livia. She would leave, and marry, and bear free children. And I would be left behind. The tears crested and rolled down across both temples as I lay on the gurney, thin wet tracks. I could not wipe them away, for Sabina held my hands to tend to them.

I stared at the blurry ceiling. "I don't know if I can do this."

Sabina bent over the table, looking directly down at me and said softly, "She must come to her husband a virgin."

"Of course," I said, sniffling loudly, arguing on behalf of the stranger who would take her away from me. "What of her time with Boaz. Wasn't she ..."

"She is intact. I told you he was a better man than most of his kind."

"This is very hard, Sabina."

The healer's tone turned contemplative. "Perhaps it would be better to have her taken away from this place."

"You must never do that! I will not allow it!" I shouted, rising to my elbows, then quickly deflating back into flaccid decorum. "Apologies. Please, Sabina, let me go to the master. Let me ask him for a *peculium*. At least grant me this."

"That is the first thing I did when I learned of your fondness for each other."

"You did not just discover it from Ludovicus?"

"Subtlety, Alexander, is one of your lesser strengths. You'd have to be blind not to have noticed the way you come apart around my daughter. But Livia, she's got more craft than a market fair. If they weren't all whores and poor as Arabs, she'd have made a great actress. She hid her feelings for you from me, and my ears were perked, I can tell you."

"Why didn't you come to me when you saw I was falling for her?"

"There was no harm in it as long as it wasn't serious, and honestly, I had no idea anything would come of it. I should have done, I see that now. I am deeply sorry."

"I may be ill." Sabina brought me a bucket; I turned on my side and held it, mouth open, breathing in short gasps.

"Look at how far you've come in such a short time," she said, her hand on my shoulder. "Crassus will grant you many favors; you will be a rich man some day."

"I could join you."

She shook her head. "My dear sweet Alexander, you will never leave this place."

I stared into the dark emptiness of the bucket. "I am undone."

"Then maybe this is the best advice I can give you: the less you see of her, Alexander, the less pain you will endure. I am finished." It took me a moment to comprehend her meaning. "Wear these slippers. The soles of your feet sustained little damage. Return to me tomorrow and I will replace the dressings."

"Have you said all these words to Livia?"

"I have. She is rebellious, but there is reluctant understanding in her eyes."

I put down the bucket, swung off the table and got my feet into the slippers. If there was anything more to say that would move her, I could not think of it. I shuffled toward the doorway and without looking at her said, "Know that I will speak with Livia again. You had better see to *dominus*."

•••

Crassus never said a word about returning the unused silver to the treasury, but then, he didn't have to, did he? He was also silent about our mad dash into the burning *insula*. He never spoke of it again. Crawling off to my own bed, I gave instructions to my secretary to disturb me only if *dominus* or *domina* called. I slept the dreamless sleep of the dead for five hours.

I awoke to a gift. Gleaming on the edge of my washstand lay the golden *fibula* from the night before. Its rubies had been cleaned, the entire piece polished. But this was not the gift that shook my heart. Inside the clasp, freshly inscribed in Greek was a single word:

## Ηρωας

Hero.

# CHAPTER XX

## 76 BCE - SUMMER, ROME

Year of the consulship of
Gnaeus Octavius and Gaius Scribonius Curio

We met by Apollo in the lull between midday meal and supper. Dark clouds churned overhead; distant thunder grew nearer. Surrounding us in partial privacy, the poplars danced a tune called by the wind, but they thrashed out of time. We sat at right angles to each other, holding hands, our backs against adjacent corners of the plinth. Apollo would cry soon, tears streaking his marble face.

"We could run away together," Livia said.

"We will not."

"I know."

"How can something sound so logical to the ears, yet make no sense at all to the heart?"

"Oh, shut up."

"What have I said?"

"Don't make this into one of your philosophical puzzles."

"Apologies."

We sat quietly for a moment listening to the rising wind.

"We should not have met here," Livia said, wiping her nose with the kerchief in her free hand.

"Why not?" I asked stupidly.

"I will humor you because you are a man," she said, sniffling loudly. "If you were a woman you would not have to ask. How can this be my favorite refuge when it has become the place of our parting?"

"It need not be so."

"Mother says you are my first love, and the first is always the hardest."

"Only if it ends," I said, squeezing her hand. To my surprise, she withdrew hers.

"If we agree to end it now," Livia said, "it will hurt less when we part."

"Your mother is wrong."

"She said you would say that." The first fat drop landed with as soft plop on Livia's knee.

"And how did she tell you to respond?" My tone escaped sharper than I intended.

"She said she would do nothing to keep us apart, that this was a lesson we would have to learn for ourselves."

"And?"

"And," she said, rising to straddle my legs and sit in my lap, "I told her I needed no more schooling." The kiss that followed was sweet as fruit, sweet as honey, sweet as freedom. I took her face in my hands and looked into the depths of her green eyes. "I do love you so."

We embraced; she kissed the lobe of my ear and said, "I love you more." A bolt crackled, the storm suddenly upon us. Thunder fell down heavenly stairs to crash above our heads, Zeus' invitation for the rain to fall in earnest.

"I used to believe I could reason my way out of any predicament," I said as we ran for the cover of the colonnades. "I was young and naïve. Nevertheless will I think on this day and night. Pray that when freedom calls your name, we will still stand together."

•••

It was near the end of Sextilis, a few days before the Vulcanalia. For all of us who depend upon the uninterrupted supply of grain to this city of insatiable appetites, and for all of that somewhat smaller group who believe that the intervention or at least the apathy of the gods makes a crumb's bit of difference on the volume and safety of the harvest, this is a very important holiday indeed. The priests would invoke Vulcan Quietus, pleading with him to ward off wildfires, protect the city's grain, even lull the mighty vents of his slumbering volcanoes to utter stillness.

Here's a bit of irony for you. The Vulcanalia is celebrated on the 23rd of the hottest month of the year. Every true Roman must honor Vulcan by beginning the day, not in darkness as is usual, but by candlelight. It pleases the god, apparently, to witness the ignition of more unintended fires on his holiday than on any other. He invariably gets his wish. His altar, the Vulcanal, was in the heart of the forum, just above the Comitium where the senate convened. Wise priests, generations long past, moved the services, which included bonfires as well as sacrifice, to the less flammable Campus Martius, the Field of Mars. There, races are held in the Circus Flaminius, and a hot and sweaty time is had by all.

Last but not least, the god of fire, to exacerbate some ancient Olympian rivalry between Neptune and himself, has developed a monumental craving for fish, and it is on this day that it is sated. Once the bonfires are lit and blazing, the priests ceremoniously hurl countless fish into the flames, imploring Vulcan's fire to spare the fields, the grain, the city, the people. These holy men rely on cheap perch to appease the god. Crassus had recently acquired two vineyards in Campania and a large millet, corn and wheat farm in Venetia near Cremona. Even a cynic such as he dared not tempt the gods where his investments were concerned, so he had had me order a thousand expensive mackerel for *his* sacrifice. "Why take chances?" he asked when I questioned the size and quality of the purchase. All I could think about was the stink, and hope that the wind would carry the proof of the city's piety somewhere else.

Walking from the master's quarters back to my office, I passed Sabina coming in from the entrance that led to the servants' house. She held her favorite bucket and cleaning rags in one hand (yes, she had a favorite bucket), and something clenched in her other fist. She ignored my greeting; in truth I don't think she noticed me; sweeping quickly by muttering urgently to herself. As she strode away I had the misfortune to hear a single, coherent word: "barefoot." I called loudly after her and she turned at last. I asked what was troubling her; she stared at me with hard eyes, her mouth a thin, tight line. She looked as if to speak, then thought better of it and continued on her way. I knew her well enough to let her be; hopefully whatever ate at her would sort itself out.

I saw her a second time that afternoon. Sometimes, when the mistress was in town shopping, I stole Livia away from her work in the baths to accompany me on one of my habitual walks in the western wood. That is the name I had given it, western wood. I have never been one for flights of hyperbole, or for that matter imagination. As we strolled, hand in hand, our words were feathers, light, soft, of little consequence. We worked hard at pretending nothing had changed between us, as if one of us had contracted a mortal carcinoma. Unlike most, we could see the end of our time together, and having just begun our journey, it was not enough, it was not fair. Though it was the last thing we wanted, the knowledge that one of us would go on and one of us would not became our own shared cancer. We tried to ignore it, but it lay beneath everything we did, everything we said. A growing stone between us, always pushing us further apart. For as long as I could, I delayed seeking out the master to beg my plight. I did not want to hear the finality of his answer. Of course Sabina had been right. To his credit, Crassus did not laugh. He was moved, yet unmoved. I would become rich by his side, but that would always be my place. The stone grew much larger that day.

We had taken the longest trail, a circuitous ribbon that skirted the boundaries of the little forest. As we neared the halfway point, both of us saw a flash of color off to our left, deep in the heart of the wood. We left the trail and made our way through the brush. A woman was kneeling before a small smear of blue and purple; it was the pale yellow of her tunic that we had spied. As soon as she heard our approach she spun to her feet and walked swiftly to meet us, but not before dropping what appeared at that distance like a bundle of rags.

"Mother! What are you doing out here?"

Sabina rolled her eyes. "Polishing leaves. What do you think I'm doing?"

"Sarcasm so becomes you," Livia said. "Isn't your herb garden by your clinic?"

"You're right. You've caught me with dirty hands. Wait a moment ... by Jove's thunderbolt, it's awfully hard to garden without getting your hands dirty."

"Mother, you're acting even more peculiar than usual."

"Actually, Sabina, your hands look lovely, as always," I said.

"Such a flatterer. That may work with some ...." Sabina looked pointedly at her daughter.

"But why must you work so far from the house?" Livia pressed.

"What do you see in abundance here, daughter, that you find little of by the *domus*?" Sabina asked.

"People?" Livia said.

"Some plants prefer the shade," I said.

"Is it any wonder the young Alexander is the favorite of the *dominus*?" Sabina said.

"It is no wonder at all," Livia said, bumping me off balance with brusque affection. "He'll have the cash to purchase ten slaves before you have bought our freedom."

"Livia, please. Your mother toils to give you the gift of gifts."

"He will have money," Sabina said, "no doubt. We have spoken of this and I have no time to debate it further."

"Those flowers look lovely," I said, peering over Sabina shoulder. "May we have a closer look?"

"Not now, Alexander. I have three poultices to make and several balms for the baths. Perhaps another time."

"Gratitude, Sabina. We will leave you to your work."

"And best get back to your own," she said. She waited with her hands on her hips, watching us until we had found the path before she returned to her herbs.

•••

Attendance at the Vulcanalia was voluntary, but who doesn't love a good bonfire? The immediate family left early to attend services at the Vulcanal, and soon after the house was almost deserted. Tessa, an Ostian, was among the first out of the *domus*. She grabbed a seat on the lead cart – there were twelve lined up outside our gates - which I had arranged to transport the *familia* to the Campus Martius. Vulcan is Ostia's patron god; no wonder, since the majority of Rome's imported grain passes through that harbor.

As soon as the family had left, I looked in on my teaching staff (in our expanded school, a building Crassus owned near the foot of the hill, we taught everything from shorthand to mathematics, from carpentry to bricklaying) and sent them all off to the festival for the rest of the day. Then I trudged back up the hill to attempt to clean up my work table; if I were able to get caught up, my appreciation of the subtleties of immolated seafood would have fewer distractions and was sure to be enhanced. As I passed through the gates, I noted that Betto had left, probably dragging Malchus with him, passing their duties off to hapless subordinates. I found Sabina hard at work in her clinic and made a joke about how devotion and holidays were rarely found in the same bed, at least not until later in the evening. She laughed politely at the first part of my jest, but found little humor in the final allusion to sexual congress. These acts built throughout every Roman holiday until late at night the only couples not fornicating were either lying unconscious in their own vomit or buried in their own graves. I supposed it was because she assumed I was talking about Livia and myself. Which I was not. I said I would try to find her later on the Field of Mars and made a hasty exit, as all misunderstood comics should.

Just before sunset, I rubbed my eyes, dropped my *calamus* in its inkwell and decided I had better go and find my master's banner up on the field. Sabina was still hard at work, but promised to find me. I told her I would send my escort back to fetch her. Down through the forum and up the hill we went, guided by the glow of a hundred bonfires. The entire field had been transformed into a bazaar, each merchant's stall punctuated by blazing cones of light and heat. People stood in line before each of these infernos, waiting to be blessed by a priest in blue robes, his cowl pulled over his head so that he was almost faceless. He solemnly received their piscatorial offering and flung it into the flames. Something familiar about the holy man nagged at me, but I could not make the connection.

I looked in vain for Livia, which was just as well. The smell of burning fish was hardly enough to dampen the blossoming ardor of the revelers, and I could not risk succumbing to the excitement of the moment in her presence. The best insurance for that policy arrived about an hour behind me: Sabina.

We rallied by Crassus' flag, but the only people present from our house were two soldiers standing guard over the almost empty baskets of mackerel. I reached into one, slipped a forefinger up through the jaws of two long-dead, slimy specimens and off we marched to the largest of all the bonfires, which also happened to be the nearest.

The line was formidable. We inched forward, seeming to make little progress. The high priest of the Vulcanalia was moving slowly up and down the line, greeting supplicants and encouraging their patience, although shaking few hands. He walked by us and, seeing the plaque around my neck denoting my house and my station, instantly summoned us to the front of the line. He was also hooded, but his robes were a rich purple trimmed in gold. Again, a memory stirred within me, a recent one at that, but I could not put my finger on it. I had the feeling that much depended upon the connection being made, but it was impossible to concentrate. Quite frustrating. While my attention was thus diverted, the high priest was happily recounting how Senator Crassus had donated a special offering; his holiness had commanded that anyone from the house of Crassus must be moved expeditiously through the line as gratitude for their service to the god. I was about to ask what service that might be when a portion of it bumped into me from behind. A terrified herd of goats and sheep was being driven past us into a corral situated perilously close to the flames. Acolytes were sprinkling thousands of rose petals upon them as they passed, which neither mitigated the noise nor the smell. The priest told us that this being a particularly dry year, these dozens of animals were being herded into the blaze as insurance against any fiery mishaps in the coming year. Sabina and I made our way back through the crowd, all of whom were struggling to get closer to what we were trying to avoid. Moments later, the specially constructed corral was folded and collapsed so that it and everything in it became a crackling, squealing paean to Vulcan Quietus.

# CHAPTER XXI

## 76 BCE - SUMMER, ROME

Year of the consulship of
Gnaeus Octavius and Gaius Scribonius Curio

There were so many servants at House Crassus that a separate kitchen had been built inside the barracks. Most of the slaves ate there; those of us who slept in the main house took our meals in the kitchen, but even we had to eat in shifts. We drifted into cliques based on seniority, and most of the original household were the first to eat after the family. Nestor chose to eat in the outbuilding.

At supper soon after the Vulcanalia, Tessa mentioned that she was experiencing some tingling and numbness in her feet and legs and asked if anyone else had noticed anything similar. Betto immediately cried "poison!" exclaiming that he, too, had been feeling the same sensations in his feet. He made it his personal duty to poll the rest of the house and to everyone's surprise discovered that three others shared these symptoms. Sabina examined each one but could find nothing amiss. She rubbed salves on their feet and told them to return to her each evening. After the incident with Pío, everyone was as skittish as an unblooded legionary. Crassus sent Tertulla and the children to Baiae. They had just purchased a vacation home on the hill overlooking the bay, and while *dominus* did not think they were in any danger, the new villa did require furnishing and decorating, a task at which he was as hopeless as Tertulla was proficient.

Within three days everyone but Tessa had improved. Although the temperature was hot throughout that week, it seemed she was always perspiring. Her tunic was drenched every time I saw her. Sabina recommended bed rest, but Tessa refused. There was too much to do, too many bouquets to cut and arrange. Besides, she said, she had no real pain; toward the end she even cut herself with her clipping shears and didn't know she was bleeding till she spied the drops painting her toes and the rich earth.

•••

You must know by now that it was Sabina's jealousy that threatened Tessa. The healer was the most intelligent woman I had ever met, but she was also arrogant. Perhaps she believed she could act with impunity. If one believes there is no risk, it is easy to gamble everything of value.

•••

When she lost the sight in her left eye, Crassus stepped in and insisted she take to her bed. He told Sabina that if Tessa's condition did not improve by morning, he'd be forced to call in outside help. Sabina admitted to *dominus* that Tessa must have been poisoned. Her condition was grave, but she would do all that she could.

When he heard this, Crassus put the entire estate on alarm: no one could enter or leave without his knowing.

By then of course, it was too late. Now that she lay abed, she was too weak to leave it. Sabina asked that she be brought to the clinic; Crassus himself carried her there in his arms. In the night she wet the bed four times; it hardly mattered for the bedding was already soaked through with her sweat. Tessa's heart raced, then slowed, and her breathing became erratic. The healer gave her *theriake,* a Greek antidote for poisoning. It was her own formula of herbs and spices ground with opium into olive oil. She worked through the night, joined by many of the *familia,* including Crassus, who stood vigil with the young gardener.

Conspicuous by his absence was Ludovicus.

Something Livia had said to her mother when we came upon her in the western wood kept nagging at me. When Sabina asked her what is found in short supply at the main house but is lavishly abundant in the forest, Livia replied "people." Her tone was mocking, of course, but it set me thinking. There was something else the healer could find a great deal of out at the boundaries of the estate: privacy. Almost in that same moment, I realized why the priests' hoods had seemed so familiar, yet somehow menacing. My uneasiness grew.

It is an effortless matter to draw conclusions from a narrative that takes you by the hand as I have done, but to believe the unthinkable in the midst of events that swirl about you in a confusion of emotion and distress, that, I hope you will see, is a more challenging task. Yet I curse myself for my slow-wittedness. I could not change the outcome for Sabina, for the law of Crassus is unforgiving. I could not recapture the look in Livia's eyes that died on that day of judgment. But I might have saved a life.

It was the night that Tessa died. All of us, myself included, believed that Sabina labored frantically to revive the gardener. But I had to know. I summoned Malchus, told him to don socks as well as his heaviest *caligae* and meet me at the tool shed. There we collected shovels and rakes, and with lanterns raised high headed to the western wood. It was easy to find the spot, for as we approached it stood out from its surroundings, natural in aspect, but unnatural in fact. A patch no larger than three by six feet was covered with a layer of moss, twigs and bark made to resemble the rest of the forest floor. We raked this aside; I warned Malchus to let nothing touch his exposed flesh.

We found nothing, except merely circumstantial evidence: Sabina had planted something here, then removed all manifestation that she had done so. This was enough to report to Crassus, but would I do so? Could I do anything that would reshape me into a wedge between mother and daughter? And that, in Livia's eyes, would be the least of my crimes should I continue down this path. I was almost ready to take relief from our failure when Malchus said he thought that perhaps Sabina merely wanted to plant some flowers. Why do you say that, I asked him, since I had told him nothing of my suspicions. He pointed deep into the hole where he had been digging. We lowered our lanterns and there at the bottom lay a single, battered, purple bloom.

"Don't touch it!" I said as Malchus reached for it. I put on a pair of gloves, exhumed the flower from its intended grave and dropped it into my belt pouch. One itch had been scratched satisfactorily, for the flower's hooded shape was a perfect mimic of the priest's cowl.

The gods, now intent on guaranteeing my undoing, laughed as they brought my own eyes to our next discovery. As we hurried away with our prize it was I, not Malchus, who chanced upon a small, pale glow beside a mossy granite outcrop. We delayed our race back to the house to investigate. The lanterns illuminated the destruction of any hope for me to remain in denial: a single daisy, its short green stem flat and mangled, its white petals and yellow heart crushed and lifeless.

•••

"Seize her!" Malchus shouted as we burst into Sabina's clinic. The legionary's inertia answered his own command as he crashed into the healer, knocking her to the floor. I slapped the spoon out of Tessa's mouth, but she swallowed involuntarily.

"What is the meaning of this?!" Crassus shouted, grabbing the sleeve of my tunic amidst the shouts and screams of those present.

"Where are your emetics?" I demanded of Sabina, who was still pinned to the floor by red-faced Malchus.

"She's too weak," Sabina said with an emphasis meant only for me. "You'll kill her."

"Give her water. Now, master, for the love of Flora, if you want her to live. As much as she can drink." Crassus released me and nodded to Eirene who ran to fetch a cup and pitcher. "In the old school room," I called after her. "It's closer."

"For gods' sake, man, let the woman up," Crassus said. Malchus pulled Sabina roughly to her feet. "Gently, Malchus," *dominus* commanded. "I will know what this is about before anyone is maltreated. No one is accused of anything. Yet."

I knew the words must come but they lodged in my throat, a lump of ruined futures.

"Alexander!" Malchus urged.

"I accuse," I shouted, as if volume were needed to regurgitate the unspeakable. Unable to look at my old friend, I stared at the floor at Crassus' feet. "I accuse Sabina of attempting to murder this woman."

The silence that followed was interrupted only by the rasping of Tessa's breath. Eirene returned. I raised Tessa's damp head and the tearful scullery girl brought the water to Tessa's lips. The little she managed to get down made her choke.

"You'll kill her," Sabina repeated.

"Eirene, step away. Let no more be done. Alexander, I have no reason to doubt you, but if you have maliciously kept Sabina from administering to Tessa, so help me .... Both of you, go with Malchus. He will keep you safe and separate till morning. The rest of you, except you, Betto, go to your quarters and pray to our *lares domestici* to preserve this woman. Betto, fetch another guard, stay by Tessa, do nothing but watch over her. We will let the gods decide if she lives or if she dies."

Just before dawn, the gods chose death. Tessa's shallow breath rose to a gasp, then stopped. Crassus sent a rider to Ostia to notify her parents and to pay their owners more than the man and woman's worth for allowing them to come to Rome for a few short days to collect the body. While we waited, Crassus held court.

•••

The day was grey but looked unlikely to rain upon us. "The accuser shall speak first," announced Crassus from his seat in the *tablinum.* He had turned it to face the peristyle where the household had gathered, standing, at my request, on the gravel paths, avoiding the few decorative patches of lawn. Livia sat by Sabina. I would have given anything to have had a private moment with her, but there was no opportunity; the first words she would hear from me would be those that condemned her mother.

"*Dominus,* if I am upheld in these proceedings, we must replace all the soil in our flower beds. To prove to you why we must take this extraordinary measure, I have asked Malchus to bring these three strays, bitches in fact, from the streets." The *familia* murmured, and I was fairly certain I heard Nestor, scrawny and hateful, 'there's only one dog I see up there ought to be put down.'

"Keep them at a distance," Crassus said to the guards holding them by short, rope leashes. "I'll not have fleas infesting the *domus.*" I emptied the contents of my belt pouch onto a table just below where Crassus sat. With a tweezers, I raised the drooping purple bloom for all to see. "In Greece, we call this *lykotonon,* 'wolf killer.' Hunters rub their arrows on its petals, its leaves, its stem, but mostly on a ground up paste made from its root."

"How is it," Crassus asked, "that a young Athenian philosopher comes by such knowledge?"

"*Dominus,* Aristotle was succeeded by Theophrastus, acknowledged even by Romans as the father of botany. I have read *De Causis Plantarums,* and have seen with my own eyes the carefully guarded corner of the Lyceum gardens devoted to *aconitum napellus.* It is beautiful, but deadly."

I instructed the guards to force the dogs to sit on disparate patches of ground throughout the peristyle. Nothing happened. "I expected this," I said, trying to sound confident. "Now the flower beds." The dogs were moved. "Make sure they sit; do not let them lie down."

"What difference can that make?" Crassus asked.

"I want to be certain their genitals come in contact with the soil. You see, *lykotonon* need not be ingested to be poisonous. It can be absorbed through the skin." The dogs looked wide-eyed and terrified, but otherwise unremarkable.

"Enough, Alexander. Get to the point. We understand that you are claiming Tessa was poisoned from contact with this flower, evidence of which is dramatically and overwhelmingly non-existent. But even if you are correct, what proof do you have that Sabina had anything to do with it? Tessa was not the only one with symptoms."

"My toes were numb," Betto called out.

"Mine too," cried another.

"Because you stopped to smell Tessa's handiwork," I said. "As you leaned in, your toes touched the soil on which Sabina had sprinkled the pulverized root of aconitum. The effect would not be lasting. But Tessa trod those beds barefoot day after day. *Dominus,* may I speak with Sabina?"

"You may."

"Sabina, are you in love with Ludovicus?"

"No. Definitely not."

Why should she help? "Let me rephrase. Is Ludovicus your lover?"

"Again, no."

"*Was* he your lover?" Silence. "Shall I ask him? He's standing just to your left."

"We have shared a bed, yes."

I turned again to Crassus. "I came upon Sabina during one of my walks in the woods at the western end of the estate." At least I could leave Livia out of this tragic narration. "She would not let me inspect the blue and purple flowers she was growing there. She intimated they preferred shade, but I know for a fact that *lykotonon* will thrive in full sun as long as it is irrigated well. The only reason, then, to plant it so far from the house was if she did not want anyone to know she was growing it. And when I first approached, she dropped what I at first thought was a bundle of rags, but which now I surmise must have been gloves with which to handle the lethal plant. Do you deny it?"

"I do not," Sabina answered.

"But," Crassus said, "you have still not established that she was growing this *lykotonon*."

"If someone will ask me," Sabina said, "I will answer."

"Are you growing this flower in our woods?" Crassus asked.

"Yes. I was."

"You *were* growing it," I said. "But not anymore, for your purpose has been achieved. *Dominus*, last night, I went back into the woods, taking Drusus Malchus with me. The site which Sabina had refused to show me had been concealed. We had to dig up the entire plot to discover this solitary flower. No leaves, no roots, just this single bloom. It is clear that Sabina did not want the place found." Malchus affirmed that I spoke truly.

"This herb," Sabina interjected, "has many beneficial uses, *dominus*. It can reduce fever, excessive beating of the heart, and I have used it many times to reduce the pain of scrapes and superficial wounds. But the *atriensis* is correct to say that it can be highly poisonous if misused. Naturally I planted it far from the house so that no one would come in accidental contact with it. And once I had harvested an ample supply for the clinic, what else should I do but remove all trace of it? I planted it far away from the house and discarded the remains so that no one would accidentally come upon it and make themselves ill."

The household stirred, leaves rustling in a wind that had turned against me. Crassus said, "Alexander, I don't know what petty grievance you may have against our healer, but I am disappointed in myself to find that I may have misjudged you."

"*Dominus*," Sabina called out above the murmuring of the *familia*. "Alexander had good reason to wish me ill, if you will hear it."

"Go on."

Sabina spoke of her plan to buy her freedom and that of her daughter, of my love for Livia and of the fact because of Sabina, the two lovers must eventually be parted.

Crassus shook his head slowly from side to side. The *familia* grew quiet. Finally *dominus* said angrily, "Get those dogs out of here."

"May I speak, lord?" Drusus Malchus said. He was holding a rake.

"What is it?"

"With humbleness, to end this hearing now would be unfair. Our proof is not yet complete."

"What more do you have to say?" Crassus asked impatiently.

"Sabina," I said, earning an instant glare from the master that made me stutter, "Sabina was jealous of Tessa." While I spoke, Malchus began scraping away the top layer of soil in the flower bed closest to the tablinum. "I noticed it the first day I came before Pío." I spoke rapidly. "Tessa stormed into the house, right through your tablinum. I remember because she did not stop to put on house slippers. She was barefoot."

When Malchus had cleared a sufficient space he picked up one of the bitches who, as he neared the flower bed began whining, complaining and struggling against him. Malchus forced it down in the cavity he had made, kneeling to hold it still with his massive arms.

"I can't remember a time I ever saw Tessa wearing sandals," I continued. "The day of the Vulcanalia, Sabina and I passed each other in the atrium. She had her cleaning supplies and must have been returning from Ludovicus' quarters where she had been tidying up. She loves to clean," I added weakly. "As she passed me, she was muttering angrily to herself, but one word was plainly clear: 'barefoot.'" The whispers swelled again.

"Sabina was clutching something in her free hand, something which I believe Malchus and I discovered last night in the woods."

"Yes, Crassus said, irritated. "We know all about the poisonous flower."

"No, *dominus*. It was this." I reached inside my tunic and dropped the cut and mangled daisy onto the table. Everyone craned to see it, and everyone knew instantly what it meant.

Betto said, "Tessa would rather have shaved her head than wear her hair without those daisies."

"Ludovicus," I called, "did Tessa come to you on or before the Vulcanalia?"

"Answer," Crassus said when the battalion commander hesitated.

"She did, but ..."

"Sabina," I asked, "did you find a daisy in Ludovicus' room and assume they were lovers?"

Before the healer could answer, the dog held down by Malchus howled in obvious agony and scrambled free. It ran in circles, panting and flinging spittle in all directions before it stopped, vomited and fell to the ground, shaking violently.

"Put that animal out of its misery," Crassus ordered. Malchus slit its throat.

"This is ridiculous," Sabina said, unnerved. "All right, yes, I admit I was jealous. And perhaps I wanted to make her sick. But kill her? Never! Walking barefoot in *lykotonon* can't kill you." Livia was staring open-mouthed at her mother.

"It can with a little help from your poison antidote."

"You are a fool, Alexander. You said it yourself: *theriake* cures poisoning, it doesn't cause it."

"May I explain, *dominus*?" Crassus nodded. "*Lykotonon* slows the heart and breath. The primary ingredient of theriake is opium, which depresses most bodily functions, including respiration. To administer this medication to a person knowing they were suffering from *lykotonon* poisoning can only be construed as an attempt to kill them."

Finally, the healer was silent. "I am so sorry, Sabina," I said. "Forgive me, Livia, I had no choice."

"You always have a choice!" Livia shouted through her tears.

Sabina looked up at me with such hostility that I understood in that instant that I had never known her. She leered at me and made to put her arm about her daughter, but Livia jumped as if she'd been bitten. "Get away from me!" she screamed. She leapt up and fled the peristyle. No one, not even Crassus, made an attempt to stop her.

Sabina's face melted from hatred to humility. "Marcus Licinius Crassus," she said, "master of this *familia,* I beg mercy. I confess to jealousy. I confess to hatred. Of these things I am guilty. But I do not confess to murder. I *did* try to save Tessa's life. I swear. Anyone could have poisoned the soil. The evidence before you is tattered, full of supposition, spoken by a man who would do anything to keep my daughter near him."

"Now I am convinced," Crassus said. "You are right, slave, there is evidence here of a circumstantial nature. But this is not a court and I am in need of no proof in order to pass judgment. Yet shall you have it. The single unassailable, indisputable fact in all that I have heard today is that Alexander himself has brought this case against you. What more proof do I need of your guilt? He loved your daughter. She has fled, not just from you but from him. Look at what he has sacrificed in the name of justice.

"Alexander, I do not like being wrong, and I do not like apologizing. More than once you have placed this meal before me and forced me to eat." He rose from his gilded chair and sighed. "Before this assembly, before my *familia* I say to you – apologies.

"Now, to Sabina I say this: you have killed an innocent girl. You have committed a heinous and brutal murder based on an assumption. Did you even confront the commander with your suspicions? It matters not. An attack on a member of my family is tantamount to an attack upon my person. But I want to hear you say it. So tell me, tell everyone here assembled: did you kill our Tessa?"

Sabina held Crassus' gaze but remained silent. A guard who had moved up beside her prodded her with his finger. Almost imperceptively, she nodded. "Say it," Crassus commanded.

"I killed her."

"Do you have anything to add before I pronounce judgment?"

Sabina turned to me. "Alexandros of Elateia, I curse you. You have betrayed a sister to these Roman scum. May Hermes give you no rest, no peace of mind, no love for all your days. I curse you, and bind it with my blood. May all the gods below harken to me and conspire against you." With her teeth she tore at her hand in the fleshy part between thumb and forefinger. She spit a bloody glob in my direction. "*Dominus*, I am finished."

"I should have you crucified on the street and let the children throw stones at you to assist in your agony."

From somewhere in the crowd, a voice shouted out, "Do it! Crucify the fucking whore! And hoist Alexander up beside her!"

"Nestor, how good of you to remind me of your continued presence in my house. Step up and stand beside the healer." Nestor did as he was told, persuaded by the butt of Betto's gladius in his back. "The sight of you has offended my eyes from the day you were branded. Why I have suffered your employment for so long is a mystery. Perhaps out of some lingering respect for Pío. No matter. Your impudence has settled your fate.

"Sabina, your blameless daughter has suffered enough on this day. For her sake, I will be merciful. You will not die on Roman soil, which I trust will please you. I am sending you home. Just last week I concluded negotiations for a silver mine near Laurion. There you will spend the rest of your days in contemplation of your sins."

"No!" The scream came from behind us. Livia had returned and was standing at the far end of the peristyle, behind one of the arcade columns.

Sabina cried, "Mercy, *dominus*. Kill me here. Kill me now. I offer you my throat," she said, tilting her head back. "I beg of you, do not send me to the mines."

"Do you want your daughter to keep you company? No? Then do not speak again. You will go, but you will not travel alone. That *fugitivus* will go with you," Crassus said, flicking a finger at Nestor. "We are done here."

•••

When her mother and father arrived at the estate, they found that Crassus had prepared Tessa as if she were his own daughter. She lay in state on a funeral couch in the atrium, surrounded by the flowers she had nurtured with her own hands. Incense burned at each corner of the *lectus*. There followed a day of prayers and mourning, then Crassus, who would not have her sent to the grave pits on the eastern slope of the Esquiline, paid instead for the expense of having the young girl cremated. Tessa's parents returned to Ostia, but not before they fell at the feet of their benefactor. He bid them rise, assuring them that he grieved with them. He instructed me to slip a purse heavy with coins into the father's hand as they set out for the journey home.

# CHAPTER XXII

## 70 BCE - FALL, BAIAE

Year of the consulship of
Gnaeus Pompeius Magnus and Marcus Licinius Crassus

"I don't hate him, sweet," Crassus said. "It isn't hatred to wish he had tripped and fallen beneath one of his Hispanic war-wagons. That's not hatred, is it, Alexander?"

"It isn't undying love, *dominus*." I stood against one of the portico's scalloped columns which was half-draped in waxy ivy. The sun was turning the leaves green-gold.

"What use are you to me if you won't agree with me?" Crassus said.

"None whatsoever," I replied. "I shall have myself thrashed directly after you've supped."

"Hush! Both of you! I'm trying to enjoy the sunset," Tertulla said.

Crassus, now forty-five, leaned on the outer wall of the portico wrapped in a large Egyptian towel dyed in patterns of apricot and lemon. Perspiration glistened on the golden hairs of his tanned arms. Tertulla stood behind him, reaching up to massage his exposed shoulders. After his successful but arduous campaign against the rebellious slave Spartacus that ended the year before, his features had taken on the hard, weathered look that only combat can press through the flesh and into the soul of a man. "*Columba,*" he whispered, reaching behind to pull her curves more tightly against his back. "My dove."

After a languorous interlude that sent my eyes to the horizon to count the colors of the darkening sky, Crassus broke their embrace to lean far out over the balustrade, turning his eyes toward Bauli, just two miles to the south. "I can't see it," he said. Pompeius' villa was hidden by the intervening hillside. "It's smaller, isn't it?"

Tertulla slapped his rump. "Miniscule. Like his balls."

"And much farther down the slope," I added.

Tertulla laughed. "All right, Alexander, from now on if there is any massaging to be done, be it to hubris or parts more accessible," she said, continuing to press her fingers over her husband's oiled shoulders, "then I shall see to its administration." As she worked, evoking another grunt of pleasure, her own towel gradually came undone. She slid her left hand under his arm, slipped it through the opening in his wrap and brought it down across his chest, letting it come to rest where the fine hairs of his lower abdomen started to thicken. She pulled him back against herself, pressing with her hand while pushing her hips forward, rising up and down on her toes.

"You are a marvelously perverse woman," he said, twisting around to nuzzle her cheek. "Isn't she marvelously perverse, Alexander?"

"As a Thracian gymnast, *dominus.*"

"I hear they're the best," Tertulla said.

"I have no personal experience, *domina*."

"Then let us attempt something, husband, so that should you ever have the opportunity, you may compare." She gripped Crassus in such a way that his answer was more throaty gasp than agreement.

"Who claims I have not?" he managed.

"Have not what?" Tertulla asked.

"Had the opportunity to compare."

"Isn't he comical?" *domina* asked of me, expecting no reply.

The sweat from the *calidarium* was rapidly evaporating from their limbs in the soft evening breeze. Throughout the estate, many of my staff were lighting oil lamps and any remaining *praefurnia* not already heating the baths from below. I preferred to manage the household in a more hands-on fashion, but Crassus almost always kept me by his side. No matter what he was doing.

The night promised to be chilly. Crassus sighed. "I wish," he said, addressing Tertulla, "you'd have talked me out of begging that aggravating little pebble to propose me for consul. Thank the gods the year is almost over." Crassus waggled his empty cup. I snapped my fingers and a wine bearer hurried forward bearing a large blue, blown-glass amphora. As his cup and then Tertulla's was refilled, Crassus said, "Unfortunately, I wager he'll hold that little favor over my head till I'm as bald as Caesar. Wait a moment, Tranio," he said, as the servant replaced the stopper and was about to withdraw. Crassus lifted the delicate chain which hung over the neck of the amphora and inspected the writing on the hammered silver label. It was a local red, and to indicate the vintage, the names of that year's consuls were inscribed on the metal. Crassus' lip curled at the sight of his name next to that of Pompeius. "'Don't think much of this new wine," he said, waving Tranio back to his station.

Tertulla let her hand drift still lower, but it was clear that her husband was as yet preoccupied with thoughts of his rival and co-consul, Pompeius. She rested her cheek against his back, curling his pubic hairs in her fingers. "You didn't beg," she said. "You asked, and he acceded, because he was afraid of what might happen if he didn't. He wants your legions by his side, not opposing him."

"That's a wife talking, albeit one who would have made as fine a senator as any patrician." He reached back and laid his hand on her thigh. "When the clarion call of war sounds, love, my legions fight always for Rome, never for Crassus. Rome is all we have, all we are."

The sun had surrendered to dusk, and shadows now slipped down the eastern slope of the hill where their Baiaen villa sprawled. Across the little bay, the light was still frantically painting the town of Puteoli in impossible shades of pink and orange. The sea was deepening to blue-black, glinting here and there as a crest rose to wink impertinently one last time at the setting sun. In the distance, a thin rope of rosy smoke drifted straight up from the summit of Vesuvius until Zephyr, lying in wait for just such a plaything, bent it sharply and blew it to the darkening east. Two servants entered and lit the portico lamps.

"Rome is a child, Marcus." Listening to his wife, Crassus admired the splendid exit Helios was making over the bay this evening, but Tertulla's eyes were closed. "The plebs' gaze will follow any bright object till the next one steals their attention. It's true," she said, squeezing him tightly, "for this brief moment they are dazzled by the man they call victor of the Hispanic wars, but I never knew anyone who followed anything but their nose when their stomach was growling. Pompeius may claim the hearts of the people for a day, but you rule their bellies and their minds. He is a distraction. You are their true champion."

Crassus turned to face Tertulla, his smile brimming like the cup of wine he now tipped to her lips. As he watched the graceful curve of her neck tilt while she drank, he said, "The Rome I serve is no child. She stands here before me, elegant, precious. You are the foundation upon which all my work stands. Without you in my life, it would all crumble into a meaningless heap."

Tertulla handed the cup back to Crassus with a look upon her face so sublime that it hurt my eyes to behold it. Once, a girl had blessed me with that same expression, but no more. Crassus leaned in to gently clean the thin line of purple from Tertulla's upper lip with a kiss. Then he emptied what remained of the wine in one exuberant swallow and tossed the cup to Tranio. Husband and wife kissed, and for a moment, the only sounds were the sputter of the torch flames and the song of the year's last, brave nightingale. Their embrace ended; their impassioned gaze lingered. Suddenly, Crassus began to laugh.

"It *was* an inspiration, wasn't it? Pompeius may have pranced into the city with a triumph for supposedly subduing Hispania, but never in ten lifetimes could he ever match such a display as our sacrifice to Hercules."

"A triumph you deserved but never received. At least we have the satisfaction of knowing your offering soured his moment of glory."

"Indeed. A feast for the people laid out on ten thousand tables: it did leach attention from that strutting charlatan, at least for the time it took the plebs to chew and swallow the meal."

"When will you ever see yourself as others do?" she asked, hugging him. "As I do? You know, it's three months now, and the slaves tell me it is still the talk of the city."

"The feast? Merely my thanks for all that Rome has given us."

"The feast, yes, but also the three months' supply of corn you lavished on every citizen."

"The people are our children, and children must be fed. Besides, the cost was a mere trifle."

She shook her dark curls and smirked, intertwining her fingers in his. "Your sense of proportion is sadly skewed."

"All right, call it an investment." He gestured with his chin to take in the villa, its fountains and gardens, and by inference, the literally hundreds of homes, businesses, quarries and mines throughout Italy and beyond which he either owned outright, or controlled through his clients. "I am no fool, dove. Who here is the true master, and who the slave? Our happiness is tied to Rome's by a Gordian knot not even Alexander the Macedonian could sever. One will endure only as long as the other prospers, and not a heartbeat longer. The Republic has become a frail old man, ruled by the fickle whims of its needy grandchildren. If you doubt me, just ask Alexander."

"Give your servants more credit than that, *dominus.*"

"Why should I? Look what happened with Spartacus. If the urban slaves ever rose up with one voice, Rome would cease to exist."

"Which is why you keep them well fed and well entertained," Tertulla said.

"I wonder, dove, is it enough? Tell me, are you happy, Alexander?"

"I am lucky to be alive. I am grateful."

"Answer the question."

"I am as happy as my condition allows, *dominus.*"

"There, you see, dove, what a scoundrel he is? I can always count on you, can't I, Alexander, to deliver a sentence well-honed on both sides."

"Brrr, let us go in, love," Tertulla said. "Don't let Alexander toy with you. He is the luckiest slave in Rome, and he knows it. See how the light and warmth have fled the sky - now they await within. I'm ready for the *tepidarium*. Bring your intellectual sparring partner with you, if you must, but let us go in."

Crassus kissed the top of Tertulla's head, readjusted her towel about her and together they padded back into the house holding hands.

"Oh, Livia. Good," Tertulla said as they passed through the smaller *calidarium* and into the large, circular space of the *tepidarium*. I followed discretely behind, nodding slightly to Livia as I passed, whose straightforward gaze never wavered.

It almost didn't hurt anymore. In Livia's eyes, I had become a child of Dis, a spirit of the underworld, a barely visible shade to be shunned. If not shunned, ignored. If not ignored, deterred. It had been thus for the past six years.

The poets sing of love as if it were forged of iron, incorruptible, shining, eternal. Perhaps it is so, perhaps the love of which the ancients sing is a love so strong it endures beyond life itself. Or perhaps the ancients were so focused on their poetry that they had never really experienced love themselves and had no idea what they were singing about. For us poor mortals, ordinary love is a fragile, delicate wisp of a thing with a very poor life expectancy.

I had not so much fallen out of love with Livia as been pushed. Was there no way I could scale the heights back in to the refuge of her affection?

# CHAPTER XXIII

## 70 BCE - FALL, BAIAE

Year of the consulship of
Gnaeus Pompeius Magnus and Marcus Licinius Crassus

Tertulla lay on her side on a couch by the warm water pool, her towel haphazardly draped about her waist. "Someone seems to have emptied our cups, the curs."

"Alexander," Crassus said, "would you please summon Tranio to see if there is any more *Caecubum*?"

"I know where it is, *domini*," Livia volunteered. "Alexander, I will go. Keep your place - remain by *dominus*." A honey bee usually dies when once it stings. Were Livia a member of the order Hymenoptera, she would be more wasp than bee. Her words could prick over and over again with impunity. If memory serves, it is only the female of the species capable and willing to deliver these little, vexing attacks.

Livia. In the years since I had robbed her of her mother, the whistling, impudent sprite had lost none of the qualities that had drawn me to her when she was little more than a child, although the first of these had diminished to accommodate a burgeoning of the second. Six more years had aroused and affirmed what everyone in the *familia* already knew, including the girl herself. What was impish and playful at seventeen had matured into stunning and willful at twenty-three.

Some well-worn turns of phrase, worked smooth by years of usage may grow stale and out of favor. Yet the kernel of their truth may yet be fresh; indeed their hoary longevity is proof of their accuracy even though the modern wordsmiths may pass them by as unfashionable. Here is one such as this: the effect Livia had on me, steadfast and unchanging since the day I realized I was in love with her: the sight of her took my breath away. This in spite of my own damnable contribution to her loveliness: a layer of sadness deep in her eyes, dead leaves in a forest pool. But she was nothing if not pragmatic. Her mother was gone, she was a slave in the house of Crassus, and since she could not avoid her fate, even as I had done years ago, she, too, determined to embrace it.

•••

Imagine you are young and in love. Something, anything, it does not matter what, destroys that affection. You weep, you plead, you separate, you never see each other again, you suffer, you heal, you go on. But suppose through circumstance you are forced to see each other almost every day. You work together, share meals together and to fulfill your duties, must often communicate together. Can you picture a more exquisite torture? Try it another way. Think of what you want most in life. Hold it in your mind's eye. Place it close by, but just out of reach. Is the image there before you? Now, deny yourself the chance of ever having it.

For six years I had tried to learn to see Livia with dispassionate eyes. Hopeless. I don't think she hated me; but those first looks of enchantment had clouded over with cataracts of repudiation. I lived in a purgatory of my own making.

Tertulla had convinced Crassus, in order to restore the tranquility of the house, he must send Ludovicus to another posting. She suggested that Livia and I also be parted, but he would not hear of it. There was no possibility that I would be sent away, this Tertulla understood. As for Livia, while *dominus* was a faithful and loving husband, he had an appreciation for beauty in all its forms. Livia, too, must remain within his sight.

I made inquiries to the mine several times a year, and without advising either Crassus or Livia, sent a monthly bribe from my own accounts to the mine manager. As far as I knew Sabina was alive and spared the most brutal travails of that hideous place. But I had no way to know for certain how she fared.

I did not revile myself for the actions that had destroyed the only love that had ever found me, but neither did I give myself any peace about it. Sabina had murdered Tessa, of that there was no doubt. But if I had listened more carefully, been a better friend, recognized the signs of her jealousy, I might have been able to influence that awful outcome.

•••

The day Ludovicus left, I found him at the stables securing his belongings and tools to the horse Crassus had gifted him to speed his journey to the *latifundium*. The Cremona farm was prospering, and a man who could repair almost anything was always in great demand. He looked fine in his sand colored tunic and maroon cloak. I noticed he wore military style *caligae* on his feet, leather laces crisscrossing up to his calves.

"I am sad to see you leave," I said, handing him his bedroll.

"I am sad to be leaving. I like the city life; the country is too noisy for me." I cocked my head. "I hate the sound of crickets. And mosquitoes? I'll never get a good night's sleep again. But," he said, scratching his shaved head, "that's what I get for putting my cock where it didn't belong. I fucked things up for you as well, and for that I am truly sorry. Any chance you can patch things up with her?"

"In another lifetime, perhaps."

"When snakes have knees, eh? Well, maybe it's for the best. She was a bit young for you, eh? Jupiter's balls, Alexander, in your position, you can get any wench you want. Just whistle and point."

I had no reply. Though our feet were planted on the same ground, Ludovicus and I lived in two different worlds; there were some words that could never span that celestial distance to be heard or understood. Instead, I said, "So it's true then: you were not faithful to Sabina?"

"Faithful? You're joking, right?"

"She cared for you deeply. She's had a hard a time of it. Did she never tell you?"

Ludovicus shrugged. "There wasn't much opportunity for conversation. She'd come to my room, I'd throw Tranio the hell out, and when we were done, he'd come sulking back to his bed. The most talking we did was, after about a week of this, we told Tranio he could stay put, we didn't mind."

"So you never exchanged words of commitment, or endearment?"

"I didn't. She may have done. Alexander, look, I get it, there was a fucking great misunderstanding. I liked her and all, I liked her a lot, but it wasn't as if we were married." He bent to cinch his saddle. "The thing I can't figure is why she didn't take one of her scalpels to me. She had plenty of opportunity."

"She and Tessa had always been at odds," I said. "If she'd gotten away with it, she must have thought she could go on with you like before. If I hadn't stumbled upon her in the woods, she'd very likely be here now. You wouldn't be packing and Livia and ...."

"Here now," he said, standing. "Come on, come here." He threw his arms around me and gave me a bone squeezing hug. "It'll be all right. You'll see." After slapping me on the back a few times, he released me and we shook hands.

"You're a good man, Ludovicus. For all your faults."

"And usually proud of them, too. Except today."

"Perhaps our paths will cross again."

"May the gods make it so." He leapt up on his horse and I handed him the reins. His clear eyes smiled down at me and for a moment, I wondered what it would be like to be a man like him: big, strong, confident, carefree, and unburdened by an excess of contemplation. He saluted smartly and rode off.

Now, I remember him thusly—wearing a centurion's helm, bloodied and ferocious, wielding a sword as if it grew from his arm.

•••

Livia left the baths in the direction of the wine room. "Not the five or the ten," Tertulla called after her, "but the fifteen, if you can find it."

"You know, she's become quite stunning," Crassus said, eyeing the lissome departure of the twenty-three year-old, whose long tresses, wrapped and tied atop her head with a fringed scarf had deepened to the color of fiery autumn leaves. "I thought she was a seamstress," he mused.

I found some empty wall space and put my back to it.

"Not today," Tertulla said.

"What do you think, Alexander?" Crassus asked.

"About what, *dominus*?"

"Don't be obtuse, man. You'll remind me of Cicero and spoil my good mood. About Livia. Is she not a ravishing creature?"

"She ... um, she whistles well enough."

"That's it?" Crassus asked, giving me an incredulous look. "Don't lie to me; you've had your eye on her for ages, you coward. You'd have more than that if she'd let you."

I winced.

"Apologies, Alexander," Tertulla said as she rose, leaving her towel on the couch. "Have you forgotten, Marcus? That business with the healer ... Livia's mother?"

"Curse me for a Cretan. Apologies, Alexander. This aged soldier's memory is flagging."

It was impossible to make myself invisible when they kept talking to me, but I stared straight ahead, trying to look through rather than at the dimples above Tertulla's hips as she descended the three steps into the lightly steaming water. "That's why you married a girl fifteen years your junior," she said, wading waist-deep to the statue of Venus in the center of the pool. "Come along then, old man."

Crassus dropped his towel, stepped into the pool and crossed the ten foot radius to join Tertulla on the submerged marble bench that encircled the statue. "Now, where was I?" he mused. "At my age, the memory starts to go."

"So you've said. Just now. Let's see, you were about to say something that has absolutely nothing to do with politics, I believe."

"Was I? That can't be right. I'm sure it was about politics."

Tertulla reached across his chest with her left hand and pinched his right nipple between her thumb and forefinger. Crassus flinched but managed to say, "Yes, I'm positive I had more to say of a political nature."

"Go on, then. I give up," she said, releasing him. As soon as he began to talk, she slid beneath the surface and stayed there, holding her breath.

When she burst up again with a gasp and a shake of her short, black hair, spraying scented water in all directions, Crassus laughed and said, "That's hardly fair! Remind me to pay you in kind next time you need to discuss your latest shopping excursion."

"Point taken. I just thought we might relax this evening."

"I *am* relaxed. All right, I admit I'll relax *further* when Pompeius has made good on his promise to disband his army and retire from public life. Have I told you how much it is costing us to maintain our own legions just to keep him from marching into the capital?"

"Several times. And he wouldn't dare."

"Actually, you're right, he wouldn't, and he won't. Frankly, I don't think my fellow consul has it in him to make a play for dictator. When we return to Rome next week, I will speak before the senate and to the people, and make a great show of amity and conciliation to the mighty Magnus."

"Is that wise? You might encourage his ambition."

"Pompeius is nothing if not vain. But in his heart, I believe his love of Rome will prevail. Or his fundamental lack of courage. And if he needs further persuading, there are many of us - plebeians, senators and I myself who have played upon his pride and flattered him with artful diplomacy. It's his Achilles heel. I couldn't tell you this earlier, but I met with him before we departed for Baiae. He asked me how it would stand with me if he were to accede to the people's demand that he assume the dictatorship."

"He didn't!"

"He *did.* I wanted badly to admonish him that great generals do not necessarily make great emperors, but the matter required all my diplomacy and delicacy. I played upon his sense of history and his place in it – did he want to be remembered as the destroyer of the Republic? Would he risk civil war to bask in a popularity so fickle a mediocre harvest or a whisper in the wrong ear could overturn it? I knew I had him then. But I kept on. I reminded him that now that he and I had swept away all the evil that Sulla had perpetrated on the government, did we not now have the best of all possible Romes? What could he accomplish as dictator which he had not already achieved as consul? Was he not rich enough? Powerful enough? Influential enough? He was the hero of the nation and his place of honor in Roman history was fixed for all time.

"I think I may have overdone it a little, for he accused me of wanting the crown for myself. After I contained my laughter, I told him, and it's true enough, my world is perfect just as it is. I could have no greater joy than to continue the status quo ad infinitem. And here is where I took the leap of faith I knew I would have to make to ensure the safety of the Republic. If he had any doubt of my sincerity, I told him, I would prove my patriotism and my loyalty by disbanding my army unilaterally."

"Marcus ..."

"I had to do it, love. And when we return to the city next week, I will make good on my promise."

"No wonder you've seemed preoccupied ever since we arrived. I should have been more supportive."

Crassus chuckled. "I can't imagine how. Unless you can perform some kind of magic and cancel that picnic at Solfatara tomorrow."

"I will if you wish it. But I think we should take the waters. The fumes will do you good. Relax you."

"I have no doubt. It's the noxious gases spewing from the likes of Cicero, Lucullus and the others we came here to escape that I would rather not inhale."

"Don't worry, my sweet," Tertulla said, rising to stand before her husband. She took his hands and drew him to his feet. Crassus watched as the motion caused a pair of water drops to fall from the rapidly rising tips of her nipples. "I'll protect you. Now come with me."

"Where to, my pet?"

"To the anointment room."

They walked naked to the small *unctuarium*, adjacent to the warm pool. I followed and found another wall. I would continue to do so until Crassus gave me permission to retire.

Livia was waiting for them. Her short, cream tunic was cinched tight about the waist, pulling its hem halfway up her thighs, the sight of which made my toes ache. As soon as she saw our masters, she began pouring the wine that she had fetched, having diluted it only slightly with spring water.

"Are you doing the honors this evening, Livia? What happened to Tranio?"

"I asked for Livia to attend us," his wife said. "I'm certain you will approve of the substitution. But first, Alexander has earned his rest. May I dismiss him?"

"Why? I need him: he is the whetting stone upon which I sharpen my wit."

"Now is not the time for rhetoric. Besides, I think you'll find Livia's tongue just as sharp. Please?"

Livia handed *dominus* a cup of wine. "Well," Crassus said, taking the offered cup, "personally I think you're working her too hard." He sipped the wine. "Gods! This is ambrosia."

"It's the best we have," Tertulla said. "Livia, join us."

"Thank you, *domina*." She poured herself half a cup and emptied it. "To the house of Crassus. May it's strength multiply like the silver coins in its coffers."

"Splendid," Crassus said. "Well spoken." He took a mouthful of wine and closed his eyes to savor it.

"Your impertinence is excusable," Tertulla said, "But do not think it goes unnoticed."

"Am I missing something?" Crassus asked.

"She mocks us, dear. You sent her mother to mine your silver in Greece."

"An Alexander in female guise. Delightful!"

"Perform your best, Livia," Tertulla said. "The past is set down in a thousand thousand indelible scrolls. But the future is a blank parchment forever in wait of a present."

"Yes, *domina*."

"Those were sad times for this house," Crassus said. "Best we put them behind us." His voice had turned as unyielding as concrete, his subtext clear: the judgment of Sabina was final.

I had been required to be in attendance during many forms of my masters' copulations, from parties with over a hundred guests to the more frequent and private meetings of husband and wife. This was the first time Livia had ever been summoned to take part. I had not thought of Greece for years, but now I found myself longing desperately for home. My gaze rose to the cove ceiling, both to avert my eyes and to keep my self-pity from rolling down my cheeks.

"Come," Tertulla said, wanting to regain a lighter mood, "let us use the new unguents we got in town today. You're going to love these, Marcus. Livia, the *rosaceum* and the crocus-oil."

"Crocus-oil?" Crassus asked. "How much did you pay for *that*? Never mind, I don't want to know." He put the cup down and raised his arms.

"With your permission, *dominus*?" Livia asked, her tone moderately strained, our master thoroughly oblivious. Crassus nodded, and she opened the two *ampullae oleariae* and handed one to her mistress. Wife and slave anointed *dominus* with the precious unguents and began in earnest to apply them.

"*Dominus*," I said. "Please, may I be excused?"

"Let him go, love. Truly, we do not require an audience."

"I see, so that's where we're headed. Well as it happens, I like an audience. Besides, Alexander may be master of all things ethereal and esoteric, but he is sorely lacking in the ways of the flesh. We do him a service by insisting that he stay."

Tertulla threw me a look of compassion, but punctuated it with a sigh. She had prepared this evening to take her husband's mind off his work and my discomfiture was not a high priority. Crassus had already moved on. He raised his wine cup to his lips, then stopped suddenly and exclaimed, "You know, I think you're right, dove. I think that when I have moved these pieces to their proper place on the board, I will have very likely saved the Republic!"

"You are hopeless, husband," Tertulla said. "Fortunately for you, I am not. Livia, stronger measures are required. Clean him up a little, but don't be too thorough. I don't want all that expensive oil off him just yet." Tertulla pressed up against him from behind, moving her hands over his chest and stomach. Livia went to a cabinet and retrieved a silver-plated *strigil* which she methodically but lightly ran down her master's arms, then legs. She collected the runoff in a small cup attached to the instrument by a golden chain.

"Darling," Crassus said, "we may need to search for a new seamstress. Livia has a gift." He stood with legs and arms spread, beginning to respond to the hands that moved upon him.

*"Dominus,"* I said, my eyes downcast, my voice low, "do not make me do this."

Everyone stopped and turned to look at me. Crassus appeared as if he were considering acceding to my request or summoning his *lorarius*. I did not care; a whipping would be less painful, or so I thought at the time. Before he could speak, Livia said, "You and my mother were so naïve." Her laugh was almost genuine. "Did you really think Boaz would not get full value from me? Watch and see what I learned."

"No." Gods above and below, Livia had pushed *dominus* to his decision. "Leave us, Alexander, and take with you the knowledge of just how close you came to reaping my displeasure."

My back ached and my stomach threatened revolution, yet I managed to find my way back to my quarters. I would never know if Livia spoke the truth, just as I would never know if being dismissed from that room was better or worse than the sights my imagination plagued me with that night. To blot them out I squeezed my eyelids shut till suns and stars blazed behind my eyes. One shining godsend careened among them: Sabina would die without ever knowing that no decent freedman would ever take her despoiled daughter for a wife.

# PART II - MASTER TO SLAVE

# CHAPTER XXIV

## 62 BCE - SUMMER, BAIAE

Year of the consulship of
Decimus Junius Silanus and Lucius Licinius Murena

"Alexander, back so soon?" asked Crassus.

It was early summer, and for the eighth year running we had escaped to the south, hoping to trade the stink and heat of Rome for the ornate tranquility of the general's Baiaen villa. This morning, however, peace and quiet were being trampled by engineers working on the new mineral baths Crassus was having installed halfway down the hillside. The sun was just beginning to warm the southern slopes of smoldering Vesuvius.

In Egypt, a daughter of pharaoh Ptolemy Auletes, Cleopatra Philopator, had just celebrated her seventh birthday. Earlier in the year, a conspiracy to overthrow the Republic was thwarted and its leader, Lucius Sergius Catilina was killed, thanks entirely, to hear him tell it, to Marcus Tullius Cicero. Pompeius Magnus had been busy in the east, his armies turning nations into Roman provinces, including Pontus, Phoenicia, the two Syrias and Judea. The Jews barricaded themselves in their temple fortress, but it fell to the Pompey's machines of war. He killed twelve thousand of the defenders, profaned the temple by entering the Holy of Holies, but left the gold and relics therein intact, ordering the temple purified and restored. For his conquests he would receive his third and greatest triumph. But my hand runs away from my thoughts.

Censor, Propraetor and proconsul Crassus, through generosity, popularity and the political lubricant of gold judiciously distributed, controlled much of the senate; save a triumph of his own, there was no honor or office left for him to garner. He had become one of the most influential men in Rome, and certainly the richest. So wealthy was he, in fact, that the people bestowed upon him his fourth agnomen; he was now known throughout the land as Marcus Licinius Crassus Dives, Crassus the Rich.

"Word has already spread," I replied. "They know you're back for the season. Half the town was up and waiting for us."

"How many loaves?"

"Fifty. The crowd was well-ordered and respectful, but the bread vanished as if by magic. Our workmen were only able to snare about half before the cart was emptied of everything but crumbs."

"How many went empty-handed?"

"I would say one hundred."

"Tell the kitchen to bake two hundred loaves for tomorrow."

"The bakers' knuckles are already deep in enough dough for three hundred loaves, *dominus*."

"I don't like it when you do that," he said, his tone unreadable.

"If my lord will elaborate on the nature of 'that,' I shall see to it that 'that' never happens again."

"Impertinence is unbecoming in a man of your station, let alone your age." He sighed. "I suppose I must thank you for attending to the little things that maintain my popularity."

"In that I have had an excellent tutor."

Crassus waved a hand in the direction of the only available open space on the table. "Put it there." I was carrying sliced melon on a golden tray, which I set down where he indicated. "I should like," he continued, his attention focused on a letter, "to be able to at least cling to the illusion that I am running this household."

Another 'Crassus compliment.' He seemed to sense that no matter how high he raised me up, there was only one advancement that held meaning for me. I sagged with the knowledge that the more I earned it, the less chance there was that it would ever be forthcoming. I had been in service to the house of Crassus for twenty-four years, five years more than my age when I was taken.

Work followed Crassus like a puppy. Scrolls and documents covered the waist-high table. We were in the rear *tablinum*, the one used as an office, not the larger one where the senator received the daily stream of needy clients who apparently took no holidays, their palms raised in petrified extension. These were the armies of well-wishing men to whom Crassus was patron and on whose votes and favors he counted. They followed him everywhere. The heavy rust-colored drapes were drawn aside so that from his writing table he could look one way into the garden of the atrium and the other out across the northwest terrace to the blue of the bay. His brown tunic was trimmed in gold but he wore no other adornment.

"What in Jupiter's name is that?"

"Melon, *dominus*. Honey melon."

"Not the melon. The tray."

"My lady bought it yesterday at the market. In Puteoli."

Crassus reached over and hefted it with both hands. "It's solid gold. How much did she pay for it?"

"Two thousand *sesterces*."

Crassus shook his head and smiled. "I begrudge her nothing, of course."

"It is good to know one's value," I said, unable to hold my tongue. I ran a finger along the dully gleaming rim. "It appears this charger and I have equal worth."

"Tut, Alexander, you are worth that a hundred times over." He meant it as a compliment. And to underscore the point he added, "Besides, my wife is no bargain hunter. She overpaid by half."

I'm one of the luckiest, I reminded myself, changing the subject. "I see you've received a letter from Lucius Calpurnius Piso."

"As a matter of fact I have. How did you know that? Have you been spying on me?"

"Spying would be pointless, *dominus*. What could I learn that you are unwilling to confide?" He agreed by nodding and raising his graying eyebrows. "The runner came from Herculaneum. Piso retires to his villa there for the season. More telling, when I entered you were wearing that grin peculiar to his correspondence."

"And what grin is that?"

"The one you exhibit when you are about to burst out laughing."

"His words do tickle, true enough. He mentions you, you know." I girded myself. "Yes, right here, he says, 'Don't pay too much attention to that Greek of yours. Absorb too much of his philosophy and your brain will become soggy and spoil. You'll have to purchase a new one in the market.'"

"Should you write him, tell Piso from me that his love of Epicurus blinds him to other disciplines, like science and the search for truth."

"You can tell him yourself. They're coming to dinner next week."

"Are they bringing Calpurnia? What a lovely child, so poised and graceful for a thirteen year-old."

"Am I interrupting?" The man who had crossed the atrium and now stood in the archway was slight of build, of average height, with sharp, hawk-like features. His crisp, white tunic was long-sleeved, fringed and loosely belted; in other words, quite eccentric. Not only his face, but what was visible of his chest, arms and legs was hairless.

"There you are, Gaius! Of course you're not interrupting. Sit, sit. I trust it was not our engineers that roused you at this hour?"

"I slept as soundly as if Cato himself knelt by my bedside to whisper sweet and endless orations in my ear."

"That is a good night's sleep."

"I have never understood the need of it. As far as I can fathom, it serves no useful purpose, save to give the wakeful advantage. Two or three hours is all any active man should require."

"Our wives must disagree, since I have seen neither of them this morning. Please sit. That's better. Well, my young friend, we've come a long way from Apulia, haven't we?

"I had no idea you were aware I fought under your command against Spartacus."

"I wasn't. But Alexander here did a little research and pointed out your name in the rolls. Come, tell me the news. And no politics. Let's have nothing to disturb our bucolic *otium,* aside from the unfortunate construction. We'll be forced to shun the gardens and picnic in the country today. How is your family? How fares your niece? I understand she had some difficulty last year with her pregnancy."

"Atia has recovered fully, thank you for asking. Octavian will be a year old come September."

"Splendid. Alexander, bring our guest some melon."

"Just water."

When I returned with a pitcher and goblets, Crassus was saying, "I didn't realize you were a man of such piety." The remark was rich with sarcasm. I poured the water and receded to my place in the shadows to study this most recent of my master's friends. Gaius Julius Caesar was in his late thirties, but he sat with an easy elegance as if on a throne, as if nothing he desired could stand against the sheer force of his will to acquire or achieve it. Ambition. You could see it leaking from every pore of his body, but no place more than his eyes. Ambition, and pride, and arrogance. He had the look of a soldier, but a man could rarely be considered great in Rome if he did not have a taste for blood. I had heard him speak on the *rostra* several years before. He claimed his bloodline to be descended not only from kings, but from the gods themselves!

What did Crassus see in him? What need of him did he have? Surely it was not a friendship based solely on amity. He set my nerves on edge, and I admit I was frightened by him. In the end, I suppose I should have been more afraid of the love of a husband for his wife, and the misguided lengths to which it would drive him.

"To serve the people," Caesar was saying, "they must elect me. To elect me, they must love me. To love me, they must see how the gods favor me. Who is more favored by the gods than the *pontifex maximus*?"

"Your logic is appalling. I shall have to hire out Alexander here as your tutor." *Athena forefend.* "What the people love are the bribes you spread to secure the election. How else could you have won without a single grey hair on your head? You must be broke."

"Not as destitute after the election as I am now." Crassus cocked an eyebrow. "You know the hill above the old naval base at Misenum?"

"The tip of the cape with the fabulous view of the bay."

"That's the place."

"It's lovely. Tertulla and I sometimes go there for a stroll. We could venture there today, if you like."

"I bought it."

Crassus barked a short laugh. "You're insane! Who did you borrow the money from? You didn't come to me."

"I expect I will. Eventually. My creditors have nothing to fear. When I earn a command, the spoils of conquest will repay all with interest. I'm thinking Hispania Ulterior."

"So you'll be standing for *praetor*."

"No army, no glory. No glory, no gold. But I'll need your support. Can I count on you when the time comes later this year?"

"Of course. Providing, as you plow your way up the *cursus honorum*, you clear an equally unobstructed path for my own interests as they arise."

"Naturally. And you know, I've been thinking. As wet a sponge as Hispania may be, from what untapped source do you think the most treasure may be wrung to lay at a grateful Rome's feet?"

"Gaul? Britannia? Egypt?"

"Parthia."

"Parthia? Sulla once spoke to me of that wasteland of barbarism. There must be easier coffers to empty closer to home."

Caesar shook his head. "Not a wasteland, Marcus, but a richly paved road. Think of it: Rome's borders reaching to the Indus, perhaps beyond. What a triumph! No door would remain closed to us, no glory withheld, no honor denied to such a man as could deliver the opulence of the East. Where Alexander failed, we could succeed!"

"I admire your spirit, Gaius, but shall credit such brashness to youthful temerity. The world is already ours;

have patience and enjoy what you have, or at least what you've borrowed. Besides, the senate would never countenance such folly."

"I'm no fool, Marcus. A good stew needs simmering. I'll be able to stand for consul in three years; that should lend substantial gravitas when I propose the expedition after my term expires."

Crassus snorted and shook his head, smiling. "Already won the post, have you?"

Caesar continued as if *dominus* had not spoken. "Even then I doubt the senate will issue enough gold to finance the entire campaign. We'll need additional resources, which is where you'll come in. But I'm in no hurry. Let's just keep it in mind, you and I."

Crassus was about to say more when an explosion thudded through the morning air followed by a commotion of shouts from outside. We all rushed to the balcony to look down across the five terraced gardens that framed the slopes of the villa to where a jet of water arced up in a decidedly unintentional fountain.

"I'd better see to this," Crassus said. Caesar offered to accompany him, but my master wouldn't hear of it. "Nonsense. Stay here. Have breakfast. We're on holiday. I won't be long – I just want to make sure no one is hurt. I'll take Mercurius with me. If he's not off napping somewhere. Alexander, see to our guest's comfort. Bring him anything he desires."

Crassus left to check on the disturbance, and fearful for the privacy of my master's papers, I suggested to Caesar he might be more comfortable in the *triclinium*. He grinned briefly and without humor, but allowed me to guide him. As I was getting him resettled in the dining room, propping pillows behind his back and exchanging his footwear for dining slippers, Tertulla found us. Her black curls were festooned with yellow ribbons. They matched the color of her tunic, whose sleeves fell just to her elbows. Each of her forearms was adorned with golden bracelets, some studded with rubies, others with sapphires. Over her tunic, she had draped a long *stola* the color of daisy petals.

My lady greeted Caesar politely, but when she heard where my lord had gone, asked why I was not with him. I answered that he had commanded me to stay behind to see to the young high priest's needs. This seemed to satisfy her, and reclining on the *lectus* adjacent to Caesar's, she ordered refreshments while we awaited his return. I hovered close by while fresh oysters, chilled mullet from our ponds, slices of honey melon, and Armenian apricots stewed in white wine were served.

"How is Pompeia this morning?" Tertulla asked, spearing an apricot half with the pointed end of her spoon.

"As witty as ever I have heard her," Caesar replied.

"She'll be joining us shortly?"

Caesar dabbed at his lips with a napkin. "She'll have to stop snoring first." I glared at the two dining room attendants who were both grinning recklessly.

"You are unkind, Gaius," Tertulla said.

"I am an honest man."

"An unlikely and unprofitable trait in a politician."

Caesar sipped his water, then retorted, "It is you who are unkind, Lady Tertulla, for your words condemn your own husband as the most colossal liar in Rome."

Tertulla let a small smile escape her. "Eat your breakfast, Caesar. Your wit must need frequent nourishment."

"My stomach may growl, yet my eyes banquet to excess."

"Then I suggest you close them, and I will have a servant guide a spoon to your open mouth." Tertulla's smile had vanished.

"These delicacies before us will not sate the hunger that gnaws at me."

"I would remind you, sir, that you are a guest in my husband's home."

"You are right, of course. Let us speak of your husband. And your marriage. It must be tiresome to be saddled with the same old horse for so long without the variety of a new ride now and then."

"Think yourself a stallion, Gaius Julius? You are an ass. If your rudeness did not appall, I would find your braying amusing."

"What would it take to amuse you, Tertulla? I long to entertain you." Caesar reached for her hand, but she slapped him away.

"Incorrigible! Do you honestly think your advances are of the slightest interest? See to your own wife."

"I have. Why do you think I am sitting here with you?"

"Your reputation, Caesar, is like your manhood: it precedes you, crashing blindly about until it is ruined. Does it mean nothing to you that you are speaking to the wife of your benefactor? Does betrayal come so easily to you?"

"It is no betrayal to compliment your beauty and my friend's good fortune. And now mine, for Aphrodite smiles on me." Caesar raised his eyes to the heavens.

"And why is that?" The hem of my lady's *stola* having slid slightly askew, she readjusted the garment and covered her legs below the knees.

"You imply that were I speaking to you without the constraints of marital propriety, you might succumb to my advances."

"Deluded *and* incorrigible," Tertulla said, irritated. "You make no advances. You make noise. Must I stop up my ears every time we meet? Are you not afraid I will go straight to my husband with your obnoxious behavior?"

"I fully expect you will. But you see, dear lady, Marcus loves and trusts us both with the naiveté of a Vestal. He knows you would never betray him, and that I would never seriously attempt to seduce you and cuckold him. An opportunity for the perfect crime, don't you think?"

"I know you, Gaius. You are like a child who clamors for a toy, and when he gets it, plays with it for a day, then discards it. I feel sorry for your wife, who sleeps but a few feet from where we sit."

"I assure you, fair Tertulla, that were my wife enjoying breakfast here with us right this very moment, she would still appear to slumber." Caesar tapped the side of his head with his knife. "A comely enough creature, but light as a feather."

"Sulla's granddaughter deserves better than to be matched with the likes of you. But," she added brightly, "there is always the chance some enemy of Rome will make her a widow. Where are you off to next? Someplace dangerous, I hope?"

"I warn you, Tertulla, I am nothing if not persistent."

"In that case, Gaius, you are nothing. Prey on some other patrician's wife. Perhaps you'll even find one who doesn't love her husband." Tertulla pointed to a glistening mullet and her myrtle-wreathed *analecta* selected a fillet and sliced it into bite-sized pieces for her. "I know! Consul Decimus Silanus is in town for the season. He is newly married - I hear his wife Servilia is a rare beauty. I shall throw a party and invite them so you can attempt to slither and hiss your way into her arms. And leave me in peace."

"First an ass, now a snake. Women are so fickle," Caesar mused unfazed. "If I must choose, I prefer the serpent. They glide into dark places with strong, determined muscles."

Tertulla laughed out loud. "Don't tell me that inept flummery actually works on your conquests?"

"Since you admit their status, you must acknowledge my persuasiveness. Come, Tertulla, you may as well relent. You know your stubbornness only fuels my determination." As he spoke, he reached across and slid his hand up her calf.

My lady had finally had enough. She smiled and leaned forward as if to embrace him. Then she slapped him so hard it turned his head so that for a horrifying second his eyes met mine. He turned angrily away, his hand flinching. For a moment I thought he was going to strike her. Tertulla broke the stunned silence by leaning still closer and spoke softly into his reddening ear. "Down, senator, or I shall convince my husband that his investments will yield higher returns elsewhere."

"Are you flirting with my wife again?" Crassus appeared behind me, splattered with mud, smelling of sulfur, his hair disheveled and the hem of his tunic dripping onto the marble floor. "You'll have better luck conquering Parthia."

# CHAPTER XXV

## 62 BCE - SUMMER, BAIAE

Year of the consulship of
Decimus Junius Silanus and Lucius Licinius Murena

My lord and lady excused themselves so that Crassus could clean himself up and change his clothes. They left me in the *triclinium*, standing awkwardly before Caesar. He wanted no more food, so I had the *analectae* clear. When we were alone, I asked if he would like me to fetch his wife. He replied that if I did, he would have me flogged. For a long while he reclined unmoving, saying nothing, holding me with a malevolent gaze, for nothing more, I assume, than the satisfaction of seeing me finally wilt and avert my eyes. When I did, I saw Livia approaching.

"Good morning, my lord," she said, her voice subdued, her head bowed. Caesar ignored her and sipped his water. Protocol and common sense demanded that she ignore me and address the *pontifex maximus*. But in the past eight years, I must admit to you that I had grown more and more delusional. Time had hewn away the sharpest edges of Livia's distaste for the very sight of me, and while I never let it show, inwardly I took this for a sign, letting my imagination grow apace with my affection. When she spoke, I imagined no one present but the two of us; in my head I even altered her tone to one of reverence and adoration.

What a sap.

There, pathetically, was the limit of my boldness. Much had changed in the past eight years, and much had remained the same.

Here is a list of what had changed:

1. Through my masters' generosity, I had become one of the richest slaves in Rome, and I suppose, therefore, one of the richest slaves in the world.
2. Livia had fallen in love.

And here is what had remained the same:

1. Livia did not love me.
2. I was still a slave.

Six years ago, a young sculptor belonging to *dominus* had become enamored of Livia. She was twenty-four. I do not know if she returned his love, but as Apollo is my witness, I never saw her look at him the way she looked at me when we stole minutes and kisses under the statue of the god.

While slaves were not permitted to marry, with the permission of their owner, they might form a *contubernium,* a union of limited rights. Do not be confused, for while the word is the same, this is not the military term meaning an eight-man unit of tent-mates.

Crassus, on a tour of his holdings in Picenum was expected to return by the end of the month. As you know, I hold little stock in the efficacy of prayer, but in the days and weeks prior to his arrival, I spent every free moment in every temple I passed with knees bent and palms raised. I bribed augurs, donated to charity, even, to my shame, let slip to *domina* several unsavory remarks about the boy's artistry. All to no avail: Crassus gave his blessing. Vows were exchanged in the atrium and it was done. Why should *dominus* deny them? Had they but time to make a family of their own, their children would have been added the rolls of men and women owned by Marcus Crassus, joining a multitude that now numbered into the thousands. The rewards were many and the risk almost non-existent. It was the perfect investment.

But less than a year after their joining the lad had died suddenly after sampling oysters he had purchased at the market for a party marking my lady's thirty-third birthday. The circumstances were suspicious enough that Crassus immediately set to work on his own private oyster beds at Baiae, placing them under twenty-four hour guard. Livia's devastation was acute and complete. Though I burned to comfort her, it was not my place; any condolences on my part would have been misunderstood, their sincerity suspect. Thank Athena my lady Tertulla would not rest until Livia's grieving and healing had run their course, except for those scars of loss which fade but never disappear. I left a collection of Sappho's poems on Livia's pillow, but the note of sympathy I wrote sounded shallow and trite: I tore it up. I don't know if she ever read the poems.

My feelings for Tertulla's seamstress had all but drowned beneath the crashing wave of Sabina's treachery. But in that deluge a tiny seed survived, ironically nurtured by the torture of seeing Livia work, fall in love, grieve, grow. I was twenty-three when I first set eyes upon her; a dancing child of twelve. Now she was a woman of twenty-nine: a long time to be tossed about together on the crests and troughs of the strange sea of our existence.

One cannot love unless one is loved in return. Of this I am certain, for I have lived it. There is no such thing as unrequited love; the phrase ought to be stricken from the lexicon. Love is a thing shared, an intertwining of essential separateness into something not quite alone. There is nothing like it under the heavens. Like bread, it will not be made with flour or water alone; the recipe requires both. Guarding each other's vulnerability provides the yeast that makes it rise, and salt from the tears that caring brings lends the finishing touch.

Because of this, it would be contradictory to assert that I was slowly falling back in love with Livia, but I will say this: whenever our paths crossed, I made ready to inhale the scent of her, a smell like cut grass or the sun on saltwater. I will say that her smile would melt ice, her laugh entice songbirds from the air and the green jewels of her eyes throw armies into confusion. Her body, now long and lithe, was an arrow taut and tense, awaiting release. When Livia filled my head, there was room for little else. In her presence, study, philosophy and debate were confounded. What was thought or contemplation compared to the pounding in my chest?

There was a word I had banished from my vocabulary these many years: hope. Unbidden, and almost unnoticed, it had crept back into my dreams and from there into my waking hours. From whom did I receive permission to slowly unbuckle my heart's armor? From she who had given me a glimpse, no matter how brief, of what elation may be possible in this life, feelings so strong they made any thought of a life beyond death superfluous. At first, Livia would not offer up any form of encouragement, no. But then, this emotion, this non-love which I could not stopper nor contain, was released by a thaw in her own conduct. Little by little, year after year, Livia's demeanor relaxed from disdain to neutrality, from contempt to disinterest. It took fourteen years; who knew what the next decade might bring? I was content, for now I had hope.

Today, as always, I glanced furtively in her direction. Her long, auburn hair fell in two rivers down the gentle slope of her breasts which were covered by a simple, beige *peplos*. She had thrown a deep blue shawl about her, and I cursed her gently for hiding the alabaster of her shoulders. She spoke again. "Good morning, *atriensis*." Polite and respectful. I cursed this Caesar, for had he not been present, she might have used my name. Then, to him she said, "My lady Tertulla requests but a little patience from my lord. My masters will rejoin you presently."

Caesar looked up from his couch and for the first time took note of Livia's presence. His eyes roamed over her as if she were a leg of sweet, roast pork and he were a man condemned to a diet of rancid goat. "Patience, charming girl?" he said, rubbing his cheek where Tertulla had slapped him. He took hold of her hand. "Patience withers before such beauty." To me he said, "Didn't your master tell you to see to my every desire?" He pulled Livia down onto his lap. "Leave us." For an instant, she looked up at me in terror, then lapsed into the posture of submission every slave learns to assume with shameful expertise.

"That's better," he said, completely ignoring her distress, cupping her left breast, testing the weight of it. He raked his fingers lightly over her nipple, seeking the involuntary response that he could falsely interpret as desire. Her face was averted, but I could see her tremble, lips crushed together, eyes shut tight.

"I thought I told you ..."

It was a difficult angle; fortunately Livia saw it coming and ducked. I punched Caesar in the face, connecting with the left side of his cheek and jaw. It wasn't a vicious blow, but what it lacked in force it redeemed in astonishment. Shared by everyone in the room. The vile man fell backward into the pillows; with my left hand I pulled Livia up and off of him. For just that instant he was too stunned to grab her.

"Go!" I urged, pushing her out of the room. She ran sobbing in the direction of the master suite. I turned back to Caesar, and stood with my hands trembling at my sides. At least half a dozen other servants had stopped what they were doing to stare at us. I tried to resign myself to my fate and summon what little dignity I could. My knees shook uncontrollably.

Caesar rose slowly. He stood directly in front of me, looking up into my eyes, searching for any remaining glint of contumacy. There was no light there, I can tell you. He brought his right hand to his chin and I flinched. He smiled, rubbing the smooth, pale skin thoughtfully. Then he twisted his upper body to the left as if something else had caught his attention. I realized what was coming as he raised his right hand past his left ear, his elbow under his chest. Only the hopelessness of my plight kept me from ducking. What would have been the point? With a force and viciousness that made both of us stumble, he whipped the back of his hand across my right cheek. The stone in his iron ring tore blood from my face and tears from my eyes.

"Hold!" Crassus came running across the atrium, wrapped in nothing but a towel, followed closely by Tertulla and Livia.

Caesar, having regained his balance, turned to my lord and as calmly as if he were buying fruit at the market said, "Marcus, how much for this slave?"

Crassus ignored him. "Alexander, is it true? Did you lay a hand upon him?" I nodded, and the face of my master sagged as if made of warm wax.

"Go ahead, name your price, Marcus. Ten thousand? Twenty? A hundred thousand? What, not interested?" Caesar feigned disappointment. "In that case, I suppose we'll have to settle for a decent scourging."

"Gaius, please," Tertulla said. "Alexander's behavior was inexcusable, unconscionable. But let us agree on some less violent compensation, I beg you. Name your price."

"I understand you are fond of him, but no. He must be whipped, at the very least. I insist. Marcus, you of all people know where such impudence can lead. Let this pass and the next thing you know you'll be traipsing all over the countryside chasing another slave rebellion."

"Don't be ridiculous," Crassus said.

"Marcus ... there are witnesses. If he were mine, I'd take the hand that touched me and make him wear it as a necklace."

"This is not right, husband," Tertulla pleaded. Livia gripped her mistress' hand. Her knuckles were white.

"Come, let's not let this spoil our day," Caesar said brightly. "Fetch your *lorarius*. I'll rouse Pompeia while you change and we can be off on that picnic within the hour."

"I'll do it," Crassus snapped.

"You'll do what?" Caesar asked.

"I keep no *lorarius* here. If not for your boorish, brutish behavior I would have no need of one."

Caesar shrugged. "As you wish. Let me know when you are ready so I may bear witness to the flogging."

"You will witness nothing!" I had never seen my master so angry.

"Marcus, by rights you should have him crucified. I think it only fair that ..."

"You are a guest in my house," Crassus said, tight-lipped. "You will do as I ask or I will have your carriage summoned." Caesar looked at my lord with a variation of the expression he wore the moment before he struck me. Unlike me, Crassus did not look away. "The choice is yours," he said.

The silence stretched like stale honey. You could see Caesar's pride wrestling with the consequences of his response, both political and financial. He must have decided this battle required a tactical withdrawal, for he bowed slightly and went off to find his wife.

# CHAPTER XXVI

## 62 BCE - SUMMER, BAIAE

Year of the consulship of
Decimus Junius Silanus and Lucius Licinius Murena

"Livia told us what happened," Crassus said. "Shameful. Had I been there, I would have put a stop to it. He had no right."

"Pardon, *dominus,* but it is I who am bereft of rights."

"*Please,* Alexander, not now. Can't you see how I am vexed?"

The two of us were walking side by side through the villa toward the place of my punishment. I was naked, covered only by a long, gray cloak. Crassus had put on an old tunic - I doubted there would be any picnicking this day. In his right hand he held a *lorum.* From the handle dangled two strips of leather thirty inches long, knotted at the ends. He held it slightly away from his side like a thing alive.

"I have no choice in this."

"Do what you must, *dominus.*"

"An example must be made."

"I am honored to provide one."

"This is hard enough for me, Alexander. Must you?"

"I am curious about one thing." Crassus half-lidded his eyes, dreading whatever might come next. "If what Caesar did to Livia was wrong, how then could it be wrong to stop him?"

"It was wrong for *you* to stop him. You should have fetched me."

"What manner of man could stand by and do nothing?"

"Any fool would know better than to assault a citizen, considering the consequences."

"I did consider them, but only afterwards. In the moment, there was only reflex. It was over before I could think about how or whether to act. Had you been there, you would have had done no less. In fact, one may interpret my behavior as acting on your behalf."

"You are not going to talk your way out of this. For even if you are correct, old friend," Crassus said, conscious of the leather-bound handle of the whip in his sweaty palm, "you will find my 'gratitude' stingy."

"I beg you, *dominus,* do not confuse friendship with dominion." Sarcasm and fear wept from my voice like the fluids that would soon seep from under the stripy lacerations on my back.

"Damn you, man, for putting us through this. Damn that girl, too." I looked at him, not understanding. "She's a sorceress. Don't think I am blind to your feelings for her. Had it been anyone else, we'd be on our way to Misenum by now."

"I am sorry to inconvenience you. And I have acted with nothing but propriety every day since you sent her mother away."

"Sabina would still be with us if you'd just left well enough alone. You and that insufferable redhead would have had a half dozen little, horned Greek daemons running in and out of the *impluvium* by now."

"And Tessa would still be dead, gone to Dis without a cloak of justice to warm her passage." I sighed. "Ignorance is a wonderful thing; look at the word – it is not so much a lack of knowledge as it is disregard for the facts before our eyes. I wish I possessed more of it."

"We must all live with the consequences of our choices, voluntary or not. Myself included." He eyed the whip. "I should have listened to Tertulla years ago and sent the girl away."

"Do that now, and what you do next will undo all."

"Damn it, Alexander! Word play and riddles at a time like this." I was hurting him, and I did not wish to do so, truly. For a time, we walked in stinging silence, letting words blow away like leaves covering a forest floor, their soft blanket now removed, revealing a grim, bare floor gnarled with roots and worms and things scuttling from the light. The kitchen loomed close. "Forgive me," Crassus said finally, staring straight ahead. "The medical staff is standing by to tend to your wounds."

Odd how he referred to injuries not yet inflicted by his own hand. Just stop. Could we not just stop? In the dark hall, the smell of baking bread and pungent *garum* rushed out to greet us. Crassus halted and turned to me.

"Alexander, before we go in, what you did ... I'm glad you were there. You have my thanks."

There was nothing I could say. Certainly not 'you're welcome.' I hoped for both our sakes he would find his humanity, but knew he would not. He could not. We walked in silence through the *culina.* As we passed the brick burners, wash basins, chopping boards, cauldrons and charcoal ovens arrayed everywhere in chaotic order, the staff turned to bow to the master and watch our passing. I could feel their eyes upon me. My bare feet padded silently on the tiled floor. I longed for sandals. I hated the thought of anyone seeing my ugly, ungainly feet. Why, you ask, did he not take me to some private corner of the villa, away from the wide eyes of those I had commanded yesterday and would again tomorrow, or perhaps the day after? The great general had calculated our route, my garb, even our destination with precision. Humiliation was the spice that made this dish memorable.

"Atticus," I said suddenly, "see to your staff. The pigeons are overcooking! Come, come, attend to your duties, people. Adriana, if you interrupt the beating of those eggs, that omelet will fall short of fluffy. The house of Crassus does not accept insipid omelets!" My voice found a new and rusty register. I was about to say more, pointing a shaking finger at the round, scored loaves of black bread cooling on racks. My cloak slipped from my shoulders and the staff turned away from my nakedness, their heads bowed. Crassus readjusted the *palla* about me and put his hand on my shoulder. "Courage," he whispered. I fell silent. My lord stared straight ahead as we passed among his people. His face was ashen, grim and stricken with dreadful anticipation. Only the whip told us apart.

Activity approached a more normal bustle after we had passed into the large storeroom where dry goods, earthenware *amphorae,* terracotta pots and brass pans were neatly inventoried. A large wooden work table stood at the back of the dimly lit room and it was toward this that we headed.

There was a commotion outside in the room we had just left. Livia rushed in. I gripped the cloak tighter about my nakedness. She ran up to us, bowed to my lord, then turned to me, twin streaks reflecting dully under her shining eyes. Laying her hands lightly over mine she said, "You are a stupid man." She put a hand on my cheek, rose up on her toes and kissed me quickly on the mouth, then fled the way she had come.

I had not the wits about me to know whether or not her action was spurred by pity or affection, but in that moment I did not care. I turned to Crassus and said, "I am ready."

•••

In point of fact, I was not. At least the memory of her touch would be an oak around which I could wrap my psyche and cling while both dignity and hide were being stripped away. Would Crassus be equally girded? Like any high-born Roman, he was raised on civility and oratory, but bred to violence. He had led armies and slaughtered thousands. He was an educated tactician and an underappreciated commander. But in his own home, upon a trusted and I hoped beloved servant, to perpetrate such brutality with personal and immediate intimacy – this was new to him. I hoped the prospect of it was turning his stomach as much as it was mine. Then I remembered the day he had branded Nestor. I shuddered involuntarily.

There was neither door nor drapes at the entrance to the storage room, but Crassus posted two men in the doorway, their backs to us. I thought to myself, the sound will carry. He bade me bend over the thick wood of the table. I called out for Atticus and another cook to come hold my arms outstretched. They begged to be excused, but I begged in return for their help – I feared I would be unable to hold myself steady for the duration of my chastisement. I shrugged the *palla* from my shoulders and handed it to Atticus. He folded it neatly and laid it aside.

Naked, I spread my hands toward the far side of the table, but as I stared down at the stained and worn grain of its surface, my bile rose and I retched pitifully on the very spot where I was to lay my head. I apologized in sputtering half-sentences as someone wiped it away. This is going to happen now, I thought, laying my cheek against the wood warmed by the acid contents of my gut.

The short length of the leather strips forced Crassus to stand close enough for me to hear his breath. I closed my eyes and began to pray. I am not a brave man, nor am I built for the rigors of the field. I had no idea what to expect, but surmised that like other distasteful events, such as a visit to a non-Grecian dentist, the expectation would be worse than the reality. It was a vain hope.

No one who has not endured the lash can be prepared for its agony. Soaked in brine, then dried to a crackling stiffness, a *lorum* is elegantly engineered to strip away stubborn defiance and expose not just flesh, but the cringing animal within, the howling thing no man wants the world to see. It is a miner's tool, designed for digging through layers of pain, searching for that rich vein of humiliation.

The beastly sound that the first strike blew from my mouth was wild and unknown to me. A shriek strangled by shame into a whimper, caused by a stinging, biting blow that made the muscles beneath my skin ripple in involuntarily waves. The first of twenty.

Crassus grunted with the effort of each stroke. Though the blows fell with equal force, each taught me a new way to experience pain. I lost count in the confusion of my own cries. My master did his best to keep the strips of hide from intersecting previous blows, but I am tall and thin and my back too narrow. It was not long before the leather thongs crossed older welts and bit deeper. As the blood started to flow, the salt began its work.

The gods took pity on me. I passed out before it was over; of a sudden I realized my body was no longer jerking in uncontrolled spasms. I had stopped screaming, at least with my vocal chords. There was sobbing, and I am fairly sure I was not the only one making that pitiful sound. I embraced the table like a lover, hoping they would never make me move from the spot. Someone passed behind me and the gentle movement of air sent swords of agony slicing through the rents in my back. I fainted again, but jerked awake to the touch of a poultice being laid upon me. Hands held me firm, but I was not going anywhere. I could not imagine how I would ever rise, let alone walk from that place. Out of the corner of my eye, I saw my lord Crassus.

He leaned against a cupboard, his chest heaving, eyes fixed on the flagstone floor, face and tunic speckled with scarlet. A girl approached, I forget her name, carrying a bucket of cool water and a large sponge. She curtsied and made to daub his sweaty brow, but he slapped her roughly away. She squeaked in surprise and fear. "See to *him,* fool!" Confused and terrified to have brought his displeasure down upon herself, she turned from Crassus toward the table where I lay, but he touched her arm and in a gentle voice repeated, "See to him."

While Baltus, the doctor who had been with us for several years, prepared the next strip of balm and grease soaked cloth, I watched Crassus turn and leave the bloody scene of his own making. He did not look at me or speak to me. Walking away, he let slip the *lorum,* supple with gore. It lay on the ground like a scarlet viper. The hand that had wielded it gripped nothing but air, muscles fatigued, fingers locked as if they still held the instrument. At his passing, the *culina* once again came slowly alive, as if thawed by the magic in a child's tale.

Almost more than the beating, I dreaded the next time I would be forced to look him in the eye. There was a pain here the doctor could not soothe and a wound that would forever be beyond healing. Later, I would mourn for what we each had lost, for it would never be the same between us.

# CHAPTER XXVII

## 56 BCE - SPRING, LUCA

Year of the consulship of
Cn. Cornelius Lentulus Marcellinus and L. Marcius Philippus

"I'd "say that was a good day's work." Gaius Julius Caesar, reclining in the dining room on the couch of lowest stature picked a bit of meat from his teeth with the sharp end of his spoon. A cold Aprilis wind whipped rain against the roof tiles of his villa in Luca, just within the southern border of his province of Cisalpine Gaul. No one knew that the estate, even though this was our first visit to it, was actually owned by my master. Rome was run on favors, and no one practiced the art better than these two statesmen.

The scars on my back had mended six years ago; white welts on a pale background. The man whose cruel arrogance and thoughtless lechery had instigated their manifestation had just now summoned a meeting of the real rulers of Rome, a conspiracy clandestine to none.

Almost two hundred senators, accompanied by more than three times that many lictors, slaves and spouses had met to renew their vows, a marriage of power tenuously held together by the three leaders of the alliance: Caesar, Pompeius and Crassus. This was the end of the sixth day of the conference, but by now most had returned to the city. Crassus, Pompeius and their wives yet remained. When we had first arrived, Caesar laid eyes on me and smiled, after which, to him, I ceased to exist. He, however, had never left my thoughts, and my dread of this meeting had increased with every mile of our approach.

The only other men lingering in the *triclinium* at this late hour occupied places reserved for honored guests. One of them was drunk and dozing, his head tilted back on the arm of his *lectus,* his mouth hanging open as if he were waiting for more wine to be poured directly down his throat. The other, by Caesar's reckoning, was not drunk enough. I found a wall against which to become invisible; it gave Crassus sufficient eye contact with me, but otherwise kept me well out of the way.

"Oh come, Marcus, surely you're content with the arrangements? Try those boar-pasties before they get cold." Caesar, at forty-four, had the knack of simultaneously appearing fastidious and soldierly. His dark brown eyes were quick to both assess and judge, and they could estimate with equal ease the tactics required for the battlefield or the senate floor. From his narrow face and patrician features to his taut, trim frame, everything about him said "advance!" His hairline was the only physical trait in retreat, but not a one of the hairs remaining was out of place. His garb for the evening was a coarse linen tunic with a fringed sleeve and a royal red military *abolla*. He wrapped the cloak about him against the chill.

"I would have been more content to have forged them privately in Ravenna. You asked that we meet there, alone. Tertulla and I make the arduous trip, wait three days, but you show up in the form of a letter saying that we must now trundle off instead to Luca. I am not a child's ball to be bounced hither and yon. Why, Gaius, was it necessary to turn our private deliberations into a spectacle? Half the senate has come up from Rome. Yesterday, I would have wagered a million *sesterces* that the Circus Maximus lay between the Capitoline and the Aventine. But today I find that no, Caesar has had it transplanted to Luca."

"A slight exaggeration," Caesar said, not smiling.

"I could have suffered the rest, but who should be the first to meet us at the gate, full of smarmy smiles and feigned friendship?"

"Pompeius is genuinely fond of you."

"Hmph. As a Vestal is fond of her virginity - what privileges she enjoys if she keeps it intact, but oh what rapture she would know if she were free of it!"

"Wine has made you a poet, Marcus."

"Why, Gaius," Crassus said, ignoring the compliment and accepting more wine from a servant, "why was it necessary to drag Tertulla and me across the entire breadth of Italy when we'd already made the trip from Rome to Ravenna?"

"Please extend my apologies to your wife. The additional miles cannot have been pleasant for her, even in a carriage as finely appointed as your own."

"Tertulla goes where duty dictates, and gladly. As do I, Gaius."

"How is she, Marcus? What with the business at hand, I have had little time for friends. I swear you are the only noble Roman I know who married for love, not political advantage."

Crassus relaxed visibly. "If men knew the source of true happiness, Gaius, they would covet my wife, not my wealth. Thirty years, mark you, thirty years. I pray that you and Calpurnia may share such a union. I am blessed by many gods and goddesses, but none greater than she."

"Piso is one of your closest friends. I am fortunate that my marriage to his daughter has added both adhesive to our commitments and joy to my home. But Tertulla, Marcus! Polykleitos with his chisel could not have sculpted such an Aphrodite."

My lord closed his eyes for a moment and smiled. "When my brother's slaughter made her a widow at fourteen, I took her in; honor demanded it. Within a year, I was entranced. Another and ... well, I can still smell the roses in the garden where she agreed to marry me. But even more than her beauty or her youth, it is her wisdom I treasure. I cannot count the times I have left home for some business dealing or another with her sage advice in my ears. You know it was she who convinced me to forsake Catilina, to spurn his conspiracy and advise you to do the same. She said, and I think this is exact, 'You and Caesar will go no further than the point of a sword if you follow that brigand.' You would be surprised how many times the mind of Tertulla has spoken through the mouth of Crassus."

A momentary expression of surprise flitted across Caesar's features. I doubt my lord would have confessed this tidbit had he been sober. From where I stood, I saw Caesar's look change from surprise to gratification, then disappear.

Crassus yawned. "Gaius, these old bones are weary. But I will know before I retire why you unilaterally altered our agreed plans."

"You must forgive me, Marcus, but I believe that circumstances did indeed require us to ... open the discussions. Grain shortages continue, there is violence in the streets and the senate seems powerless to suppress it. I need your help, old friend." Caesar raised his bowl to Crassus, then sipped his water.

"Oh, I have no doubt you felt it was necessary. But it strikes me that all this traipsing about, this wrangling and politicking is for no one's benefit so much as it is for the boon of Caesar."

Caesar seemed genuinely nonplussed. "I am hurt to hear you think so. You, Pompeius and I have sworn to take no action without the approval of the other two, and I have lived by this accord. We have just affirmed it this morning."

"And here I thought our original appointment in Ravenna, by excluding Magnus, would be the beginning of a new, smaller-by-one, coalition. I see that I was mistaken." A shutter blew open across the room and rain spattered across the stone tiles. The oil lamps hanging from nearby floor stands sputtered and almost went out.

As I rushed with others to set things aright, Caesar said, "I knew we should have dined in the south *triclinium.*" He wrapped his cloak more tightly about him. "I had seriously considered a duumvirate, yes. But thanks to the feud between Milo and Clodius and their bloody street gangs, I concluded that more than four hands are required to contain the problems now facing the city."

"That's odd," Crassus said, drinking the remainder of his wine. "I was under the impression you felt it could be accomplished with but two."

Caesar smiled thinly. "We both need Pompeius in Rome. Unless you've had a recent change of heart and are more interested in counting grain than gold."

"No, let's leave that dull responsibility to his bureaucratic expertise."

"Well, then ...."

"Well, then, of all the men who would cast aspersions on my purported avarice, I'd have thought you would be one of the last. As I recall, you have done quite well from the use of my gold - eight hundred thirty talents' worth, if memory serves?"

I saw the brief twinge in Caesar's expression, probably cursing himself inwardly for making such a careless remark. But my master was too far in his cups to notice. "Your generosity is legend, Marcus. I could not have achieved half as much without your patronage. You must be certain how keenly I know this. But is it not true that we have all made gains together we could not have achieved alone?"

"I don't know, Gaius, is it? Certainly your own fortunes and those of Pompeius have soared in the past four years. Admittedly, I was well situated before our accord, but while you and Magnus have risen to the heights, I seem to be wandering around the same plateau as when we began."

I could practically read Caesar's mind by the light of his facial expressions. What more does the old Croesus want, he must be thinking. He was never adept at concealing his feelings, though he would be the first to deny it. "A plateau that rivals Olympus, Marcus. Only opportunity has given Pompeius and me more military achievements. That aside, who in Rome is your rival? There is no finer orator, statesman or politician. Your influence in the courts is matchless. And that is why I need to count on your continued support. Rhetoric and persuasion are no less critical to our success than the legions at my command. We are each generals in our own way."

"True enough, I suppose. But this commander, Caesar, is ready for retirement. Here lies the crux of it. You and Pompeius are men who 'want.' I, on the other hand, am a man who 'wants not,' and is getting to that age where he cares little whether or not he acquires more. Therefore, any agreement between such as we must by definition *take* from me and *give* to the two of you. I'm beginning to wonder what my support means to you, and what, in the long term, it will garner for me which I do not already possess. You see before you a man satisfied."

Caesar was clearly becoming exasperated. "Marcus, you well know that the political stool upon which you, Pompeius and I sit cannot stand firm unless all three legs are of equal length and strength. You yourself heard Lucius Domitius say that if he wins the consulate, he'll make good on his threat to take away my armies. For all our sakes, we cannot allow that to happen. That is why you and Pompeius must win next year's election, whatever it takes."

"Oh, I understand full well why *you* wish it so. And all things being equal, as your friend, your desires are also my wishes. But is there parity, Gaius? Where is the profit? Why should I subject myself to another year of bickering with Magnus over every petty decision. It wasn't pleasant the first time; it will be no less irritating now."

"If we do not act now to secure the futures we deserve, we risk losing them." Caesar sat up, now truly concerned. It was clear he had misjudged my master.

"No, Caesar," Crassus said. "With respect, *my* future is secure. It is not I who ran off to Gaul before getting the senate's approval. It is not I who has pissed into the cups of more *optimates* than I can count. And it is not I, Gaius, who will stand trial for impeachment when your *imperium* expires. You may fool the likes of Pompeius into believing our actions are for the good of Rome, but kindly afford me a little more respect. Do not confuse me with the players on the stage of your mime. Like you, I sit behind the curtain as author, producer and director. I understand what is happening here. To continue down this path is to imperil all that I have acquired. Such a singular risk must be minimized ... if I am to help place you on your throne."

Caesar considered my master carefully before speaking. "I did not realize you were unsatisfied, Marcus. Tell me, what result of our deliberations is not to your liking and I will see that it is corrected to your satisfaction."

"You miss my point, Gaius. Perhaps it would be better, now that you have invited half of Rome to join you in your scheming, if I were left out of it. That way, should your machinations fail, I might at least preserve something in what would surely to be a messy aftermath."

"Marcus, you know that is impossible. Without you as consul next year, nothing will come to fruition. Pompeius will flounder without you. There must be something else you desire, something that will make your participation more ... more palatable. Another province, perhaps?"

"Another? I cannot fathom what to do with the first."

"I thought you wanted a proconsulate?"

"I would appreciate its novelty, certainly, but what on earth am I going to do with Syria? You're not suggesting I crawl off to Antioch to retire, as is the fashion these days for well-to-do businessmen?"

"I rather thought you would wring it like a sponge."

"There's a coincidence. That is precisely how I feel at this moment - like a wrung sponge. Perhaps it is the hour. Late in the day ... and late in life." Crassus sighed and put his empty wine bowl down too close to the edge of the table. It fell to the floor. I snapped my fingers and an *analecta* came running to replace it. The noise elicited a snort from the man on the third *lectus*. "We depart tomorrow morning," Crassus said, struggling to rise. "I will consider all that you have said and will send word to you within the month. Will that satisfy you?"

Caesar leaned forward and shook the dozing man. "Marcus Junius, bestir yourself. We still have guests to entertain." Caesar motioned to the wine pourer to fill Crassus' bowl yet again.

"Enough," Crassus protested, "this is not a *commisatio*."

"Did I hear someone say drinking bout? Excellent!" The young man sat up, rubbing the crick in his neck. He looked at Caesar, who nodded. Something passed between them that pricked me to pay closer attention.

Caesar rose. "Marcus Licinius Crassus, Marcus Junius Brutus. Brutus' mother, Servilia Caepionis is a good friend. And Brutus studied philosophy in Athens so I'm sure you'll have much to discuss. Brutus, Crassus is going to be consul next year, remember? After that he's off to Syria."

"Syria? How wonderful, sir. I understand that Antioch is the jewel of the East. I've just returned from Cyprus with my uncle. Not nearly as exciting, I can tell you. Not much philosophy in administration."

"Are there any jewels left in Cyprus?"

Caesar said, "Marcus Licinius, I do believe you're drunk. Marcus Brutus, keep an eye on my old friend here. Don't let him go wandering off." He laughed and clapped my master on the shoulder. Brutus was not smiling.

Crassus lowered himself back onto his couch, resigned. "I have heard of the young and accomplished Brutus. Tell me, lad, how fares your uncle?"

"Now, Marcus Licinius, don't blame the child for the sins of his relatives. Brutus is a good lad, and will some day be a great defender of the republic."

"I am certain of it," Crassus said without conviction. "Cato," he persisted. "He is your uncle, is he not? I haven't confused you with another have I?"

Brutus sat up and said rather too loudly, "Sir, yes, I am proud to call Marcus Porcius Cato 'uncle.'"

Crassus looked up with incredulity. "Your friendship with his mother must be strong indeed, Caesar, to find favor with this family. Cato cost you a tribute, tying up the senate with his prattling until dusk till the vote could not be taken. Just as Pompeius clipped that same rose right off the vine from under my nose."

"Yes, Marcus, every Roman schoolboy remembers your heroism during the slave uprising. You were unjustly denied," Caesar sighed. "As for Brutus, what can I say? I like the boy."

"Please do not mention that name," said Brutus with clenched teeth, "or we shall see the wine in my belly poured a second time."

"What name is that?" Crassus asked with feigned innocence.

"There, you see," Caesar said. "You have found common ground in your dislike of Pompeius." Brutus grimaced. "Talk about that. What?"

"Very good, Julius," Crassus said, smiling. "A fine joke." Caesar furrowed his brow, not understanding.

"Common," Brutus said, "as in provincial, not of patrician heritage. Pompeius elbowed his way into the nobility."

"Since it was not intentional," Caesar said, "I shan't take credit for it. I'll say goodnight then. You two trample that well-trod *earth* to your heart's content, but remember, deeds define us, not words. Till morning. On that other matter, we will talk more, Crassus, as you say."

"Good night, Gaius. Your hospitality, as always ... oh! You will remember to deliver my letter to Publius?"

"Your son is one of my finest legates, a courageous, spirited officer. He does your family proud."

I could see that Crassus was torn. He watched Caesar depart, wishing he could leave as well, but did not want to appear rude. He'd stay a few minutes to be polite; that was his way. I was exhausted myself, and longed for my sleeping pallet.

# CHAPTER XXVIII

## 56 BCE - SPRING, LUCA

Year of the consulship of
Cn. Cornelius Lentulus Marcellinus and L. Marcius Philippus

The two stared at each other in awkward silence after Caesar had left. I offered to bring in more sweetmeats, but Crassus waved me off. My master appeared to know neither what to make of the nephew of his senatorial rival nor whether he could muster the energy to give it much thought. After a while he said, "It is hard to lose a father."

"You know?"

"That Pompeius had him executed for supporting Marius, yes. My own father shared a similar fate for his neutrality."

Brutus appeared not to have heard Crassus; or more likely there was no room in his heart for commiseration. He would wave his bloody standard and let none fly higher. He spoke slowly, almost accusingly, as if all the world were culpable. "Father had surrendered honorably.

Pompeius had him beheaded." The word turned between them, a scorpion looking for a way out.

"'The adolescent butcher,'" Crassus said finally, almost to himself.

"What?"

"Pompeius. He earned that nickname many times over in those days."

"You also fought for Sulla, did you not, sir?" The scorpion struck, swelling the last word with venom.

Crassus smiled thinly, though his face reddened. "I feel no burning compulsion to submit my justifications to you." He looked as if he would add "boy" but stopped himself. "However, had you been paying attention just now, you might have heard one. For the sake of civility, know this: I received the benefit of Sulla's proscriptions, but took no part in them." My master sighed, the flare of anger passing, leaving him deflated. "Young man, this is an unseemly hour for dispute. Your father was a statesman, and deserved better. I seek no quarrel with you."

"Nor I with you!"

"Then if you will forgive the advice of an old man ... ?" Brutus nodded. "It is we who move through time ..." Crassus said, pointing unsteadily in the direction of his empty cup. He began reaching for it before the servant finished pouring. "... not the reverse. When we walk beyond any one of life's instants, it becomes nothing more than a receding milestone. We can look back, but we cannot retrace our steps. The past remains stationary, while we are doomed to move ever onwards. To do otherwise is against nature."

"And what of justice?"

"A noble metal, but affordable by few. The young, lacking seasoning, believe it may be more cheaply bought. How old are you, twenty-seven, twenty-eight?"

"Almost thirty," Brutus said defensively. "Perhaps the young believe justice must be bought at any price."

"Well, the thing is, even if you pay the price and make the purchase, you never know till it is beyond undoing whether what you bought is what you expected. The scales are rarely balanced." Crassus drank. I curse myself as I write these words, but in that moment I feared to be shamed by a rebuke. I could not bring myself to interrupt their conversation.

"Let me tell you a thing or two about justice!" Crassus was unstoppable now. "They say you've returned from Cyprus a rich man. You've become a practiced and clever moneylender, have you not?" Brutus sipped sparingly at his wine, saying nothing. "Do you owe your fortune to fastidious Cato for employing you there? He would blanch if he learned his nephew, the incorruptible Brutus was a base usurer. 48% interest to those poor people of Salamis. Tut, tut, Brutus. Do not shame yourself further by denial: I have spent a lifetime cultivating loyal clients more numerous than all your *sesterces*. Oh don't worry, I don't give a fig for your illegal gains. Let me tell you whose feet you should be bathing in gratitude: not your uncle's, nor those of Matinius or Scaptius who fronted for you (I know *all* that passes in the senate). No, it is to Pompeius, your avowed enemy, that you owe gratitude! Don't look so incredulous; two years before you put your little scheme to work, it was he who subdued the island and brought it under the aegis of Rome. If not for Pompeius, your uncle would have had nothing to govern and you would have no decent citizens of Salamis to fleece. Where is your justice now? Shall I help you compose a letter of thanks to Magnus? Better still, let us determine his commission. Stone and earth are good for funerals, but nothing buries a feud so durably as silver and gold."

I gathered my loins and said softly, "Sir, the hour?"

"All right, Alexander. You are a cruel taskmaster. I'm coming."

Brutus buried his face in his hands. "Oh my," Crassus said, "I've gone too far."

The young man sniffled. "No. You have gone to the mark. My father's honor and service were enough to earn him his tribunate. I must let it stand." He raised his head and smiled meekly; his eyes were neither red nor wet. "Do not hold my actions in contempt, I beg you. Today one must have a full purse to climb the *cursus honorum*."

"I'm sure you'll do fine, lad. Stay close to your uncle. He may be misguided, but his honor is unimpeachable. He has some followers in the senate and will find you a place."

"My uncle does not approve of my being here." Brutus tore a chunk of bread from a loaf and dipped the end in a bowl of honey.

"I should think not, considering the company you are keeping. Why *are* you here?"

"I respect Cato's Stoic beliefs, I do, but I am no ascetic. My uncle would have me in sackcloth, exercising five times a day and eating birdseed. You should taste the wine at his table: it is unfit even for his slaves. To answer your question directly, I am here at Caesar's bidding. He need but ask and I will see it through."

"He does not share your politics. He, like myself, stands for a new Rome, a people's Rome."

"My friendship is immovable, but I may yet nudge his devotion away from the *populares*. Rome has had its fill of kings. The senate must remain inviolate to protect us against a return to dictatorship."

"Truly, your uncle is a greater influence upon you than Caesar. I am more of a pragmatist. There are more citizens than senators. Ironically, of the three of us, Pompeius may be more easily moved. That is, if you don't conspire to kill him again."

"The conspiracy was never proved and the charge dismissed! Three years ago."

Crassus smiled and emptied his cup. "True, yet your name held a place of prominence in the debate."

"You bait me, sir, but I shall not rise. For if you know this much, you also know that it was Caesar who had my name stricken from the list of conspirators. Another reason for my loyalty."

"Caesar is nothing if not persuasive. You will never find a more loyal supporter. One does wonder, though. If I make a list for the market, does that list not imply my intent to go shopping? Well, the hour grows beyond late." Crassus swung his feet to the floor, which awakened something in Brutus. He also rose to a sitting position.

"At least let me applaud you for 'winning' the consulship a second time. I am surprised, though, that you chose Syria for your proconsulship."

"*If* fortune favors me and the people demand it, yes, I would serve again. As for Syria, who can say what a year will bring. Truth be told, if it should come to pass, I wasn't actually planning on going."

"Why on earth not?"

"Why bother? One of my *legates* will do just as nicely. The money will come in all the same, and these bones are not quite as fond of travel as they used to be. Did you know Pompeius isn't going to Hispania? He also plans on remaining in the city. I fear more for the fate of Rome. He is an inept governor and a worse politician. Pompeius will make a mess of it if I don't stay close by." Crassus began gathering his robes about him.

"Notwithstanding any other disagreements we may have between us, at least we may agree regarding Pompeius."

"What's the time, do you suppose?"

"Isn't it bad luck to look for a water clock in the midst of a celebration?"

"The celebration is long over. I'm tired. My wife will be worried."

"A wife. Yes, I must arrange for one as soon as I return to Rome. There is nothing that gives one's career a boost so much as a politically advantageous union. That, or a successful military campaign. But I don't need to tell this to the champion of the Servile War, do I?"

"Do you mock me, boy?" That time my master did use the word. I was well pleased.

"Never! Caesar was wrong to dismiss the injustice done to you with his denigrating tone. Few will admit it, but Spartacus was a worthy adversary."

"Spartacus was a rabid dog that needed putting down. What could you know of the uprising? You were no more than a child at the time."

"Forgive me. I meant more than mere respect. I intended admiration. Every Roman who values the safety and sanctity of the republic is indebted to you. And I was twelve, by the way."

"Then you will know that it was Pompeius who received the honor for that victory."

"The man comes running with a mop after you have scoured the house clean from top to bottom, and they give *him* a *triumph* for it. You were passed over, sir, plain and simple. Politics defeated you, not Pompeius. The senate had no choice. Their public position had to be that this was nothing more than a minor irritation from a mob of unruly slaves. To do otherwise would create panic among our citizens and hope among those who serve us. They gave *you imperium* to defeat Spartacus; how then could they confer upon you the Republic's highest honor if the rebellion was the minor scuffle they advertized?"

"They gave it to Pompeius," Crassus said bitterly.

"It was a war and every Roman knows who won it. No more difficult or demanding campaign was ever fought on or off Italian soil."

"It pleases me to hear you say so. It pleases me very much indeed." I watched Brutus smile into his drinking bowl. There was no friendship in that grin. Marcus Brutus was plucking the strings of flattery, and my master was all too quick to leap to the dance.

"*Dominus*, forgive me, but I must ... "

"No you must not!" Brutus shouted. "Can't you see we're talking here, man?"

Crassus sat up with a grunt. "It's all right, Marcus Brutus, the hour is late, for young and old alike. Let us put an amicable end to it, shall we?"

Brutus cracked the kinks from his neck by rolling his head around. I watched him glance at one of Caesar's slaves standing in the shadows in a corner by the entrance to the *triclinium*. This man glanced outside the dining room to a floor lamp in the hallway whose wicks remained lit. The servant subtly but clearly shook his head. "Forgive me, general," Brutus said. "I had purposed to ask you earlier, but your good fellowship has made hours grow wings. If I may, I need your advice on a delicate matter. If you wouldn't mind ..."

"*Dominus*," I said, risking a beating, "I really must speak with you."

"Damn it!" Brutus yelled. "What insolence is this?"

"Alexander, if you wish to retire, I will see myself ..."

"No, *dominus*. It is not for myself. It is a matter of some ur–."

"Have you no control over your people?" Brutus asked. He turned to me and hissed through clenched teeth, "Shut your fucking, contemptuous mouth."

"All right, son, that's enough. Just a few more minutes, Alexander. Go on, Marcus Junius, but I must ask you to be quick about it. We must all retire."

"Many thanks," he said, searing me with a glance. "Apologies – a moment to compose myself." Brutus adjusted his toga, ran a hand through his short, wavy hair and took several calming breaths. He called for more wine and took his time bringing the cup to his lips. Every action superfluous. He was stalling for time, but *dominus* could not see it. "Here's the thing of it," he said finally. "It is true that I have returned from Cyprus with a respectable sum. First I would ask for your confidence in this matter. As a supporter of the merchant class, you know it is an impossible law that prevents honest men from making a living while they seek a life in politics." Crassus nodded. "You are also aware that even a talent of silver grows weak if it is idle and not exercised from one year to the next. I can think of no Roman who may better advise me how to invest this capital."

"I am happy to do so. Forgive the brevity of my answer, Brutus, but know that a simple response makes it no less prudent. Diversify, that is the advice I give you. Place some of your investments in *latifundia,* for the large farms will always prosper as long as the world has mouths to feed. But do not neglect the city: *insulae* have always made money for me. Look for quality: the best real estate will always appreciate in value. Do not restrict your properties to Italy. The mints are ever-active; buy productive mines wherever you may find them throughout our provinces. Finally, and I can think of no better advice for a man of business: treat your tenants and your workers well, create loyalty with generosity; do not stint on those who daily bear the responsibility to make your money grow. You will see the largest returns from *that* investment."

"I am in your debt. I was right to seek your counsel."

Marcus Brutus held Crassus in conversation for several more minutes. Crassus would have retired, but every time he tried to rise, Cato's nephew found another way to detain him. Over such trivialities may lives be made or unmade. Crassus rose finally and steadied himself on the arm of the *lectus*. "Forgive me, sir. If I stay one more minute, it will be the end of my marriage. I've enjoyed the company and the conversation, but now, I'm for bed!"

"Wait! One more amphora. How many chances does one get to celebrate the reaffirmation of such an alliance? One sworn to uphold the republic and the sanctity of the senate. And what two men better qualified to hold Pompeius in check than Caesar and Crassus. Your wife will not begrudge you, surely?"

"You do not know Tertulla, sir, for if you did, you would perceive she does not begrudge me anything. Nor I her. And as much as I have enjoyed these indulgences, I want to save at least some of the night to share Caesar's proposals with her. I'm sure you understand. Come!" he said, pointing to Caesar's slave waiting at the entrance to the dining room. "Light my way.

"Alexander, I am too tired to talk more. Go to your rest. We will speak in the morning. *Salve*, Marcus Brutus. I would wish you good night, but I do not think there is much night left."

# CHAPTER XXIX

## 56 BCE - SPRING, LUCA

Year of the consulship of
Cn. Cornelius Lentulus Marcellinus and L. Marcius Philippus

In the aftermath of the war with Parthia, Tertulla, long past a grief she once believed inconsolable, wanted to honor in some small way those who had perished to avenge her, though most did not know her name, much less the real reason they fought and died. To let the truth uphold her virtue, and to shame the memory of the man who had dishonored her, her husband and Rome itself, she told this sad tale to me. For thirty-five years I have kept its secret, for no good could have come from its revelation. Innocents would have perished, both friends and family, and the story would have been obliterated like one of Sulla's proscriptions. Now that I am old and safe in this island refuge, and most of those I cared for have gone ahead of me to their rest, it is time for me to set it down. There will be little good to come from the telling even now, save for its release from my bosom, and the faintest hope that some day both Gaius Julius Caesar and Marcus Licinius Crassus will be seen in a light more clear than that which shines upon them now.

•••

"Marcus. Sorry, I tried to wait up for you." Tertulla stretched and rolled over to face the doorway. "The rain – it's like a drug. And so much wine ..."

It was very dark. The wick in the bronze lamp on the chest across from the bed guttered, its oil almost spent. The single window that opened onto the *peristyle* was shuttered against the downpour and drapes were pulled in front of them. She could not make out the face of the man in the doorway, but she knew immediately that it was not Marcus. Whoever it was had pulled the portiere partially aside and was now standing just inside the room. He casually unclasped his cloak and threw it in the corner.

"Who are you? Where's my husband?" Tertulla scrambled from the bed and pulled the coverlet around her.

"Oh, he's still contemplating the fact that I am going to make him even more rich and powerful than he already is."

"Caesar." Her voice was flat, but her heart began pounding like the ramming rhythm of an attacking trireme. What was this satyr doing in their bedchamber, with her husband only steps away? The infamous philanderer. Even his soldiers sang of it in the streets.

"You don't seem pleased."

"I am *not* pleased. You must go." In a louder voice she called, "Esther?" Cicero had said that Caesar had been at the root of Pompeius' divorce from Mucia. She hadn't believed it, of course, for why would he risk political suicide for a moment's dalliance?

"Shhh. Lower your voice," he said in a mock whisper. "You don't want a scandal, do you? Don't worry about the *famula* in the hall - I sent her off to more comfortable quarters." As he spoke, he walked slowly toward the end of the *lectus*.

"What do you want?" Tertulla took a step backward, wondering if she could get past him to the door. Her mind fled back six years when he and Pompeia had visited the villa at Baiae. She had left no room for misunderstanding, and he and his soon-to-be-divorced wife had departed shortly thereafter. Since then, she had kept out of his way, feigning illness or some other excuse whenever Marcus wanted to socialize. She had seen Caesar maybe half a dozen times in as many years.

Now he was in her room in the middle of the night. Whatever lie he was about to tell her to explain this inappropriate intrusion, she knew the truth behind it. No honorable Roman would invade a matron's privacy thus. She was stunned by his audacity. Would he attempt to seduce her with her husband close by and liable to return any second? Was he mad? Unless he *knew* there was little risk of being discovered. Suddenly, she became truly afraid.

"Frankly, I need your help. I want to talk to you."

"That's fine, Julius. Let's talk in the morning." Tertulla could not keep the waver of fear out of her voice. She must think. He was right about creating a scandal. Even though it was common knowledge how much she and Crassus cared for each other, tongues would wag, and humiliation and disgrace would follow. Yet Caesar must know that he could never come between them. What truly worried her was how closely her husband's fortunes now depended on the general's success. Their fates were now interwoven beyond unraveling. Crassus promoted Caesar's scheming in the senate, he had loaned him millions to stage huge entertainments for the plebs, and of course there was that business with Catilina. If Caesar fell, it would be almost impossible for Crassus to avoid being pulled down with him. She had warned him of the risk, but he had persisted. For better or worse, they were now tied to the proconsul's ambition. And should the alliance end badly, with the two of them as enemies, her husband could very well be destroyed. Marcus might think he was a match for Caesar, but as much as she loved him, she knew he was wrong. She must protect him. She must find a way to get rid of Caesar with no one becoming the wiser.

"This can't wait. You're leaving in the morning, and I need to know things have been settled before you go."

"I don't know what you're talking about."

"Good, then let me explain."

"All right. Wait outside while I dress, then we can find some place comfortable to talk."

"I'm quite comfortable here. I see, however, that you are not. Let me get to the point, and then you'll be rid of me." Caesar came round in front of the bed and sat down. He patted the mattress by his side, but Tertulla backed further away. She now had a slight chance of getting to the doorway. The room was so small though. Would he try to grab her? She wished Marcus would return, then realized her folly. He must *never* know. She must do this herself.

"Speak quickly, Julius. You risk my marriage." She wrapped the coverlet more securely around her, but pulled it up away from her ankles so she wouldn't trip on it when she ran. Moving toward the far side of the chest near the window, she wondered what story she could dredge up to explain why she was running around the villa at this hour. First I have to get away, she thought. She now stood in the place that offered the best angle for escape, if he would just stay on the bed.

"Oh, I think not. If you do as I ask, your union will be safe." Caesar paused to take a swallow from a small bottle of wine she had not seen when he entered. The sight of it, knowing how rarely he drank, only increased her anxiety. He held it out to her and when she refused, he shrugged and took more himself. Then he set the open container on a small table by the bed.

"You see, your husband is having second thoughts about our agreement." He proceeded to tell her the details of the results of the conference, much of which she already knew from the other wives and servants who'd been paid to snoop. "We spent almost a week getting everyone to agree, and now he's thinking of backing out."

"He must have his reasons," she said coolly.

"Lady Tertulla, do you realize what will happen to him, and to you, if he does? If I am *persona non grata,* if charges are brought, proscriptions reinstated, you could lose everything. Do you want that to happen?"

"Of course not. But that is between you and him, and perhaps Pompeius. I am willingly married as much to my husband's fate as to the man."

"That is well, but I have made no such vows. I cannot afford to lose this accord. We must proceed as planned."

"I have nothing to do with it."

"On the contrary. I have recently learned that at this most delicate point in our negotiations, you may have everything to do with it. I know how he trusts your judgment. I need you to convince him to accept what we have already decided, nothing more."

"That is not my place."

"But my dear, I am making it your place." Caesar spoke in a tone so gentle and friendly it was ominous. "I know you, Tertulla. You are a smart woman. You see the truth of my argument, don't you."

"Yes," she said. There was no doubt of it.

"Then you will speak with him, tonight when he returns?"

"Yes. Now please go."

"Unfortunately," he said, sighing, "I cannot rely on your charm and wit alone. I must have something else from you, some little secret that only you and I share that guarantees you will be successful in persuading him to do the right thing." Tertulla knew exactly where this was leading, and she did not need to hear any more. He had not moved from the bed. This was her chance. She bolted toward the door, but as she crossed in front of him, he reached out and got hold of a handful of the bedcovers to which she clung. She spun away, trying to extricate herself from the blanket, but lost her balance. Caesar was up now.

He threw the coverlet aside and grabbed her thin tunic as she stumbled. The cotton stitching on the top left side of the sleeveless gown ripped and bared her shoulder. As they tussled, he upset the wine bottle, knocking it over. It spun on the floor, leaving an arc of dark liquid, a crescent moon, symbol of Astarte, ancient goddess of sexuality and war.

"Where are you running?" he asked, pulling her roughly to him, his wine-soaked breath on her cheek. "You see, I was right – you *are* a smart woman. You know exactly what secret we need to share."

"Caesar, don't do this. There is no need. I will do as you ask."

"I suppose you're right," he said, "there probably is no need, per se." He spun her around and pushed her the short distance to the chest of drawers, never letting go of what remained of her tunic. He shoved his body up against her from behind, pinning her against the wooden chest. He was strong, for such a small man. She reached out for balance and knocked the oil lamp to the floor. It's tiny flame extinguished in the rush of air, and the clay shattered with a crash on the far side of the dresser. At the noise, they both froze, for neither, in their vastly different ways, wanted to be discovered.

A second later, Caesar slapped her on the back of her head. "I hope you didn't do that on purpose."

"You coward, you cockroach," she spit through clenched teeth. She tried to elbow him, but he blocked the blow. Reaching round with her right hand, she struggled to find his eyes or his hair. It was a desperate, silent contest. Tertulla continued to fight against him, until suddenly she felt cold, sharp metal pressed against her throat. She froze and Caesar withdrew the knife.

"Tertulla, you are such a beautiful creature." She could feel him pulling the belt from his waist with his free hand. "How long have we known each other, fifteen years? Ironic - your husband is exactly that much older than both of us. Not much between statesmen, granted, but don't you think he's getting a little long in the tooth for you?"

"Leave now, Caesar," she implored, "and I shall say nothing of this."

"Well, you see, that's the thing of it. It's occurred to me that I am *certain* you will say nothing, no matter *what* transpires in this room. I know, because you love your husband, and you will not see him disgraced. Neither will you see him risk financial and political ruin by breaking with me. You would do anything to protect him. I believe this of you. I believe it so strongly that I expect you to prove me right, right here, right now." He stopped pushing against her just long enough to yank her tunic up to her waist. She felt him naked against her.

"No!" she groaned. But even as he pressed against her stiff legs with his knee, trying to part them, she knew she was lost.

"Come, Tertulla, do as you're told," he whispered sweetly in her ear. "Open for me, you arrogant, little whore. You're all whores, in the end, aren't you?" Caesar knew he had her when he felt the almost imperceptible release of Tertulla's thigh muscles, enabling him to push her legs slightly apart. He pushed at her again, until her feet slipped apart on the cold floor.

I am going to let him rape me, she thought. Oh, Marcus! Forgive me! I love only you. I swear before all the gods, I belong to you alone. Juno, hear my prayer: let him leave no mark upon me, I beseech you. Protect my husband.

Even though she had now exposed herself and was offering no resistance, she was hardly ready for him, and he struggled to get inside her. The more he strained, the angrier she became.

"Know this, *little* man," she said with all the venom she could inject into her voice, "when you have shriveled and departed, I *will* avenge myself upon you."

"I shall hire a slave to do nothing but walk behind me," he replied sarcastically. "And one more to taste my food." Tertulla bit her lip, stifling a cry of pain, and Caesar moaned with her, for he had found that which he sought. Tertulla winced, and tears filled her eyes. She kept talking to herself to keep her mind as far away from what was happening to her as possible. She said prayers to all the gods, both Roman and any who might listen: to Juno and Inanna, Diana and Atargatis, Astarte and Ishtar; to any goddess who reviles the mistreatment of women and the vainglory of men. And when all her prayers were exhausted, she began listing the ways she might take revenge should the deities forsake her.

Caesar continued his frantic thrusting, but Tertulla had disappeared into her prayers and curses - she was hardly there. She did not resist, neither did she participate. Before long, Caesar found his conquest becoming a chore. Sweat beaded his brow and his breath became labored. All he wanted now was to be done with her. Her body may have yielded, but he felt as if her spirit stood apart, laughing at him.

This rebellious vision was almost confirmed when she said, "Haste, Julius, or my husband will discover how boring you are." Her last word was turned into a grunt as Caesar responded with a vicious thrust that practically lifted her off her feet. The tears filled her eyes once more, for speaking to him had snapped her back into the present. She twisted her head away from him and prayed for the end of this nightmare.

That is the moment when she saw her husband staring at her in dumbfounded disbelief from behind the portiere. She knew it was him even though he was no more than a silhouette. His head jerked and she thought he was going to vomit. She felt her own gorge rise. Something glinted below his face – a dagger! He's looking down at it. She willed him to look back at her, and he did! She warned him off with a shake of her head and the hope that he might somehow see the expression of desperation on her face. He must withdraw, he must! Caesar will kill him. The *pugio* he had held against her throat was somewhere nearby, but she could not see it. At his age and in his condition, Marcus would be no match for Caesar, even if he struck first. Could they overpower him together?

She would never know, for as she pleaded with her eyes for him to depart, his face slowly passed from view like a pale, lifeless moon disappearing behind clouds. His expression broke her heart.

A spasm shook Caesar, and while one part of Tertulla's torture was now over, she knew another was just beginning. She found that she did have something for which to be thankful. She gave her silent gratitude to Juno for sparing her husband the final moment of her degradation. But as her mind returned to settle on her violation, her body joined her spirit and revolted: she leaned over the side of the chest where the lamp had fallen and emptied her stomach. Afterwards, wiping her nose and sucking lung-fuls of air through her mouth, she stooped to pick up the bedcovers, using them to clean herself as best she could. She kept a wary eye on Caesar.

"I suppose your youth gives you some advantage," Caesar said with disdain. "But for that, you are not much use to men, are you? Remember this, Tertulla, if you fail to do your part with your husband, I will put it about that the wife of Crassus is not as chaste as her reputation. And you know I will be believed. So perform better with your husband than you have with me, and you can grow old and gray spending every *denarius* he owns. The alternative will be far more costly, I assure you. Now clean this place up. He'll be back soon." And with that, Caesar left the room.

# CHAPTER XXX

## 56 BCE - SPRING, LUCA

Year of the consulship of
Cn. Cornelius Lentulus Marcellinus and L. Marcius Philippus

"This is not the way. We're in the wrong wing! Give me that!" Crassus seized the torch from the slave. "See my *atriensis* in the morning and instruct him to flog you. Ask for Alexander. Now be gone!" Pahnehesy, the slave who was part of the conspiracy to delay Crassus and who had now misled him to the wrong end of Caesar's villa, padded off to his quarters. He'd done the best he could. He hoped the few extra coins he'd been promised would be worth the stripes he'd just earned.

Crassus pointed the sputtering torch down a dark hallway and saw that it was too short to be his own. Ah, here's the *culina,* he thought. No, couldn't touch another bite. No one about. Even the slaves are abed. He was still quite drunk.

Syria.

He wondered what the food was like. Proconsul is no small achievement, and he supposed Caesar was right, he could make a sizable contribution to his already astounding fortune as a result of the governorship. I'm so tired, he thought. I could sleep for a week. Well, we'll see what Tertulla thinks of all this. Maybe she'd like a vacation abroad. He headed back through the villa, passing columns that threw sweeping shadows like grasping arms. As he made his way through the garden atrium, rain splashed into the *impluvium* and blew spray in gusts over the slick tile floor. Crassus slid on a wet spot and fell to his knees. The torch skidded, hit a clay planter head-on and went out with a hiss and a small explosion of sparks.

Cursing, he got to his feet and groped along the walls until finally, he found the right wing. As he turned into it, he heard a woman's voice, low and urgent. It didn't sound like his wife. More words, then a grunt as if someone had been struck. He drew his *pugio* from its scabbard. As he made his way down the hall, past two empty *cubiculae*, the sounds became clearer and he realized whoever this person was, he or she was not being attacked. He squinted at a wall painting, recognized the image of Orpheus and Eurydice, the viper curled around her ankle, and confirmed that he was indeed in his *cubiculum's* hallway. The knowledge, instead of spurring him to greater speed, turned his feet to stone. He thought they must surely scrape on the stone floor as he dragged himself forward. He did not want to see what he now feared awaited him.

The *cubiculum* had no door, and the heavy drapes that separated it from the hallway were partially drawn.

Crassus peered past the curtains. The room was dark, and he could hear more than he could see. The rhythmic grunts of the man in the room were occasionally echoed by a woman's groan, whether in pain or pleasure he could not tell. There was also the intermittently rhythmic thump of a chest of drawers as it was knocked up against the wall.

Forms began to be discernible out of the murk. Two bodies faced the wall, leaning over the waist high wooden chest. A man whose head was turned away from the doorway had his tunic pulled up above his waist and stuffed into his belt. His pale, exposed buttocks moved in a short arc, up and down, like comic moons unsure whether to rise or set. Crassus could make out the prominent bald spot on the back of Caesar's head as he hunched over a woman's right shoulder. Had he come to the wrong room? Crassus tried to equate the hunched and sweating man before him with the proud, armored general mounted not on this woman (who was she?) but on a snow-white steed leading the charge against the Nervii. He couldn't do it.

This has to be our room, but where has Tertulla gone? His mind fought with his eyes, trying to blind them, but they would not be fooled. His fear spread like a stain. If I slip away now, he thought, there will be no betrayal because there will be no proof. I won't know for sure who these fornicators are. Tertulla can tell me in the morning that she grew tired of waiting, went to search for me and got lost as I did. She found other quarters in which to take her rest. And I would believe her, or any other story she might wish to tell me, because I cannot bear to face any other truth. If I take a step forward, my world will end; and yet, if I turn away, will not doubt eat at my insides till nothing is left?

The fate of worlds may hang on the slightest hesitation, and Crassus had waited too long. Had he been able to turn away, the lives of twice ten thousand men might have been spared. But before he could retreat, shutting his eyes and ears to the truth of what he was witnessing, the woman spoke, and his last shred of hope vanished with the unmistakable sound of his wife's voice.

"Haste, Julius, or my husband will discover how boring you are." Her last word was turned into a grunt as Caesar responded with a vicious thrust that practically lifted Tertulla off her feet. Crassus gagged. He thought, she jests with him and makes sport of me even as she spreads her legs for him. Bile and wine rose in his throat and it was all he could do to swallow it back down again. He stared with grim fascination as Caesar's hands gripped Tertulla's breasts for support and more. The front of the long tunic she wore as a nightdress swung at her ankles with each lascivious stroke. The back of it was mashed up above her thighs, held up by Caesar's pumping hips. The left shoulder of her tunic was torn. Could there have been a struggle? Or was this just more evidence of their ardor? Her own arms were fully extended, hands gripping the edge of the chest to keep her head from bumping into the wall with each of Caesar's thrusts. Crassus followed the slender line of her bare arms up to her shaking shoulders, her twisted neck, the ringlets of her hair which half obscured her face. He was so absorbed with cataloging her treacherous features it was a moment before he realized she was looking right at him.

In this instant of recognition, in the one moment when all the gods called out for decisiveness, for retribution, for action of *some* kind, *any* kind, Crassus moved not a muscle. His wife's gaze pinned him like an insect, and although the light was still very dim, he knew with absolute certainty that she saw him standing there. It was hard to tell, but he thought he saw a look of terror pass over her face at the sight of him. This was immediately replaced by an expression of unbearable sorrow.

Crassus wanted to die. The meeting of their eyes was far more terrible than the sight of her rutting. Before this moment, had he accepted the title, he could have claimed the moral high ground of accuser. Now, with each passing second, he became the accused, complicit in their sin, his voyeurism almost paramount to their infidelity. The longer he stood there, the more his shame grew. For every action of theirs for which there was no re-action from him, he lost a piece of himself. Each moment he lingered, shards of the man Crassus fell away and were lost. If she would but close her eyes or turn away, he would be free to move, to act. But she held him with her gaze, and every thrust from her lover was a blow to his shattered heart. Tertulla's look riveted him to the spot just as surely as the nails that pierced Spartacus' rebels had fixed them to their crosses.

Cold sweat pooled around the hilt of his dagger till he felt it would slip from his fingers. With immense effort, he broke eye contact with his wife and stared down at the blade. He considered which way to point it. He had three choices and each seemed equally reasonable. Just when he finally decided that it was Caesar's throat that desperately needing slitting, Tertulla made a small, frantic gesture. She shook her head in a clear imprecation for him to do nothing. Her eyes widened and only because of thirty years' intimacy with that face, could he see she wanted him to slip away, to depart – to continue to do what he had done since he had come upon them - *nothing*.

It was a blow worse than any that had come before. Anger, like the bile that had tried to erupt before, rose within him. How could she expect him to do nothing? How could she *ask* him to do nothing? Her gesture had finally provided the impetus to reveal his presence, but the gesture itself pleaded for silence. His mind cracked like an egg. In his chest, there was a thick knot of rope where his heart had but a moment ago beat only for her. Yet he knew he would obey her. Even in betrayal, it was a reflex of love he could not abandon. And the core of him, already broken in two, found it could shatter into even smaller pieces. He took one step back and let the curtain come between his eyes and hers, between a joyous past and an empty future.

# CHAPTER XXXI

## 56 BCE - SPRING, LUCA

Year of the consulship of
Cn. Cornelius Lentulus Marcellinus and L. Marcius Philippus

Crassus wandered the drafty hallways, refusing to return to his bedroom, and instead found me. He sent me to find an empty *cubiculum*. It was difficult to leave him alone, even for a moment, such was his distress. Once I had him resettled, I foolishly asked him what had happened. My master was curt and rude, telling me to tend to my own business and leave him to his misery. I knew it must be something horrible, for even on his worst days, like the one when I received a flogging at his hands, he never spoke to me thus. I feigned departure, leaving the portiere half-open, then, barefoot, tip-toed back to watch over him. Curling up on the floor outside the door to his new quarters, I tried to remain alert in case he should require my assistance.

He sat on the small room's bed staring at the floor till dawn, rising only once to vomit. I could hear him mumbling to himself, running the gamut of emotions from the soft keening of shame and humiliation to the clipped whispering of cold anger.

For awhile there was silence, but then in a voice so composed it frightened me, he said my name. I thought I must be dreaming. "Alexander," he repeated, "I know you're out there. I would speak with you."

I obeyed, and he waved me to the only chair in the small, unadorned room. Without preamble or preparation, Crassus proceeded to confide in me. I winced at the surgically precise and cold recounting of each sordid detail. When he was done, I felt his eyes on me, but I could not raise mine off the floor.

"Have you nothing to say?"

"If I knew the words that could annul your own, *dominus*, I would say them."

"I am *dominus* of nothing." His voice had gone hoarse, pushing back tears. "What home am I master of? There is a house, but it is empty. There is a bed, but I can never sleep in it again."

"You are certain you saw *domina*?"

"There is no doubt," he said bitterly.

"Then what you saw ..." I hesitated to say the word, "this was rape, *dominus*."

"No. Not rape. She spoke sweetly to him, I could swear it. I was drunk, I know. But no, I think not rape. " He stared at nothing, replaying the scene, stabbing himself with the memory, over and over in his mind's eye, as if that might mercifully blind him to it. When we are sane, we may realize this torture would have the opposite effect, painting the scene with indelible strokes. But no man, faced with such immediate, terrible loss could put down that blade of recollection.

"I almost left without her, but then I realized it was not I who needed to skulk away in darkness like a thief. Oh, Alexander, I am bereft. The fine metal of my life has rusted, its foundation crumbling. My love is gone, my marriage a travesty. Tell me, my friend, in what vault shall I deposit the devotion, the passion so freely lavished on my Tertulla each and every day for the last twenty years? There is no place to pour this torrent of affection; without the proper cask, this sweet wine will spill into the gutter, a wash of ruined vinegar."

"This is a horror beyond measure." I shook my head. "Lady Tertulla hates Caesar. This I know; I would put the *lorum* in your hand myself if it be untrue."

"It is your hand where it belongs, Alexander. I did *nothing*! I am dishonored, a coward. Yesterday, I had worn honor like a crown; today I am wrapped in a mantle of disgrace."

"My lady would never betray you, *dominus*. She loves you as Baucis loved Philemon; she is as faithful to you as Penelope to Odysseus. Everyone in the *familia* knows this. The house of Crassus is a generous, loving house; it could not be otherwise if there was discord between you. I myself have heard dinner guests on many occasions marvel that the two of you act as if newly wed."

"They were not here tonight. Their words would sour on their tongues had they seen what I have seen."

"*Dominus*, look at me. You did not bring me into your confidence to hear feckless words of commiseration. You have always trusted me. I beg you to do so now. Caesar and Brutus plotted against you. Brutus delayed your return intentionally, with malice and terrible purpose. Your wife is faithful; she was raped by Caesar."

"You tried to interrupt our conversation. This I remember."

"And Brutus would not allow it. I did not know what he was plotting, but there were signs, looks between him and Caesar and the servants. You are the victim of a cruel conspiracy."

"How will I face her in just a few hours time?" Crassus felt for the dagger on the bed. "I had the chance, yet I did not strike."

"*Dominus,* you could not have bested Caesar. He is fifteen years younger, fifteen years stronger, fresh from the battlefield. He would have killed you, and after you, *domina,* to leave no witnesses."

"Your logic is impeccable, Alexander. But it is irrelevant. I stood by and watched; that is my eternal shame. Better to die protecting my honor than to stand idly by. I should be dead now, if not by Caesar's hand, then by my own."

"Certainly," I said angrily, "die like a Roman and your troubles will be over. What of the children? Do they deserve a life without their father? You must talk with *domina,* and you must act."

Crassus turned away from me and curled on his side in the dark. "Act? There is nothing I can do to set this right; nothing she can say."

"You *know* Lady Tertulla. Talk to her. She is wise and brave, and your truest friend."

"So I thought. And so, too, I thought of Caesar. What of him? Am I that despised? Is my measure of men so poor? I am nothing to him. I am a bank, a villa, a line of credit." Crassus choked on his words, as anguish overwhelmed him again. "I have nothing I call mine that he cannot use or take away. I am a latrine for his defecation, a sty for his discarded scraps. There is no amity between us, no honor, no trust. In their place crouch perfidy, enmity and sham. Nowhere is safe, for he invades and ravages all I hold dear as easily as he storms through Gaul."

There followed a silence filled with the clamor of grief and betrayal. I fought an urge to cross a line that could never be breached: to reach out to this man, place my arms around him and bestow the consolation of human touch. He needed this more than anything, but would not, could not receive it from me. Of a sudden, out of that wordless cacophony, Crassus sat up, reached across the space between us and grabbed both my hands in his own. "He is my enemy and he has declared his war. I will pray to the gods, Alexander, make sacrifice and rekindle my faith in them: they must show me how I may confront him and prevail. If it was not my fate to die tonight, then there can be but one agenda to justify life: I will have vengeance." He released me and rose to pace about the small room in silence. I was just about to break it with a plea for reason when he stopped and spoke in a clear voice, as if he were alone in the room.

"I cannot hope to win this campaign on the battlefield. My finest soldiers are not men, but money and influence. Yet though they are great, I doubt even they are sufficient.

It would be a mistake to overestimate their power. They cannot match his legions, or his cunning as a general.

"What if my counterstrike were more personal, say the blade of a knife, or poison? This could more easily be arranged. I can think of a hundred senators who would beg for the chance to stick him, and cry tears of elation at his funeral. But no, death is a gift; I will not bestow it upon him. A man can be killed only once, and once, for Caesar, is not nearly enough. I want to see him die a thousand times. The blow must be struck in some other way.

"What does he wish for most, and how can I take it from him? What one assault will bring him low even as it raises me up? He craves power as much as they say I love gold. It is true, he has no regard for the Republic. He would see it die and himself crowned as the new Alexander. Dictator is not enough for Caesar. He will not stop till he is King and the Republic dead at his feet. This is my task, then. I will see him fall, and when his world is as defiled as mine, I will let him know who it was who had ruined him. I will use him a while longer, as he has abused me."

Then, in an instant, Crassus jerked abruptly and stood unsteadily, reaching behind him for the bed. For a moment I thought he was suffering an attack of the falling sickness from which Caesar himself reputedly suffered. I leapt to him and helped him sit. His mouth was open, a look of wonder upon him, his face all at once alight. He took my hands once more and pulled me down to kneel on the floor before him. "Alexander," he whispered, his grip almost painful, "I have it! Caesar himself has put the means of his undoing into my hands."

"What is it, lord?"

"Caesar loves to speak of our league as a three-legged stool which will not stand unless he, Pompeius and I are all of equal strength. He must think me as dimwitted as a Numidian. Gaius wants no stool; he seeks a throne. Let him have his fantasy.

"There is another triangle, Alexander; he who possesses all three of its sides may rule Rome. Money, political power and military might. No one man can hold sway over the aristocracy, the plebs and the government without all three. I have spent my entire life amassing two of the three, with no thought until tonight of what I might do with the third. In spite of my success with Sulla and against Spartacus, Rome has never recognized my military service. Do you know why, Alexander? Do you?"

"No, lord, no." Crassus was practically aflame with excitement.

"Because my victories could never be seen as more than domestic squabbles compared to a successful campaign on foreign soil. This is the missing third of the triangle, Alexander, and Caesar has unwittingly shown me the way to acquire it.

"In the meeting earlier this morning - can it be such a short time ago - we had drawn lots to see who would be the proconsul of Hispania and who would govern Syria. Look, Alexander. Dawn approaches, and with its light I realize the gods have blessed me with great good fortune - because the eastern province fell to me. Let Pompeius have the west, its wealth pales by comparison. Bordering Syria lies the pearl of my revenge; all I need do is stoop to pick it up. And when I return with it in my pocket, the people will declare it to be a jewel worthy of eclipsing any other pretender to power, even Caesar."

"*Dominus*, you cannot be thinking of ..."

"Parthia! She has long been a thorn in Rome's side."

"But we are at peace with the Arsacids."

"No more. Her size and wealth is an insult and an irritation, Alexander. Why has a country so close, so vast remained outside Rome's embrace? Now, I say let it fall under the sword of Crassus, before Caesar takes it for himself. The timing is perfect. Their monarchy is in such disarray, they know not in which direction to turn the assassin's blade. They are uncivilized barbarians, disorganized, decentralized, and will surely wither and blow away before the discipline and training of but one Roman legion. Who knows if they even have an army to speak of? One thing is a certainty: their capitals and their temples are over-brimming with riches, gold beyond measure, wealth beyond counting. Alexander, I will bring it all home for the glory of Rome and Caesar's undoing."

I took a deep breath. "My lord, forgive me, but consider how much you risk. Is vengeance worth so many lives? Is it worth your own life?"

"It is worth all I have, and all I am." Crassus' tone had hardened, and I knew I had reached the limit of my insolence. "I will take the consulate," he said stonily, "and go to Syria, not with a governor's stilus, but with an army. And when I return a conqueror the city will open its doors to me. I will feast the citizens for a month, host the most extravagant games ever witnessed, and lay treasure in heaps upon every household. Then I will go to the *curia* and turn Caesar's coalition to dust."

"But even if you succeed, *dominus,* how can you be sure a conquered Parthia will be enough to dislodge Caesar?"

"In three months I can raise seven legions. Who could stand against such a force? We will squeeze the eastern provinces and sack the treasuries of Seleucia and Ctesiphon, and if enough gold cannot be sifted from those sands, we will march on to India, perhaps even to the Eastern Sea beyond. It will be the greatest conquest Rome has ever witnessed. I will make Caesar look like a schoolboy playing at soldier."

"Such an expedition will require many years. Your business interests will suffer without your guidance."

"My wealth will serve but one purpose now: to finance this war and strip Caesar of everything he values. The people will forget him like day-old news. And after my triumph, with the senate enriched and in my pocket, he will be overthrown, cast out, finished. Deprive him of his one true love - as he has done to me, that is my task. Strip him of power, influence, glory – yes, there is meat in that revenge."

"I fear for you, my lord. I beg you to think on this."

"My purpose is fixed, Alexander, as the earth is in the heavens. Fear not. With what agony can death threaten me which Caesar has not already made real? Someone once asked him, if he had the power to choose it, what kind of death he would prefer. He hesitated not a moment before replying "an unexpected one." Crassus looked out through the doorway into the darkness of the villa. "There are many kinds of death, Gaius Julius, and the one I have in store for you will most certainly grant your wish."

•••

*(Editor's note: the following two letters, dated respectively June, 56 BCE and August, 56 BCE, are reproduced from the archives of the British Museum's Department of Greek and Roman Antiquities. We have placed them in this location due to their chronological relevance.)*

To G. Julius Caesar

Rome, Junius

I trust you and your army are well and enjoying the improving weather in Gaul. I write to tell you of my misgivings about our recent treatment, or rather, dare I say, my part in your treatment of the old man. You have been a most steadfast friend to my mother and myself and my loyalty to you is boundless. This you must know in advance of all else I write here. Crassus seems a likeable, even venerable statesman, a revered conscript father, and I had thought your indispensable ally. Politics is a complicated business of which I understand little, but I regret causing harm to anyone whose enmity toward Pompeius equals my own. In the end, we must all do our part to preserve the Republic, but I confess I do not see how this deed serves our lofty purpose. Here is the crux of my letter: do you think he has any idea what transpired in Luca? What if a confession were forthcoming? Do not underestimate the man, Caesar. He clasped your arm and met your eye well enough when he took his farewell. If he did this aware of what you had done, I would not value his mettle too cheaply. An old war horse like that would know to avoid a frontal assault on a veteran such as yourself. He may try to outflank you! I wish you all success in your campaign against the Veneti. M. Junius Brutus

To M. Junius Brutus
Celtica, Sextilis

My dear Brutus, I was gratified to receive your letter. As you know, it has been a difficult year for the army, especially for the 7th and young Publius Crassus, son of our esteemed friend. These heathens do not withdraw to take up winter quarters, but harry us the year round, detaining tribunes and demanding the return of hostages. Insane, audacious and vexing. Young Crassus, however, has acquitted himself so well, I have sent him to subdue Aquitania. Ironic, is it not? As for the boy's father, you fret unnecessarily. Even if all were made known to him, Crassus must accept the consulship for several reasons. Do not disesteem the counterbalance of his avarice. He will gain a province, his first; he'll not pass up that rich harvest. Second, the man's a coward. He would never confront me. Finally, upon reflection, the poor fool will realize that nothing is worth upsetting the lucrative bargain he, Pompeius and I struck at Luca. No, do not fret, Brutus, we have nothing to fear from Crassus. You know what they say about him, don't you? He's a brave man, anywhere but in the field. I hope this campaign does not separate us for too long. My best to your mother. Do not neglect your studies in my absence. G. Julius Caesar

# CHAPTER XXXII

## 56 BCE SPRING, VIA CASSIA

Year of the consulship of
Cn. Cornelius Lentulus Marcellinus and L. Marcius Philippus

I did not learn of my lord and lady's reconciliation until after we had made the six day return trip to Rome. I have patched together the narrative of what was said along those 300 miles from the subsequent confessions and confidences of both my lord and lady. I dramatize this lamentable tale to you here, as I expect it would have unfolded.

•••

My lord, on horseback, rode behind his lictors. Tertulla sat by herself in the ornate and commodious *raeda* which was drawn not by the usual two, but by four horses. All the shutters were closed. My lady had been looking forward to the journey home through northern Etruria, especially since it had rained on most of the journey north and she had seen little of the countryside. Now, her body and spirit as closed off as her carriage, her mood raced like the clouds between despair and rage as we wound our way toward Pistoria on the Via Cassia.

Before we had gone ten miles, Crassus halted the procession, summoned a groom to take his mount and rapped smartly on the carved door of the vehicle. "Tertulla," he said in a tone just below civil, "I wish to ride with you awhile." There came the sound of a bolt being pulled back, and the door swung open.

Crassus entered, flipped his cloak out of the way and sat with his back to the front of the carriage, facing her. Tertulla lowered the hood of her sea-blue *paenula* and waited, her eyes lowered. He pulled a shutter aside, gave the command to proceed and closed it again. In a moment, the *raeda* lurched and they were on their way. The two of them sat without speaking in the dim light of the cabin. The constant grinding of the iron-rimmed wheels on the flagstones paved over their silence. Tertulla ached to tell him how sorry she was, to explain, to do anything which would make him look at her in the way he had done only yesterday, in the way she feared he would never look at her again. Her heart was pounding with the knowledge that these next few moments might determine how they would spend the rest of their lives, yet she could not speak first. That was her husband's prerogative, and so she waited.

At last, Crassus looked up and said, "Do you remember when we first built the villa at Baiae, that mouse in the bedroom?" His voice was sad and distant.

"Hercules." Tertulla, said, her voice too timid to be hopeful.

"You made a pet out of him."

"Only because you could never catch him."

"I would have done, if you'd let me tell the slaves to do it."

"But you were my hero. You were so diligent: devising traps, laying bits of cheese about the room."

"At least you allowed the slaves to clean up the mess. And the droppings."

"And that time you stayed up, sitting on the bed in your nightshirt, ready to pounce on him with your helmet .... I could not breathe for the laughter."

"I did catch him, if you recall. That's when you named him. Alas, he ate through the box."

"And you held a manumission ceremony in absentia!"

"More for me than the mouse. I gave him his freedom so I would be free of having to chase him. Remember that little bed you made for him from a jewelry box? He never went near it. Thought it was another trap. A smart little rodent - you should have called him Alexander."

"Our Greek would have been insulted."

He sighed. "Did we ever find out who let the cat in the house?"

"No. Poor Hercules." She waited, hoping he would say more.

"Those were happy times," Crassus said at last, putting his hand to his forehead. He seemed ready to sink back down into silence.

"Marcus? Talk to me. Please?"

Staring at nothing, he asked, "Have the years turned me into such an ogre? Or have Caesar's laurels charmed you?" He looked into the blue of her eyes. "Do you love him?"

"Oh gods, Marcus. He raped me!" She reached across the coach to take his hand, but he pulled away.

Crassus looked up and met her gaze. "It did not look like rape." His words fell like lead from his mouth. He felt diminished, compacted, separate. He could see truth in her green eyes, but a carapace of convention kept him from touching her.

"But for the darkness, you would have seen my tears."

"Why, then, did you not cry out? Why did you not resist?"

The carriage bounced over a rough spot and they both grabbed for their handholds. "Do you think after thirty years I would betray you for that hairless vulture? Think, Marcus. I let him do what he did for the same reason you did not stop him! How long did you stand at the doorway? Who do you think sacrificed more last night, you or I?"

"I do not know what to think. I do not know why I did not stop him."

"Then please, my love, let me set your mind at ease. You did not interfere because, when our eyes met, you saw my warning and knew that doing nothing was the only path left for us. If I had screamed before you found us, or if you had intervened, everything you've worked for these past ten years would have been lost. Honor would have demanded that you divorce me and break with him. Caesar would have become your enemy."

"Caesar *is* my enemy."

"But *he* does not know that, and we must keep that pearl of knowledge very safe, between only the two of us. He must remain an ally for as long as possible. Caesar thinks he was born with *imperium*. He came to me to force me to convince you to take the consulate. At least that was his convenient justification for his perfidy. I knew he wanted more. He has coveted me for years. You, too, have seen it, but given it no credit. I did not complain because I knew you needed him, just as he needed you. I stayed away as much as I could." She looked out at the monochrome sky. "I should never have come with you to Luca."

"We have both sinned greatly."

"We have paid dearly, husband, but if, by my acquiescence and your silence your plans are assured, was it not worth the price? I knew what this day meant to you. So yes, I let him take me - I could retch hearing those words fall from my lips. Caesar has grievously used us both. He knew we would submit to his blackmail. Because think, Marcus, if the alliance fell, your dreams would have been tossed aside like so many soiled bed sheets. The coalition would have dissolved and your march to power and glory would not have made it out of that bedroom. You know that this is true."

"I have had more than my share of each. I would trade it all to regain your virtue."

"No, I will not accept this. You could be the most powerful man in Rome if you but wished it so. We will avenge ourselves upon Caesar; let us use him as he has used us."

Crassus looked up to see the fire in his wife's eyes. He leaned across the compartment, grabbed both her hands in his and said, "Swear to me he forced you. Swear on your ancestors, on the heads of our beloved sons."

"I so swear," Tertulla said, tears springing to her eyes. "May Diana strike me down if I lie."

"Is it love or folly that makes me yearn to believe you?"

"Believe me, Marcus. I beg you."

Crassus sat back in his seat. "Trust. It is a word whose meaning I shall have to learn anew. The sight of you with him is burned here ..." he struck his forehead with the heel of his hand, " ... like Nestor's brand. But it smolders on the inside of my skull. I will never purge the image from my mind."

"We have time, Marcus. Time that will blast our scars as smooth as stones polished by the desert wind. Juno help me, I love you so much." Tertulla's tears fell in drops to her lap.

"Time may indeed ease our pain. But I will take my own shame with me to my grave."

"It is a shame we share, Marcus. We, both of us, allowed this to happen."

"Mine is the greater disgrace," Crassus said, shaking his head. "You let him take you for my sake, so you say, and it may be true. I want to believe you. But I ... I let him ... and did nothing."

"I sent you away, Marcus. You had to go, for both our sakes."

"If only I had come to bed at a decent hour. But that Brutus, he would not stop talking."

"Marcus Brutus?" she asked. "Isn't he Caesar's man?"

"Caesar has a fondness for him. He's Servilia's boy; I suspect she is the basis of his affection. Every time I tried to rise, he poured more wine and found some new topic on which he simply had to have my opinion."

"He was a part of it," Tertulla said with conviction. "I will place his name next to Caesar's own when I write my curses."

"You may be right. Come to think of it, the servant who led me to our room took me in the wrong direction. I became quite lost."

"He has been planning this since before we left the city. And he knew I could not stop him without great risk to you. He counted on it."

"My fortune is nothing without you," Crassus said. "I would dump it all into the Tiber to undo this monstrousness. You should have screamed, and loudly. And I should have plunged my blade into his neck. Nothing is worth a sacrifice so great. Now look at what he has done to us. Look at what I have done."

"I will go to the temple and apply for purification. Then we must seek revenge."

"I have thought of nothing else."

"You must be very careful. Greed has blinded everyone who attended the conference. I'm sure that brave words were spoken about consensus and the good of the Republic, just as long as every senator's strongbox was sufficiently stuffed full of silver. But nothing was decided at Luca that does not further Caesar's aims."

"That is precisely what I said to him."

"Then he was your enemy long before he left the *triclinium*. He will use you and discard you when he has what he wants."

"As he did you."

"Yes, Marcus, just as he did me."

•••

I had served the *familia* of Marcus Crassus for almost three decades, indeed had counted myself a part of it for almost as long, but it wasn't until after Luca that I came to realize that those of us who made our home under that roof were like denizens of the deepest seas, living our lives unmindful of the medium that sustained us: the amity in which we lived and worked. The affection between *dominus* and *domina,* their rigorous devotion to their children - this contentment was, in great part, what gave me license to accept my own truncated existence.

Other patricians took and discarded wives the way children trade coins. They married to form alliances, mend fences, latch onto fortunes and gain influence. But then, should a more propitious match become available, the bond would be summarily broken.

This vile game was never played by Marcus Crassus. Though the custom had fallen out of favor, my lord followed the ancient ways, taking Tertulla into his own home when she was widowed by the death of his older brother. They married, and within a year realized to their delight that they had fallen in love. For three decades thereafter, almost without exception, theirs was a congenial home, a marriage unblemished by strife or division.

I weep to think of what might have been had we never gone to Luca. Caesar's crime was heinous; I cannot imagine the agony my lord and lady suffered to feed that villain's ambition. He would go unpunished if my lord were not his judge. But at what cost? Crassus was sixty when he led his army to Parthia; he had no material wants and a steadfast love standing right before him. How could they endure a separation of years and the dark nights of worry? They broke asunder a life as perfect as any dream, all for the sake of vengeance. Could I have refrained from retaliation had I been in their place?

But I am not in their place, am I. A vision of Livia darts before my eyes and quickly flits to weigh upon my heart. How I miss the grating sound of her whistling upon my ears. I remember how I cast her mother into the abyss, shattering the only love I ever had, all because I did not stop to think that I might have had a choice.

How sad that only a moment before I had just been thinking, I shall never understand these Romans.

# EPILOG

## 19 BCE - SPRING, SIPHNOS, GREECE

Year of the consulship of
Quintus Lucretius Vespillo and Gaius Sentius Saturninus

Reflecting day after day upon the minutiae of one's life is a taxing business. Should you embark upon such an exhaustive audit, I suggest living a shorter life. If that cannot be arranged, be more circumspect in the selection of your memories. For myself, I have become a meticulous chronicler, examining the lives of those close by, and yes, I suppose, my own stumbling journey. The honest witness must be ruthless: every artifact of remembrance must be unearthed, brushed free of dirt and debris to be scrutinized anew, even those recollections pressed deep into the ground, long buried, thankfully, by the balm of years.

I had not realized the task would be this hard.

I sit staring at a fresh scroll of parchment, unbloodied as yet by the stabs of my pen. The path lies clear before me, yet I fear to take another step. Contemplation of all that is to come pulls me up short, an old horse come upon a pit of vipers. Loiter no longer, Alexandros; the time has come to tear down the bulwarks that have stood against memory for over thirty years, to pry open these eyes and see again what man was never meant to witness. By the gods, it gives me pause; my rebellious heart shakes in its bony cage. The slope of my narrative rises ever more steeply, and the memories - chaotic, heroic, tragic - grow as difficult to relive as they are to set down. But this is my purpose, and I will see it through.

•••

I am eighty-six years-old and a free man. Though I have lived two lives, I cannot say whether I was damned in one or blessed in the other. But this I know: choices are the dominion of free men. For almost half my adult life I had been liberated from the necessity of having to make them. Let me tell you, there is nothing so poisonous and seductive about life as a slave as the freedom from having to choose one's own path.

Marcus Crassus had no such excuse, but like a slave whose decisions are not his own, my master was carefree of the consequences of his actions. He was as close to a god as any man could hope to come. But godhood, it turns out, is a trap: the burdens and responsibilities are just as great as the privilege. Aristotle once said, *"Virtue makes the goal right, practical wisdom the things leading to it."* My master was virtuous, but he was not wise. What need has a mortal god of perspective, when a god may suit his morals to his needs? Men like Crassus see what they want, reach out for it and it is theirs. Consequences to their own wellbeing are weighed, but what of others? What of the multitude who follow him like flowers chasing the sun? What are they to a god?

Should a small man choose unwisely, though the future repercussions of his error are unknowable, the immediate ripples of causation are most often also tepid and contained. When a man like Crassus chooses his fate with clouded vision, the gods themselves may avert their eyes. My master dragged fifty thousand souls behind him on the rushing tide of his miscalculation. Only a handful of the multitude that followed him into the desert realized that they did so, not for conquest or the glory of Rome, but for one man's love, for the restoration of his honor, and for the administration of his vengeance. Marcus Licinius Crassus would have his war. And Alexandros son of Theodotos would be by his side.

###

## AFTERWORD

Any book describing events taking place two millennia in the past must necessarily be a work of fiction. However, I have taken several conscious liberties interpreting the life of Crassus, based on the premise that because of his singular defeat at the battle of Carrhae, his story was rewritten by pro-Roman historians. (It isn't as if there has been no precedent since we first began describing events that occurred before our time.) For this reason I have cherry-picked some of the details of his life. My errors, hopefully, were more of omission than commission, with the possible exception of his home on the Palatine. It is unlikely that the house was as grand as I describe, for like his father, Crassus lived modestly and without ostentation. As Mary Agnes Hamilton says in *Ancient Rome: The Lives of Great Men*, "at a time when he owned half the houses in Rome, and so many members of the Senate were in debt to him that they dared not vote against his wishes, he built for himself only one house, and that of moderate size."

Some may find glaring my omission to recount in any detail the Third Servile War (73 BCE - 71 BCE). The story of Spartacus and his ultimate defeat by Marcus Crassus has been told and retold, built upon the paltry scraps available from the actual historical record. *The Bow of Heaven* trilogy is not meant to be a complete biography of the triumvir; it is a story about the man, his family and the people who served him, primarily in the latter part of his life. For these books, what interested me most was the answer to the question, what could goad Crassus to leave everything behind - his wealth, his power, his wife of over three decades - to seek war and conquest 1,500 hundred miles from home? Historians say he greedily hungered for more gold (he was already known as "the richest man in Rome") and that he was jealous of Caesar's and Pompey's military achievements. This last may be true, but how much fight can be left in you when you're 60, two decades past the average Roman lifespan? That's how old Crassus was when he left for Parthia. I have proposed that his motivation might very well have been something else, something much more personal. Now that you have finished the book, you know what that is. Caesar's licentiousness, at least, is not conjecture. From Suetonius, *The Lives of the Twelve Caesars*, speaking of Julius Caesar: "It is admitted by all that he was addicted to women, as well as very expensive in his intrigues with them, and that he debauched many ladies of the highest quality; among whom were Posthumia, the wife of Servius Sulpicius, Lollia, the wife of Aulus Gabinius, Tertulla, the wife of Marcus Crassus, and Mucia, the wife of Cneius Pompey."

I ask those of my readers whose knowledge of ancient Rome is second only to their love of this glorious, insane time in history to be patient with one new to their ranks.

Andrew Levkoff

Phoenix, March, 2012

An excerpt from *A Mixture of Madness, Book II of The Bow of Heaven* follows the glossary.

# GLOSSARY

Abolla A loose, woolen cloak.

Acheron One of the five rivers leading to Hades: the river of woe.

Aediles Municipal magistrates and record keepers.

Ala Wing, of a house; also, a cavalry unit.

Amphorae Storage vessels, usually large, to contain liquids.

Ampullae Jugs or bottles, usually clay.

Ampullae oleariae Bottles of oil for bathing, sometimes perfumed.

Analecta Dining room slave.

As Roman coin worth one-quarter of one sestercius.

Atriensis Chief slave or majordomo of a Roman household.

Aureus Gold Roman coin worth 400 as, 100 sesterces, 25 denarii.

Caecubum According to Theodor Mommsen, "the most prized of all" wines before the age of Augustus.

Calamus Reed pen, writing utensil.

Calidarium Roman steam bath.

Caligae Boots.

Capena Gate The gate through which the Appian Way enters the city of Rome.

Cenaculum Apartment, flat; plural: cenacula.

Century Roman army unit composed of ten contuberniums, or eighty legionaries.

Clientes Clients: those who depended upon the power and influence of their patrons.

Columba Dove.

Commisatio Drinking bout.

Comitium The center of all political activity in Rome.

Compluvium An opening in the roof of a Roman atrium which let in light and air. Rainwater would fall to be collected in a pool below called an impluvium.

Consuls Similar to co-presidents, they were joint heads of the Roman state and were elected to a one-year term.

Contubernium The basic eight-man unit of the Roman army in the first century B.C.E. Also the term used for an intimate relationship between two slaves, who were not allowed to marry.

Cubiculum Bedroom in a Roman house or villa.

Culina kitchen.

Curia Where the senate met in the *Comitium.*

Cursus honorum The progression of offices each magistrate had to climb on his way up the Roman political ladder.

Denarius Silver Roman coin worth four sesterces.

Domina Mistress of a Roman household.

Dominus Master of a household.

Domus House.

Familia The family members, including servants and slaves, of a Roman household.

Famula A female slave, handmaid.

Fibula Clasp or brooch.

Fortuna Goddess of Luck.

Frigidarium The bathing pool in the Roman baths that was unheated.

Furina Goddess of thieves.

Furtum Theft.

Garum Aromatic fish sauce.

Gladius Short sword, plural: gladii.

Grammaticus Teacher.

Imperatore General who has won a great victory.

Imperium the power of magistrates to command armies and (within limits) to coerce citizens.

Impluvium A shallow pool, usually to be found in the atrium, that captured rainwater from an opening in the roof (the compluvium).

Insulae Apartment houses.

Kalends The first day of the month in the Roman calendar.

Lares Domestici Minor Roman deities whose function was to guard and oversee all that transpired in the home.

Lararium Household shrine usually found in the Atrium.

Latifundium Large Roman farming estate.

Lectus Couch, bed.

Legate Commander of a legion; one with authority delegated by a consul or magistrate.

Lora A cheap wine for slaves made from grape-skins, pulp and stalks left in the vat, soaked in water and allowed to ferment; a thin, bitter brew.

Lorarius A slave whose job it was to punish other slaves by flogging; also, in the arena, a person who encouraged reluctant animals or humans with a whip.

Lorum A leather whip.

Ludi Public games.

Ministratore Servant, waiter.

Nobiles Patrician families possessing most of the power in the Republic.

Optimates Conservative, aristocratic senators who wished to limit the power of the popular assemblies in favor of the senate.

Optio Junior officer, assistant to a centurion

Orarium A small, linen handkerchief for wiping the face.

Ornator Slave who adorned or dressed his master; f. *ornatrix* (who concentrated more on her *domina's* hair.

Otium The Roman concept of leisure, ideally occupied by pursuits of philosophy, art and music in a natural setting.

Paedagogus A slave or freedman in charge of educating children of rich Roman households.

Palla Cloak.

Pater The seventh and highest level of Mithraic initiation. Only the pater was allow to marry.

Paterfamilias Head of the household: the father.

Peculium Money or property acquired by slaves in the course of conducting business on behalf of their master. While technically any such gains belonged to the slave's owner, the master might allow these sums to be considered the slave's property, and might even allow these assets to be used to purchase the slave's freedom.

Peplos Long sleeveless tunic worn by Roman women.

Peristyle A spacious courtyard, open to the sky, framed by a covered colonnade.

Petronia Amnis Stream running along the Quirinal Hill.

Pilum Roman throwing spear; plural: pila.

Plebeians Free, non-citizens of Rome, also called plebs.

Polykleitos Greek sculptor, ca. 430 B.C.

Pomerium The spiritual limits of the city of Rome, marked by cippi, small pedestals used as boundary posts.

Pontifex Maximus Supreme supervisor of all things religious, and of matters of worship both public and private. Guardian of the ancient customs. The Pontifex was not subject to any court of law or punishment. The pontifex maximus was elected for life.

Populares Aristocrats, like the optimates, but favoring stronger representation of the people in the popular assemblies and tribunes of the plebs who wielded power to veto senate rulings.

Praefurnia Ovens used to heat Roman homes and baths.

Praetor Chief law officer and deputy to the consuls.

Pugio Dagger.

Quaestor In charge of military and civic treasury, as well as record-keeping.

Quirinal One of the seven hills of Rome.

Quintilis The seventh month of the Roman calendar, i.e. July.

Raeda 4-wheeled carriage, usually pulled by two, sometimes four horses.

Rosaceum Roman perfumed oil for bathing.

Rostra The place in the Comitium where consuls and other magistrates spoke to the Roman people.

Salve Good Day! Good Morning! Also used in bidding farewell.

Sambucus Berries from the elder tree, used by the Romans as a cure-all.

Scutum Roman shield.

Sestercius Brass Roman coin worth one quarter of a silver denarius; plural: sesterces.

Sixth hour The Roman sixth hour of the day was always noon; The sixth hour of the night was always midnight.

Somnus Roman god of sleep.

Stola Long sleeveless tunic worn by women over other tunics; a symbol of marriage.

Strigil In the Roman baths, a curved metal tool used to scrape dirt and sweat from the body.

Subligaculum Underwear worn by either men or women, usually a wrapped loin cloth.

Tablinum Room usually between atrium and peristyle where guests were received and records kept.

Taburnae Retail shops usually located on the ground floor of insulae.

Tali Dice made from the knucklebones of sheep or goats, used in possibly the most popular game in ancient Rome.

Tepidarium The warm bath where Romans soaked after the steam bath, then cleaned themselves before venturing into the frigidarium, or cold pool.

Trireme Originally Greek, then Roman galley

Triumph The crowning achievement of a Roman general. City-wide celebration of a great victory awarded to the returning victor.

Unctuarium Roman anointment room, where perfume and oils were applied and sweat and dirt were scraped off.

Urbs City.

•••

# A MIXTURE OF MADNESS
## BOOK II OF
# THE BOW OF HEAVEN

On the fields to the east of Brundisium, before the troops prepared to board the ships, Crassus assembled the army. There he offered up many cleansed and garlanded sacrifices: seven lambs, seven bulls and seven pigs. Seven sets of three throats to be slit to ensure the safety of each legion. A city augur, proud of girth and unashamed of excess, possessed of such capacious jowls they'd have made a roomy pair of mittens, this practical priest had allowed his mouth to be stuffed with bribes too prodigious for a lesser man to swallow. A positive result having thus been secured, the relief of the gathered thousands was no less genuine when, after the sacred birds had been released, the blessed father interpreted their flight as an auspice that our enterprise was looked upon favorably by the gods.

Crassus had had crafted seven of the most exquisite and opulent standards, taller and richer than any soldier had ever seen, crested with eagles of hammered silver and gold. The priest had blessed and anointed each with sacred oil. They were mounted in a row at the back of a raised reviewing stand, seven sanctified emblems that were the soul and strength of each legion. Beneath them, rustling gently in the slight breeze were many mounted, tasseled, purple *vexilla,* banners numbered with gold thread and images of wild animals, woven from the finest Tarentum lamb's wool. Before these flags and standards stood the senior officers of the army, their helms and breastplates shining as brightly as the standards above their plumed heads.

It is said the Hebrews would march to war carrying a small cabinet containing stones marked by the hand of their god. With this gilded ark leading them into battle, their armies would be blessed and protected; their god would not let them suffer defeat. Now Judea and its boxed god, their people rebellious and troublesome, squirm under the heel of Rome. Every army finds some pretty mystery on which to pin their hopes of victory: success proves faith justified, but defeat will not strip it away, for faith is impervious to calamity and disaster. Yet here they were: seven blessed standards, and every soldier who saw them, even the skeptics, believed with all or some part of his heart that with them marching before us, we could not fail.

I dimly remember possessing this glazed look of wonder as a child. When I grew to manhood, I discovered that one of three things was true: either the gods had abandoned me, I was beneath their notice, or they did not exist. Soon the elegant proof of a boot in the back had me rethinking the lessons of childhood. The logic of starvation, when the most appetizing offering on the menu was a maggoty hunk of something that used to be bread, this evidence argued relentlessly for the reevaluation of the idea that someone above was keeping a lookout for me. The irrefutable theorem illustrated by men unafraid to meet your eyes as they beat you – these daily insults were better proof of the way of things than anything I had been taught as a child. They filed away at the chains of my reliance on the gods till they broke, and with almost no effort at all I was able to turn my back on them. Finding myself spiritually on my own was a revelation. I was alone, and better for it.

Unless everything has been taken from you and your soul scraped clean of the last stains of foolish dependence on help from above, you cannot imagine how freeing it is to depend on nothing but your wits and the occasional bit of good luck. No, I put no stock in those seven eagles staring down upon us with cold metal eyes. I took far more comfort from Malchus' sword arm, multiplied and compounded by thirty-five thousand men with hard eyes and rigid discipline.

•••

I had arrived in the port city weeks ahead of the army, to meet with the priest, inspect the ships, inventory the cargo and smooth the way for our departure. I took quarters in the finest inn Brundisium had to offer, The Whistling Pilum. The name made me think of Livia, who was on the Via Appia at that moment, in all likelihood annoying one of the other healers with her tuneless tunes. I wished she was here to annoy me. When the engineers began arriving, they went right to work building a city of their own on the fields outside Brundisium's walls.

Hundreds of citizens poured from the port to watch, but were rebuffed when they offered to help. They were told they'd only be in the way, which was true, but feeling slighted, many returned to their tasks behind the walls.

•••

At a trumpeted signal from two dozen *cornicines* standing on a separate platform, men secreted among the 420 centuries raised thirteen foot tall standards stacked with bronze disks, silver wreaths and purple tassels that ended in a honed and oiled spear point, itself over eight inches long. (As I have said, the warlike Hebrews marched into battle with but a single divine emblem of their invincibility; Roman history was rife with evidence that where one sacred symbol was good, hundreds were better.)

As each decorated pole was offered humbly to every century's standard bearer, the shout that went up from the troops created such a noise that within the city walls those that were not already watching the spectacle were joined by everyone else, bringing commerce, shipping and the entire city of Brundisium to a standstill.

As he mounted the wooden steps to the main dais, Crassus handed his plumed helmet to me and smiled. I marveled at the weight of it, but he seemed to wear his armor lightly. His eyes were alight as they had not been since before Luca, the grievous events at that meeting having both darkened and narrowed his vision. He stepped crisply up to the raised wooden platform, his armor glowing dully under the overcast sky. The roar of the army escalated to madness as soon as his grey head could be seen climbing the steps. He took his time, greeting and complimenting his lieutenants, warmly grasping their forearms, each in his turn: Cassius Longinus, his *quaestor,* brave Octavius, loyal Petronius, ursine Vargunteius, Antoninus, Ignatius, and the one remaining officer whose memory I dishonor by my shameful inability to remember his name.

Giddy with the enormity of this spectacle, I imagined what it would feel like to don the general's helmet, to wear, just for a moment, the trappings of a god. Until that moment, I suppose I had never truly understood the power of the man to whose fate my own had been lashed (though ever since the night of our return from Baiae, the assistant who had become my replacement had succeeded in unnerving me on just that subject).

As the general spoke, his slow, careful words, having been memorized by the banner-bearers, were repeated loudly from where they stood so that all in the great multitude could hear. The timing was imperfect, creating eerie waves of words, cresting and falling in dissipating ripples.

"Have you ever seen a legionary weep?" Crassus shouted. "I don't mean the man who has lost at knucklebones ten times running; that poor wretch has cause to cry." The general waited for the light breeze of laughter to pass. "I speak of a soldier, battle-dressed, armed with *gladius* and *pilum,* brilliant in polished helm and painted *scutum.* No, not this man, trained, strong, deadly: this is not a man who weeps. Yet today, your general stands before you, water welling in his eyes. Shall I tell you why? Because in my forty years of service to our people, I have seen and fought with many armies, but none such as this. The cohorts that blanket this field are the finest group of veterans that Rome has ever assembled! We are a Roman army - there is none finer in all the world! So, should my tears fall," he shouted above the roar, "should my tears fall it is because I stand here, now, with you and for you, at the proudest moment of my life! And because you men of valor have chosen to stand here with me...," Crassus continued to speak, but his final words went unheard, buried in an avalanche of cheers.

"You all know we march to Syria. Do you think proconsul Gabinius is such a poor governor we must come to his rescue with such a force? Last I heard, Antioch still stood." Now Crassus' voice rose in volume and authority with every sentence. "Does this look like a relief force?" The "NO!" that answered each question was a thunderclap. "Are you nursemaids for infants?" "NO!" "Will you be content to gaze at palm trees from the safety of a sleepy garrison?" "NO!" "Are you armed and girded for peace?" "NO!" "I know men on their way to WAR when I see them!" The cry of affirmation was deafening. I had to put my hands to my ears, almost dropping the general's helmet.

Crassus waited and let his eyes sweep across his legions. "You must also know that the senate has withheld its blessing." Boos and whistles swarmed like locusts. "The day *that* decision was made the senator's *wives* must have gone to the *curia* while the men rummaged through their houses searching for their testicles!"

While he waited for the laughter to subside, Crassus looked down and scanned among the closest ranks, men of the first century of the first cohort. Then he looked up again and called out, "Would you like to know the secret of our invincibility?" He was departing from the script and the banner bearers were forced to keep up as best they could.

A legionary shouted, "We march for the First Man of Rome!"

"Gratitude," Crassus said, pressing the cheers to silence with outstretched arms. "But our strength does not come from me, nor from any you see upon this platform. For the answer, I shall demonstrate. "You," he said, pointing. "Leave your shield and ascend the rostrum."

Behind me, a stunned Drusus Malchus hissed under his breath, "Furina's feces!" He broke rank and the safety of anonymity to join his general. Behind Crassus, the legates were smiling. The stair planks creaked as Malchus climbed, gripping the rough-hewn hand rail for the equilibrium that had suddenly forsaken him. A large splinter speared his left hand and before his mind could stop his mouth he shouted, "*Fucking* son of a whore." His brain reminded him where he was before he finished speaking so that the last word was more miserable whimper than curse. Face flushed with crimson, he let the long sliver remain rather than risk any more unmilitary outbursts. He could be whipped for such an offense. If that was his fate, he'd have plenty of company: those within earshot, and there were many, laughed out loud with as much lack of intention. It was hard to say who was more embarrassed.

To break the solemnity of such a moment was surely an ill omen. Next to me, Flavius Salvius Betto clucked his disapproval. Crassus saved the moment by laughing along with his men. Betto clucked even louder, but with such lofty permission, the wave of fellowship spread until Malchus had made the top of the stage. He came to parade rest several feet from the general, as if the aura surrounding Crassus were an invisible shield he could not penetrate. Even with cradled helmet, Malchus was still a full head taller than anyone on the dais and half again as broad. Yet pulled from his place in the ranks, the poor man looked like a gasping fish tossed up onto a hot beach; the sea of his brothers-in-arms beckoned just beyond reach.

"Do you need a medic, son?" More guffaws. Drusus shook his head spasmodically. "Let's have a look then," Crassus said, motioning him closer. There was a stirring of awe as their godlike leader took the legionary's hand in his own. Crassus gave a crisp, hard yank and pulled the two-inch sliver from Malchus' palm. There was a tumultuous cry as he held it aloft.

"Let this," he shouted over the cheers, "let this be the first and last casualty of our campaign!" Crassus grabbed Malchus' hand and as he finished his next sentence flung it aloft as if the legionary were the winner of an Olympic wrestling contest. "Let Mars Invictus cause Parthian spears to fall as harmless splinters against our Roman shields!"

By my side, Betto whispered, "They'll have to be very tiny Parthians."

Crassus waited for the noise to die back down, allowing the men a good deal more license than he would once we were on the march. "Tell us your name," he demanded. Then, under his breath, "You're a good sport,

Malchus. This will all be over in a moment and you can take cover."

Malchus nodded gratefully. "Drusus Quintilius Malchus, sir."

"Any women in your life, soldier?"

"Several, sir." The requisite answer, which still got a laugh.

"Well then, Malchus, your sweethearts will want to hear about this day, but they're not likely to take your word that you stood with your general and his legates before the entire army. Get some witnesses: let them hear you back in the sixth cohort. Again!"

"DRUSUS QUINTILIUS MALCHUS! SIR!"

"That's more like it," Crassus said, taking a step backward, his left arm extended to present the soldier to the army. "I give you Drusus Malchus, legionary: first century, first cohort, first legion." Thousands cheered and whistled, none louder than his *contubernium* mate and best friend, Betto. His especially raucous praise was a mixture of pride and relief that the general's pointing finger had come so close yet passed him by.

"Well, Malchus, I shall have to commend the cooks. You have obviously found no fault with the food." My friend reddened and grinned, but kept silent, his inventory of replies having been exhausted by remembering and saying his name.

Now Crassus paced slowly across the stage as he spoke, tens of thousands of eyes following his every move. "Legionary Malchus achieved his status of rank through constant training and practice, expert sword and shield work, applied in the only furnace hot enough to temper his skills to the hardness of steel - the field of battle. I know this without asking because the same is true of every man in his century, I'll wager in his legion. They could not have earned their posting otherwise. With whom did you serve, son?" he asked with a wink.

"With you, sir. Against the rebel slave Spartacus."

"And I remember you well," Crassus lied. "Like Malchus, most of you served under Pompeius, or Caesar or Lucullus. To face and engage the enemy, there is no substitute for this metal - forged with strength and rigorous training it is a most deadly alloy. And those of you whose sword points are as yet unblooded - know that every century is crammed with men of experience ready to guide you."

Crassus walked to the edge of the platform. "Training, strength and experience. A most deadly triumvirate." He pointed back toward giant Malchus, who flinched at the gesture. "Legionary Malchus has them all. Is this what makes us invincible?"

"Yes!" cried the multitude.

Crassus raised his arms as if to enfold the entire field. "You are my children, and as a father loves his sons, I swear by Jupiter, I love each and every one of you. And so, to keep you safe, I must answer 'no.' These things makes us deadly, but they are not what makes us unconquerable. Know that each day we march I will sacrifice to Mars Invictus so that when this war is over, we may *all* return to our beloved families and homes. Every one of your lives is precious to me; that is why you must heed me now and learn this lesson above all others. Those who have been tested know this truth, but all must share in the sacred secret of our indomitable strength."

The silence that followed was stunning and strange amongst that throng, especially after the good-natured jesting and camaraderie. The general paused to let the stillness grip every man, then called out, "Legionary Drusus Malchus did not come to this field alone. Nor should he stand here, alone upon this stage. Bring his tent-mates forward."

Betto and six other serious faces marched up the stairs, their joyous relief at not being singled out short-lived. "Come, come," Crassus said, gesturing with his hand, "stand beside your worthy companion here." He spoke directly to the soldiers on the stage, but his voice was loud and carried far. "I will trouble you with no more questions, but speak plainly. When we bring the battle to the enemy, when *pila* are thrown and swords are bloodied, when ranks are closed and the press of bodies weigh upon your shields, remember for whom you fight.

"You do not fight for Rome.

"You do not fight for glory, or for riches.

"You do not fight for your centurions or your legates.

"And you do not fight for me."

There were no looks of puzzlement from the legionaries on the stage, but two of the officers standing behind the general, Ignatius and Antoninus, frowned and shifted uncomfortably. I would mention this to Crassus when the day was done.

"Look at the men around you," he continued. "Meet their eyes and take their measure. From this day forward, for as long as we march together, your tent-mates are your brothers. Your mother is Rome; she spat you from her womb to stand side-by-side with your brothers-in-arms. Fight for *them*. Protect *them*. When they stumble, *you* help them stand. When they tire, *you* give them encouragement. And when the enemy is but a gladius length away, you *kill* for *them*. Do this, and they will do the same for you.

"You think you fight for fame or spoils? Do not let the play of your anticipation distract you from the work of your sword. You think you fight for your sweetheart or a child left behind? Your wives are far away, but your brothers are right beside you. Fight for them, and live! Fight for each other, and we will return to Rome with such treasure it will take a thousand mules to bear the weight of it!

"I make this promise, witnessed by these officers: when we return victorious, laden with Parthian gold, a bonus of 5,000 *denarii* awaits every fighting man!"

When the uproar had died down, aided by the outstretched arms of the general, my master said, "One final burden I must place upon you." That made the troops grow very still very quickly. "Many of you veterans, if you are like me, have either misplaced or worn out much of your equipment. When you fought with Pompeius or Lucullus or Caesar, the army supplied your weapons, your shield and your helmet. Everything else, from your cook pot to your armor came from your pocket or your pay. Is it right that the man fighting next to you is better protected just because his purse is heavier than yours? No, it is not right, and in my army, *every* legionary will be as safe as I can make him.

"Centurions! See the posting outside the *quaestorium* for your appointment time. Cassius Longinus and his people will supply each legionary with freshly forged *lorica hamata,* chain mail in every size and for *every* soldier!"

It started somewhere in the middle of the army but rapidly built to a crescendo, a single voice amplified thirty-thousand times: "Crassus! Crassus! CRASSUS! CRASSUS!"

###

## ABOUT THE AUTHOR

Andrew Levkoff grew up on Long Island, New York, got a BA in English from Stanford, then put that hard-earned degree to dubious use in the family packaging business. After a decade of trying to convince himself to think 'inside' the box (lots of them), he fled to Vermont where for eight years he attempted to regain his sanity by chopping wood and shoveling snow off his roof.

Since 2005 he has been taking the cure out West, where his skin has darkened to a rich shade of pallid. Andrew lives in Phoenix with his wife, Stephany and their daughter, Allison, crowded into close proximity by hundreds of mineral specimens Stephany and he have collected while rockhounding. "They're just a bunch of rocks," says Allison. Ouch.

www.andrewlevkoff.com

Made in the USA
Middletown, DE
27 June 2016